The Doc Namdaron, Part Two.

Michael Porter

Copyright 2017 Michael Porter

All rights reserved.

ISBN:1978069685
ISBN-13:978-1978069688

DEDICATION

For my long suffering sister.
Who has finally come to terms with the fact
that she can't change me.
All the love to you and yours.

"No matter how evil may assail you.
Remember, there is still love in this world."

FOREWORD.

Namdarin, the Lord of Namdaron found his house destroyed and all his people dead. Swore to end the evil priesthood that had perpetrated this act. Part one told of the beginning of his journey, the first faltering footsteps along the road of revenge. He made some friends and some enemies, helped some people and killed some others, loved some and tortured some. In part two we meet some of the dark priests, their story is as much a part of this as is Namdarin's.

CHAPTER FOURTEEN

Kevana surveyed the remains of his troupe, only one horse had so far expired from the cold. His own, a once a beautiful black stallion with a proud curve to his neck, is now a back broken, head drooping, waddling old carthorse, the only reason it was still alive was that when the others had died the pace had to drop to the pace of the horse carrying two. The long race to the forest of the sleeping willow had nearly killed their mounts, to find the great sword and the gold plundered and the watcher Crandir dead was too much to bear. The only purpose of their small outpost was to provide an escort for the sword when the watcher called for it. Two hours rest to give the old man a decent burial and to load the gold had not been enough for the horses or the men, though the men got little rest, Kevana observed that the axe that had killed the tree was the same shape and size as the one that stuck down the old man. He had obviously come to investigate as soon as he felt the tree die, and been killed by the robbers. He did send a clear message as was his duty, this had been followed some time later by a mixed up and garbled message that spoke of a nemesis, a wild man and a small group of soldiers without uniforms, the old man's talent for long range transmissions was undeniable, but the message was so garbled as to be almost useless. There was no doubt in Kevana's mind that this nemesis had killed the old watcher and that he had stolen the sword, their tracks in the snow would be easy to follow, Kevana's troupe would catch them and take back the sword and the gold.

Kevana now saw the folly of his confidence, after a quick meal they set off in pursuit of the robbers, only two hours across the snow the first of the exhausted horses died on its feet, its rider was thrown to the ground but unhurt, ten minutes rest for the others whilst the gold and rider were re-distributed then off again at the same gruelling pace. Another hour and another horse fell. This time the gold was buried and its location marked on the map that Kevana carried, the corpse of the horse was laid over the gold so that hungry scavengers would hide the evidence of the digging. Kevana could see from the spacing of the hoof prints that the people they were after were moving faster than they could, every step put him further behind, walking the horses through the rapidly approaching night might gain them some distance, but every delay cost them ground. Despite the much reduced pace another horse fell in the night, the cold was too much for their seriously weakened condition, now with only five mounts between eight men they were forced to walk, the constant pace was beyond anyone even Kevana was forced to allow rest stops every hour or so.

    At one of these rest stops in the middle of the night two of Kevana's men lay down in the cold snow and died, they just surrendered to the cold. From this point on Kevana began to hate the robbers that he was chasing, horses were expendable but men were not, to lose men of his command in this way was unforgivable. He would extract vengeance from the skins of the robbers who had plundered the vault, devising the form of this vengeance took his mind away from the cold seeping up his legs to the knees, all feeling was already gone from his feet and shins, but this only made walking through the knee deep snow easier. The intense cold of the night killed another horse so by dawn they had only four horses and six men to the party, the rising sun brought no relief from the cold, it only brought the added danger of snow-blindness. Eating on the move and melting snow in their water flasks by putting the flasks inside their clothes and using their own most valuable body heat to give themselves water to drink, the strain of this journey was more than any had every experienced before.

Before midday they came to a place where the robbers had stopped for a while, from the tracks it seemed to Kevana that they had met someone and then continued on their way. After a few moments rest he waved the ragged band on, one of the horses refused to move and fell over, it was plain that is was going to die in a few minutes.

"Hell, its still warm." Shouted one of Kevana's men and then he skilfully punctured the horse's carotid artery, a short fountain of blood came from the wound which the man collected in his empty water flask. He placed his hand over the wound in the horses neck and the bleeding stopped, he drank deeply from the flask and looked into the shocked faces of his friends.

"It is warm and rich like red soup, it is sustaining even if it does taste bad and seem wrong." They were all convinced and each drank at least one flask of the warm blood. The vampiric feast over they continued on the trail each a little disgusted with himself, and each with a minor case of indigestion, the human gut is not designed for blood. The meal seemed to give them a little more energy and with that a little more hope, not that they would catch their quarry but they would at least survive to hunt on. As the afternoon wore on their progress slowed, the stops became longer and more frequent, no amount of shouting and cajoling from Kevana would make them go any faster. The slow steady pounding of their footsteps was almost hypnotic in its persistence, it along with the cold drove them all into a state not unlike an hypnotic trance, Kevana's thoughts turned to his home town, a city many miles to the south, where snow was a magical rumour not a cold reality, where heavy clothing is a waxed coat that the spring rains will run off. It was entirely his own fault that he was stuck in this white wilderness. He had been such an unruly youth that the local courts had given him to the priests of Zandaar, their task to tame him, this they did quite thoroughly, they realised that he had no aptitude for learning of the academic kind, but his large frame and quick fists made him a perfect addition to their military arm, here he progressed fast through the ranks until he was finally honoured with the guard post near the forest, this he won by defeating an invading fleet from the southern continent, almost single handed he sank half their ships with a fire raft. His timely intervention saved many of the coastal villages from plundering southerners, his warning launched a naval counter attack that left only a few surviving invaders to run before the wind. It made him very angry that his first failure was going to be a task that should have been so simple. This failure was brought on by the people at the end of these tracks he thought looking down to find that the tracks had vanished. He turned to see his men stumbling along behind him, paying no more attention to the ground beneath their feet than he had been up until this moment.

"Stop." he shouted, "We have lost the trail, turn round and find it again."

With a mixed muttering and grumbling the six turned about and followed their own trail for a while before they saw the track of the others off to one side, they followed the change of course until it entered a group of trees, in the middle of which they found a large burned out circle, a huge fire had burned here, the tang of wood smoke was still in the air.

"We camp here for the night." Said Kevana even though the sun would still shine for an hour at least. He knew that they could not go any further without rest and food. Delegating the relevant tasks, collection of wood for fire, and snow for water, he decided which of the remaining horses they were going to eat, he picked the one that he thought would not survive the night. The thought of a fire and a hot meal gave his troupe a surge of energy, he could hear the hatchets crashing into the trees, before the first of the logs was hauled to the fireplace he had the horse killed skinned and butchered ready for roasting. Before long a big fire was raging in the same place that Jangor and the rest had camped only the day before, large pieces of horseflesh were thrown on the fire and heated, not cooked properly just heated until a warm, charred, wood smoke flavoured hunk could be torn off and stuffed into a waiting mouth, such an uncivilised barbecue had not been seen in ages.

    Kevana planned while he sat beside the fire, the heat brought his injured limbs back to painful existence, he could feel the frostbite had taken hold in both his feet and the tip of his nose seemed to be completely dead, his plans however were simple, they must survive the cold and find shelter, then continue the hunt afresh, with new horses and hurts tended. He set the guard rota for the night and wrapped himself up in his tent, no one could be bothered to erect the tents properly they merely encased themselves in the fabric and attempted to keep some semblance of warmth inside.

    During his turn at guard, the duty of the guard was more to keep the fire burning than to protect the sleepers, he thought about where they could get help in the hunt for the robbers, the house of baron Melandius was fairly close so he decide to go there and force the baron to help him. The mere threat of Zandaar involvement usually ensured assistance was forthcoming. Every few minutes he got up from his seat and stabbed a knife into the remaining pieces of roasting horse, when they were cooked he removed them from the fire, they would make a few good meals for the walk to Melandius's house. When his turn at guard was over he returned to his tent and slept a little, his dreams were disturbed by visions of cold, white, ice stallions chasing him across unbroken fields of snow. Before morning the wind had changed and indicated an improvement in the weather, it was noticeably warmer long before the sun dragged itself above the high mountains in the east. Loading the last two horses with the tents and the remains of the third horse, they started the march for Melandius's house, spirits were much higher after a nights sleep and a good breakfast of cold horse, the only one of the men who did not like the meal was the one whose horse had been chosen by Kevana the night before, he may not have liked it, but he certainly ate his share.

   Kevana kept checking his map all through the morning, he was amazed to find that though he was following what he believed to be the most direct route to Melandius's home they were still following in the footsteps of the robbers, he finally concluded that they must have gone to Melandius as well, the deep hoof prints in the snow showed a string of pack horses that always stayed in line and an indeterminate number of other horses that seemed to move around this line in a purely random fashion, this was obviously not an organised military expedition, he looked back at the ragged remnants of his own expeditionary force, they where in strict formation, a single file that never changed and left a single confused track behind it, these robbers were amateurs. Following the trail with his eyes he saw ahead a strange group of bumps in the snow, and a few dark patches scattered about them, when they reached the spot he changed his opinion of the foe. They were not amateurs at all, they had faced down a hungry pack of the biggest wolves he had ever seen, and taken no losses doing it, not even one of the pack horses was sacrificed, yet all the wolves were dead. Trudging through the carnage he came to understand that this was going to be no easy hunt, the quarry was well armed and quite skilled, care would be needed to avoid any more deaths in his depleted force. The sun was just beginning to go down when one of last two horses fell to the ground and refused to get up again, Kevanas own black horse was the only one left alive and it now was loaded with all the tents and the remaining food, the dying horse gave the men a last bloody meal before they had to press on, the march to Melandius's house was their only chance of survival. They stumbled on through the night, the cold was lessening all the time though they were getting so weak that they could hardly notice the changes at all, with the rising of the sun the snow all around them started to melt from the trees and fall to the ground in huge slushy lumps, small puddles began to appear in the snow anywhere the sun shone on it. The degeneration of the snow didn't however make the walking any easier, the wet slush was very slippery and extremely cold to the touch, their boots were leaking in places and their clothes were getting thoroughly soaked by every splash and slip that threw the cold now muddy coloured snow up at them.

Kevana consulted his map at mid-morning, for the hundredth time, it was only a few miles to go. 'The house should be visible once we get over the next rise.' He thought, sharing this information did not bring too much joy to the group, they were looking at the last rise and thinking that it was too high for them. The pace of the march fell in direct relationship to the inclination of the slope, it was just about noon when the finally cleared the top to find that Kevana's skill with maps had not let them down again, the road down to the house was now smooth and more importantly it was most definitely down. Kevana wondered which way the robbers had gone, he had missed their trail sometime in the night, but was loathe to change his plans of going to Melandius's warm house.

Once they were within a few hundred yards of the front gate Kevana noted that the entire house seemed to be in some state of agitation, there were very obvious sentries on duty in the towers at the corners of the walls, the gates appeared to be shut, which should have been unlikely during the daylight hours, after dark all big houses close their gates, but in the day they are generally open. Kevana could only speculate as to the cause of the nervous panic that was evident before him, 'Perhaps they have been robbed in the night.' He thought with a wry smile, 'This is the way the robbers were coming.' Kevana watched the gate closely as they approached it, they were wearing their priestly robes, though somewhat dirty and dishevelled, the gate should be opened so that the people inside can give the priests the aid that they so obviously needed, the gate stayed firmly closed and the guards around it only increased in numbers.

"Why don't they open the gate?" Asked one of Kevana's men.

"I have no idea." Was the answer, though the questioner was

not really expecting any reply at all.

The approach to the gate was slow and tense, there was no relaxation of the guards, and when Kevana was about to knock on the gate arrows appeared over the top of the wall and through the narrow windows that surrounded the gate, these where arrows drawn and ready to fire. Kevana paused and looked slowly around before shouting for all to hear,

"I am Kevana of the Zandaars, we come in need and require entrance."

"We have orders to admit no more robbers." Came the shout from atop the gate.

"If your master will not except our pay for the services we need then you shall all be made to pay." He paused to allow the threat to sink into the slow minds all around, "You will pay by the silver fire from my hand and the black fire that falls from the sky."

There was no reply, but the sound of rapidly receding footsteps could clearly be heard in the cold air. Shortly the footsteps returned to the top of the wall, they were not hurrying and carried with them the sound of confidence.

An unclad head appeared above the wall, grey haired but clear eyed. The eyes surveyed the force before the door.

"You and your army of," a pause for a very theatrical count, "five, yes five, dare to threaten the house of Melandius." The head tilted backwards and a great booming laugh issued from the open throat, the ridicule was too much for Kevana to bear, he reached inside his robe to the pouch that hung concealed there, taking from the pouch one of the small silver flames that he kept there, he held it in the palm of his right hand and formed the thought in his mind as clearly as he could, the thought that would bring fire to the cold metal, he felt the cold of the flame disappear, he reached the arm behind the shoulder and then brought it forwards in a fast arc, releasing the flame just before it became hot enough to burn the flesh from his hand.

A brilliant white lance of fire leapt from his hand against the hard wood of the gate, the harsh whiteness splashed across the surface of the door like a liquid thrown on the floor, it spread in an instant until the whole of the huge gate was awash with the hard white radiance. For those standing inside the gate, they felt the concussion of the fire striking the door and the heat that came on the blast wave was enough to make the cold men start to sweat. They saw the door outlined in white and then it began to eat its way through in places, the patches of light on the inside growing together as the fire burned hotter than ever, gradually they were guarding a door made entirely of hot white light, the heat became so intense that they were forced to retreat, the light so bright that covering their eyes with their hands only succeeded in blocking some of it. As suddenly as it came the fire was extinguished, the guards felt the sudden in rush of cold air, that brought a shiver and gooseflesh to them all, but this was not caused by the cold, they looked towards the gate, around the pink spots that the fire had burned into their eyes, it was gone, burned to nothing more than a dark stain around the opening that it used to close. They stared open mouthed at the remains of a gate that had stood against many sieges and more years than any alive could remember. The metal hinges and bindings that had held the great door together were left in small piles in the opening, blurred by the heat and almost unidentifiable.

Kevana stood in the open doorway with his right hand inside his robe, caressing another silver flame.

"If we must leave here unaided, I will call down on your heads a hotter flame that burns a beautiful black." The stunned silence of the residents response was like music in his ears as he turned slowly away and, along with his men, began a stately procession back along the road by which they had arrived. Once Kevanas back was turned to the house and his hood was settled firmly on his head he allowed a small smile to cross his lips, this sort of demonstration of power always had the same result, abject surrender. Soon enough he heard the sound of a fast horse coming after them, the horse galloped up behind them and then swung around them in a wide arc, the rider did not want to get too close until he had no other option. The small horse came into Kevana's field of view and skittered to a halt directly in front of the black robed man, Kevana kept walking towards the horse until the young man riding it was forced to make it walk backwards to get out of Kevana's way. While the horse was stepping backwards the young man spoke.

"The baron Melandius apologises for any offence caused by his earlier refusal offers the total services of the house to aid the brothers of Zandaar, any assistance they may need on their obviously urgent quest is theirs, they have only to ask." The young man continued in this vein for several minutes until he was forced into flattery and an almost begging attitude by the constant advance of Kevana, the young messenger became worried that his horse may fall into the ditch, the constant twitching of his head finally brought Kevana to a halt. The young man stopped his horse and sighed in relief.

"What, exactly where your instructions?" Kevana asked of the startled youngster.

"Convince you to come back or die?" he stammered.

"Had you failed they would all have died before the sun went down." The young man saw the truth in Kevanas eyes and fainted dead away, one of Kevanas men caught him before he fell from the saddle and turned him around throwing him back across the saddle, a quick slap on the horses rump sent it back to its stable. Kevana and his cohorts walked back through the remains of the gate that he had so recently demolished, a thoroughly disturbed Melandius was waiting to receive them, he was hopping from one foot to the other in agitation.

"I am sorry for the welcome. My lords." he said almost

fawningly, "We have only recently been invaded by robbers, they came in the night and held me prisoner, they forced me to give them silver to release me."

"You thought us thieves in the night?" Asked Kevana imperiously.

"No, No, No, I left instructions that were over zealously obeyed. Anyone can see that you couldn't be robbers. What is it that you need? How can I help you?"

"Food, warmth, horses and a day and nights rest."

"On the instant a good meal will be served in the great hall as soon as you get there." A savage glance sent servants running to carry out the unspoken orders. Leading the black clad men into the houses main entrance Melandius guided the men through the corridors until they reached the main hall, through the tall double doors they walked into the great hall, this was the place where all the banquets and feasts where held, the high table at one end was almost set, though servants still ran around it like disturbed bees. Kevana took a long look about the hall, hanging from the walls were rich tapestries and battle flags of silk, each commemorating a victory .The panelling on the walls had the richest carvings the he had ever seen in his life, the skill of the carvers was glowing in the shapes and pictures of the huge panels. By the time they had all walked between the lesser tables, the high table, which sat underneath the banners of the house, was set ready to receive visitors. Melandius seated Kevana in the place of honour, to his left, the rest of the men were seated at either side of Melandius's centrally placed throne, this was the only chair in the entire hall that had arm rests. From their places the men could survey the whole room but not the family tapestry that hung on the wall behind them, this heavy hanging could have concealed a number of doorways and a hundred men. The tapestry depicted a large house in a green valley, not the current house of Melandius but possibly an older one, maybe the original. Kevana gave it close inspection before he took his seat at the table. Kevana noted that Melandius was exceptionally nervous, though he decided that this must be because the Baron was almost trapped here in a room with complete strangers and no bodyguards at all.

"What is the nature of your obviously urgent mission?" Asked Melandius, while the first course of green soup was being served.

"We are hunting robbers who stole a great treasure from the tomb of an ancient Zandaar master."

"What manner of treasure?" asked Melandius in a greed tinted voice. Kevanas eyebrows raised at the distracted look on Melandius's face. 'Greed drives this man.' he thought, 'I won't tell him of the gold.'

"They stole a great sword, it is the sword of a god, for a mortal man to touch it means instant death, so far none of the robbers have touched it."

"What does this sword look like? So that we can bring it to you if we discover it somewhere on our lands."

"It is said to have a long blue blade and a black hilt with a large black stone in the pommel." He said knowing the baron was more likely to try and sell it to them than just hand it over. The baron nodded and filed the description away in his mind, drawing an elaborate picture there so that he would not forget it. Once he had the picture fixed in his mind he knew that he had already seen the sword it had been strapped to the back of one of the robbers.

"I thought you said that no mortal man could touch the sword and live?"

"That is true." Said Kevana, paying very close attention to the confused face of the baron.

"One of the people who robbed me was carrying such a sword

on his back, the black stone in the pommel was clearly visible above his right shoulder."

"That should not be, no man can touch it, it must be brought to Zandaar still in its black box." Kevana was very puzzled by this, he had been told not to touch it because it would kill him, yet the baron had seen it on a man's back.

"Did you see him touch the sword?"

"No, but one of my guards carries the imprint of the pommel stone on the side of his head where he was knocked unconscious." The baron was greatly pleased by the discomfort his words were causing the black robed invaders. The second course was served, a thick meaty broth that was kept cooking in the kitchens at all hours, so that there was always something ready to be eaten. Kevana's men devoured this with the same speed that they had demolished the soup. Kevana was eating much more slowly, he had a lot to think about.

"There is something else you may like to know." said the baron, softly.

"What?"

"The man with the sword says that he killed my minstrel, the minstrel was found dead in a locked room, to which he had the only key, he died in his sleep with not a mark on his body, only a look of utter terror on his face. The man with the sword said that he would send my own nightmares to kill me if they were followed from here." Melandius almost smiled when he saw the blank expression that slowly came over Kevana's face, even Kevana's men stopped their feasting.

"He sounds like one of our own." Said Alverana, Kevanas lieutenant.

Kevana made no reply, he sat unmoving for what appeared to everybody to be a very long time. Eventually the uneasiness all around him pierced his shell of thought,

"That man I will kill. We will need horses and supplies ready for dawn, until then we sleep." His still hungry men looked at the food spread before them, they were dismayed at the prospect of leaving it uneaten, their eyes flashed from the plates to their leaders face, flickering from one to the other.

"Finish the food, then sleep." He said to a universally happy response.

"We ride with the rising of the sun, and we will not stop until the thief is dead or we are." His hand was on the book of Zandaar, that was concealed beneath his robe, all the men knew that he had spoken an oath that would bind them all. Faces fell and silent prayers were whispered in troubled minds, prayers for absent families and friends. The meal took a depressing turn but proceeded and a much faster pace, in only few minutes Kevana was demanding beds for himself and his men.

A small barrack room was set aside for them near to the main gate, it used to be the guard room for the gate guards when they had a gate to guard. The beds were hard and lumpy but they were at least warmer than the snow that Kevana had slept on in the last few nights. None of the black robed monks undressed, they just dropped onto the bunks and seemed to fall into a deep sleep not unlike a coma. Melandius stood in the doorway looking at all the resting forms and wondered if he should have them killed in their sleep. Kevana opened his eyes and turned his head to look straight at Melandius, no other part of his body moved at all.

"We may seem to be sleeping but there will always be one on guard, to protect us all from treachery." Melandius stared hard into the eyes 'Can these people read minds?' He thought. He watched Kevana's eyes close slowly. 'They must get any help that they need, anything, just so long as they leave soon.'

As he walked away from the sleeping monks Melandius was sure that Kevana had been reading his mind, he increased his pace until he was nearly running away, worried what they would find in his head.

Sensing the departing fear Kevana smiled to himself and went to sleep. Through the rest of the day Kevana and his men slept, the guards commented to each other when the time came to change over that they had never guarded so many corpses in their lives, not one twitch, not one snore, and none running to the latrine, one guard even observed that they had not even been shown where the latrines were. Speculation was rife all through the house about the nature of these strange people, were they human or not? None could tell for sure.

Through the night the guards changed at the usual intervals, no sign of life came from the men in black until about two hours before the sun was due to rise. The guard, who was dozing in the doorway, heard a rush of wind as all the sleepers took a deep breath and woke, sitting up and stretching the cramp from their limbs. The guard was astounded by the accuracy of their timing. How could they all wake up at the same instant after more than fifteen hours of sleep?

"Fetch Melandius." said Kevana.

"My lord will be sleeping and should not be wakened at this hour of the day." the guard said.

"Fetch Melandius, now."

Seeing that the priest would not be denied the guard left at a run, going by way of the temporary guard room he detailed another to watch the priests while he went to wake Melandius, certain that he would suffer some awful punishment for his rudeness. As he ran down the corridor to Melandius's quarters he was surprised to see that the guards were missing from the door, he flung the door open and rushed in, almost impaling himself on the point of a drawn sword. The door guards were inside and ready for anything, behind them paced Melandius, he looked very unhappy.

"Well, what do you want?" Shouted Melandius. The panting guard tried to slow his breathing down so that his message would sound better.

"The priests had awakened, my lord, and their leader wishes to speak with you."

"About time too, I thought they would sleep forever." He flipped a cape from the arm of a chair and threw it about his shoulders.

"You two stay here." to the door guards, "Well come on, lead the way." Pushing the other out of the room. Melandius headed for the guard room with the struggling guard in tow. When they looked through the open doorway into the guard room they saw only three men in black, one of which was Kevana, and no guard.

"Where are the others?" demanded the baron.

"They have gone to the latrines, when they return we three will go. We will all eat in half an hour, and you can tell us everything you know about the thieves."

When he had finished speaking the three returned and Kevana left without another word. The Baron sent the guard to tell the kitchen and stable staff that the visitors would be eating and leaving very soon, then he sank down onto one of the still warm bunks and watched the complex, almost balletic, exercises of the priests. He realised that these were fighting men, not like peaceful village priests at all. When Kevana returned from his ablutions he ushered a disgruntled baron from the room saying, "We need privacy for our prayers." Melandius stood by the door and heard the bolts slam home, the door rattled as someone on the inside tested the fastenings. Standing outside the silent room he felt like a small boy awaiting a punishment from the angry father he knew was inside and waiting for him. Melandius felt the strange uneasiness build until he could stand it no more and moved away from the door, as he moved away the feeling dissipated with surprising speed, only ten strides and he was wondering why he had moved away, one stride back towards the door and he knew, retreating from the influence of Kevana was better than trying to stay by the door and discover what was going on inside.

Once the door was secured and tested the Zandaars formed a circle holding hands and facing outwards. Kevana began the slow soft hum that locked all their minds into the right pattern, then together they projected a small circle of fear around themselves to prevent a sudden disturbance, then Kevanas mind showed them a picture of the sword, it was taken from an old book that had been held in a monastery, this picture was given to the leader of the swords honour guard so that he could recognise it if the chance arose, Kevana shared it with the last five of his men. When the picture was steady they began the search, each man in the circle covered one sixth of a rapidly expanding circle, mile after mile they reached and as they reached the area to be searched became bigger, so the expansion rate had to fall, twenty miles in the first minute, ten in the next, five in the next, after ten minutes the circle was expanding very slowly indeed but they did not falter, after fifteen minutes they were moving at less than speed of a running horse, but they did not stop. After seventeen minutes they all felt the twitch that meant they had found their target, it was nearly forty miles away. This was at the extreme range of a six man search, the circle split at a point directly opposite the man who's segment the sword was in, Kevana released the hand of the man next to him and the circle unfolded to produce a crescent shaped line of men, the focus of the crescent was the sword, though the range was long they received a good impression of the swords whereabouts, it was jogging along on a man's back, it was getting further away with every moment that passed. They felt the presence of other people around the sword but could not get enough information to enable them to fix on the people, only the sword remained clear and it was fading rapidly. Kevana decided to break the connection, it was getting weak anyway and showed no sign of revealing anything helpful, he signalled to the collective mind and the search was ended. All the monks were staggered by the amount of energy that had been expended in the search, two almost fell to the ground but were supported by their neighbours.

"At least we know now which way they are going, and that they are not too far away." Said Kevana, trying to force a hopeful note into his voice.

"Even so short a distance can be beyond reach at this time of year." Said Alverana. Kevana's cold stare told him that no distance would be beyond reach in this hunt. Alverana lowered his eyes and feared for a more verbal rebuke, none came.

"Let's eat." said Kevana and the others followed him out into the corridor, they retraced the path by which they had come the afternoon before, soon they were back in the great hall sitting in the same places at the table. Melandius was already there waiting for them, his face was paler than normal and he seemed to be shivering, perhaps he was cold, Kevana's cruel smile told Melandius that Kevana knew it was fear that caused the trembling. The meal was well started before Melandius spoke.

"What more do you need to know about the robbers?" he asked timidly.

"Nothing." said Kevana, Melandius frowned and Kevana continued, "We know where they are and we know which way they are going, we only need horses and supplies and we will catch them soon." Melandius's puzzled look did not dissipate, and Kevana would not elaborate, for a whole minute they stared at each other, one questioning the other implacable. Melandius returned his gaze to his plate thinking that he really didn't want to know how he had discovered the location of the robbers, it was probably some wicked magic as far as he was concerned. The priests cleared the table of food twice before they were ready to leave it, they knew that this would be their last good food for a long time, until the robbers were caught and killed they would get little rest and less food.

"We leave now." said Kevana when he was ready, the men almost sprang to their feet and stepped back from the table, Kevana waved Melandius up and said, "Lead on to the stable." Wearily Melandius levered himself away from the table and heaved himself to his feet, "This way." he muttered. In only a few minutes they were walking across the flagged yard towards the huge double doors of the stable. Melandius showed them the small postern gate. "They appear to have simply climbed over the gate and let themselves in." Kevana examined the small opening carefully. "One of them must be very thin, or possibly an acrobat." He turned and walked into the dim stable, his own horse was waiting for him, it looked a lot healthier than it did the last time he saw it, it tossed its head as soon as it recognised the tall black robed figure. Behind the black horse were five more riding horses and two pack animals full loaded, a covey of stable boys stood well back in the darkness of the rear stalls, a short look and a quick nod were all the thanks they got from Kevana for the care they had given his horse.

Alverana and the rest stationed themselves by the sides of the horses they had selected, but they did not mount, not until Kevana had pulled himself up into his own saddle with the single fluid movement that spoke of many years of practise. The only sound in the stable was the creaking of leather and the clopping of the horses hooves as they settled the weights on their backs.

"The priests of Zandaar thank you for your aid." Said Kevana in a loud voice looking straight down into the upraised face of Melandius.

"We will leave by the same door as the robbers did." Melandius did not even get a chance to issue orders for the gate to be opened, two of the boys ran forwards without instructions to unlock the door. Melandius watched the horses troupe slowly out of the stable, he saw the men's heads dip as they passed under the wall, and as the wooden gate closed behind them he sighed and fell to the ground in a dead faint.

    Kevana heard the gate bang shut and kicked his horse, picking the speed up to a quick trot they moved away from the big house, and up into the hills before them, the sky was lightening with the coming dawn and the snow all around them took on the deep blue colour of the sky, before the house was lost to sight behind them, the sun appeared above the peaks and the dazzling red and gold light made the search for the tracks very difficult. By mid-morning Alverana was certain that the tracks they were following were those of the robbers, they were going in the right direction and had not been crossed by any other human sign for some distance. All the time they climbed up into the hills the temperature seemed to be rising, the wind was blowing warm from the south and the sun was hot on their faces, the horses began to sweat beneath them and the ground started to turn to mud, the tracks of the robbers vanished along with the snow, only remaining in the patches that were shaded from the rays of the sun. Kevana could spare neither the time nor the energy, for a mental search, so they followed the direction they had discovered that morning, steadily they climbed into the hills, the path getting steeper and more difficult, at any flat section they kicked their mounts into a fast trot, hoping all the time to catch up some of the distance separating them from the target of their journey, the robbers who had stolen a gift from their god.

CHAPTER FIFTEEN

Namdarin awoke from a deep and untroubled sleep, to feel the warm body of a woman resting inside his crooked arm, it was Jayanne. He felt a sudden rush of pleasure at the activities he remembered from the night before. There was as yet no light creeping through the flap of their shared tent, but he knew that something had shaken him from a deep sleep.

"Move your lazy backsides." Came a shout from without the confines of the dark tent, it was Jangor's best military voice and it was admonishing them to action. With a simple twitch of the left arm Namdarin woke Jayanne and said softly, "We must be starting to move now." Jayanne looked up into his eyes and smiled, her arm tensed across his chest and she rubbed her soft white cheek against the course hairs around his nipple.

"Let's get going." She whispered in a voice made husky by sleep, though she made no actual move away from the warm resting place of his armpit. With a hard shrug of the shoulder he dislodged the beautiful face and then rolled over, so that he could not see the look of disappointment on her face. He started to collect his clothes together and wondered why Jangor had elected for such an early start, without light it was going to be very difficult to make any real progress through the snow that Namdarin knew was all around them, and would be for the foreseeable future, still he made no overt objections and started to get dressed in the clothes that he had discarded only the night before. Jayanne rapidly followed suit, her clothes were all mixed up with his and it took some joyful and giggly time to disentangle their relevant garments. Namdarin felt like a young man again, in that he woke with a woman to whom he had no idea at all what he should say. When the disturbed pair staggered from their tent the packing of the other tents was already under-way, lowering their tent with the occasional knowing glance was as close as they got to real communication.

The sky was still full dark when Jangor called them to mount the horses and start the journey of the day. They rode out of the small depression in which they had spent the last few hours and moved quickly up into the hills, the thaw continued as it had before they went to sleep, small rivers formed on the surface of the snow, the constant drip of falling water was louder than the horses feet sinking into the rotten, and increasingly brown, snow. Climbing slowly up the valley Namdarin began to feel more and more uncomfortable, almost as if something very unpleasant was following him. He kept twitching from side to side and looking over his shoulder, Jayanne who was riding alongside him noticed his unusually jumpy behaviour and asked him what was troubling him.

"I don't know." He answered, scanning the horizon for the hundredth time, "I get the feeling that someone is watching me, but I can't tell where from." Reaching over his shoulder with the right hand he held the hilt of the sword and the feeling dissipated a little, but as soon as he released the black hilt the fear came rushing back. Holding on to the long black bindings he felt that the presence was closing in all around, the feelings of imprisonment became stronger and stronger until in an instant the touch of fear shattered like a broken mirror, splinters of it scattered all around, but no image of it could be found in his troubled mind. What ever it was that had been hunting him was gone, as if it had never been, he was glad to the point of joyous excitement that the black cloud had lifted from his brain, he turned and smiled into the concerned green eyes that were staring at him, at her puzzled look he said, "It is gone, whatever it was."

"What was it?"

"I have no idea, it felt like a searching, or a reaching, a watcher staring at my back, I don't know how to describe it, it felt supremely uncomfortable."

"Are you sure that it is gone?"

"Oh, yes there can be no doubt about that, as to how much information it was after, I cannot say. If it was only looking for me then it found me, if it was after more then I would say that it missed the extra, it felt like it was sure that I was here but could find nothing around me." He was shaking his head from side to side, unsure about the words even as he spoke them.

"I am glad that it is gone," she said quietly, "but I think that it will bring the pursuers all that much quicker to our trail." After a moments thought Namdarin kicked his horse hard and galloped up the line to where Jangor was slumped almost asleep in the saddle.

"Wake up." said Namdarin.

"I am not sleeping." Was the terse answer.

"I felt a presence watching me a while ago." Jangor sprang to attention in the saddle, various emotions flashed across his face.

"Did this presence find anything?"

"Only me and the sword."

"They must be the honour guard that Crandir spoke of."

"That is the most logical explanation."

"If they know where we are, they will be coming quickly." Namdarin just nodded. "We must pick up the pace and try to lose them in these hills." Continued Jangor. Then he shouted, "Kern, speed things up a little." Without turning the big scout gave his horse a little more rein and took the pace to fast walk.

The sun was bright on their faces, and the glare was intense on the snow, but neither was at all warming, the path that they were following up into the mountains was steep and winding, it followed the line of a stream that must have flowed in the summer, but was now a small river of ice below a thick covering of snow. Before the sun was half way up the sky Kern suddenly reined in hard and forced his horse to a skidding stop. The line of people stopped behind him. Jangor pulled up alongside Kern and asked what the problem was.

"Up on the hillsides ahead." was the soft answer, far softer than the big man's usually soft voice. Jangor stared for a moment or two, scanning the hills for signs of trouble, he saw no tracks at all, no signs of danger, nothing that he thought should stop their passage.

"I see nothing."

"On the ridges high above our heads, there are huge curved formations of wind sculpted snow, if the temperature continues to rise, or the sun gets too strong, those snow banks will come crashing down into this valley and kill us all. A single loud noise could even start it off."

"Then we had better be very quiet then, hadn't we." Turning slowly he walked his horse back down the line and told each member of the group to be as silent as they could. Once he was stationed at the tail of the line he waved to Kern to start them all moving again. Now the pace was painfully slow, Namdarin became nervous at the thought of the others following, he could almost feel their hot breath on the back of his neck, 'This is how a deer must feel when it knows it is being hunted.' He thought. Staring hard up onto the ridges at both sides of the valley he could clearly see the snow formations that Kern had warned them of, there were huge jutting prominences with thick black shadows under them, the flashing of the sunlight on the icicles hanging from the edges was exceptionally beautiful, but equally frightening. The southern ridge held a bank of snow that was smooth and looked very hard, 'The wind must have been blowing to the south.' thought Namdarin. He looked up at the top of the northern ridge where the huge snow cornice hung like a curtain of death, waiting to drop on any unsuspecting traveller. Shivers of ice ran up and down his spine, his feet trembled in his boots and his knees shook against Arndrol's nervous flanks. Calming the horse with a gentle hand, the man visualised a wall of white death falling down the slope at an acceleration rate that even Arndrol could not hope to match. His hand felt the tension drain from the horses neck and this helped to quieten his own jangling nerves. Progress through the narrow section of the valley was very slow, every sudden footfall caused a momentary holding of breath and a juddering restart. The jingling of their equipment seemed to take on insanely large proportions, Namdarin rapidly lost his patience with all the noise, trying to prevent a dozen things from banging together with only one hand free was too much, so he lets them rattle and closed his eyes, leaving Arndrol to follow Stergin's horse as best as he could. Arndrol was acutely aware of Namdarin's disturbed state and endeavoured to make the ride as smooth and quiet as he could, the horse did a much better job than Namdarin had. Just before the sun reached it height, the group came up against a steep wall of snow that entirely blocked the valley from one side to the other, it appeared to be twenty or thirty feet thick in places.

"This is an old avalance." Whispered Kern.

"We will have to force our way through," said Jangor, "the people following us will catch us in the valley if we try to go back."

"It is only a few more miles ,"said Jayanne, "before we have to leave this valley, I think."

"What we need," said Jangor, "is a draft horse to drive through this snow."

"I think that is Arndrol's talent, don't you?" asked Namdarin.

"Go ahead." Namdarin moved to the front of the line and eased Arndrol into the deep snow, it was almost as high as the horses head, which he was tossing from side to side in fear, he had no wish to be buried alive in the soft white snow. Namdarin's firm control of the reins reassured the horse that he was in no real danger if only he could control his own fear. After about fifty nervous yards the depth of the snow decreased markedly, it was suddenly only to the horses whithers, this he could cope with, though the chill would soon become a problem, the other horses behind him were not forcing a path so they where not in direct and constant contact with the snow. Namdarin hoped that the snow would get shallower before any permanent harm was caused to his old friend, his hopes proved true, the steep slope and rapidly narrowing walls of the valley meant that the amount of snow that had fallen down the windward slope lessened to such an extent that it had not reached the middle of the valley, and Arndrol was picking his feet above the hard white crust and kicking the snow about in his usual manner, his coat was matted with ice in places but this was quickly melting.

"There." Shouted Jayanne without realising the danger of the noise.

"Be quiet." whispered Jangor harshly.

"Sorry. There is the valley that leads to Granger's home." She was pointing to a small notch high on the southern ridge, it was nearly hidden in the glare of the sun, "I am almost sure that is the way."

"Almost?" asked Jangor.

"There was not as much snow about the last time I was here, all the other landmarks have been hidden."

"Is this valley a dead end, or does it continue through the mountains?"

Her only answer was a shrug.

"Kern could you lay a false trail in all this snow?"

"No. It would be a complete waste of time, I could not hide the fact that I am a lone horseman, not from a tracker of any worth."

"So we pray for some heavy snow and soon." said Jangor then he waved Namdarin on. Namdarin turned Arndrol towards the notch and squeezed him with his heels, the big grey walked slowly up the slope not sure of the footing under its thick covering of snow and ice. Any loose rock seemed to have frozen solid and they had no real problems, other than the occasional minor slip, climbing up to the high valley entrance. It was a narrow v shaped valley that curved left and right but maintained a roughly southerly direction for almost a mile before it made a sharp turn to the east. All the way along the valley the amount of snow became less and less until it was only a light dusting, after the eastward turn they were confronted by a steep bank of scree that had no snow or ice to bind it together.

"How did you get past that?" asked Jangor staring hard at Jayanne.

"I had forgotten about this," she said, "I was on foot so it was a slow walk, I had no horse worry about."

"I wonder why it is free of snow?" asked Jangor of no one in particular. At the upper edge of the slope he noticed a haze rising, a small rippling distortion of the background above the scree, a heat haze.

"This place is warmed from underneath, there is most probably a hot spring under there somewhere." he said, "But that helps us not at all."

"If we stay near this wall," said Kern, "here in the shade, where the sun never reaches, it may be cold enough for a little ice to hold it all together."

"I agree." nodded Jangor. "Mander you and Stergin can go first, it may be that we will have to leave the horses here."

"Why must I always be stuck with this amoral tom cat?" asked Stergin.

"And why must I be put with this stuffy swordsman?" snapped Mander.

"It is because you two get on so well together, now move." The argumentative pair could see that Jangor was in no mood for their usual banter, so they dismounted without another word and walked gingerly onto the slope. As the gradient increased they were soon forced onto hands and knees, the rocks under them tipped over and crashed down, slipped sideways, or just wobbled enough to unsettle the climber. After ten minutes of painstakingly slow progress there was a low rumbling noise and the face of the slope rolled down where the men were.

A cloud of dust gathered about them and they vanished in a tangle of arms, legs and grey rubble. Once the noise had stopped and the dust blown away on the light breeze that blew up the slope, the two erstwhile climbers staggered to their feet coughing mightily and beating the dust from their clothes.

"Any injuries?" Asked Jangor.

"Only pride." Stergin repied.

"And a sore arse." Said Mander, rubbing the indicated area with both hands.

"Well, we cant go that way," muttered Jangor, "Is there any other way in?" he asked Jayanne.

"No. That is why he has few visitors, even the Zandaars, who hate him, don't try to invade."

"Then we have to get up there somehow." He walked slowly away from the base of the slide. Studying the walls of the canyon he rejected the idea of climbing them, they were covered in ice and snow and showed no obvious ledges that would help the traverse. Peering through the haze he saw the top of a large rock jutting from the snow above the fall. 'If we could get a rope around that, then the climbers would be in no danger of falling, but how?' he mused.

"Andel." he shouted, "How much rope have we?" Andel considered the pack horses loads before answering.

"We have about two thousand feet of heavy climbing rope, and five of light duty for guys and packing."

"That should be enough. Namdarin could that bow of yours throw a rope around that rock up there?"

"I have no idea, an arrow certainly, but pulling a rope, who can say."

"Andel. Break out the rope, two thousand feet of each." The man swung a leg over his saddle horn and slid to the ground, he went straight to the pack animal which he knew was carrying the rope and started to unload it.

"Namdarin, see if you can put an arrow behind that rock from this side and then bring it back on the other side." Namdarin walked to the right side of the canyon and fired an arrow so that it missed the rock by only a few feet, it sailed on out of sight. Namdarin moved to the other side of the canyon and reached with both hand and mind to the arrow that he could only visualise not actually see. He felt the familiar tug as it came free from the snow in which it had lain, then the steady force as it slid through the unresisting air, he opened his eyes and saw it only a hundred feet away drifting quickly to hand as all the arrows always did, a slow spiral flashing alternately green and gold fletchings in the weak winter sun.

"If I can repeat that when the arrow is carrying a rope then we may succeed."

Andel had the ropes free of the packs and was carrying them over to the right where Namdarin had fire the arrow from. Stergin and Mander helped him to stack the light weight rope in a loose coil so that it run as freely as possible after the arrow. Once the stacking was complete Namdarin took the loose end and tied it securely to the tail of an arrow, standing with the coil to his right he took careful aim, shooting high and pulled the bow, giving the whole of his right arm to the pull, holding the bow against a tightly locked left elbow, when the tension was just right he released. The huge bow twanged and launched the arrow into the sky, Namdarin knew as soon as it left the bow that it was not going to go the way that everybody hoped, as soon as it had gone far enough to pick up the stationary rope lying on the floor it started to curve, its course turned gradually right and down until it crashed into the scree ten feet from the top and fifteen feet from the right-hand wall.

"Try again." said Jangor, Mander was already reeling in the line and stacking it for the next shot.

"I'll stand behind the coil and shoot higher this time." Said Namdarin embarrassed by his failure with the first attempt.

Namdarin took his stance behind the second coil and looked up the slope,

"Kern." he said, "Throw as much of the rope up the slope as you can. " The scout nodded and picked up the whole coil he passed the loose end to Stergin and then after a single swing, slung the coil high in the air, it curved over the slope and scattered itself almost a third of the way up.

"Stergin, pull as much of it back as you can, but don't move the highest piece any closer, the further up it starts the better the chance." When Stergin had finished, the rope ran from the arrow in Namdarins hand straight up the slope nearly a third of the way and then came back in a wavy line to a small coil lying at Namdarins feet. Namdarin pulled the bow to its limit again, his arms twitching and shaking under the strain, he aimed at almost 45 degrees, to give the maximum range possible, the bow twanged and the arrow howled as it punched a hole in the air. The line followed the arrow in a high arch that looked like it would clear the entire pass not just the slope of unstable rocks, when the line had been lifted all the way to the place where it turned back down the slope, the sudden increase in mass as the arrow picked up the whole length of rope that was laying down the slope, caused the arrow to dip quickly downwards, it cleared the prominent rock by a few feet and disappeared from the view of the watchers. Namdarin waited until the rope had all fallen to the ground and then he walked slowly to the opposite side of the canyon. He closed his eyes and tried to visualise the arrow where it lay in the snow, a streamer of rope hanging from its tail. He held out his right hand and called with his mind to the arrow, 'Come to me. Come home to me. Come home to me where you belong. Come and be as one with the bow again.' The mental commands went on in this fashion, each one more insistent than the last, each one more powerful than the last, each one increased the strain in his arm, until his shoulder screamed and his back howled in pain and his legs trembled in fatigue. His mind stayed strong, the imperative of the slope could not be denied, it was essential to the man's life to reach the top and the return of the arrow was necessary. He felt the arrow release itself from the snow, but there was no easy drift after the freedom, the pressure on his arm and mind stayed, if anything it became more intense, the rope began to slide slowly up the slope, Stergin picked up the coil that was left at the bottom, and after standing on the loose end he hurled the coil up the slope, he could see from the sweat on Namdarins face that the ex-lord needed as much help as he could get. The sudden relief of the drag on the rope caused the arrow to leap into view above the upper edge of the slope, it was on the right side of the big rock, the rope was obviously behind the rock, they hoped that it would stay there. The progress of the arrow was painfully slow, most of the pain being Namdarin's, just before his legs buckled under the load Kern placed a huge arm around Namdarins chest and held him upright, instants later Kern's face was red and sweating, his arms and legs shaking, Jangor lent his own not inconsiderable strength to the contest and the arrow continued in its slow path the load getting heavier with every inch that in moved.

"Andel." groaned Jangor waving one arm up the slope. The lightest of his men understood instantly, he began the slow climb up the tricky slope, to meet the arrow coming down. Namdarin's mind was a seething morass of agony, the red light of pain was lighting up his very soul, only his will maintained his consciousness against the incredible pressure to surrender to the blackness of collapse. Namdarin was sure that he had no more to give, he was certain that all was spent when he felt the cool hand of Jayanne on his shoulder, hope fired in his heart, and power surged in his head, the arrow rushed towards the waiting hand of Andel. Andel snatched the arrow from the air and Namdarin released the force in his mind, collapse followed in a moment. Namdarin would have fallen to the ground had not his friends been supporting him, they were weakened by the struggle but not to the same extent as Namdarin.

The soft touch of Jayanne's cold hands on his face soon

brought Namdarin back to wakefulness, his eyes flicked open to stare into the deep green pools of the woman's eyes. "Did I succeed?" The question brought only a nod, the others were already puling the heavy climbing rope down the slope making a long two stranded loop that they could climb with ease.

"Who goes, and who stays to watch the horses?" asked Crathen.

"I go." Croaked Namdarin.

"And I." Whispered Jayanne, still with her eyes firmly fixed on Namdarin's face, the dreadful strain clearly visible for any to see.

"I would go." said Crathen hopefully staring at Jangor. The old warrior studied the young man's face for a moment, then nodded. Crathen heaved a sigh of relief.

"I go." Said Jangor, "and Stergin. You three stay and guard the horses and the stores, remember that there may be somebody after us. Crathen you are lightest, you go first." Before Crathen could get a hold on the ropes Kern had picked up the lowest point of the loop and pulled it tight, his large bulk merely leaning against the tension holding the rope taught parallel to the slope he said.

"That will make it easier to climb." Crathen nodded his thanks to the big man and taking the rope firmly in both hands began the slow steady progress up the treacherous incline. The rocks beneath his feet skittered and slid, bounced and pitched, each one trying, or so it seemed, to throw him down the slope. As he got nearer to the top the effect of Kern's weight on the ropes became less and they hung nearer to the surface of the slide, it almost seemed that he would fail right at the last step, but he crawled on his belly up the last few feet and disappeared from view over the edge. The entire group at the bottom of the slope held it collective breath, for what was a subjective eternity, until a head came into sight at the top and arms waved and a small voice cheered.

"Stergin, you're next." The same slow climb with the same eventual result.

"Jayanne." Said Jangor, looking down at the woman who was cradling Namdarin in her arms, her hand strayed towards the axe and defiance flared in her eyes.

"Me next." said the ex-captain. "Then you and last Namdarin. Kern you make sure that Namdarin is secured to the rope and the rest of us will pull him up."

Leaving the red haired woman stroking a tired head he started his climb. Jangor soon found that this journey was not going to be as hard as it first had seemed he was a strong man for his age, but time always leaves its marks, the heavy jerks on his arms every time a rock moved under his feet made his shoulders scream and his back clench, he feared for his ankles with every boulder that suddenly turned over, and for his life every time his grip on the rope slid an inch. He was soaked with sweat and too tired to stand by the time he crawled over the edge onto the flat open grassy place that was the resting place of the other climbers, he staggered to his feet and gave the quick wave that sent Jayanne on her own way up the scree. Surveying the scene he observed that both Crathen and Stergin were resting with their backs to the huge rock that projected like a broken tooth through the grassy surface. Jangor felt unusually warm, the air above the scree was almost spring like in its freshness and scent, there was a tang of growing things in it. The fatigue in his shoulders and legs gradually faded away and he was soon able to look over the edge and watch Jayanne's perilous ascent. He was astounded to see that she was almost at the top, she appeared to be skipping from one rock to the next, like a mountain goat, though not quite so gracefully. On the most difficult section just below the summit she abandoned the rope entirely and simply ran up the skittering rocks swinging the axe and shouting gleefully.

"You are mad." He murmured as she passed him.

"That was fun." She panted.

"Clear that rope you two." he shouted over his shoulder as he watched Kern fastening the rope around Namdarins waist. Once he was secure Namdarin himself made certain that his sword was not trapped under the rope, he drew it from his scabbard with a flash of blue steel, a blue arc curved in the sunlight and vanished into its scabbard in an instant. The bow and quiver were across his left shoulder, he was ready, a wave to the ones already at the top, and they knew.

"You guide us," Jangor said to the woman, "while we pull." She stood right on the edge, her face still flushed and her breathing still ragged from the climb. Jangor took the anchor man's place at the back of the short line, he being the heaviest, the other two settled nearer the edge.

"Take up the slack." said Jayanne, they walked slowly backwards until they felt the tension in the rope rise as they started to lift Namdarin's weight.

"Slow." Came the command. They shuffled back half a pace at a time, as Namdarin stepped up the slide, his own weight not a problem, just the placement of his feet to worry about.

"Stop." She shouted and the three held perfectly still feeling the rapid changes in the pressure on the rope, like fishermen waiting for a huge fish to tire, the twitching and twanging of the rope stopped as Namdarin regained his feet, a delicately balanced boulder having dropped him on his backside. He had a serious problem standing up again because the end of his longbow kept getting tangled in his legs and the sword felt like it was falling from its scabbard, he finally stood upright holding the sword hilt in one hand and the bow in the other, determined to loose neither. The calm green eyes waited until they were certain that Namdarin had achieved some sort of equilibrium before she turned and said, "Slowly." The inexorable progress resumed, Namdarin was hauled up the incline almost against his wishes. Jangor was getting worried about the lack of free space behind him, the ground under his feet was getting both rocky and slippery with the occasional patch of ice or snow. He was looking down for clear places to put his feet when the tension in the rope suddenly disappeared and dropped him firmly on his behind, the shock made him yelp, and the pain of a small pebble digging into his ample left buttock made him shout. "Bastard." Looking up he saw Jayanne with her arms around Namdarins neck, they were staring into each others eyes like lovestruck teenagers.

"Isn't it sickening the way some so called adults behave?" asked Stergin, with a suppressed, almost jealous, smile. Crathen pulled a very sour and definitely jealous face and turned away. Jangor got up from a large depression in the snow and rubbed his offended posterior, that precisely matched the indentation.

"You two secure that rope to the rock and throw it back down, the others may have to get up here in a hurry." As he walked towards Namdarin and Jayanne she released him and untied the rope from his middle.

"Which way now?"

"There is a narrow track up through those boulders over there."

"Lead on."

They all turned towards the rocks that she had indicated, they saw a man, he appeared to be unarmed, and almost undressed, he wore a light white tunic, which revealed his skinny tanned arms, white trousers that flapped in the light breeze, as if there were no legs inside them, and soft white slippers. His face and body looked very old, but his eyes were bright and fast moving, they flicked from one face to the next in an instant, the flashing blue eyes had an instantaneous hypnotic effect on everyone they touched. Everyone froze in place, unmoving and unblinking, no hands move towards weapons and no minds strayed towards violence, only peace poured from the deep blue eyes, peace that could not be denied.

"Who are you, and who brings the old magic to my place?" The eyes locked onto Jangor, the voice was light and smooth, soft yet impossible to ignore.

"We come seeking aid for our friend in his fight against the Zandaars, and to discover the true nature of an oath he swore."

"You are the friend." said the old man, looking straight into Namdarin's soul.

"Your oath is more powerful than you know, and you brought the old magic."

"Who are you?" asked Namdarin, his voice weak and cracking with the strain of combating the old man's trance inducing glance.

"You are a strong one, for sure. You carry much anger and hate, but also much power. You hold a sword of power, and the bow of Morgandy."

"I know little of these weapons and at the moment feel completely powerless."

"Never the less there is power in you. Jayanne, you I have met before, but you have changed a great deal. I seem to remember a tale of an axe like the one you carry, but I cannot put a name to it. The others I know not." He stared at Jayanne awaiting her introductions of her fellows.

"This is Jangor and Stergin and Crathen," each man came to attention and gave a small bow, "they are friends and soldiers of fortune."

"I do not like having soldiers or weapons in my demesne."

"We seek only your advice, if you are Granger, and then we go about my quest." interrupted Namdarin, the old man looked harshly for a moment then his gaze softened.

"I am indeed Granger, though I don't know if I can be of any assistance."

"I have heard that you are a magician of power, and that you can at least identify the true nature of the oath that binds me."

"There is no doubt that I can do that and much more besides, but should I?"

"Why shouldn't you?"

"I could be stepping on the toes of some god or other, that would cause me some serious difficulty."

"I have spoken to Xeron, he says that the time of the old gods is over and Zandaar must be made to surrender his existence here." The old man's eyes opened wider than ever and bored into Namdarin, who held the stare for a moment of eternity.

"Where and when did you talk with him?"

"I went to the very edge of death and met him at the entrance to a golden tunnel." Granger thought for a while before answering.

"He could not have told you any lies there, though he may not have told you the complete truth." He waited silently while Namdarin recounted as best he could the conversation he had with Xeron. Then he spoke of the meeting in a dream.

"The dream world belongs almost entirely to the gods, he could have lied to you with absolutely no risk. I must consider this carefully before I decide. You may come up to my cave and stay a while." He turned away from them and stepped behind a boulder, vanishing in an instant.

"Granger." said Jangor. "We have more friends and horses at the bottom of the scree and Zandaars pursuing us." Granger re-appeared.

"That I can help you with." he walked slowly to the edge of the grass, opened his arms wide and began a soft and deep chant, the rocks echoed to the rumbling of his voice and the whole valley was filled with a reverberating grating noise. Tendrils of blue fire washed down the scree, jumping from the top of one rock to the tip of the next, fastening the entire slope in and eerie blue light. Once the light was set and stable, Granger said. "Bring them up I cannot hold this forever." Jangor stood right on the edge, the toes of his boot glowing in the blue fire, and he shouted, "Kern. Mount up. I want every one and all the horses up here now." Kern pulled the picket line that had been set up and tied the horses together, Namdarin whistled weakly but it was enough for Arndrol to hear, the big horse reared and screamed, then ran at the slope, he hit the bottom at full gallop and surged upwards with great heaves of his wide hindquarters, sixteen strides took him to the top and three more to Namdarin's side. The strain of the horses thunderous passage was plain for all to hear in Granger's chant, but once it had past Granger's voice seemed to modulate in strange way, the deep chant to the rocks was still there but he was talking in a normal manner to Namdarin at the same time.

"That is a beautiful horse."

"And a good friend." Granger's chant settled and the blue light in the rocks intensified, the others started to climb and the chant took on a tense but not over strained note, this was easier than Arndrol's run, the others were walking up the slope some of the horses carrying far too much weight to run up such a steep incline. As soon as every one was safely on the grassy sward Granger withdrew the blue fire, the scree settled a little when the restraint was gone, but no major slides occurred. The old man turned away from the edge and looked tiredly at the waiting crowd.

"That was not easy, I am going to have to practise that one more often."

Walking slowly between them he went on, "Follow me, I have a nice warm cave that should easily accommodate you all." He walked between two high boulders and vanished from sight. Namdarin walked cautiously over to the place where the old man had disappeared, to his right was a cliff face and to his left a jumbled pile of rocks, one of the darker shadows of the cliff was in fact an arch like opening that lead onto a well hidden path, it was revealed as such by a wrinkled old hand that suddenly came in to the light and signalled for Namdarin to follow it, the old man had simply stepped under the arch and passed into the darkness. Once through the archway the path turned sharply left and steeply upwards, it was wide enough for the horses but not so wide that the men could walk alongside them, Namdarin felt Arndrol's warm breath on the back of his neck.

"Move along." Grumbled Jangor, who was directly behind the grey.

Namdarin followed the rapidly retreating back of the old man, who was moving quickly, but seemed to be in no real hurry. Jangor looked upwards and saw that the pathway almost closed over their heads, the jagged opening was wider in some places than others, as if there had been a solid roof up there but it had fallen through in places. An occasional snowflake came through the roof but there was no snow lying on the ground, 'It feels strangely warm in here.' Thought Jangor watching a flake gradually melt where it fell into a patch of light in front of his feet. 'This whole mountain must be a volcano, an old one, but still warm enough to keep the snow away.'

An awed silence came over the whole group as they climbed the path through the middle of the mountain, the strange formations on the walls followed exactly the line of the path, they were striations that stretched the whole length of the path like small shelves. 'This was a lava pipe.' thought Namdarin. 'It probably leads to the main crater, or less likely a secondary vent.' Glassy patches in the walls helped to scatter the light from the roof opening, the floor of the path was not well lit, but there was enough light for the people and the horses to step over the boulders that had fallen from the roof, when Namdarin was carefully stepping through the fragments of a large rock, his eyes were downwards, looking up he saw that the old man had vanished again.

"That is beginning to irritate me." Muttered Namdarin. The slope of the path became gradually easier and the light at the end of it became more clearly defined. The path eventually opened out onto a large bowl shaped depression.

"An old crater." Whispered Jangor. There was surprising warmth to the air, considering their altitude, and a distinct tang of sulphur in the air. A column of white smoke rose from the very centre of the crater, it blew into a steep spiral before it reached the fast moving air above the walls and was blown away as a smear across the sun. Approaching the fire Namdarin discovered that he had made a mistake, there was no fire, only a small pit of boiling mud, it was certainly hot enough to serve all the useful purposes of fire except one, it gave no light. Granger was standing against the wall of the crater directly opposite the point where they had all entered. When Namdarin looked at him he bent over and went into a cave, the entrance was far too small for the horses, so they had to be left outside, Namdarin left Arndrol in the sunny part of the crater with a direct instruction to stay, then he followed Granger into the cave.

The deep blackness of the cave was broken by the constant flashing of multicoloured lights that were imprisoned in large many faceted crystals scattered about the walls, which ever way he looked a crystal seemed to shinning its light directly into his eyes. Namdarin was entranced by the lights, the blues and the greens, the reds and the yellows, and the other colours to which he could put no names. He heard the footsteps of his friends behind him, but could utter no warnings because his mouth would not work, he heard them gasp as the lights ensnared them, but he could not sigh because his lungs were controlled by the weird flashing. He sensed that one of their number was not held as tightly as the rest, a deep rasping breath and a panting of the effort told Namdarin that one of them was trying desperately to break free. Namdarin caught sight of movement from the corner of his frozen eyes. The movement was all he saw, he did not see Granger carry a crystal and place it in the writhing hand of Kern, who became instantly quiescent. The entire company was now firmly held in the thrall of the strange crystalline light. Granger walked amongst them, staring into each ones eyes, his piercing blue orbs cutting straight to their souls, or so it seemed to the human statues. Granger came to stand in front of Namdarin for the second time, he paused before speaking.

"You are the driving force behind this invasion of my lands. What do you want here?" The old man made a strange gesture in front of Namdarins face, it appeared to leave streaks of light in the air for only an instant and then they were gone. Namdarin found that his voice would work but none of his other muscles would so much as twitch.

"I want your help to defeat the Zandaars." he croaked, a simple whistle would have brought Arndrol to the rescue, but the damage the horse could cause to both friends and enemy was unacceptable. Unable to take his eyes from the lights he concentrated his mind on moving the muscles of his right arm, somehow he knew that the sword would help him, all he had to do was reach it. Sweat stood out in beads on his forehead, but the arm remains stubbornly stationary.

"You cannot escape the spell of the lights. Why should I help you?"

"The Zandaars know where you are and they will come to kill you soon." The arm remained fixed in place.

"How do you know?"

"They told me at a monastery south of here that you were a wicked charlatan, and that one day they would finish you. That was before I killed them all, but now some others are following our tracks, they will be here within a day or maybe two."

"You and your band killed all the monks at the monastery?"

"No. I was alone then."

"The sword must have been a great help."

"I only found the sword more recently." Granger's cold eyes unfocused for a second as if his thoughts had wandered. Namdarin felt a slight twitching in his arm, but that subsided the moment Granger's eyes focused. Namdarin's thought turned to the sword. 'If the sword could help me against the Zandaars magic, perhaps it can help me here.' He said a silent prayer to the sword, felt a moments movement, but nothing more.

"You killed so many of them. Why take such a risk?"

"They killed my whole family, and destroyed my house."

"I feel something else behind all this, what is it?" Though Namdarin had no wish to tell the truth he could not stop himself.

"I accidentally swore an oath to one of the old gods."

"Which one?" asked Granger urgently, glancing at the sword hilt above Namdarins right shoulder.

"Xeron." Granger stepped backwards, shock plain upon his face.

"And now you carry what appears to be his sword."

"His sword?" asked Namdarin.

"Is its blade blue and yellow?"

"Yes."

"Then it is without doubt the sword of Xeron that was lost over a thousand years ago. Where did you find it?"

"In a vault beneath a tree that killed all that came too close by putting them to sleep." Granger stepped back again.

"You defeated the sleeping willow. A worthy deed. I wondered what that tree was hiding, the sword of Xeron indeed." Granger turned away deep in thought, he was blatantly shaken by Namdarin's words, he knew them to be true because the lights would allow no lies. Namdarin gave up the physical reach for the sword and tried to move it with the power of his mind. Calling silently to Xeron for the strength to reach the sword, he pictured in his mind, as clearly as he could, the sword rising slowly from its scabbard, gradually revealing more and more of the blue blade. Did he actually feel it move? Was it really responding to his mental instructions? Did he actually hear metal scraping as it rose? Granger must have heard it to, because he turned, his eyes opened wide in amazement, Namdarin had a moment to study the fright on the old man's face before the black pommel stone fell through his line of sight into his open right hand. A rush of power surged through Namdarin's cramped muscles, the sword lunged forwards like dark lightning until the point rested in the hollow of the old man's throat. The deep blue flash of the moving sword pulled the fixed eyes from the entrapping light for an instant. In that moment of freedom Kern threw the crystal to the floor and closed his eyes, he fell to his knees and began to crawl from the cave. Jayanne twisted her wrist and took the haft of the axe in her right hand, this released her from the spell of the lights, with a howl of previously impotent rage she flew at the old man, axe held high and murder in her eyes.

"No." shouted Namdarin, the axe stopped inches short of the fatal blow, a wicked snarl on the pretty face.

"Release my friends." Said Namdarin. Granger made a slow gesture with one hand, and the lights settled into a much slower rhythm of reds and greens that filled the cave with a steady glow. A shuffling of feet told Namdarin that his friends were free.

"Your turn to answer some questions." he said as calmly as he could, "Why should you live?"

CHAPTER SIXTEEN

Granger's face froze like ice on a winter river, his eyes focused far off into the utmost reaches of infinity, for an eternal moment he said nothing. Then his mouth started to form the words as slowly and carefully as it could.

"I know the sword of Xeron, and the bow of Morgandy, the axe I might have some knowledge of, in the old texts. These things I can help you with. Your oath, I may be able to discover something about. My actions against you and your friends were only precautions to ensure my own safety." His old eyes locked firmly on Namdarin's, a thin trickle of blood ran down his neck from the tip of the blue sword.

"You will help me without reservation?"

"Certainly."

"Can we trust him?" Asked Jangor, before Namdarin could move the sword.

"What option do we have? If we kill him and go on with my quest, then we may be missing some important information."

"He may mislead us."

"If he does, then the last survivor will come back here and kill him. I think he understands that. Have you any other information with which to bargain for your life?"

"I know a defence against their iridium weapons." Namdarin's eyebrows raised in surprise, Granger knew that he was now safe.

"What is this defence?"

"Do I live or die?"

"You live." Namdarin jerked the sword away the wrinkly old neck, the tiny cut bled for a minute or two before it stopped, leaving a thin red stain down the front of Granger's white tunic.

"I have come many miles to ask for your aid," said Namdarin, "we have fought many battles recently, you must understand our caution when we are captured by some strange magical means."

"You must understand my wariness of strangers of any sort. Jayanne, I approached because she seemed lost and helpless, this state has since been rectified to a truly remarkable extent, I would not have given odds on her surviving a few days."

"Which only goes to show how fallible you are." Snapped Jayanne. Granger bowed towards Jayanne by way of an apology.

"Can you read?" asked Namdarin.

"More languages than you know of." snorted Granger, with a sour look.

"Can you read this?" Namdarin threw him a small book. The old man's reactions were good enough to snatch it from the air. Having snared the book he gave Namdarin a disgusted look, 'How dare he treat a book this way?' was the thought that they all could see in the glance. Looking down at the treasure he now held Granger's eyes and mouth made three round ohs of surprise.

"Where did you get this?"

"From a priest, he had no further use for it."

"This is the teachings of Zandaar. In it self it could be very useful, but one of the master copies would be better, they are available only at monasteries."

"I have one of those as well."

"You do." The old man's voice rose in pitch almost to a squeal. "Fetch it, fetch it quickly." Namdarin went outside to his horse leaving the old man hopping from one foot to the other in excitement. Namdarin returned with the cloth wrapped bundle under one arm.

"Will you help us?" asked Namdarin.

"Of course." said Granger in a rough whisper, his hand reaching urgently for the book. Namdarin released the bundle and the old hands moved with startling speed, they ripped the covering away in tattered rags, they turned the book over so that he could read the title inscribed in large ornate letters on the front.

"It is. It is." He muttered to himself, before he almost crashed to the floor, his legs crossed and the book resting on his bony knees, he opened it almost reverently. His head turned slowly from side to side as he read the large flowing script, the occasional sounds escaped his lips but made no sense to the ones that heard them. The heavy pages fluttered as he turned them, rustling loudly as they flashed across in front of the old man's eyes, the merest second was too long for his eyes to be away from the writings.

"He is lost." Said Jangor. Namdarin frowned a question.

"He is in a world where the book is the only existence, he will come back when he is hungry." Namdarin nodded thinking of all the times that same saying had been used to calm his worrying wife, referring to their son. The memories brought tears to his eyes and a catch to his throat.

"We will stay here for a while then." he said, his voice roughened by the emotions of memory.

The whole group settled down in Granger's cave, they selected sleeping places and unloaded their belongings from the horses, they had little provision for their mounts but they would come to no real harm to do without until morning.

None of their voices disturbed Granger, none of their movements moved him, only the smell of Mander's cooking in the mud pot finally broke the old man's trance.

"That smells good." He said softly.

"It may smell good but it still tastes of sulphur." Was Mander's disgusted answer. "Is there no way to get rid of this awful taste?" His question was more rhetorical than anything else. Granger shared their meal but did not stop reading. Namdarin noticed that the pages flashed over at exactly the same pace as they had when he was using both hands, 'But he is using both hands, for eating.' He leaned forwards watching very closely, the left hand was holding a wooden bowl of Mander's soup, the right hand held a large spoon, the spoon never stopped it slow cycling, bowl, mouth, bowl, mouth, it went, not pausing always moving, and so suddenly that Namdarin jumped, the book turned over its next page with absolutely no help from either of the old man's wrinkled hands . 'That certainly looks like magic to me. How can the

Zandaars call him a charlatan? Perhaps they are more frightened of him than they want anybody to know? Maybe they don't want anyone to come to see him? I wonder why?'

Kern came into the cave and talked quietly to Jangor for a moment. Once Kern was settled down and eating Jangor spoke to the group in general.

"Kern has had a good look around, there is only one way up here, the way we came, there is no way out of the crater other than the way we came, this place is easy to defend , but could just as easily become a trap, I think we should leave as soon as possible."

"I agree." said Namdarin, "But I must find out what Granger can tell me before I go. Perhaps he can be persuaded to come with us."

"Every day we wait puts the pursuers a day closer."

"That cannot be helped, they will have great difficulty with the rock slide, they may even spend a few days looking for another way in."

"What if they post guards at the bottom of the slide?"

"Then we kill them and escape while the rest are elsewhere."

"There are far too many ifs for my liking." said Jangor shaking his head slowly from side to side.

Darkness began to fall outside the cave, the brightness of the flashing crystals seemed to increase in a direct relationship, though the pattern of the pulsating was certainly calming it was no longer mind numbingly hypnotic. Namdarin found himself watching a single crystal closely, its slowly changing light made him very sleepy, three times his chin fell against his chest and woke him up. After the third occasion he stirred himself and stood up, once he turned his eyes away from the light, the drowsiness vanished. 'It is merely our own tiredness that makes the lights so inviting.' Granger was still sitting cross-legged on the floor, the book of Zandaar open on his lap, every two or three minutes a page would turn over. 'How can he read so intently for so long in this pulsating light? 'Walking over to the old man's resting place Namdarin noticed that the light on the pages of the book was a cold clear white, steady and bright, though with no apparent source . He waved his hand over Granger's bowed head, its shadow passed across the book, his hand glowed white in the strange light that seemed to come straight down from the roof of the cave. Looking for the source of the light Namdarin could see one of the strange crystals embedded in the roof, it was dark and appeared to be giving no light at all. Namdarin put his head in the beam and looked straight into the source, it did indeed come from the crystal in the roof, a narrow white beam, that was perfect for reading.

While Namdarin was looking into the beam the light changed, it took on the same red and green flashing as all the others, Namdarin looked down at the book, the pages were once again lit by the white light, but now it came from another crystal. 'This old man performs some clever tricks with these lights, I wonder if they can be made to work by any one?' All the crystals seemed to be firmly fixed to the rocks, except for the one that Kern had smashed earlier, each of the fragments that still lay on the floor was flashing like those in the walls.

Namdarin gathered up the largest of the fragments and sat down to inspect them. They looked just like ordinary quartz, with the same hexagonal type structures and the same angles, of the six he held, four were long and pointed at each end, quite beautiful in fact, the other two where short and jagged. 'I wonder if these can be worked like normal quartz?' He put the four good ones in his pouch and tried to smash the others into a more aesthetic shape, using a handy sized rock that just happened to be between his feet at the time. Each time the improvised hammer struck the crystal it produced a shower of bright sparks, some red, some green, and some indeterminate shades in between. The fountains of sparks leapt away from his hands but extinguished themselves before they reached the ground, as short lived as any sparks from a fire. 'Perhaps there is a size below which these crystals cease to function.' Namdarin tried to investigate this thought by finding the smallest of the shards that still showed any colour. The difficult part was not finding the glowing splinters, but finding the dead ones. For many minutes he searched and discovered none at all. All the ones he could find were flashing just like rest of the fragments. 'Exactly like the rest.' Gathering a handful of the shards together he found that indeed they did all change colour at exactly the same time as if they were still part of the same large crystal. Sifting through those in his hand he picked out the smallest, it was less than a quarter of an inch long and about half that wide. Placing the fragment carefully in a small depression in the rock floor in front of him, so that any tiny pieces would not be too far away, Namdarin crushed it with his rock. The flash of light was so bright that his eyes closed reflexively, a large bright green blur was clearly visible on the inside of his eyelids. When he opened them again the blur did not coincide with the place where the splinter had been completely destroyed, no tiny splinters were anywhere to be found. It was only after he had given up looking for the remains of the splinter that he realised that the blur was in the wrong place. Carefully resuming his sitting position he saw that the blur was in almost exactly the same place as the biggest piece of the crystal. 'Striking the small one must have made the big one flash.' He tested this thought by moving the big one around so that he was hitting the small one where he could not possibly see it, it took a few tries before his makeshift hammer actually struck the small crystal, when it did the result was just as had been expected. The big crystal flashed brightly as the small one was crushed. Namdarin decided to check this to be sure it was not just a lucky coincidence, he turned round and found that he had not hit the small crystal squarely, he had merely clipped it, it now lay in four small flashing pieces that lit the depression in the floor quite brightly. 'Total destruction is not necessary. I wonder how small an impact on one will make all the others flash?' Eventually he found that simply by tapping one crystal against a rock, with no where near enough force to cause it any damage at all, would cause all the pieces from the same crystal to flash a little, not enough to be seen in strong daylight, but certainly visibly on a cloudy day or at night. "I wonder if this could be use for signalling over some distance?" He whispered to himself.

"So I have heard." Replied Granger, who had finished reading some time ago and had been quietly observing Namdarin's experiments with the crystals.

"How? Knocking them against hard surfaces is going to cause damage and restrict the useful life of the crystals."

"Well, a gentle tap will make all the fragments from the same crystal flash, as you have already discovered. Then a direct thought communication can be set up."

"How much training does this need?"

"I have no idea, I never bothered to try it, it may not work at all, it could be just an old wives tale."

"How do you know of it then?"

"I read it in one of my many books, I have a fairly extensive library."

"So did the monks, until I burned it." Granger could hear the hate in Namdarin's voice and shook his head in horror at the destruction of so many treasures of knowledge.

"Come with me." Namdarin stood up and followed him into the darkness at the back of the cave, noting as he went that all his friends were fast asleep. They went out of the main cave and down a narrow passage that turned sharply to the right, Namdarin had to feel his way along because the light from the cave did not reach much past the entrance. The walls were rough and obviously not man made. The passage opened onto a small cave that was illuminated by more crystals in the roof, but these were giving a soft almost white light, it seemed to have a tendency to pulse slowly to a yellow but the pulsing was so slow and so slight that Namdarin could not be sure that it was actually there at all. Around the cave were row upon row of shelves, each one full to overflowing with books. The whole room was filled with the characteristic smell of old and musty books. The centre of the cave was taken up with a large table, it was a rough piece of furniture to say the least, the ends of the planks that made up the top were badly cut and unevenly fitted, the legs were merely planks nailed together along one edge, the chair beside the table was constructed in a similar fashion. 'All the materials had to come in through the passage and be assembled in here.' Thought Namdarin turning his attention to Granger who was now rummaging through the books on one of the shelves, "No. No. No." he muttered inspecting the bindings carefully. Finally, "Ah, this is the one." He pulled the book from its resting place and turned to the table. He put the book down on top of the pile of open ones on the table, crashed down into the chair, which let out a loud groan at the sudden impact. 'If I dropped into that chair it would collapse.' Thought Namdarin. Granger flicked through the pages with practised ease, from the ruffled edges it was clear that this was a much used volume. Namdarin moved around the table to peer over the bony shoulder, the flickering scribblings on the pages as they fluttered by meant absolutely nothing to him.

"Here it is." said Granger stopping the frantic search through the book. "It mentions the flashing stones that can be found only in certain old volcanoes, it talks of an affinity between fragments broken from the stones, they appear to have grown out of the rock and so have a sort of wholeness that cannot be broken by separation of the individual fragments. They react as a mass even when widely scattered. It doesn't mention the actual sizes of the pieces but it does say that the larger pieces have a greater range. It is all very confused, there are no clear instructions, it seems very vague about the whole matter, that is why I have paid no attention to it before now. Mind you, I have no wish to talk to any one, near or far, on a regular enough basis to warrant any real effort or experimentation."

"How can a lump of, admittedly pretty, rock join two minds together?" Asked Namdarin.

"I am not sure." Replied Granger, without looking up from the yellowed pages of the book, "It must collect the thought patterns, or what ever they are, and send them to the rest of itself, where the other brain decodes the information. This is of course total guess work."

"How do we find out?"

"By experiment naturally. Go and get some of the bigger splinters." Namdarin frowned at the way the old man issued orders, but he produced two of the best crystals from his pouch, and handed them over. Granger turned them over and over in his hands, he had only ever seen them in the natural rock bound form before.

"They are pretty, aren't they? They could certainly make some interesting jewellery."

"If this is going to be a long range communicator I would prefer it to be secret, the more fragments there are the more people would be listening in."

"I see that. To start with I will try and send a picture of something to you. Clear your mind and hold the crystal to your forehead, that puts is as near to the brain as possible." Granger put the crystal to his head and closed his eyes, Namdarin did the same. Namdarin felt a strange itching sensation at the back of his eyes, as if a beetle was crawling into his head. Then he saw a picture of the mud pot in the middle of the crater, it was blowing bubbles of alternating red and green. A moment later the picture was gone, Namdarin gasped, and tried to reach the picture again, but it was nowhere to be found.

"Did you get that?" Asked Granger.

"Was it a picture of the mud pot blowing coloured bubbles?"

"You received it then. Was it clear?"

"Only for an instant."

"That is strange it felt as if it was perfect to me. The picture could not have been clearer, I think the crystal helps visualisation, it seems to make things more solid in your head. You try." He put the crystal to his forehead and waited with his eyes tight shut. Namdarin put his crystal to his brow and thought of Arndrol standing outside the outer cave, shifting his weight and stamping his feet, the horse became very solid and utterly lifelike in Namdarin's mind.

"A horse." Said Granger, "I see a horse."

"What sort of horse?" Asked Namdarin looking at the ornate saddle with his minds eye.

"A horse." Said Granger, "The details seem vague, almost blurred."

"The picture was perfect."

"The one I received was not."

"There is something wrong here." said a bemused Namdarin.

"Perhaps we need a better contact with the crystal."

"What do you mean?"

"Something more fluid, put the crystal in your mouth. That way there is a fluid contact that covers much more of the surface." Granger put his crystal in his mouth and turned to face Namdarin, who followed suit. Namdarin looked down at the old man sitting on a rickety chair with a crystal in his mouth flashing green and red, he then saw himself standing with the same crystal flashing in his mouth, 'Like children playing....'

"With silly stones." Granger finished the thought and Namdarin spat his crystal into the palm of his hand like it had burned his tongue.

"Well we now know how they work. That was an amusing picture you painted of us." Laughed the old man.

"Lets try again, this time only touch the stone with your tongue." Each of them held a stone near their mouths and reached out with their tongues to touch it. When both had only the tips of their pink tongues touching their respective crystals, they had an impression of the others mind, Namdarin felt an aching loneliness, and Granger a raging hatred. Together they turned away from the frightened faces.

"These things can show things that should not be seen." said Granger.

"They tell things better left unsaid."

"One must be sure of the message to be sent before one uses these stones."

An awkward silence fell between the two and they were each absorbed in their own thoughts. Granger thought of having friends around him again, ones that he could trust not to brand him with charges of witchcraft, though that was obviously his chosen profession. Namdarin thought of the uses of the crystal communicators, if Granger would consent he could be of great assistance without ever leaving the security of his cave.

"Granger." said Namdarin wakening the old man from his reverie, "Can the priests of Zandaar reach out with their minds to find me or perhaps the sword?" He had remembered the incident of that morning when he had the feeling of being hunted.

"Oh yes, but it does cost them a lot of energy, they still seem to be very inefficient in their use of their magic. From reading their book I would say that is a deliberate ploy on Zandaar's part, I think he may be afraid of a real adept coming along to displace him."

"Is he really that weak?"

"No. But he hopes that he has reduced the risk to almost nothing. How ever, he was not able to go and get the sword for himself, so he does have certain restrictions, the trick will be to find out what they are and use them against him."

"Does the book give any hint to his limits?"

"Only in the things it doesn't say."

"What do you mean?"

"It makes absolutely no mention of any form a accumulated energy. The priests all work with only the energy they have to hand, they don't store it in any devices, nor do they use what is all around them, they use the energy of their bodies only, that is a serious restriction to ones total output."

"What sort of devices?"

"Well, the sword is one, the axe that Jayanne carries may be another, the bow, is and isn't both at the same time."

"That makes no sense."

"I'll start with the sword. You have probably noticed a feeling of power, strength, what ever when you pull it from its scabbard." Namdarin nodded. "It feeds energy into you, energy it has taken from those it has killed, now being a gods sword it can also be charged with energy by other means, those I will tell you of later. The axe, I think, I am not sure, gets its power only from killing, but it is very efficient. The bow is different. It takes energy from the user, channels it into the arrow, the arrow remains passive in flight and transfers the energy to the target on impact, except where the user redirects the arrow, then some of the impact energy is used for the direction changes. When the arrow is returning it uses energy from all around it, heat, light, it cares not. This means that the bow is a temporary storage device, as is the arrow, though the arrow is also a transmitter and receiver of external energies, it is very complex."

"I think I begin to understand."

"Take my staff." Namdarin glanced at the innocuous looking piece of wood that Granger used to help him walk around, it was seven feet long, smooth and straight, both its ends were shod with iron, or maybe steel, feet. It seemed to be an ordinary walking staff, if a little long for an old man. "All day, every day I feed energy into it from the surroundings, notice how it seems to be a rich dark wood." Namdarin nodded. Granger muttered something unintelligible under his breath. The staff lightened until it was the colour of a peeled pine stick. Then it shifted back to its original colour.

"Why the colour change?" asked Namdarin.

"The dark colour means that it is absorbing light from the air, the pale colour is the natural colour of the wood. You saw the blue fire at the rock slide that was merely a little of the energy released from the staff. The reason it was so hard for me was that the staff was so far away, it was exactly where you see it now, I had to be the channel for the power to hold the rocks, holding a pathway open over all that distance is very difficult, and the energy had to come directly from me, I could not tap the power in the staff to open the pathway to the staff, if you see what I mean?"

"Yes, I think so. How much power can the staff hold?"

"If I was to release all of it at once it would probably take apart the whole of this mountain, but both me and the staff would be destroyed as well."

"Is there no way for you to survive such a blast?"

Granger thought for a while before answering thus. "It may be. It might be possible to project the energy as an expanding sphere, with me at the centre, if I can make the surface of the sphere hard enough and push it outwards fast enough, then all the debris would fall away from me, but if the balance was not exactly perfect, the sphere would burst like a soap bubble, and the back blast would destroy anything at the centre. I haven't spent much time on the offensive uses of magic, I have been devoted all my life to self preservation and the search for knowledge."

"There must be some important information in the book of Zandaar, all their methods must be in there somewhere."

"Oh yes. Including a method for beating their iridium weapons."

"What is it?"

"All it requires is a stronger mind than the man using the weapon, to beat him you must take control of the weapon as he is about to use it, taking it in the air is more difficult and taking control after it has burst is in one way easier but in another much more difficult. I think that it is possible to stop the expansion of the fireball and re-compress it back into its metallic form, but the quantity of energy needed can only come from the consumption of some of the target, which means that the damage can be limited but not stopped entirely."

"What of the lightning bolts?"

"Ah, there was no mention of lightning bolts in the book, that must be a new development, I would have thought that stopping a lightning bolt once it has hit its target would be impossible, because of the speed with which it acts. You would have to take them in the air or in the hand."

"How do they work?"

"As usual with the Zandaars, it is merely a question of visualisation and belief, see it with the mind, believe it will happen and it does. Most of their magic is of this extremely simplistic nature."

"How have they lasted longer than all the other old religions?"

"Numbers mainly, and the fact that their god doesn't seem to tire of meddling in human affairs, the other gods got very bored very quickly, but not Zandaar, perhaps he's not the brightest of the bunch."

"He's not short of followers, or cunning."

"True, we'll no doubt find out in due course."

Namdarin thought for a few moments before deciding that it was time to tell Granger everything. He struggled for a while to find the words, he stammered and stuttered but once the tale was started it flowed all on its own, it appeared to have a will to be told, a life to live and a wish for expression. Granger did not interrupt once, questions he had but he left them unasked. The village in the forest with it guardian heads shocked him, Namdarin's destruction of the monastery amazed him, and Namdarin's meeting with Xeron at the edge of death astounded him. Finally the tale was told and Namdarin's creaky voice ground to a halt. Granger sat perfectly still, his eyes glazed and his mind free. Namdarin felt a pressure all around his head, like the hangover after his coming of age, only more so, and increasing and all pervading presence, he put his hands to his temples and felt nothing there except for the rising force crushing his mind, 'Not the head, the mind. I must resist. How? A wall, a good and strong stone wall.' He visualised the wall of his old home, it was high and strong and solid, nothing could breach that wall. The pressure eased until a raging black fire came and tore the wall the wall down. 'Not a wall of stone, a wall of ice.' A massive glittering edifice of flashing ice appeared in his mind, the cold was extreme but the pressure was almost gone, a roaring blast of heat and the ice washed away in rivers, the pressure returned doubled. Namdarin could feel his mind shrinking under the load, 'Resistance does not work, I must counter this strange force.' He felt that he was being crushed at the centre of a collapsing bubble, 'To make a bubble bigger one must increase the pressure on the inside.' he started to push back, he pushed harder and harder, the pressure rising all the time, logarithmically it rose, doubling every second, until, after what seemed to be an eternity, it burst. Namdarin's mind almost blew itself apart in the instant of the expansion, the soundless concussion echoed in his empty head. Slowly the scattered pieces of his consciousness gathered themselves together in the pattern to which they had become quite accustomed. Namdarin shook his head and opened his eyes, his vision was blurred and his head hurt abominably, but he was at least alive, he was not at all sure that the same was true for Granger, the old man's head was resting on the book in front of him, he was not moving at all, Namdarin could detect no signs of breathing, only a slight pulse in the veins at the temple showed that he was actually still alive.

"Are you all right?" asked a voice that Namdarin failed to recognise for some time. Turning he saw Jayanne in the passage way.

"I think I will be fine, but I am not at all sure about him."

"The air around you was filled with yellow light."

"Was it?" Namdarin was totally confused by the conversation and was still waiting for Granger to wake up. With a loud groan the old man finally stirred.

"Ow." he said holding his head gingerly in both hands. "That hurts. I have never felt a mind as powerful as yours before. What did you do?"

"Were you the one attacking me?" Asked Namdarin, Jayanne raised the axe above her head and prepared to strike, Namdarin held one hand up, a sign for her to restrain herself, this she did with some reluctance.

"Yes, I was only trying to assess your strength of will."

"Did I pass your test?"

"You beat me. You are stronger than me. You resisted at first then suddenly you threw everything back at me, the power kept bouncing one way then the other, each bounce higher than the one before, until I gave way, not you, the amateur, but me, I am far more experienced in this sort of trial, and you beat me, I cannot judge your strength because it exceeds my own."

"Did I injure you?"

"No. Have no fear for me, I am only extraordinarily tired. I must rest." He wobbled uncertainly to his feet and left the small library to the younger two, one with an exhausted, and one with an anxious expression.

"What time is it?" asked Namdarin.

"It has been fully dark for some time. How are you?"

"I will be fine, I just need some rest, let us go and get some sleep." He stood up, staggered and fell against her strong shoulder, she guided him into the passage, as he left the small room he turned for a moment and made a small gesture with his right hand, the lights were extinguished, as if they had never been. He looked at his hand, though he could not actually see it in the absolute darkness that suddenly engulfed them, he wiggled his fingers and wondered, 'How did I do that?' Shaking his head in disbelief he went into the main section of the cave and collapsed into his blankets, though sleep seemed to be actively avoiding him, the same was not true for Jayanne, her head was resting on his chest, the slow rise and fall and the hypnotic thumping of his heart soon sent her into a deep sleep. Namdarin's thoughts were a confused and chaotic jumble of unconnected and disjointed ideas, some with no obvious source. Finally he came to the most likely conclusion that this mess in his head was caused by the crystal link that had existed for so short a time between himself and Granger, 'I wonder if Granger has pulled as much information from my mind as I have from his?' A quick glance at the raised platform where the old man was snoring loudly was evidence enough, he had not. 'Time for a little snooping, I think.' Practice had improved his abilities greatly, he made the link to the collective consciousness of the horses in an instant, he was greeted as usual by a mental nuzzling and reassuring warmth, reaching further to find any others he could detect none. 'Either they are out of range or the rocks restrict contact between groups. Or more unlikely they are all dead.' Passing on to the human sleepers was easier than he had expected, none were having dreams of any significance, none showed any influence from the Zandaars, Granger's was of interest though. He dreamt of words, millions of them in serried ranks on white and yellow papers, parchments, vellums, even old plant leaves, they marched in endless lines, in perfect formations, generally to war, one script warring on another. Namdarin stepped away from this dream, choosing to go on to Jayanne's dream, by comparison to Granger's it was like diving into a cold, clear pool of green water, exactly the shade of her eyes. A picture of pure tranquillity, not any real forms just peace all about. A soft light of green and gold illuminated and area where she sat, holding in her arms a bundle of rags, as Namdarin approached she looked up and smiled at him, the golden light brighten with the smile and a deep warmth filled him, from within the bundle came a small chubby fist which waved somewhat spastically about searching not for anything in particular but merely moving for moving's sake. The fist was attached to a narrow wrist and thence to a fat forearm, a dimpled elbow and a round upper arm, a small shoulder to a slender neck, a round fat face, the only feature that was clear on the face was the eyes, a strange blend of blue and green that appeared to cycle between the two, a colour of an undecided nature, shifting endlessly from green to blue and back again, the black pupils grew bigger and bigger until they filled all of his view except for a narrow band of changing colour around the edge. It was like falling off an icy precipice into a frozen lake in the middle of the darkest night of a year, cold blackness surrounded him, it ate into his bones and chilled his soul.

Slowly, so slowly as to be almost imperceptible the scene changed, it seemed to take many hours of coldness before something came into view. Coalescing from the blackness of deepest night, came small lights and large buildings, hey were spread out over the entirety of his vision, dark grey walls and small windows lit with yellow light that danced and flickered like candles in a draught. A sprawling network of narrow streets, that twisted and turned in unpredictable manners, the depth of the shadows in some of the streets was such that nothing of them could be seen at all. Namdarin moved his head and the view changed, this was the first sign that he had any control over this dream. Where ever he looked the buildings were the same, the same dull grey, the same small windows and the same depressing outlook, there was no decoration, no colour, no flags, no flowers, no gardens, just buildings, passing closely over the sloping roof of one such he saw below him a wider street, on it were people, some walking, some riding, on horses, or in carriages, they were all going one way, Namdarin decided to follow them, he had become used to the fact that he was flying over their heads, none looked up, none saw him, none would have seen him because his presence was ultimately slight, merely a dream shadow drifting in the night. As he flew along the lines of citizenry he noted that every one joining the main flow from the smaller streets turn in the same direction as all the others, not one turned the other way, the pace of travel in the street was dropping as it passed its carrying limit, people were shoulder to shoulder pushing and shoving to make headway against the static mass of humanity, Namdarin wondered what it could be that was pulling these people so strongly, what was so important to them that they must rush out in the middle of the night, 'They are wearing their night clothes.' he muttered noticing for the first time that most of the crowd below had not even bothered to dress. Something had taken them from their sleep, something that would allow no time for anything but movement. Flashing over their heads he sought the cause, the main street opened onto an even larger one, it was lined both sides with large trees, they were swaying as if a gale was blowing, but the wind was not of the air it was a tide of people washing against the boles of the trees, shaking them from twig tips to roots. The flow of people was more organised on this boulevard, they seemed to have settled into a marching pace each stepping forwards at the same time as his neighbours, though the pace was slow and rhythmic it moved them along quicker than on the smaller street he had just left. Namdarin could seem the waves of movement rushing down the street towards him, they came from a building at the end of the boulevard, as he approached he could see the people crowding into the building from other tree lined thoroughfares, six of the great roads coincided at the temple, for such it was, beyond any shadow of doubt, for it was the only ornamented building he had seen, its high walls were painted an intense white that was almost glaringly bright even in the darkness all around. It had no windows but appeared to glow with a strange inner light, that seeped through the surfaces and illuminated everything around. The pale faces of the people showed more strongly as they neared the walls, the huge open doorways admitted six abreast, though each admission was checked by the hand full of guards stationed there. The guards seemed to be looking for a specific face, or possible one that didn't fit.

    Namdarin drifted slowly towards the nearest door, the opening was more than high enough for him to pass inside without coming near to the people below, the closer he got to the blank walls the more frightened he became, he felt his insubstantial chest tighten as the guards looked over the next rank of people, he held his breath then wafted in with them, two of the guards glanced around quickly, as if they had forgotten something, or caught a sign of movement out of the corner of an eye, they were nervous about something. Once through the doorway the corridor inside was considerably higher than the people, Namdarin stayed as close to the ceiling as he could, though his vision was becoming more and more confused by the intensity of the light all around him, it leaked through the walls and the floors, it permeated the very air with a glowing nimbus that was difficult to see through. The speed of the people below him slowed down to a very slow walk, they were packing closer and closer together, shoulder to shoulder and chest to back they squeezed along the narrowing corridor, still firmly fixed in their collective blank faced rapture, their steady pace not changing rate only length, until they were almost marching on the spot. Namdarin had no sensation of temperature, though he could see the sweat pouring from the bodies all around, the air became so dense with evaporated water and thick light that his insubstantial body was having difficulty breathing, he felt constricted and imprisoned, though he was not a claustrophobic person he was slowly creeping towards the verge of panic. He realised that the main cause of the panic he felt was the destination of all these hypnotised people, he had no real wish to lay eyes upon the source of their dreadful compulsion. But he was being pulled along just as they were, he struggled to back away from the door ahead, but he could not, his mind remained definitely his own, but he could no longer us it to control his movements. Only feet from what he now assumed to be the last doorway he thought of the sword, he drew its picture in his mind, the edges and colours kept loosing their coherence, and the visualisation kept scrambling itself into a mush that showed no intelligible design at all. Some force was interfering with his mind, the light from the doorway was blinding, even with his eyes shut it seemed to punch holes straight into his brain.

'Its the light that is controlling all these people and now me.' he thought. Suddenly his brain picked a piece of a recent conversation from memory and replayed it as a shadow play inside his head. "The dark colour means that it is absorbing light from the air." Granger had said it, Namdarin wondered if he could do something similar to get rid of the awful brightness in the corridor. He thought of the sword, a hazy picture formed in his mind, the blue blade with its yellowed edges, wavered and wobbled, the plain cross piece, shimmered and shook, the hard black of the pommel stone was clear and sharp, it glittered with a black radiance, every facet showed a blackness deeper than night, colder than the spaces between the stars, more empty than the deepest pit. 'Fill it, fill it with all the light all round.' he thought, begging and pleading that it would suck up the light like a dry sponge. With every thought the stone appeared to swell, the harsh white light was torn to tattered streamers that sped into its black heart, Namdarin's progression towards the final door stopped, the steps of the people below him faltered, they stumbled one against another and fell in confusion to the floor. The black jewel increased in size rapidly and engulfed Namdarin in cold darkness. His control returned and he breathed freely for the first time in what seemed to be hours, his breath came in huge shuddering gasps, as if he had been starved of air for many minutes. Once the gasping was under some sort of control he opened his eyes, to find himself back in the cave, Granger and Jayanne staring into his face, twin looks of concern, Namdarin's head resting on her knees.

"Are you alright now?" She asked, her free right hand twitching next to the haft of the axe.

"I think so." Said Namdarin, one word at a time, in between lungs full of air.

"What happened?" Asked the scratchy voice of the old man.

Namdarin sat upright and related as accurately as he could the experience, Granger nodded occasionally but did not interrupt.

"You travelled to Zandaarkoon." He said when the story was told.

"You mean that I was actually there? It wasn't a dream."

"Your body never moved from here, but your essence, or spirit was in Zandaarkoon. This sort of travelling is quite common amongst the adept of certain religions. They say that some can travel all over the world in a single dream."

"Then it was a dream."

"Yes and no. These things are not always clearly one or the other."

"What does this maybe dream mean?"

"I don't know, I think that Zandaar himself was creating the hypnotic light, it was most likely his way of feeding. Gods are fed by prayer or belief, probably the people of Zandaarkoon believe in the light of Zandaar, and follow it to its source, where Zandaar takes their energy to himself. If this theory it correct, when you go against Zandaar, you will be taking on the massed spiritual might of the entire city."

"The pommel stone of Xeron's sword took energy from the light, I felt it."

"Yes, but could it hold enough to beat Zandaar himself? I doubt it."

"So we need some way to separate him from his energy reserve."

"Either that or force him to expend it faster than he can absorb it."

"How can it be possible to deplete such a reserve, against the tide of energy coming in? It would be like bailing out a river with a bucket." Namdarin shook his head, the enormity of the task ahead was finally beginning to show itself.

"You can dam a river and reduce its flow to almost nothing."

"But eventually you have to either let the water out or the dam will break."

"If the dam breaks then the ensuing flood generally destroys the old river, and replaces it with a new one."

"You're suggesting that we, by some as yet un-devised means, make him take on more energy than he can cope with, forcing his power level higher and higher until he actually explodes." Namdarin's voice crept up the scale in disbelief.

"As an available option, yes." Granger nodded.

"If such an explosion could be engineered, how could any one nearby, or perhaps even the whole world, survive?"

"That would be a problem."

"I grow weary of all this theory, dawn cannot be far away and I need some sleep." Said Namdarin, laying down and almost pulling Jayanne with him. She lay against his side, and draped one arm across his chest. Granger instantly realised that there would be no further discussions of the problem that night and retired to his own bed with a disgruntled huffing. Jayanne pulled the furs high around both their bodies and wriggled closer to the warm hairy chest. Namdarin half rolled towards her and slowly slid his hand inside the light shirt that she wore for bed. Gently he cupped her firm breast and rubbed the rough edge of his thumb across the rapidly hardening nipple, her breath tightened in her throat and her chest heaved against his hand, once the nipple was fully erect he rolled it between the finger and thumb, he could feel the excitement rising in her. Slowly he reached his head down to hers and kissed her softly on the mouth, his tongue flashing inside for a mere moment.

"Good night my dear." He said as he turned his back on her and pulled her arm tightly around him. She was disturbed by his sudden withdrawal, she wanted much more of his gentle caresses, but didn't know how to tell him, she could think of no words that would tell him how she felt, she had never felt this sort of empty longing before, his chest rose and fell slowly under her arm, sleep had taken him utterly. When his grip on her arm relaxed she slowly slid her hand down the hard ridges of his lower ribs and across the muscles of his belly, wriggling her fingers under the loose waistband of his trousers, she soon encountered the coarse bush of hair, she toyed with it, twisting and twirling it about her slender fingers, growing bored with this game she reached further, she found the root of his manhood, it was soft and warm, like jelly in her hand, it held a slight pulse that was fractionally behind the one in his chest. It felt very different from the equally flaccid members she had removed from the corpses of Blackbeard's men, the mere comparison in her mind caused her to shiver, the thought of this one separated from its owner was terrible to her. Releasing the resting penis her hand moved on, it cupped his scrotum and felt the soft bulges therein. 'A quick squeeze and he would be helpless.' the thought rushed through her brain, followed an instant later by a trembling of fear. How could she think such a thing about this man? He had done her no harm and showed her only friendship and pleasure. 'And pain, at the willow tree.' She argued with herself for no reason other than the habit of hate. Her swirling mind spun down into a disturbed sleep, troubled by instantaneous flashes of dreams, momentary pictures of disconnected scenes. Granger did not fall immediately to sleep, he lay for a while listening to the world around him, his world, changed subtly by the presence of so many strangers. This was not the place he had come to know so well, this was somewhere new, something different. 'Was this change going to be permanent? Or would things return to normal after these people had left? Could things ever be as they where? Namdarin had come into his cave and brought his enemies with him. What would happen when Namdarin and his friends left? Those enemies would still come here looking for Namdarin, baying like wolves at the door, and find an old man, whom they already mistrusted, now having two reasons to invade his mountain hideaway they would come in force, to defend this place he would have to kill many of them, but the more he killed the more would come. Would the Zandaars run out of soldiers before he was overwhelmed? Not likely. What ever the outcome his hand was already thrown in with Namdarin's, realisation brought relaxation, there was nothing more to be said or thought about it, they were tied together by a bond forged of hate, hate of the Zandaars and their dogmatic following of a god who should have gone long ago.

CHAPTER SEVENTEEN

Kevana and his shrunken group were racing upwards into the hills, pushing their mounts as hard as they dared, the horses were sweating and blowing, dripping foam in the warming air of the slowly climbing valley, the stream that ran up the middle of the wide valley floor was only narrow but was flowing quicker and quicker with every hour that passed, not only was the gradient getting steeper but the snow that was melting was adding greatly to the quantity of water in the valley. The whole area seemed to be turning to a swamp beneath their feet.

"Once we get above this warm air the ground should get firmer." Said Kevana.

"You hope." Answered a pessimistic Alverana. A sour look from the leader ensured that he said no more on the subject. Riding two abreast was a good thing for those in front, they being Kevana and Alverana, those behind were getting very dirty and very cold, though the mud was certainly liquid it was definitely cold. The last two in the small troupe were in an even worse state, though they weren't going to risk opening their mouths to complain, the mud tasted even more horrid than anything they could remember having eaten. The only sounds they could hear were the clattering of their own gear and the soggy thuds of their horses hooves, there were no birds singing and no wind to speak of, the sun was hot on their faces when it shone through the rapidly thinning clouds.

"I think it is going to keep on getting warmer." Said Alverana, when they paused in a group of trees beside the stream so that the horses could drink, none got down from the saddles and they chewed on some dried meat and hard biscuits, Alverana washed his meagre meal down with the last of the water from his bottle, then showing off some of his skill he hooked his left leg over his saddle horn and leant down to fill the bottle, never actually setting foot on the wet grass beside the stream. One of the others tried to emulate him, but lost his balance and fell head first into the icy water, to gales of laughter.

"Petrovana." Said Kevana, looking down on the bedraggled monk. "You are a fool, we can afford no more losses on the trip and you take stupid risks." The soaked man bowed an apology to his angry captain and remounted his horse, the animal showed every sign of being truly amused by its riders sudden fall. It tossed its head and rattled its bit along its teeth, then received a solid kick in the ribs for insolence, imagined or otherwise.

"Petrovana." Said Kevana quietly, "You take the last position in the line. Keep a sharp eye on our trail, I feel that some one may be following us."

All the members of the group knew that this was just another excuse for an additional punishment for the wet monk. Unhappy looks past between the monks but none was prepared to make any comment in case a similar punishment was handed out. Kevana was a notoriously strict taskmaster, there was none stricter.

Morning was all but over before another halt was called by the leader, the same quick meal beside a still, or recently, unfrozen stream, the horses drinking and finding whatever coarse brown vegetation they could reach.

"The signs are getting more difficult to follow." said Kevana.

"There are still enough good marks for me to track them, you need not worry, I won't lose them." Answered Alverana, more confidant in his tracking abilities than the morose leader, whose mood seemed to be getting worse as time passed.

"But are we catching up with them?"

"I am sure that we are travelling quicker than they were at this point, but how we will fare if the ground gets any boggier is another matter entirely."

"How far ahead are they?"

"More than half a day but less than a whole one, I can be no more accurate than that."

Kevana turned away and slammed his flat hand against his thigh, with a report like a falling tree. Scanning the sky and the narrowing trail ahead, the valley behind, he searched for any sign that they were nearer than the tracker said they where. There was nothing to encourage him, he hoped to see the thieves come charging over the ridge, waving their swords and shouting their battle cries, so that he and his trained soldiers could cut them down like so many stalks of wheat, and end this dreadful chase that had already cost far too many of his men. His hope was vain, no charge appeared, the only unusual sound was that of an icicle falling from the end of a branch, it dropped with a thud and a shatter that scattered white crystals everywhere around it. Looking upwards Kevana saw that the sky was a cold clear blue that seemed to reach up to infinity, the sun a hot yellow ball that blinded when looked upon and blinded by reflection from the rapidly melting snow banks that filled the valley floor. Alverana was right, the cold had held a lot of water above the ground as snow and ice, all of this would be released today, by tomorrow all the snow would be gone, and following the thieves would be almost impossible.

"We have no time to stand around, we move on now." He shouted, wrenching his horse's about and heading up the valley at a quick trot. The others exchanged concerned glances before following somewhat slower. Alverana caught up with him before he had cleared the next ridge and said.

"If we go too quickly we will kill more horses, and yours will be the first to die. It is already struggling to maintain the pace you have set, the others are not working as hard, but they have had more food in the last few days, and a lot more rest."

Kevana was astounded that his second could speak out so defiantly against his direct instructions, but after a moments thought he could feel the strain in his mounts movements so he nodded to the younger man and slowed down a little. The others soon caught up at the new slower pace, no one spoke but their tiredness was beginning to show, they had only had one nights rest and two good meals, this did not repair the damage done in two days of freezing misery. It was only a matter of an hour before the horses were really starting to labour up the steep and slippery slopes, all the riders felt that sudden jolt as a hoof breaks loose from its hold on the icy surface and starts to slide down the hill, every such slip was recovered if not immediately then before any ground was lost, or the rider thrown, Kevana's horse seemed to handle the treacherous conditions better than the others, but then it had been trained for such hard conditions, the horses borrowed from Melandius had probably never been out of the stable in these dreadful conditions. Petrovana began to grumble quietly to himself about the awful state of his life, he cursed every decision he ever made to join the priesthood of Zandaar, he belaboured the fact that his inability to learn the, for many, simple task of reading and writing had placed him in the hands of a madman who insisted in chasing after more madmen rather than returning without the sword. Through all these curses his eyes were firmly fixed on the horn of his saddle, he rolled from side to side and pitched forwards and backwards with the natural skill of a true horseman, but failed to notice that his voice had gradually increased in volume until everyone could hear his displeasure. He was woken from his almost trance like state by a cold voice close by.

"If you are so unhappy why don't you just lay down and die like the fool that you are?"

Petrovana jerked upright and stared at the source of the voice then looked at the ground mumbling apologies, as Kevana kicked his horse hard and moved to the front of the line again. When Petrovana finally looked up again he saw his friends looking back at him with only pity in their eyes, they knew that Kevana was going to make life very hard for the young and inexperienced monk.

"It is starting to get colder." Said Kevana two hours after noon, he had noticed that the snow had stopped melting and the mud now had a thin crust of ice over it.

"That is the altitude." answered Alverana, "It will get much colder from here as we get higher up these mountains."

"How much colder? Surely not as cold as a few nights ago."

"Who can say. Once the sun has gone down the temperature will fall very quickly."

"We still have a couple of hours before that happens," said the leader, "we can make up some more of the distance."

"Travelling over this sort of terrain in the dark is very dangerous." Alverana knew what Kevana was thinking even though he had said nothing about the night to come.

"Is the great Alverana afraid of the dark?"

"On unknown ground like this I most certainly am, to fall off a cliff would kill even Kevana, unless he has learned a few tricks from the birds and told no one about them."

Kevana just shrugged but made no other comment. Their progress up the mountain slowed down soon after as the sun was blocked by a large bank of heavy clouds, thick and black they were, snow clouds beyond any doubt, a deep twilight fell and they were forced to guide their horses very carefully, going around the icy boulders and frozen puddles, a sudden plunge through a crust of ice on a deep hole could easily break a horses leg, and then somebody would be walking, a fate that none of them wished to repeat.

Every time that a horse missed its step, slid on the ice, or stumbled over a rock it failed to notice in the gloom, the rider cursed or swore or made his displeasure felt in some other way. Kevana was not immune to such errors, any more than the rest of his men. If anything his curses were more colourful than the others, had the horse been able to understand his language, it would have thrown the man to the floor when its own parentage was questioned, but when its grandsire was likened to a spavined donkey it would certainly have trampled the man until he was a red stain upon the snow, and then trampled the snow until it was gone. The men followed Kevana's lead when he started to eat his rations without dismounting or stopping, they all ate and drank as they rode, which caused even more slips, and a few desperate snatches at saddle horns.

"We must stop for the night." Said Alverana.

"No. We ride on a while longer."

Alverana shook his head but followed his instructions, slowing down even further as the light failed completely. Petrovana took a torch from his saddle bag and lit it ,the jumping yellow light was used to kindle other torches and soon they were a line of bobbing fire wraiths moving up the valley, stumbling and swearing all the while. Alverana came to a bank of frozen snow, it was knee high on the mounted men, the glistening whiteness seemed to stretch across the whole of the valley, Alverana turned to Kevana and said.

"We cannot get through this without hurting the horses. It may look like snow, but the sun has been shining on it all day, the crust of ice is an inch thick, we should camp here."

"The thieves must have crossed this somewhere, you go that way and look, Petrovana can go the other, when you find the place where they went through shout and the rest will come to you."

Alverana looked at Kevana in disbelief, never had his superior ignored his advice in this way, he was sure that Kevana was loosing his mind, but he could not bring himself to disobey, not yet. As he trudged along the shinning wall of ice he thought of all the times that Kevana had followed his suggestions to the letter, instantly and without question in some cases, but now there were other things that were more important than life itself. It was failure that Kevana feared, this was the first time he had failed, and failed at what was supposed to be a simple task. But then the simplest tasks are the easiest to fail. Go and fetch were the orders, it sounds so easy, but they had encountered more difficulties than in a host of battles, more bad luck than in a hundred man hunts. It was the prospect of having to report a serious failure that was driving Kevana on at this reckless pace. 'What will be happening when we don't return to our base?' Alverana asked himself the question and knew the answer. More soldiers would be sent to look for them, scouting parties would be out everywhere, having to report that he had lost half his men and not recovered the sword to a sergeant that tracked them down would break Kevana.

Alverana was so deep in thought that he very nearly missed the narrow gap in the ice where Namdarin and his friends had pushed through the snow. Reining in hard the horse slid to a halt and Alverana held his torch high staring intently at the gap, through it he could clearly see the tracks of the group they were chasing. Looking back across the valley he could see the small cluster of torches, shining pinpricks on the black velvet of the night. Beyond the cluster was a single torch that he knew belonged to Petrovana. He stood high in the stirrups, waved his torch above his head and shouted.

"Captain. I have found it." There was no response so he shouted again, this time as loud as he could. A torch waved and the rest started moving slowly towards him. Sitting quietly on the horse Alverana listened to the echoes of his shout die away, a smile came to his lips as thoughts of his childhood and the echoes in a canyon near his home dashed through his brain. Then he heard a dull crack, this made him sit up and listen more carefully. There was a distant rumbling, soft and low, like a far away waterfall. He knew the sound should mean something, but what? He saw Petrovana suddenly speed up, his torch jumping wildly, only to vanish suddenly, as if it had never been. He remembered.

"By the gods." He whispered. Then stood in the stirrups again.

"Avalanche!" He screamed. "Avalanche! Ride! Ride for your lives! Avalanche!" He stopped shouting because the horses had started to move, they were galloping down the slope towards him as fast as they could, though the horses were tired they were galloping their hardest, here and there encouraged by a swift thump from a burning torch on the rump, there were no whips to hand and a shower of sparks behind them urged them on better than any whip. Closing fast on their tails was a seething wall of snow, though they could not see it the men could feel its icy fingers clutching at their necks, leaning forward in their saddles they urged their dying mounts on, Kevana was pulling away from the group, his horse though much mistreated recently had been bred for speed and power, Melandius's steeds were bred for endurance but they had no speed worth mention, and they certainly could not race with free falling snow. A horse tripped in the dark, a man fell and a light went out. The other three carried on, leaning forward in their saddles, screaming in the horses ears, kicking them in the ribs, and belabouring their singed rumps with burning brands. Alverana manoeuvred his horse in the gap and waved his torch for his friends to see, at the last possible moment, just as they were swinging away from the ice to make the turn into the opening as quickly as they could he move inside to show them the way, first Kevana then after a moment another man, and then just as the snow struck another made it to the comparative safety of the bank of snow and ice. They were covered only by the very fringe of the avalanche, a freezing whiteness that extinguished their lights, and weighed them down. Alverana kept on shouting Kevana's name as loudly as he could giving his friends something to follow, he kept moving in as straight a line as he could though he had no landmarks to navigate by. He was as blind as the others. The suffocating mass gradually lessened as they forced a path away from the avalanche, finally they could see each other by the light of the major moon that was showing through a small hole in the cloud cover, they looked like white ghosts walking on a white background, their camouflage was almost perfect, the only dark patches showing were the horses bellies.

They stopped and beat the frosting away from themselves and their horses, the cold had their teeth chattering and their bodies quaking with unstoppable shivering. "We need a fire." stammered Kevana.

A nod was all the answer Alverana could give as he pulled his tinder box from its usual hiding place in the warmth of his jacket, he soon had a spare torch lit and providing some small warmth to frozen fingers. The heat on their skin gave waves of pain as the feeling came back, they were not actually frost-bitten but it was definitely close.

"We need to camp." Said Alverana, it was Kevana's turn to nod. Alverana turned towards a stand of trees a few hundred yards away, just when he was sure that he was going the right way the clouds covered the moon again, the only light was now the torches and they did not show the trees, Alverana muttered a swift prayer to the god and tried his best to maintain a straight path. Presently he nearly crashed into a tree. Rapidly a huge bonfire was built and set alight, the branches of the trees were collected in a most unsubtle manner, ropes tied a branch to a horse and the horse pulled the branch until it came away from the tree, had it been summer the green wood that would have fallen to such activity would have been impossible to burn, but in the depths of this winter the sap had long since retreated from these branches and they burned quite nicely with only a little coaxing. The horses stood so close to the fire that a sudden switch in the light wind and they stopped steaming and started smoking, but still they would not move away, at least one side was warm even if the other side was still cold. The men made a fast meal and wolfed it down like they had not eaten for ages. The tension between them kept rising though none would speak, Kevana knew what was going to be said, and he would do nothing to start the conversations. Finally it was Alverana that spoke first.

"Now we are four." The rest of the statement remained unsaid.

"It was my fault they died." said Kevana.

"We are outnumbered by the thieves."

"We are trained soldiers and they are merely amateurs."

"If they are amateurs how is it that they have lost no-one."

"They have been lucky."

"How can you call it luck, they have come through everything we have, and they didn't have Melandius's help, well not willingly anyway. They have lost no-one and nothing. I think you keep on underestimating them. You are hurrying too much, we must begin to look on this as a long chase, because it is not going to be over in one more day. You could not have foreseen that the sword would be gone, stolen before we could arrive to claim it, and then the weather did turn against us, but if we had been walking through this valley in daylight, we would have seen all that snow ready to fall. We are going to have to slow down, these horses are nearly dead, they need some rest and so do we."

"We must get that sword or we will be a laughing stock. The easiest station in the world, with only one real task, and we messed it up." Answered Kevana bitterly.

"With the losses we have taken we are already a laughing stock."

"Maybe." Alverana thought about this single word for a moment.

"You intend to bring back a forest of heads on poles, to prove a glorious victory, of course no-one in command knows as yet what a beating we have taken. You have lost more than half your men, and we haven't even seen the thieves yet. What is going to happen when we meet them?"

"Briana and Fabrana still have their bows, they can kill them from a distance, hopefully before they even know that we are there."

"I have four arrows." answered one man ."And I, three." said the other.

"That will just have to be enough."

"We are not even sure how many there are." Said Alverana.

"Melandius said there were eight of them, and one of those a woman." Sneered Kevana.

"Women can fight too." Said Briana. Kevana turned and stared hard at the young man, unused to his sudden outspokenness. Briana wrenched his eyes away from the leaders cold stare, and looked at his own feet.

"If Melandius is right, and it could be that he didn't see the whole of their number, then we are outnumbered a mere two to one." Said Alverana.

"Good odds for a soldier."

"And at least one of them can kill with a dream."

"If Melandius is to be believed." said Kevana.

"Your belief in Melandius seems to be very flexible, you believe his word as to numbers but not as to occult abilities." Alverana was pacing back and forth, getting more and more irritated by Kevana with ever word he spoke.

"Melandius can certainly count, but he knows nothing of our magic or anyone else's." The logic placated Alverana and he sat down, but he was not at ease. "We will rest until the morning and then we continue the chase."

"Wouldn't it be better to find some more men? There are bound to be some out looking for us already."

"No." Kevana almost shouted the mono-syllable. "I refuse to be beaten by a handful of common thieves."

"There you go again. How do you know they are common thieves? Judging by their considerable success so far they are distinctly uncommon. Their party seems to contain, by their know activities, a magician, a thief, a military mind of some skill, and some warriors of extreme bravery. I would not have liked to face those white wolves. If these be common thieves then nobodies purse is safe."

"We will have to be very careful."

Alverana just shook his head and climbed into his sleeping furs, a quick prayer to Zandaar to protect him in his sleep, and then to sleep, with the speed that only trained soldiers seem to manage. Kevana's training was of no avail that night, he tossed and turned, he kept putting wood on the fire but only got a few minutes sleep before the pre-dawn light woke the others. Though his sleep was short it was filled with images of demons chasing him, and him chasing them. He never quite caught them, but they never quite caught him. One of these short dreams was so frightening that he found himself fighting to wake up, fearing that a magician was trying to kill him, once he was awake he knew that no one could kill him in his dream unless they had met, if not in person, then at least in a dream, he could think of no character from a dream recently that was sufficiently clear to be a real person. The only contact he had made was a momentary link with the blue sword, and that was tenuous at best, definitely not enough for even the best magician to identify him and target him accurately.

The logic of these thoughts did not help him to get to sleep. He was stirring the fire when Alverana woke up.

"Did you sleep, at all?" He asked, noticing the haggard look in Kevana's eyes.

"A little. Not much, but a little." Alverana nodded and went about the business of making breakfast and getting the others out of their beds. Once breakfast had been eaten and they were all resting near the roaring fire, wondering why Kevana was not pushing on after the thieves. Their moment of relaxation was broken when Kevana cleared his throat.

"I have decided that we will search ahead and find these people. It is time to let them know that we are after them. Prepare yourselves." They all went through their toning and tuning exercises until they were ready. Kevana looked at them and saw that there was little energy for and extensive search so he decided on a sweep search of the area rather than the extended search they had used the day before.

"Channel through me and I will guide the search ."

"That is dangerous." said Alverana.

"My life to risk, I can't ask anyone else to do it." They formed a circle around the fire each holding hands with two of his friends, Kevana was the only one facing outwards the others felt the heat of the flames on their faces.

Kevana began the slow chant of the search, the others joined in, they knew that while they were locked into the circle none could break it, and breaking it Kevana, as searcher, would die. To simply release a hand and the leader would be dead and this dreadful race through the ice would be over. Kevana's trust in them gave them a feeling of strength, power, and fellowship. Kevana let the energy in their search build slowly for many minutes, he felt it like light in his bones and heat in his head, when he judged the level to be right he leapt, not with his body but with his mind. Howling across the frozen waste he sped, like an arrow, following and unmistakable track in the snow, suddenly it was gone. The track below him had vanished, instantaneously he stopped, and scanned around, there it was it had turned suddenly up a steep bank and into a smaller side valley. through the valleys twists and turns he tore, he knew that the supply of energy for this excursion would not last much longer, around the final turn and he faced a veritable wall of scree, with no snow, but that was were the tracks lead, no doubt. The energy of his friends started to fail, like a candle guttering in the wind, cracking and relighting, he rushed back to himself, to be caught too far away when the power failed completely would certainly cost him his life, he felt the flicker again as he turned into the main valley, and again as the camp came into view, as he returned to his body, still standing in the circle around the fire, Briana collapsed breaking the circle, he fell face first towards the fire, Alverana held his wrist and heaved him away, almost falling into the flames himself, Fabrana sat down in the snow with a solid thump, that would and knocked the wind from him if he had had any left. Kevana was in far better shape than the others, though he was breathing very hard.

"I have found their trail, I think we are getting very close."

"Did you see them?" panted Alverana.

"No. The trail ended at a rock slide and I had to return before I could investigate further up. Rest now we will leave in a little while." Kevana started dismantling the camp while the others lay on their furs recovering from the strain of the search. When things were almost ready for them to leave Alverana spoke to Kevana. "We nearly lost you then."

"I knew you would not fail, and that you would give me enough warning to return safely."

"It was still a foolish risk."

"Possibly, but you were right in one respect, this mission is now, as it always has been, all or nothing. If you and the others wish to leave me to it, then I will not think any the worse of you, many have died already and there is only room for volunteers."

"If just one of us makes it back to base and reports what has happened your reputation and your command is gone."

"The great infallible Kevana has already made his mistake, you three are all that is left of my command, whatever happens now my reputation is destroyed, know this, I will not stop. I will present the sword to Zandaar from my own hand or I will die in the attempt."

"I will not leave you to die alone." Said Alverana clasping his friends shoulder with his left hand and putting his right fist to his left breast in a military salute.

"I thank you my friend." Kevana looked at the other two, who had both climbed to their feet during this exchange.

"I have sworn to obey my commander and will not break that oath now." Said Briana, making the same salute.

"I will not leave either." Fabrana's salute was more perfunctory and his voice carried no enthusiasm. Suddenly there attention was attracted by the jingling of a harness on a horse, Kevana turned and saw a white horse coming towards them, on its back it carried a hunched figure with a vary pale face that was partially shrouded by the hood of a white cloak, the horse was walking slowly towards the camp, it seemed utterly fearless, the man's dark eyes showed little sign of life. He made no move and said nothing just continued the sedate plod towards the group of standing men. At a gesture from Kevana Fabrana strung his bow and set an arrow to the string and held it half pulled, but not aimed.

"Who are you?" shouted Kevana.

The horses ears twitched at the loud noise, but otherwise there was no response.

"What do you want?"

The same reaction.

"Stop or you die." A slight hand movement and Fabrana pulled the bow kissed the string and stood ready to fire.

"He looks like he is already dead." said Alverana softly.

"I may be." whispered the figure.

"Who are you?" asked Kevana again.

"I am one you abandoned. You left me to die."

"Petrovana, is that you?" Asked Kevana, Fabrana threw down his bow as if it had bitten him, he was sure.

"I think so. Though my head doesn't seem to work too well at the moment."

Briana ran to the horse and helped the rider down, nearly carried him to the fire, Fabrana started to collect the pots and food to make some breakfast for the obviously frozen monk. Alverana took care of the horse, he brushed the heavy layer of snow and ice from its coat, and returned it to its natural chestnut colour, it nuzzled him while he fed it some of the hay they had brought along, there was not much left but he gave it all to the hungry animal a handful at a time.

"How did you survive? I thought you were certainly dead." asked Kevana his hands shaking with uncertain emotion.

"I panicked."

"How did that help?"

"My heels clenched against the horses ribs, I dropped the reins and gripped the saddle horn, I hung on in total panic and screamed. The horse left to its own devices turned down the slope gathered some speed and then turned and jumped over the wall of ice, there must have been a low section. He was chest deep in crusted snow but still he managed to run across the slope, away from the path of the avalanche, we were rolled a few times and I lost all sense of direction, and consciousness I should think. I woke up about an hour ago, the horse was walking slowly down the hill and seemed to be heading for a fire, your fire, I left him to it. That horse saved my life." As the tale was finished Fabrana placed a hot mug in his hand and Petrovana's face vanished in a cloud of steam, the slurping noise as he gulped the hot soup was the only sound in the shocked camp.

"I was sure you were dead." muttered Kevana.

"Not yet." Petrovana's dark eyes seemed to punch holes in the cloud around him. "But I am sure you will soon remedy that over sight."

"I am going after the sword, these three have said that they will come with me. If you wish to return to our castle I think you would find help long before you got there, you may leave or stay as you please. I need volunteers, not conscripts."

"If I left, would I survive another night in this dreadful cold alone?"

"If you choose to leave, Fabrana will go with you, I think he only decided to stay because of the thought of the journey home on his own."

"If I choose to go, I take a quarter of your force with me." Petrovana smiled.

Kevana remembered the harsh way he had dealt with the young man the day before. Petrovana thought of the same things, he smiled at Kevana, a small knowing grin. The grin of a merchant who holds the only cure for a plague, and can sell it at any price he so desires. Kevana was waiting patiently for the price, wondering how high it was going to be.

"I stay, but we take no more stupid risks."

"Good." Kevana breathed again. "We move immediately."

"Can't a cold man finish his soup?" asked Petrovana.

"Eat as we ride, we may just catch them today." The unshakeable leader was back. Petrovana heaved a massive sigh and stared longingly at his soup, climbed gingerly to his feet and said "Alverana, how is my horse?"*

"He is warming up nicely, and appears by some miracle to be completely unharmed."

"He is indeed a miraculous mount." Petrovana had nothing to do with the packing up, all of his gear was still on his horse, he sat by the fire as long as he possibly could, and stared lovingly at he flames as Fabrana shovelled snow on them. Fabrana clapped him on the shoulder and waved him towards his horse with a polite bow. "Your mount, my lord."

"Why thank you, my good man." He strutted over to the now chestnut horse, patted it on the neck, and stood by the saddle with his right leg lifted, waiting to be boosted into the saddle. A whole minute past and no-one even offered to help him, he turned to Fabrana ,"Well. Help me up."

"Drop dead, your lordship." Gales of laughter tore from the tired throats, as a moments humour made them feel like a real troupe of soldiers again, not the half defeated, totally bedraggled bunch they looked. Fabrana and Petrovana were the last to mount and once they were firmly in their saddles Kevana turned his horse up the valley, along the track he had already scouted. Progress was fast, once they had gained the path Namdarin and his group had taken the snow was beaten down and they could move at a fast walk for most of the time with an occasional burst into a trot, which quickly had the horses blowing huge clouds of steam and throwing lumps of snow everywhere.

"We are making very good time here." said Kevana.

"Yes," Answered Alverana ,"but the horses are going to need food before much longer."

"There is a place with some grass up ahead."

"How can there be grass growing in these mountains?"

"I don't know, but I saw it just below the rock fall."

"There must be something very warm up there to keep the snow away."

"We shall find out soon enough."

The day warmed slowly though the clouds above didn't blow away on the swift southern breeze, all the riders were constantly watching for snow slides, checking the valley rims for the tell tale build ups of wind blown snow that usually start avalanches, there is nothing quite like hindsight for sharpening the senses. The path they were following was so clear that a blind man could have followed it, this fact gradually impinged on Alverana's mind, it was too easy.

"This path is too straight and too clear, I don't like it." He said.

"Why?"

"Where would you set a trap for someone following?"

Kevana thought for a while before answering, "True, but they don't know that we are following."

"Can you be sure?"

"The first time we searched for them I could nearly feel the man carrying the sword, there is no chance that he could feel my search."

"Are you willing to bet your own life on that? If so are you underestimating him again?"

"I feel sure." Kevana's brow creased deeply with a frown, his eyes almost closed as he considered the prospect of finding out the hard way. "I think that a little caution is called for. You may ride ahead, and keep a careful watch of the trail."

Alverana nodded and muttered, "Me and my mouth." He flicked the reins hard against his horses neck and sped off to check out the path. Kevana chuckled softly as Briana came alongside.

"Where is Alverana going?" he asked.

"Chasing wild pigs I hope."

"I hope he catches one." said Briana missing the meaning entirely.

"Alverana," said Kevana with a sigh, "has gone ahead to check the path because he feels it is too easy, he is looking for traps and such like."

"Ah. I'm sorry, but I am hungry, I thought you meant real food."

"You're always hungry, and see everything as food."

"Only if it sits still long enough." Laughed Briana.

"Well so long as its not moving too fast." Said Fabrana.

"Just so that it can't outrun an arrow, he'll eat it." Said Petrovana. All four were laughing so hard that Alverana stopped and turned to look at them.

"Quiet, you three, Alverana was wary of the path and as soon as he goes ahead we all start laughing, it will make him paranoid." Said Kevana.

"Make?" Said Petrovana, holding on to his aching sides. Gradually the laughter subsided and they returned to their own thoughts and a nearly silent ride through the white wasteland. They saw nothing that moved only a bird high in the sky it was circling on a updraught from the ridge to the south, the only signs they saw were those of small animals, nothing bigger than the small white fox, which had they seen it was as big as a large house cat. It stood very still and watched them walk by, they passed with fifty feet of it, and were ignorant of its wary watching, its coal black eyes fixed on them until it felt safe to move again. Once they had passed it dived into its burrow in the snow, and decide to investigate the intriguing smell of something recently dead, at this time of year there was no real rush to find food, it had no competition, nearly every other carnivore was sleeping. Alverana reached the place where Namdarin's party had turned up into the side valley and waited for the rest to catch up.

"I don't think they have laid any traps, we have passed several perfect places for an ambush. I don't think they even thought of it." He said as Kevana came near.

"You're probably right, they are in too much of a hurry to worry about us catching them."

Following the much trodden path up the steep side of the valley caused a few minor slips, but no falls, even though the horses were beginning to get very tired. The narrow upper valley was well lit and felt warmer to all the riders, they began to open their previously tightly closed coats and put their gloves under their belts, Alverana took off his large fur hat and showed a shiny pink circle of a bald patch right in the middle of his head, it gave him a most comical appearance, it was almost clown like, a perfect circle on the top of his head, bright pink and glistening in the sun. No one would laugh, no one would snigger, no one would giggle, for in such a young man baldness of this nature was considered generally to be ridiculous. Any one who so much as pointed it out was dealt with in a most savage manner, this was the main reason for Alverana's lowly rank. Every time he was promoted, a new group saw his bald patch and had to be taught not to mention it, this usually involved some form of fight or threat or disastrous joke, after which Alverana was instantly demoted. In the warmth of the winter sun they turned the corner of the canyon and faced the enormous rock slide.

"There are a lot of horse tracks here," said Alverana, "and many footprints as well."

"But they didn't go out the way we just came in, did they?" asked Briana.

"No."

"Then where did they go?" Demanded Kevana.

Alverana said nothing but turned and looked up the slope.

"How could they have gone up there? No one could walk up that, let alone lead a horse up it."

"That is the only other way." He searched around the grassy section at the base of the scree. He found four big hoof prints, two of them close to the last rocks, wide apart and cut deeply into the soft turf, slightly further away from the rocks were the other two, close together and cut deeply at the front edge.

"What do you see?" Asked Kevana. Alverana turned and stood so that he was looking over the hoof prints up the slope.

"A big horse was galloping just here."

"Which way was it going?" He looked from side to side wondering where a horse could be going in such a hurry and where it had found enough distance to get up to a full gallop, there was not enough room from one wall to the other.

"That way." said Alverana raising his right arm and pointing up the slope.

"You're telling me they just rode up there." Kevana was very close to shouting.

"The signs say to me that a large horse reached this point at a flat out gallop and was going in that direction. If you look carefully at the slope you will see the places where his shoes smashed the rocks. The white splintered areas, those are where is hooves hit, and by the gods did they hit hard. The others followed more slowly, probably being led, but there are still some places where the edges of the rocks were crushed by their iron shoes. I can see the occasional grey stripe where a hoof slipped down the face of a rock."

"Petrovana, try walking up there." Petrovana handed his reins to Briana and walked very slowly up the bottom of the slide. Then gingerly stepped onto it, as he went forwards the gradient rapidly increased until he was standing upright and his outstretched had touched the highest of the rocks. Soon he was climbing using both hands and feet, his feet were slowly sinking into the jumble of rock, suddenly there was a crack and the whole area around him moved, it slid down and rolled him over and over until he was ejected at the bottom.

A bashed and battered man hoisted himself to his feet and beat some of the dust from his clothes, there was a hole in the knee of his breeches, through which a red raw graze could be seen.

"That hurts." He said, "I don't see how a horse could get up there. If I had a rope to climb up I might be able, but otherwise forget it." He sat down with a thump and began to examine the damage to his knee, the occasional grunt was all the conversation he was capable of for the next few minutes.

Alverana and Kevana cast around for a place on the sides of the canyon where they may be able to climb up, but found nothing, not a ledge, or even a crack, or a suggestion of a fault in the smooth rock faces, absolutely nothing to help them climb above the rockslide.

"There must be a way up." Kevana said stamping across the short grass.

"I don't see one."

"They went up there and we must follow."

"There may be another way up."

"Where?"

"Somewhere else, but definitely not here."

"You may be right, but what if they decide to come back down this way?"

"We could leave someone here to watch for them, but don't forget the other option, there could be another way down, into another valley perhaps?"

"So, we either split our force in two, or we all go off to find another way up. Either way we stand a chance of loosing them."

"If we split up we can still maintain contact."

"I know, but none of us are really good at that sort of thing. I certainly wouldn't notice if some one was trying to reach me while I was doing something else." Kevana said shaking his head, neither he nor his men were adept in the more arcane disciplines of the Zandaars.

"If we set aside a given time of day for communication to be set up, then with both ends reaching it should be possible, even for incompetents like us."

"Incompetent." Kevana raised his eyebrows in objection, but knew that his friend was right. "We are. Our field is battle not mysticism, in the field we are the best there is." Alverana bit his tongue, he didn't voice the comment that burned in his brain. 'We are fewer of the best than we were.'

"If we say sun down and sun rise," Alverana said, "these are easy to judge, even when the weather is bad, noon is possible but difficult to judge accurately."

"That is a good idea." Kevana thought for a moment, then the decision was clear in his mind. "How many stand guard and who?" Alverana looked around for the position of the other men, seeing that they were out of earshot.

"Fabrana and Briana stand guard, I am not sure of Petrovana's feelings after the avalanche, he says the right things but somehow the sincerity is missing."

"I agree. Petrovana can come with us." Together they walked back to where the others were resting, Petrovana still bemoaning the pain in his knee, the other two staring dispassionately. Kevana addressed them. "I have decided that you two will stay here and prevent the thieves from coming down this way while we three go in search of another way up." Before the men could answer, he saw something move from the corner of his eye. Looking up the slope he saw an old man wearing a short white tunic and carrying a long dark staff he was standing on the very edge of the rock slide.

"Who are you?" he shouted, Briana and Fabrana jumped to their feet stringing bows and nocking arrows as they came.

"I am Granger, you must go back."

"Help us to get up and we will talk about it."

"No. You are forbidden to come to this place." He old man's voice was crystal clear and not at all loud, but still they heard it perfectly. Kevana on the other hand was shouting as hard as he could, his voice seemed to fall into nothingness in a moment.

"Throw down a rope then we can come up."

"No. You must leave."

"We will find a way to get up there. You can be assured of that."

"If you attempt to climb the slope you will be killed."

"You are a very brave old fool, it is you that will die." Kevana was not at all used to being threatened by old cripples who needed a stick to help them walk. He responded in a like manner, taking a silver flame from his pouch inside his jacket he held it up for Granger to see.

"Do you know what this is ,old man?" Granger shook his head, even though he knew exactly what it was.

"It is your death. It can kill you before you can move. Throw down the rope that the others used and I will let you live."

"They used no ropes, and you cannot come the way they did."

"You have only moments left to live, and I know how the old value each instant of life."

"You cannot threaten me in my home." Granger stepped away from the edge. Kevana drew back his arm and threw. The flame transformed only feet from his hand, it arched through the air leaving a glowing trail, a flickering after image, behind. As it screamed its song of death towards the old man, Kevana felt a strange sick feeling in his head, at the last moment the bolt of liquid fire turned aside and disappeared from view, they didn't see it spend itself harmlessly on the rocks behind Granger. A deep frown furrowed Kevana's head as he pulled forth another flame, then changed his mind, a lightning bolt would be better. He threw, a white blast of death howled through the air towards its stationary target. The flashing white light threw the rocks and boulders into stark relief, the shadows hard and black, moving as quickly as the bolt. Kevana felt no sensations this time as the bolt flew true to its target, at the very last moment Granger swung up his staff, pointed one end at the bolt, and released a blinding flash of vivid blue light, the light was so hot that the white was eclipsed before they touched and when they touched the white was totally absorbed, the back blast tore through Kevana's mind and knocked him to the ground. The heat from Granger's energy bolt was plain for all to feel, their faces reddened as if too close to the fire. Granger looked down and waited until Kevana was back on his feet, then he turned and slowly walked away.

CHAPTER EIGHTEEN

Namdarin woke up with a start, something had disturbed his sleep, he scanned the cave rapidly but could see no obvious cause for his sudden feeling of uneasiness, he stood and went out into the open to relieve himself and to allow the cold morning air to clear the cobwebs from his mind, and cold it certainly was. As he walked around the gently rumbling mud pot he saw that the horses were all festooned with icicles and frost, only Arndrol showed little difference and that was due to the fact that he was nearly white to start with. The sun was creeping over the edge of the crater, and showing about a third of its great orange disc, though there was little heat to be felt in the air. A steady plume of steam rose from the mud and stayed as a thick column for about a hundred feet until it suddenly met the moving air higher up and then it was torn to tattered rags and hurled across the sky at an astounding pace. Namdarin stretched and began to regret coming out without first dressing, the cold was starting to make his limbs tremble, turning he saw Kern standing in the entrance he was watching.

"The horses will need some attention today." Said Namdarin in a conversational tone.

"Yes. They will need taking to some food as well, it has been a few days since they had anything proper to eat." Said Kern.

"I think we should take them down to the rock slide, there is good grass, just what they need." Kern nodded and started to put his heavy clothes on, Namdarin followed the scouts example and before long they were leading the horses down the path to the rock slide. When the horses were released from their tethers they ran around the small area of soft green with all the abandon of foals. Kern laughed at the sight of the horses running and kicking, Namdarin sat beside Kern on a large rock, and enjoyed the sight just as much though he didn't actually laugh aloud. At least not until Arndrol lay on the ground and rolled onto his back and kicked all four feet in the air.

"They really love to be free," whispered Kern, "they don't get enough chances to be real horses any more."

"They certainly take advantage of every chance that comes along." Namdarin lapsed into a thoughtful silence, Kern observed him very carefully, he could tell that something was disturbing his friend.

"Ask." Said Kern.

"What do you mean?"

"You have been wondering how to ask something for the last

five minutes, just ask." Namdarin shook his head and sighed, there was no way to hide things from Kern.

"Something woke me up, but I have no idea what it was, and it still bothers me, I don't know why but I feel I have missed something important. Have you any thoughts?"

"I felt it too, it was like a deep foreboding, a hidden threat, but these words aren't right either. It was something without a name, I am not helping much am I?"

"I am just glad that I was not the only one to feel it, now I am sure it was something important, perhaps it was connected to those that follow us."

"It may mean that they are nearer than they were."

"It is almost certain that they are catching up because we have not moved for many hours, and I don't believe that they will be resting much." Namdarin jumped to his feet as if an insect had bitten his backside.

"What is wrong?" asked Kern looking carefully at the rock and then frowning up at Namdarin.

"How can I be so far away from my sword and bow?"

"That is an unusual lapse for a warrior." said Kern his hand resting on his swords red bound hilt.

"And why in such a peaceful place as this do I suddenly feel so frightened that I am armed with only a knife?" He pulled the small knife from its sheath in the lining of his jacket, holding it point up he turned away from Kern and assumed a typical knife fighters crouch, legs spread wide weight well forward, knife low and point up.

"Calm yourself, there is nothing to threaten you here, unless you believe that I will cause you harm." While Kern spoke, Arndrol sensed his friends disquiet, stopped cropping the lush grass and walked over to see what was going on.

"Now you have upset your own horses' breakfast, put up your blade and sit down here beside me." Kern's soft voice had the same effect on the man as it normally did on animals, he relaxed a little and trusted the cool voice instinctively. Once Namdarin was settled on the rock the big grey returned to its feeding, not wanting to miss the opportunity for fresh grass, though he didn't stray far.

"The horses will be safe here." said Kern. "Let's go and see to feeding ourselves, I am sure they can find their way back up if they get lonely."

Kern stood and offered a hand to Namdarin helping him to his feet as if he were an old man in need of a strong arm to lift him, Kern was not too far wrong Namdarin was feeling particularly weak, and a little unsteady on his feet. As they turned into the path Arndrol followed them.

"Send him back to eat some more." said Kern and Namdarin waved an arm at the grey who was forced to back out of the passage as it was too narrow for him to turn round. As they walked quickly up the steeply sloping path Namdarin's feeling of anxiety slowly lessened, fading into an uncomfortable edginess that kept him moving as fast as the subdued light of the rock corridor would allow. Coming into the brightly lit area of the crater was just as much of a shock to their eyes as it had been the first time the day before, blinking against the sudden intensity they both staggered a little, Namdarin wandered to the left, and Kern stumbled to the right, shoulders collided and Kern's quickly mumbled apology fell on entirely deaf ears, Namdarin flew into a rage, his right hand snatched the knife from his belt and he spun towards Kern swinging the knife upwards in a fast slashing arc. Kern heard the hard basaltic gravel crunch under Namdarin's left toe as his weight moved across in front. Kern's eyes had still not recovered from their emergence into the light, but they did pick up the flash of sun on the rapidly moving blade. Kern was unbalanced and unable to make any real counter to the surprise attack, his only option was to fall, this he did with such alacrity that it was Namdarin's turn to be surprised, not so much by the fall itself but more by the things that happened next .As Kern fell he used his falling momentum to generate a turning force that made him spin, then just before his hip hit the ground he shot out a stiff right leg that struck Namdarin at his knees. Namdarin felt the leg strike and his own legs leave the ground, he pitched over onto his back, his head landing on a rather prominent rock, darkness took him .

Kern was still on the ground and getting his legs underneath him when Jangor came running over.

"What is going on here?" he demanded.

"He just attacked me?"

"Why?"

"I don't know. He was nervy about something, and when we came into the light we stumbled into each other and he went for his knife and swung at me."

"What knife?"

Kern looked around with a shocked expression, there was no knife in view.

"I saw the blade flash in the sun." Jangor lifted Namdarin's head gently his hand was wet and sticky with fresh blood, he felt the handle of a knife lying under Namdarin's left shoulder.

"How is he?" Asked a worried Kern.

"He still lives as yet. Head injuries are difficult to predict." Jayanne came running from the cave, her red hair flowing in the wind, her green eyes flashing hatred at the big man, her uncontrolled temper was clear in the red flush of her face and the rapid flickering on the muscles of her legs and arms, Jangor knew she was looking for a target, so he stood between her and Kern, he put his strong right hand against her heaving chest and pushed her slowly away. At any other time his thoughts would have turned to a more sensual theme, his hand resting between her heaving breasts, feeling her heart pounding in her lovely chest, her strong arms and legs fetchingly displayed by the short tunic that she wore to sleep, short enough to reveal the curve of a buttock if she turned too quickly, but Jangor could not take his eyes from the wild green of hers, the axe was dangling from its thong only a twitch away from her hand.

"He will be waking up very soon, it was only a small misunderstanding, that got a little out of control, please don't make it any worse than it already is. There is something very strange going on here, I would like to know what it is." Mander crept around the two of them fixed in a battle of wills he moved as smoothly as he could so as to create the minimum of disturbance, a sudden shift in the conflict could trigger violence, they had all seen her wield that axe to good effect and had no yearning to feel its deadly bite. Mander knelt down beside Namdarin and poured cold water over his face and into his hair. Namdarin's eyes clenched tightly shut when the coldness washed over them, Mander trickled some of the water between Namdarin's partly opened lips, with a coughing splutter he sprayed glistening droplets all around.

"What happened?" He asked.

"You attacked Kern, he knocked you over and you hit your head on a rock. Does that ring any bells?" answered Mander.

"The only bells I hear are in my head."

Mander laughed rather too loudly, the joke was not that good but the tension of the situation needed some defusing. Kern stifled a small laugh and reached down with one huge hand to help the fallen man to his feet. Jayanne was not mollified by their actions, and asked, "Are you all right?"

"I think so." Answered Namdarin almost dangling from Kern's right arm. The back of his head was matted with slowly oozing blood. Granger came from the mouth of his cave and walked slowly over, he appeared to be trying to look into Namdarin's eyes though he was having some difficulty making the younger man look at him.

"Look at me." He almost shouted. Kern jumped at the sound and nearly dropped his friend. Namdarin's head twitched up, his eyes fixed on the old man's.

"What is wrong with me?"

"I think it is the sword that makes you forget who your friends are."

"How do you mean?"

"You are away from the sword, it begins to feel lonely and it calls to you, but its very nature makes the call one to violence, a call that is very difficult to resist."

"So, if I pick up the sword again this urge will go away?"

"Most probably." Namdarin was supporting his own weight now and shook off Kern's arm, then staggered towards the gaping mouth of the cave.

"Wait." said Granger.

"What for?"

"If the sword can call to you when you are absent, perhaps you can call it to yourself."

"Shout its name and it will come to me like a lost hound." Sarcasm dripped from the acid words. "I don't know its name."

"You know enough to make a call. Draw it in your mind, like the magic of the Zandaars, believe, and it will be."

"I will give it a try." So saying he sat down where he was, a few feet from the cave entrance, he cleared his mind as best he could of all the un-necessary thoughts that normally rattle around, this seemed to be more difficult than it had been of late, his practise against the Zandaar priests had improved his mental discipline greatly but for some reason that he could not fathom, the accustomed speed of preparation was just not there. It took several attempts over a period of many seconds before he could visualise the blank wall on which to draw the picture of the sword. Starting with the black jewel of the hilt he slowly worked his way down to the hard yellow point gradually accumulating an accurate picture of the sword, when then picture was drawn as clearly as he could muster he projected it into the space that surrounded him, hoping, and waiting for the contact that would bring the blade to him. Finally his mind felt the wrench of the weight of the sword, it was like lifting a horse with one hand, he was panting and puffing like an old man walking up a steep hill, but still he did not relinquish the contact that he was sure was bringing the sword of Xeron to him. When he felt that the time was right he held his right hand out in front of his face, his fingers were open and his palm flat waiting for the slap of the black wired hilt that he knew was to come. Slap. His fingers closed hungrily around the black bindings and energy flooded through his wrist and down his arm, a delightful warmth that surpassed any before, a deep feeling of well being that reached down to his soul and lifted his spirits to the stars. He let out a non-vocal shout and a deep sigh of pleasure as his amazed friends looked on. From their point of view the sword had drifted out of the cave, a few feet from the floor, Its point held upright in the cold morning air, it moved in a smooth and unerring fashion straight to the hand that awaited it, it touched the hand without a sound and nestled there for an instant before Namdarin shouted and sighed.

"That was amazing." Said Granger. "Only yesterday you knew almost nothing of the magic arts and now you call a sword to hand as if it were your favourite hound." He shook his head from side to side for a while before going on. "You have come a long way in a very short time."

"I have good reason." Muttered Namdarin getting to his feet. He turned slowly to Kern, looked him straight in the eyes and spoke softly in the small voice of a guilty child, "I am sorry, my friend, I know not what came over me, I have few friends left in this world and I hope that you will remain amongst their small number."

"A select band they are indeed, I am sure you will get the opportunity to redeem your behaviour soon enough." The big man offered his hand to Namdarin who took it with a great sigh and a look of sincere thanks. Namdarin turned to Granger and asked. "How does this magic work?"

"I am not sure. I think it only takes will and concentration. It is the latter that most people lack. Your purpose gives you the total single mindedness that is necessary to control matter with the mind. You have no thoughts other than the fulfilment of your oath. This gives you a strength of mind that usually only comes after years of intense training and practise, you have great potential, which we must begin to realise very soon. I feel that something is going to happen today, something that will effect us all." The stares of disbelief did not surprise him in the least, he glanced at Mander just as he was taking the breath to speak.

"Before you ask." he said disrupting Mander's voice while it was beginning and causing him to choke on his words, "No. I cannot see the future, but when I get a feeling that is this strong it is not often wrong." Mander's coughing faded away slowly. Granger held both hands high above his head and stood stock still, he appeared to be holding his breath or breathing so shallowly that no one could detect it. A dark streak cave from the cave accompanied by a deep thrumming sound like the sound of a strong wind on a tight guy rope. There was a single slap as the streak reached his open hands, his staff was there.

"I can perform this minor magic as well, but it took me many years to learn."

"I get the feeling that I will have to learn very fast just to stay alive."

Granger looked at Namdarin and felt the truth in his words.

"I am hungry." said Mander.

"You can think of nothing but your stomach." Shouted Stergin. A smile came to most of the faces as the usual banter raised everybody's spirits.

"I can think of other things than food." said Mander staring pointedly at Jayanne's long and delightfully exposed legs.

"You animal." Stormed Stergin stamping into the cave.

"It was your thought," said Jangor, "you make it." Mander nodded and continued doing exactly as he had been, making breakfast for every one.

"Jayanne, you come with me and we will see if I can find any reference to your strange axe in my books." Namdarin felt a surge of emotion as she calmly followed the old man into the dark seclusion of his small cave. The very shape of the cave mouth was suddenly distorted by his disturbed mind, an opening not unlike a widened vertical slit with coarse bushes growing up each side and over the top.

"Don't be stupid." he mumbled to himself, shaking his head to remove the extremely uncomfortable image. "I have got that woman on the brain."

Jayanne followed Granger's slightly bent back as he squeezed into the small cave that held all his treasures, for such were his books. As soon as the old man crossed the threshold the dim light brightened until it was almost like daylight, not blazing sun light but more than strong enough to read by.

"Now, let's see." He muttered, as he rummaged about on one of the long and crooked shelves, "No, not that one." He said discarding a book he had just lifted from it's dusty resting place, it fell from his hand to add to the already large pile on the table, one leg on which groaned quite alarmingly.

"Why don't you tidy them up every once in a while?" asked Jayanne.

"Because I know where they all are. Each one in its place."

"Which one are you looking for?"

"I am not sure, but I will recognise it when I see it."

She laughed, "You are just lazy."

"That also is true. Until now there has been no one to notice."

"You mean no one ever comes here."

"I get the occasional visitor, a trader now and then, or someone desperate for my help, other than those almost none, certainly none who would risk offending me by pointing out my untidiness."

"I would rather be offended by the truth than flattered by lies."

"We are much the same."

"When did you start your studies?"

"Many years ago, long before your were born, probably before your father was born." His eyes un-focused and seemed to be looking through her into the past, to a time that only he remembered. "Yes,a long time indeed."

"Why?" He reeled before her monosyllabic question, it struck him like a blow to the chest. He sat down hard in the rickety chair, his eyes clouded with pain.

"I am sorry." she said, "I ask too many questions."

"I have already said that we are much the same." She raised

her eyebrows, hoping that he would go on, but not actually asking any more verbally. He stared into her lovely green eyes for a minute before he told her how he had started on the path that brought him to his current home.

"I was always asking questions. Why? How? Those are the ones that started it all. Why should things be the way they are? How does this happen? Always the questions. My parents soon tired of them all. They had none of the answers, well that is not entirely true, until I was about thirteen I was happy with whatever answers they gave me, then the trouble really started, I began to question their answers. Why is magic wrong? That one always upset them, they would look around to see if any had heard me. They told me that magic was a fantasy, it didn't really exist. But the stories they all told to the children had some magic about them. Then they told me that it was evil, the devils work. I showed them that it was simply a matter of concentration, I turned the pages of a book with my mind. They screamed and ranted, they raged and howled, they called me all kinds of evil names, demon, devil, sorcerer. Then they calmed, it was like an unseen force had thrown a bucket full of ice into the room. I can still hear the dreadful silence roaring in my ears. No one must ever know that I could do this wicked thing, I must never do it again, if anyone ever found out they would be tainted with the same evil as I was. For some weeks this restriction worked, I didn't practise any old or attempt any new tricks, but being an adolescent I could not see any reason to obey for very long. Soon I was practising at every available opportunity, always when I was alone. Never when any one was around, until one day I was told to stack some hay bales in the barn, and I really wanted to go down to the river to swim in the late afternoon sun with all the other boys. I closed the barn door, I was very careful about the door, I settled down in the corner where I could see all the bales and the place where they were to be put. Without moving physically from my place I moved them, slowly at first, then faster and faster, with practise it became easier, I was moving two and three at a time, high up the stack they flew to land perfectly placed and just in time for the next to land on top. It couldn't have taken me more than a few minutes, but in those few minutes Johnquel, came to see if I could come swimming with the rest. My mother told him I was in the barn. He didn't even try the door, he climbed over one of the horses stalls and into the barn that way. He saw me sitting, unmoving, sweating like I had run all day, he saw the bales flying and he screamed. The distraction spoiled my concentration and I lost all control of the hay bales, some sort of backlash struck me, the whole world went black. I woke in a dark cellar, it was cold and damp, I was chained to one wall. There was a lot of commotion outside, I could here a rumbling through the wall, it was like a herd of horses galloping a mile away. I waited for an eternity, not knowing what was happening, worrying about my parents more than myself. Finally two men in black masks came into the cellar, a third stood by the entrance steps and held a lantern so that all could see. They said not a word, but came over and released my arms from the wall and almost carried me to the steps. I pleaded for a drink, or leave to pass water, but I could get no response from the silent three. At the steps the one with the light went up backwards and the others stood behind me pushing. Once we were outside it was clear that a whole night had passed, the sun was just rising, half a red disc had cleared the houses at the end of the village. There was a huge crowd gathered in the middle of the open green. The crowd separated and a path cleared towards its centre. I looked into the tired and drawn faces of my friends and neighbours, they had been awake all night, that much was obvious from the dark rings around their eyes. There was something else in those eyes that took me some time to recognise, it was fear, a terror beyond understanding had taken them all. I reached the centre of the crowd and saw that a huge pyre had been built and at its height three tall stakes were arranged, two of them already held victims, my mother and father. We were to be burned alive. Mother was crying, father was cursing, he yelled and screamed. He cursed me to hell, and called me devil. While the black faced men tied me to the upright beam the priest stood forward from the crowd and turned to face them. He spoke of devils and demons, he said that I was one of those but he was not certain which, according to the scriptures both can only be purified by fire. The parents of demons must also be burned or their evil may infect others. He gave a torch to one of the masked men and told him to bring gods holy fire to cleanse the evil. The man ran to the temple and returned with the torch brightly burning. Fear drove my mind away, my bladder let loose and soaked my trousers with its contents. More torches were lit from the first one. Seeing the fire seemed to suddenly crystallise my thoughts, panic was banished in an instant. A cold intensity took over my entire being, I held the control over my initial impulse to escape, timing would be very important, I waited, ready. The crowd moved back from the pyre, the torch carriers spread all around and at the word of the priest they plunged the torches in the dry kindling. The greedy red and yellow flames spread quickly around the edge, but the centre where all the heavy wood was stacked would take some time to light. I waited. Over the roaring of the fire I could hear two human sounds, one the frightened screams of my mother the other the joyful chanting of the crowd. I waited. The thick smoke swirled all around me and I struck. Taking all the burning wood in the grip of my mind I scattered it through the crowd, only one human sound to hear now, screams. I ripped the ropes from the arms of all those imprisoned. Hurled the stakes high into the air, put one arm around my mothers waist and grabbed my fathers hand and led them both through the carnage. It must have been a most unusual sight to see, a youth leading both his parents to safety, though there was none to see it, the entire crowd had fled. We walked across the common together and alone, even the priest had scampered off hide. Out of the smoke, across the green, out of the village, down the road to our farm, we walked side by side, and saw not a soul. When we arrived at the farm, father seemed to come to his senses, we talked for an hour, which tired me more than any time before or since. Though my mind was still fixed in the cold, clear and emotionless mode that supported my magic, the tiredness was beginning to show. It is only now with the advantage of hindsight that I see my fathers deception. He said that we must leave, and then we could be safe from those religious fanatics, he said that together we would build another farm in another land, far, far away. I trusted him, and my mother, who agreed with every word he said. He told me to rest and we would all leave once everything was packed and loaded on the horses. The efforts of the day before and the last few hours meant that as soon as I relaxed, I fell asleep. When I awoke the sun was almost down and I was alone, the house was empty. A quick search showed that the only things gone were the horses, saddles and small but saleable items. Looking through the windows I saw a crowd gathering, between the house and the barn, they appeared to have regained some of their courage, how much was of a liquid nature I could not be sure. There were no women in the crowd, only men and boys older than I were there. Above my head I heard a crash, looking out I saw someone running away from the house, I knew he had thrown a torch on the roof, they were going to burn the whole house to get me. The priest was standing right at the back, I could just see the top of his pointed hat above the heads of the rest. First came anger that parents had left me alone, then came hatred of the people who had been my friends, then came strength fuelled by these intense emotions. My mind cleared as never before, the rush of power was unbelievable to me, who had some, if small, experience of such things. A roar filled my soul, and the windows of the house blew out in shards of deadly glass. A howl filled my brain and the door flew into the crowd leaving death in is wake. Stepping through the open doorway, I saw the crowd of torch bearing killers with a thought of anger I flung them this way and that, scattering them like a farmer sows seeds. The ones that tried to run I tripped, the ones that froze I knocked to the ground, I waded through a sea of fallen people until I reached the priest, a look of total terror on his face, his holy book held before him, I thought of flame and it burned. He flung it aside like a venomous snake. 'I am no demon.' I said, 'Demons are those who burn people alive for being different. I am leaving, you will never see me again, maybe one day you will realise how much help I could have been to this village.' I pushed him too his knees, and walked around him, leaving my home was hard but I slowly made my way to this land where magic is not hated to the same extent. I never found my parents and they must be long dead by now. My story is similar to yours."

"Where is this land?"

"It took me ten years to travel this far, I never stayed more than a few days in any place, I came slowly north, I took working passage on three ships and crossed five oceans. My birth place is very far away, this place is home to me now."

"But you have no people to share it with."

"I do not need reminding of that."

"How many years have to been alone?"

"More than you have known, more than your parents have known, more than your grandparents have known."

Jayanne remained silent for a minute while she worked out the number of years that he meant. Ten travelling, fifty for her grandparents, fourteen until he left home, that makes sixty four.

"That makes you sixty four." she paused, "But you don't look over fifty."

"I may have missed some out, I am actually over ninety." Her jaw fell open in disbelief, it flapped for a while like a fish as it lay on the bank of a river.

"Close your mouth my dear, it is most unattractive." Her teeth clacked as her jaw slammed shut. Then it opened again , this time in a more purposeful manner.

"How do you look so young?"

"My life is very slow and peaceful, I have no worries or stress, generally that is, I feel that is about to change. Perhaps my work helps to keep me young."

She stared but her questions seemed to have dried up,

Granger was surprised at himself, he had told his story to no one before this day. After only a few moments silence he spoke.

"Enough ancient history, tell me of this axe."

Slowly she told him everything that had happened, where Namdarin found it, how it never seemed to need sharpening, how it felt good in her hand, the flush of energy it gave her with every successful strike, how she chopped a man in two from head to crotch with a single blow, how the power roared in her head when she cut the sleeping willow. He asked a strange question about her own injuries in all these battles, she told him that they always healed very fast, but not before she found the axe, only since.

"I think I know whose axe this was but I need to test it to be sure, I need your permission to do so. Do I have it?"

"Of course." She said handing over the axe like it was her most prized possession, her hand was loathe to release the haft, "You won't harm it, will you?" The question quavered in the air.

"It will come to no harm." His calm assurance settled her fears, she released the leather bound wooden haft into his hand. His arm twitched and his eyes half closed as if the wood was too hot for him to touch.

"It does indeed carry a lot on energy, but I wonder whose." He placed the axe on the floor beside the table. Taking his staff from where he had left it propped against the bookcase he pointed the end at the wide blade of the axe, muttering some words that she could not hear. The soft light from the roof of the cave was completely swamped by a surge of harsh blue fire that jumped from the staff into the axe blade, it flared for an instant on the surface then vanished, a constant stream from the staff that was absorbed into the axe. Granger stopped the flow of blue fire, reached down and picked up the axe, it was undamaged but not unmarked. In the very middle of the head there was some very delicate engraving, long flowing letters of a script that Jayanne could not read.

"What does it say?"

"I don't know." Said Granger. "I recognise only one word, Algoron."

"Is that a place?" Jayanne thought that it sounded like a place her father had mentioned one day when talking to a merchant.

"No. It is a who. Algoron was one of the old gods, I have not heard of any mention of him in any of the book for over two hundred years. Though it is said that he was a great warrior, I remember a quote for an old history. 'Algoron waded through the advancing ranks of Horinites chopping them down like wheat stalks his axe flashing in the blazing sun.'"

"It never gets dirty." Jayanne said.

"What do you mean?"

"As soon as it cuts it some how absorbs the blood. Even dried blood from a horses coat."

"Then it is indeed the axe of Algoron, which gives you the weapons of three of the old gods. Xeron's sword , the axe of Algoron, and the bow of Morgandy. Truly a formidable arsenal, your quest is favoured by the old ones. I think that I will join you. Though the final passing of the old gods will most probably reduce my powers. Let's go and tell the others what we have discovered."

Jayanne held out her hand so that he would pass her the axe.

"No. My dear. It was difficult enough for me to hold earlier, now it has all the energy I had to give it to make it tell me its name, if I touch it again it will most certainly harm me. I advise you to handle it with care." She nodded and moved slowly round the table, the engraving on the head had already disappeared only clean steel showed where it had been. She picked it up by the wrist thong, being very careful not to touch the haft, she wriggled her delicate feminine wrist through the thong, and gingerly took hold of the clean wooden shaft.

   Her scream was so loud that it attempted to wake the sleeping volcano that was the heart of Granger's mountain home, it was a mixed howl of both agony and ecstasy, Crathen was the first to arrive at the narrow entrance followed by Namdarin, who was tripping over the younger man's heels. The sight that confronted the startled two was amazing. Jayanne was holding the axe in both hands, it was raised high above her head, her scream reached on, punching holes in their brains making their heads hurt with its high overtones, the intense harmonics re-echoed by the small cave seemed to shake their very skulls. The blade of the axe shone with a cold blue light, that illuminated everything it touched, but cast no shadows, everything in the small room reflected a blue glow. The only things in the whole room that had not shifted into a monochrome blue world where two sharp green eyes, eyes that mixed pain and joy in equal parts, eyes that looked over a young shoulder into the blue depths of another's eyes. Jayanne saw lips move and felt voices raised, but she heard only a distance hissing, like a far off waterfall, a silent roaring that filled her mind, it was the distress on the faces before her that brought her down from the heights that she had suddenly attained. She pushed the roaring away, into the distance it faded, the crackling power that had shone so brightly fizzled and failed. The blue light vanished and was replaced by the more mundane illumination of the crystals, for the three men in the room it was like darkness had fallen, their vision was blurred for a little time, Crathen's sight cleared first, his were the youngest eyes, he saw a band of blue light creep up the haft of the axe and vanish completely into the head. For Jayanne true darkness fell like a clap of thunder and the world went away. Crathen stepped forward and caught her before she crashed into the table, she was not heavy but her falling weight would have done serious damage to the already rickety structure.

   "Careful of the axe." Said Granger. Crathen had been giving it no thought but had not actually touched it.

"Why?"

"It has just expended a great deal of energy, it will be hungry." Namdarin looked very worried.

"She will be fine soon," Granger said softly, "take her outside where she can warm up, I will explain everything. Do not touch the axe, not haft nor head, the thong may be safe if it must be touched, but never with bare skin."

Crathen walked out into the main cave following Namdarin, who was walking slowly backwards. Granger watched them leave and then he picked up his staff, he groaned and leaned on it heavily, he had tried to replace some of his recently expended energy from the reserve that was held within the wood, the staff was empty, utterly discharged, a state that it had not been in for many years, not since his last fight with the priests of Zandaar, it had sustained him then for five consecutive days of battle, today it had been drained in a moment. 'Perhaps the axe wont be so hungry after all.' he thought. He caught up with Crathen and Namdarin as they were laying Jayanne down beside the mudpot, the morning sunlight was flashing off the wide blade of the axe, he was almost sure that the faintest of outlines was visible, where the engraving had appeared earlier.

Slowly with the end of his staff he pushed the axe away from her body so that the head hung over the edge, in the column of rising steam.

"Namdarin. Put your sword in the steam but keep hold of it." When Namdarin had followed the instruction Granger placed his staff similarly in the hot gases. After a brief instant Granger felt the energy begin to flow, once he had a small reservoir he used it to open a wider channel and pushed his staff down into the bubbling mud, heat energy rushed into both the staff and himself. He sighed and stood up straight, he hadn't even realised that he had been hunched over like a tired old man, he had not felt that tired for a long time.

"Namdarin try to see your sword in your mind, make it open itself to absorb the heat of the mud, like a flower opens to the sunlight, you may find it difficult at first, but it is a far better way to feed the thing than killing, which is its normal method."

"Never mind that, what is wrong with Jayanne?"

"She will recover in a little while, I had to feed the axe a great deal of power to make reveal itself, when she picked it up again the energy surged through her body, it seemed that her mind was enthralled by the power. She began to collect it from all around her, she emptied my staff utterly in moments."

"I thought you said that was dangerous."

"I did. She found some way to channel it safely. The axe was the channel, but exactly what it did with all that power I have no idea, perhaps we will find out when she awakes."

"It does appear to be a much more powerful weapon than I first took it for." His eyes were fixed on Jayanne, the mere thought of loosing her was causing him intense pain, it had echoes in the pain that he still felt for the loss of his family. The two pains seemed to be mixing together, blending with each other in an unusual way. By closing his eyes he brought to the forefront of his mind a clear picture of his wife and son. Their faces were still fixed solidly in his memory, and would be until the end of his days. Conjuring Jayanne's picture was much easier, it appeared by comparison to by more intense, more lively, more vibrant. He decide that this was entirely due to the fact that he had seen her face only moments before, he opened his eyes to see her face again. He watched her chest rise and fall for a moment or two, the steadiness of her breathing was a calming influence in itself. Her breath caught in her throat, her green eyes flashed open, the irises huge to start with, but shutting down rapidly in the bright light of day.

"What happened?" She asked.

"Can you tell us?" Was Granger's reply. Her brow creased in concentration. She sat upright and looked at the friends that had all gathered around.

"I remember picking up the axe, it felt suddenly hot, I tried to drop it, then there was a blue light and I saw Namdarin behind Crathen in the entrance, they looked very frightened, then I realised that it was me they were frightened of, or maybe for. Then the blue light flickered and was gone."

"Is that all?"

"That is all I remember."

"How do you feel?" Asked Namdarin, reaching a hand towards her. She took his hand in her left, reaching across her body to do so, she was unwilling to move the axe.

"I feel great, like I have just woken from a good nights sleep, I am a little hungry though." Her gaze flicked to each of the men in turn, all their looks showed the same sort of concern, though Namdarin and Crathen were clearly more worried than the others. Finally she fixed Granger with her gaze.

"What actually happened?" she asked.

"You remember me feeding power to the axe?" She nodded.

"You remember the engraving that appeared on the blade?" Again a nod.

"I warned you to take care handling it?" Nod.

"When you touched the haft, there was a flash of blue light, and you screamed. You held the axe above your head in both hands and blue light filled the cave. The light came from both you and the axe, it was a tremendous power surge the like of which I have never seen. I couldn't look. It was too bright. You drained my staff and Namdarin's sword seems to have lost some of its normal shine. What did you do with all that energy?"

"I have no idea. I feel that it was going somewhere, or perhaps I was going with it. It certainly felt good I felt strong. I still do."

"What stronger than you normally would?"

"I think so."

"The energy from the axe must have been using you as a conduit, travelling through you on to somewhere else, I wonder just where that was? There was certainly plenty of it. Have you any idea at all of where it was going?"

"No, but I do get the impression that it was a long way off, but also very close, perhaps it was not distance but time that is the important factor."

"You think that the energy was travelling through time to feed what?"

"I felt a moment of deep, intense hunger, a mind swallowing emptiness that had waited millennia to be filled."

"Did you fill it?"

"I think not, I can't be sure, everything was happening so quickly, I only got vague impressions at the best. I feel that the emptiness is still there and still waiting, though now it is more alert, more awake, more ready to suck in power to feed itself, what its final purpose is I don't know."

"Could it be trying to get out of it's current location and invade our world?"

Jayanne was beginning to tire of these unending questions, her replay was almost rude, "I don't know."

"I am sure that we will find out sooner or later." Said Granger, he sensed that she would soon become very unresponsive, her irritation was beginning to show in the tenseness of her arms and the slow flexing of her fingers. Granger sat very still and closed his eyes, he was obviously meditating on the things he had just heard, Namdarin was still looking intently at Jayanne. "Are you sure you are all right?" He asked.

"I am fine, but I would be better with something to eat."

"Breakfast will not be long now." Mander shouted.

"It may not taste too good, but it will be quick." Laughed Andel.

"Could you do any better?"

"Could I do any worse?"

Jangor shook his head but said nothing.

Namdarin snorted a short laugh, and Jayanne smiled. Crathen who was just across the mud-pot from her saw the smile as entirely for him, his heart leapt at the thought that she was happy. His mind wandered off into a sensual day dream of hot sweaty bodies and deep feelings.

Mander finally brought out the food and distributed it evenly amongst them all he complained all the time about the taste of sulphur, though the others had ceased to notice it. The morning progressed slowly with little action Granger, Namdarin and Jayanne all were somewhat drained by the excitement before breakfast, Kern went down to the grass at the head of the rock slide to tend to the horses and to check for any sign of pursuit. Stergin and Mander had a little fencing practice while Namdarin tended the fletchings of his arrows. After another relaxed meal Jangor was beginning to get restless.

"All this sitting around doing nothing is getting us nowhere." he said. "We must decide a few things and quickly."

"I think that Zandaar himself knows that we are moving against him." Said Granger.

"So," said Namdarin, "you definitely side with us now."

"I think so, it is time I took some interest in the world beyond my little valley and this seems to be a good enough challenge to keep me amused for a while."

"Have you any thoughts as to how we should proceed?"

"Quietly."

"What do you mean?"

"If we storm through the lands laying waste to all the monasteries we can find and killing every person we meet who happens to like the colour black for his clothing, someone is going to notice. If we can keep Zandaar from knowing where we are, we may be able to get close enough to do some serious damage."

"I can see that we will have to be very careful, but even so I don't see our chances as at all good."

"There must be some chance for victory or the old gods would not lend so much support, three weapons and such a mix of people is probably the best way to go about this quest of yours. I think that we must find a good story to cover our trail, something that everyone will want to believe, it must provide us with a good reason to be travelling so far from our homes, does anyone have any ideas?"

A long silence settled on the group, broken only by the bubbling of mud and the gentle whisper of the wind. A loud clatter came from the path told them that at least one of the horses was coming up to find out what was happening, Namdarin was not in the least surprised to see that it was Arndrol, the grey walked straight up the Namdarin and nuzzled his chest.

"What are you after?" asked the man.

The horse merely nudged him harder and turned his head away a little.

"You want your ears scratching, don't you?" Namdarin obliged, and soon progressed to rubbing down his entire coat, soon it shone, silver and grey in the sun, even though Namdarin had something to distract his mind he began to feel more and more uncomfortable.

"Jangor." he said looking at the soldier, "Something is going to happen soon, I don't know what but I can feel it getting closer."

"I feel the same." added Granger.

"Kern." said Jangor, "go and get the rest of the horses up here." After Kern had run down the narrow path he continued. "If someone is coming they may see our horses and thereby know that we are here, if they don't see them they can't be sure." Jangor drew his sword and sat cross legged on the ground, his usual posture when waiting. Once Kern had returned with all their mounts, he looked at Namdarin and said, "If people are coming they will be riding horses."

Namdarin nodded, then turned to Arndrol and place his forehead against the horses. The merest moment was all the time it took for the man to establish contact with the horse and through him the herd, the local herd was well known but further off were the horses that he didn't know, they were much closer than they had ever been before, they were climbing a steep path in the sunlight, they were both warm and hungry, and could smell growing grass ahead. Namdarin broke the contact.

"They will be reaching the scree very soon."

"How many?" asked Jangor.

"How can you know?" asked Granger.

"They are five, and I can feel the herd of horses, their horses are tired, hungry and working hard."

"What are we going to do with them?" Demanded Jayanne, her fist clenched tightly round the haft of the axe.

"They cannot climb the scree without help." Said Granger. "I will go and discourage them, I have done that sort of thing before."

"They may be more persistent this time." Said Jangor, "They will at least suspect that we are here." Granger merely shrugged and turn towards the hidden path. The rest followed him down to the small plain of grass at the top of the scree. They waited in the bright sunlight out of sight of those they now knew were approaching rapidly. Kern was the first to speak.

"I hear horses at the bottom." His voice was hardly above a whisper, but a sharp gesture from Jangor told them all to be quiet. There was little noise from below until they heard a man slide down amongst the sharp rocks. Granger waited a while then walked slowly to the edge of the grass, he stood on the brink of the slope, calmness personified, even when threatened by the Zandaars he barely blinked. The confrontation was short and surprised the Zandaar.

CHAPTER NINETEEN

Kevana was astounded by the power of the old man's magic, he sat on the green grass for a few minutes, his men just watched him, they could tell that it was only his pride that had been damaged, no words were spoken, for none were needed. Kevana had much to think about, so they gave him the time he required.

"Our plans have just changed." He said. "We now know that our prey lies above this treacherous slope. We cannot just walk away and leave them up there, we have no idea how long they can survive without leaving the security of their castle. There has to be another way up there, we have to find it."

"How?" Asked Petrovana, looking down at the still seated man.

"We will divide our forces, two will stay here and prevent the thieves from leaving and the others will search for another entrance."

"I hate to remind you," said Petrovana, with a wicked grin, "but that old man just beat you to the ground, and you are the best of us at this sort of magic, the rest of us are soldiers. If you go off to find a path that may not even exist who of those left could stop him? He could fly down that slope and walk right on over us."

"Why assume that I would be going?"

"You cannot climb this slope and you would most certainly want to be in the group that gets to the top. You would not be guarding the known entrance to the magicians lair. Division of our force is ridiculous, the old man put you down, and I believe he could have killed you on the spot, had he so decided. If we separate now they will come down from their safety and escape, I no longer believe that we are enough of a force to stop them at all. The power that the old man just demonstrated is way above our abilities, he must be Granger. We have all heard the stories of Granger, how he is a charlatan, a trickster and a fairground illusionist, these stories are filled with hidden hate, hatred of some one who will not be controlled like all the others. How many times have our soldiers gone against this lonely old man?"

"The stories do not tell." Says Fabrana.

"No-one boasts about their losses, the tales are designed to keep us away from him. How many times Kevana? How many times have we failed?"

"In whispers it is said that our most accomplished magicians and most powerful priests have all failed right here. No-one counts the numbers, but every once in a while some one will come to believe that they are ready for the greatest challenge and come here to face it. So far few have lived, Granger seems to know when they come with the intention to beat him or die trying. Usually they die. There are two that I know of that have survived combat with Granger, they both took some one to look after their physical needs, the carers were the ones who brought the priests home. I say that they survived, but I would not call it life, they are as babes in arms, they need to be fed and cleaned, their minds are completely gone."

"Which of us have you chosen to die?"

"None. We cannot separate, you are right. They would just walk away from this place leaving dead behind them. We shall have to come up with a better plan."

"If we all stay here could we hold them?" Asked Briana.

"Their group was already bigger than ours, and now they have an accomplished magician to guide them. Much as it irks me to say it, I see no way that we can beat them here."

"Then we must face them on a ground of our own choosing." Said Alverana.

"So. We must leave here and ambush them some where else. Every where around here is white with snow, not what I would call ideal ambush country. We have to be able to surprise them, we cannot do that around here, and we cannot survive for long simply tagging along behind them."

"We don't know who they are." Said Petrovana. "You called them thieves and that is all we have envisaged them to be. I think that they are much more than just thieves out for a profit. There is no profit to be made from the likes of us. We are usually safe from thieves and such because they all know the price that they will be made to pay. These seem not care, they killed Crandir knowing he was one of us. They took the treasure that only Zandaar himself can hold. They brought their prize straight here to some one who is almost certainly going to help them, in whatever it is they are attempting to do. We need to know more about these people before we can find a way to defeat them."

"How do we find out all this information? What questions do we ask? And who do we ask?"

"You are the leader. These are your problems. We could go to the monastery that lies south of here and ask there if any one knows any thing of this band. But they would soon identify us and our supposed task. Then the world would know how we had failed."

"It begins to seem to me that we could never have beaten them anyway. Their skills are beyond ours." Agreed Fabrana.

"I don't believe that." Said Kevana. "The old wizard Granger, he is the one that will cause us problems, the others are only soldiers at best and we can defeat them I am sure. Perhaps the monastery can give us something else that we need, a priest strong enough to distract Granger while we kill the others and take the thing that should be ours back."

"That is a much better plan." Said Alverana. " We only have to convince the abbot that we need his help with Granger, he might even be glad to help us, the prestige to be won from such a battle could be enough to bring him round to our side, he would have to keep it secret until the outcome is known, because failure would reflect badly on him. To be involved in the bringing down of the wizard Granger could bring an abbot promotion to somewhere warm, like Zandaarkoon, old abbots like their comforts."

"Alverana , you have a cynical mind. But I think you may just be right." Said Kevana.

"We still need more information about these people," said Petrovana, "we need something to give to the abbot so that he will help us."

"But does it have to be the truth?" Asked Alverana.

"Lie to an abbot." Gasped Petrovana.

"They are only men such as you and I. They cannot see a lie unless they look for it. If we tell him the truth that he wants to hear he won't even look for any lies."

"We will stay a while longer." Said Kevana. "I wish to investigate their dreams, if I can. It has been far too long since I tried such a thing, but it may give us some clues as to what these people are up to." The others started to set up camp it would be a long day and possibly an even longer night, Kevana watched the slope and waited for something to happen.

Granger walked back from the top of the slope, he was much more tired than he seemed to the ones waiting below. The combat had taken far more out of him than he had expected. Kern helped him to the cave entrance where the others stared, it was the first time that he had seemed to be as old as he actually was.

"I have held them at the bottom, but I do not believe that they will leave for a while, their magician was actually quite strong, his mind was fast and clear. Taking the weapons from him was harder than I expected. Ye gods! I am out of practise at this."

"Will you be all right?" Asked a concerned Jayanne.

"I need rest and energy." With this his staff drifted over to the mud-pot and immersed itself completely.

"We have to decide what we are going to do." Said Jangor.

"We cannot stay here for much longer, though they have not as yet sent for re-enforcement's I think that they will do so soon." Answered Namdarin.

"How difficult would it be for you to hold the scree whilst we descend?" Asked Jangor.

"Impossible at the moment. I am far too tired. Though it takes little energy it requires much concentration."

"Then we must stay until you are rested. When we leave will you come with us?"

"Yes. It is time for me to leave and make something important of my life before it is over."

"We will have to kill those priests before we can go, but how shall we travel without being noticed too much, if word of us gets to our enemies then we could get into some serious difficulties?"

"If we were on a pilgrimage then none of the monks would question us too closely, there are many such groups travelling at all times of the year, most of them expect some form of protection from the priests."

"That sounds like a good idea. Lets rest for the remains of today and set out at first light or just before while they are still asleep down there." Jangor nodded his head in the direction of the monks camped at the bottom of the slope.

"Namdarin." Said Granger ."Set your sword in the mud, Jayanne you do the same with your axe. It will be a long time before we come across an energy source as good as this one. Let the weapons recharge until it is time for us to leave." They started sorting through the supplies that they had, Granger started the difficult job of deciding which of his precious books he was to leave behind, it took much cajoling to convince him that he couldn't load a horse with just books, the horses were for food and other supplies as well. He finally gave in when Namdarin explained in detail the size of the library at the monastery, Granger was almost dribbling with anticipation to get to the next monastery so that he could raid their library. Namdarin failed to mention that the monks were not likely to be all that hospitable.

But then Granger was not thinking of asking their permission.

It only seem like an hour or so when Jangor noticed that the sun was starting to go down, he told Kern to let the horses go down to the greensward at the top of the scree to feed, it was too dark for the Zandaars to try shooting at them with arrows, even if they had a bow that could reach that far. Arndrol led the way as was his wont. He went straight to the edge of the slope and stared down at the small camp below, then he stood up on his hind legs and screamed his challenge to the black clad priests. Kevana stood up and watched the horse, knowing for the first time that the ones they sought were indeed at the top. He settled down in his tent not intending to sleep but preparing himself for the mental battle that was about to be joined. He had eaten only a little, so that his stomach would not be too full as this would have been an undue distraction, his skill in the arcane was feeble enough without adding any other disruptions. Fabrana and Briana were sleeping, Alverana was looking to the horses, Petrovana was pacing slowly around the camp muttering to himself, but doing it so quietly that no word could be divined.

Kevana waited until it was fully dark before he tried to contact the dreams of his enemies, at first he felt nothing at all, for some time he was almost sure that none of them were asleep. Until he made contact with a small dream, one that had no real order , but was intensely bright, a million colours flashing in kaleidoscopic array around his head. He broke away from this and realised that he would need the help of his friends.

"Come to me." He shouted. "I need you all this is going to be even more difficult than I first imagined." He waited until the others were all close by before he spoke again.

"Form a circle and be ready to feed me your energies I may be in great need if I come up against any great resistance." They settled into a circle each one hold the hands of one to each side.

"I will start." spoke Kevana in a very soft voice, "We will build energy into the circle slowly, I will pass the energy on to Alverana. He will pass it on to Fabrana, on to Petrovana, and to Briana, then back to me, each time you pass the power on you add a little of your own, so that the energy in our ring gradually increases, until I have enough to reach out to our foes. This is a standard method used by the better trained priests to increase power by fusing minds into groups, the biggest group ever was two hundred minds in a very large circle, it was a mistake. By the time the initial surge came back to the start point it was so large that the man's mind exploded and so did his head. I do not think that we have enough energy in our little circle to cause our selves any lasting harm no matter how many times we go around." He then gave them a moment or two to gather their thoughts and said "Let us begin."

Slowly at first then with gradually gathering speed the energy pulse travelled around the circle of friends, with each pass around the circle its peak level reached slowly higher, Kevana was amazed at the amount of power available in their tiny group, after only a few minutes of intense concentration he was ready to make his attack. Taking all the power in the cycle he gathered it for a moment then hurled it outwards, up the mountain he soared like a rising wide, he rushed up the slope and washed across the grass at the top, upwards he raced until the cave was visible in his minds eye, this power was unlike any he had felt before, the clarity of the view was so intense it was better than being there in person, the forms of his enemies were all about him, he studied each one in turn, the old wizard, Granger, was not asleep but was resting in an almost comatose state, there were no dreams for him to invade. Next a woman, good looking and tall, she was asleep but not dreaming, next to her was a man, he appeared to be a little taller than her but seemed to be a lot larger, not in physical size, but bigger, he was still awake and very much alert. A young man, smaller and slimmer, lying on his side in the back of the cave, his dreams a dark swirling mass. Kevana dived in the twisting spiral of the dream, into a dimly lit room, the hearth was large and held a huge fire that gave little light or heat, the room contained all the normal furniture that one would expect in an affluent house. The young man was sitting at a dark wooden table eating, while behind him stood a woman, tall and red headed. 'Not unlike the one sleeping over there' thought Kevana. This seemed like a good place to start, Kevana sat down at the table and talked to the man.

"What is your name?"

"I am called Crathen, who are you?"

"Who is the woman? Is she your wife?"

"No. She is Namdarin's woman, though she should be mine, she is much too young for him. She is beautiful isn't she?"

"Most certainly, she could be yours."

"How?"

"If he were not here, she would be yours."

"He would not leave her behind."

"He could have an accident, he could die."

"No. They say that even death is only temporary for him, he is reborn every time that some-one kills him."

"You could make his death permanent, if you kill him with a dream he will certainly die, and nothing can bring him back."

"And then the woman would be mine?"

"Yours to do with as you please. Do you like this idea, you could spend the rest of your life with her."

"He will not be that easy to kill, he has a strong mind and unstoppable will."

"You must find a way. I can help you."

"If I kill him his friends will know and they will kill me, or she will know and hate me forever."

"They cannot find out unless you tell them, she will not be able to disobey you if you kill him, I will show you how to control her absolutely."

"Her strength is almost as his, I don't believe that she can be controlled at all."

"You seem to have her pretty much controlled as she is now."

"This is only an image of her, I know that, it cannot be the real her. She would not be mine, this is a dream. And you are the enemy, I will listen to you no more."

"You cannot just throw me out now, I have been here too long this dream is now as much mine as it is yours."

"You can show your true colours now Zandaar. I know what they are. The are the black of death. The very smell of it hangs about you, like the stink of corpses, I see the flesh rotting from your face. Can you feel it."

Kevana began to get a little worried, this young man seemed to be too good at the dream games, he decided to leave the dream, a fast fade out, and he was gone from Crathen's dream. Crathen made no attempt to follow he had no idea how to do that, but he had managed to frighten Kevana away.

Kevana passed on to another dream, a middle aged man with some greying hair and a well muscled torso. The dream was of combat , the man was fighting for his life against a many headed monster, every slash of the sword that removed a head only produced two more heads in its place. Kevana appeared in the dream, dressed in green , the green of fresh summer grass, he raised his hands and struck the monster with a blast of green fire. One of its heads fell to the ground and the neck grew no more heads.

"That is not how this game is played." Said the soldier.

"You call this a game."

"Of course, did you think that it was for real. This is merely a training exercise."

"But how can you ever win? It just keeps getting stronger."

"It currently has ten heads each filled with poisonous teeth, every time I cut off a head the game gets more difficult, the more heads it has when it finally gets you the better you are at the game. There is no way to win, if you stick to the rules. But I don't suppose that you ever stick to the rules do you?"

"No. I usually like to make my own as I go along."

"But then you have no standards to test your progress against. You change the rules to suit the way you feel, this is no way to play any game."

"Some things aren't a game."

"Life is a game, what is there more than life? It has it's rules and its rule breakers. The simplest of its rules is survival. Survival of the fittest. How fit are you?"

Kevana turned to the monster that had been almost stationary as if listening to their conversation and bathed it in hot green fire, the fire roared and consumed the serpentine necks until the wreckage fell to the ground. "I seem to be fit enough for this game."

"There is more than one game to play here." The man swung his sword around to face Kevana.

"You would challenge me?"

"No. I would kill you. This was my game and you have disturbed it."

"I can kill you as easily as I did the serpent."

"No. I will not be that easy."

Kevana formed his hands into a ball and rolled them around as if a gradually expanding sphere was held within them, a harsh green light escaped from between his fingers and a ball of solid green lightening grew in his hands. Once it was the size of a man's head he released it towards the man. He did not throw it , it appeared to know where is was to go, it left his hands and accelerated towards the man. Who stood very still, waiting calmly for it to arrive, as it approached he lifted a round iron shield, a shield that Kevana had not noticed before. Kevana was not sure whether the shield had been there earlier or whether it had appeared just for this purpose, but appear it had. The green light touched the shield and exploded, it expended its fury outwards away from the shield, Kevana felt the heat wash over him and he took two steps backwards. The green light fell from the shield into the grass and was consumed by it, the grass was very hungry. The shield passed behind the man's back and he advanced with his sword raised in both hands. Again Kevana retreated from the dream. 'These are indeed strong minded people, one more.' He thought.

The next dream that he found was of a deep dark forest. But it was strangely light, the darkness was so thick that it could be tasted, yet everything was clearly visible, the trees, the leaves on the tress, the bugs on the leaves on the trees. It all seemed to shine with an internal light. A man was sitting by a pool of clear water, the pool was a spring, because a stream led from it. The cool water was bubbling up from below the ground forming slight ripples on the surface of the pool, there was no breeze to cause them.

"Who are you?" Asked Kevana.

"I am who I am. If you don't know who I am then I won't tell you."

"I have come to kill you, I will tear your forest down and rip out your heart."

"This is my home you will not destroy it."

"How can you stop me? Kevana conjured yellow fire in each hand and spread his arms wide.

"I will not stop you, but you will be stopped."

"Tell me who you are, and I may let you live."

"I am what you see, but what you see is not me."

"You talk nonsense."

"You see nothing."

"I see fire that burns."

"Burn what you can." The man shrugged and turned half away from Kevana, almost ignoring him.

Kevana's rage burned hot is his heart, he cast his yellow fire about, washing it over the trees, over the bushes and the flowers. Where the fire passed smoke rose in the air, but the trees were unharmed, the bushes unburned and the flowers un-scorched .

"You have no influence here." Said the man. "This is my place, this is my home, this is me. You may leave, if you choose to return and bring fire to my forest again it will most certainly eat you." Kevana watched amazed as the trees started to lean towards him their branches became grasping arms, their twigs grabbing fingers, he fled again.

Kevana opened his eyes, released his friends hands, and shook his weary head from side to side.

"Those are not just thieves they are strong minded people. We must leave before first light. Get some sleep."

"They beat you again, didn't they?" Accused Petrovana.

"I was trying to get information from them and that I did, I didn't kill any of them though I did frighten them a little."

"They are scared like little rabbits now." The words dripped acid sarcasm.

"No. But I know their weakness, one of their number can be turned against them. His hope can become our victory."

"How?"

"There is a way to tear their group apart from the inside, jealously is a very powerful weapon, one that I intend to use to its fullest extent."

"That sounds interesting."

"The youngest of the men wants the only woman of the group all to himself, but she is attached to one of the others. Instil a little jealousy, add a spark of hatred, and that whole group will explode in a hopefully fatal manner. Then we walk in and pick up the pieces that are left."

"We can do this on our own?"

"No. we will need some help from our brothers, but not a whole platoon of warriors, we could come out of this better than I had hoped."

"We could even come out of this alive."

"You want to live forever? Rest, we leave before dawn."

As the dawn light appeared above the rim of the crater Kern awoke with a start. He almost remembered something, it hovered on the edge of his mind, it was something important, he kept chasing after it, like a dog chewing on its favourite bone, long after all the taste is gone, he just could not let it go. He climbed out of his bed and stalked around the cave mouth trying to snare this errant thought. He felt that it was something strange, or unusual, but had not the vaguest idea what. He move outside and went to talk to the horses about it, he always found that talking to horses helped him to organise his mind, they were always attentive but never interrupted the slow flow of his thoughts. Arndrol walked up to Kern and placed his chin upon the man's shoulder, he could tell that the man was disturbed about something. Kern found the horses presence very comforting, but this didn't help at all with his problem, something was wrong, very wrong, and he had to find out what it was. It was something to do with fire, harsh yellow fire, the sort that he usually only saw in the driest of summers, it was a forest fire. But there is snow on the ground there can be no fires at this time of year. This is no clearer. Kern put his arm around Arndrol's neck and leaned against his flank, the slow breathing of the horse and the steady thumping of his heart was loud in Kern's head, the liquid noise typical of horse digestion was a soothing as all the other sounds, Kern relaxed almost unto sleep. Like a flash of light he awoke, knowing the dream in it's entirety, and knowing that their enemy had been in it. He ran back up to the cave. And shook each of his friends in turn, each woke in his ,or her, own way. A hand leapt to a sword, a curse fell from the lips, a grunt, a muffled groan.

"What's the urgency?" Demanded Jangor.

"Our enemy has been in my dream."

The moans stop and all pay close attention to what the scout has to say as he describes very carefully the dream that had been invaded.

"You beat him off?" Asked Mander, unbelief clear in his voice.

"The dream did. That dream is where I truly live. I have had that dream all my life, it is mine, and mine alone, no-one can take it from me."

"This is the seat of your strength." Said Granger. "It would be very difficult for any one to invade it, this would be a good defence of all of us. To build within the dream world a house that is our own, where we each have total control. It will take some training in thought control but it should be possible for us all. Any one else with strange dreams this night?"

"I remember a dream." Replied Jangor. "A dream of battle, I was fighting a monster, aren't they always monsters in dreams?" He laughed. The others nodded. "A man came to help me, he burned the monster and killed it with bright green fire. Then he tried to kill me he tried hard but failed, is seemed that his heart was not in the battle, like," he shook his head, searching for the right words. "Fire wasn't his weapon. It appeared unwieldy in his hand, a weapon that he was not used to. I took his fire on an iron braced shield and then he vanished. It was very strange."

"What did the man look like?" Asked Kern.

"I don't remember, he wasn't very clear."

"Anyone else?" Asked Granger, looking around the faces, searching for more clues, only one didn't shake his head, he avoided Granger's gaze completely, "Crathen, What of you? Any unusual characters in your dreams?"

"I don't remember any dreams. Nothing at all." Still he didn't look into the old man's eyes.

"I think that at least two of us were visited by a Zandaar, that they both survived may be testimony to either their strength or the priests weakness. Both Kern and Jangor met the enemy inside their own strongholds. The enemy was unable to breach their defences and was forced to depart or face defeat. I think that he was trying to gather information, about who we are and what we are about. He cannot have gathered much from his encounters as far as I can tell. But dreams are always hard to interpret, it could be that we all were visited but don't remember.

I wonder if they have left yet." He looked directly at Namdarin, who nodded. Namdarin focused his mind on the horses, Arndrol's huge vitality came through sharp and strong, the other horses almost as clear, then further out, horses working hard and moving fast, five horses.

"They have all left, or their horses have all left. They are travelling fast, faster than they should, the horses cannot hold that sort of pace for very long in this cold."

"How long have they been pushing hard?"

"Not long, probably only since the light came up. Though they started out when it was still dark."

"They are moving with purpose." Said Granger. "They have something in mind, something that is not going to help us. They have a plan. But what?"

"How can you tell?" Asked Crathen.

"They left when it was dark. They didn't even have one more try against us. I don't think they would have left any of their number to watch us and taken away their horses, so they have all gone. In a hurry, with a destination in mind. They think that they can find us again when they need to, they must know which way we intend to go. How can this be?"

Silence descended like a heavy curtain on the group. They hadn't even decide for themselves which way they were to go. Namdarin was filled with an inchoate dread, a feeling of unnameable terror that began to creep into his brain, something was going to go painfully wrong for him and his friends, of this he was very sure.

"We have to make some plan." He said. "We have to do something."

"We will begin our pilgrimage as soon as we can decide which way to go." Replied Granger, "Any ideas?"

"We should follow them."

"No. That is probably what they expect us to do. I think that they would be very happy to have us somewhere near when they get to where ever it is they are going. We should put some distance between them and us if we can."

"But our paths must go the same way for a while at least."

"I think we should head south, Zandaarkoon, their city, is on the southern shore." Said Namdarin.

"Not directly south." Said Jangor. "A little misdirection can always be used to our advantage."

"So which way?" Asked Crathen.

"East." Answered Granger. The others frowned, waiting for an explanation that was not slow in coming.

"Over these mountains, there is a long river that runs almost directly south, passage along the river will be quick and fairly easy. However, the crossing of the mountains will be anything but. There are many perils in the high passes, some that few men have ever seen, and fewer survived. But the gains to be made once we reach the river are incredible. The river flows smooth and fast for a thousand leagues, which will take only days to travel. With a little luck this should put us out of reach of anyone following, and hopefully inside any perimeter that they can set up."

"What if the followers use the river as well?"

"They will have to stop at every landing place to be sure that we have not left the river, that will slow them down a great deal, once we are on the river they should not be able to catch up with us. Providing of course that we suffer no serious disasters."

"We will have to leave immediately." Said Namdarin.

"There are things that I have to do before we can go." Said Granger.

"How quickly can you be ready?" Asked Jangor.

"An hour or two."

"Make it quicker than that, we have to go before we loose too much of today."

Granger nodded and went into the small rear cave to start organising his books and the defences for his home, he wanted there to be something to come back to, if he survived.

Jangor organised the preparation of the horses, while Namdarin used his short dagger to lever some of the largest crystals from the walls of the cave, thinking about experimenting with them as they travelled, they could be of some use if the group got separated. Kern took the loaded horses down to the field at the top of the slope so that they could feed for one last time before the journey through the snow continued. Arndrol was acutely aware that they were going to leave and was as excited as a colt, he was jumping around and racing about, pawing the ground and shaking his mane, he refused to settled down until Kern grabbed him by the ear and explained to him that he would not see real grass again for some time, then he began eating the grass with urgency.

"Let us leave." Shouted Granger eventually. Everyone cleared out of the cave and Granger stood for a moment in the entrance, he held his staff above his head and spoke some words that no-one could understand, a deep rumbling came from the cave, like heavy boulders grinding one against another. First a wisp of smoke then a gradually thickening column that reeked of hot steam and sulphur came pouring from the cave mouth.

"What have you done?" Asked Mander.

"Opened one of the old vents, no-one can go in there now, in an hour it will be so hot that nothing can live in there for more than a moment."

"Wont all your books burn?"

"No they are protected. Some things may be damaged , but I think that it is unlikely that I will return, though some one may find a use for this refuge sometime in the future."

The group of friends moved slowly away from the cave entrance as the fumes started to corrode their throats.

"How are we gong to get the horses down this?" Asked Mander, waving at the slope.

"Horses do not like going down hill at any time and this sort of surface really will frighten them." Said Kern.

"I can hold it still, like I did when you came up." Said Granger. "But not for very long, so you are going to have to hurry them along."

"Blindfold them, it will be easier." Said Stergin.

"But slower." Answered Kern.

"Arndrol will not be blindfolded, he will go were I tell him." Said Namdarin.

"Will the others follow him?" Asked Granger.

"Possibly. If I help them all." Namdarin thought for a while in total silence. Then he nodded as he had come to a decision.

"When I am ready I will let you know, then Granger you must freeze the slide, and the rest of you must guide the horses down as fast as you possibly can, they shouldn't need much in the way of guidance, they may even guide you down. I will try and hold them together."

Namdarin climbed up onto Arndrol's back, Arndrol shook his mane and stamped his heavy feet in the grass, he knew that they were gong to leave and the only way out was down the slope.

Namdarin slowed his breathing down, long slow breaths in and out. Spreading calmness through his entire body, almost as if he was going to sleep. Reaching out for Arndrol with his mind he passed on this cool calm feeling, Arndrol stopped fidgeting, and stood very still, slowly at first, then with increasing speed the relaxation spread through the horse, until his right hind leg cocked forwards and the toe of the hoof rested on the ground.

"Arndrol's gone to sleep." Whispered Kern. A sharp look from Jangor and Kern looked at the ground. The group waited and watched, hardly daring to breathe. Namdarin reached further and spread calm to the other horses. Before long the other horses had almost fallen into the same state as Arndrol. Namdarin nodded to Granger. Who touched the top of the slope with his staff and sent the blue fire running down the rocks, with a soft crunching sound the slide was fixed. Namdarin started down the slope, the horse beneath him had barely enough awareness to put one foot in front of the next, the rest of the horses followed in a similar fashion. Their progress was slow and painful to watch, every time a hoof slid off a rock or skittered to one side the people all held their breath's hoping that Namdarins cool hold on the horses would not break. Stergin and Mander were guiding the bulk of the pack animals, these were the ones most likely to bolt, should any thing go wrong. Even the horses tails stopped their flicking from side too side, so deep was the trance that held them. Once the last horse was on the slope Granger started his descent, keeping the tip of his staff in contact with the rocks at all times was difficult but essential if the locking spell was to hold. A large black cloud suddenly obscured the sun, a darkness which was by contrast as of night covered them all, a horse twitched, Namdarin felt its awakening and pressed his calm thoughts into its mind with all the force that he could muster.

It stopped, standing very still, then slowly its legs started to fold up underneath it. Its belly settled gently to the rocks, then it rolled over on its side and snored loudly. Mander pulled on its reins, trying to get it to it's feet. Jangor waved him away, no words, but a harsh gesture. This horse was lost. Arndrol walked onto the grass at the base of the slope and ambled slowly forwards, gradually stopping, the rest followed until they were all down. Granger was the last to reach the bottom, he had paused beside the fallen horse hoping that he would be able to help it if it awoke. It did not. As Granger approached the end of the slide Namdarin signalled that he should stay at the bottom and wait for the horse to wake up. Granger stopped one stride from the end of the slide, his staff firmly wedged in a crack in the rocks, his blue fire sparkling from the points of the rocks all around. Jangor realised that Namdarin was going to wake up the horses, he signed to the other to take control of the reins and to be ready. Namdarin slowly released his hold on the horses, they each woke up in its own good time, they all seemed a little confused as to how they came to be where they were. The one asleep on the slope stayed exactly where it was, it showed no sign of awareness at all, Jangor turned with a questioning look to Namdarin. Who raised a hand to indicate that he was still holding the sleeping horse in its trance, once the rest of the horses were properly awake and the people freed to help the sleeping one Namdarin slowly release his influence trying to wake the horse just enough for it to stand up, however this was not to be. The horse woke with a sudden fright, as if from a nightmare, it kicked its feet under it and leapt upwards. Kicking far too hard against the surface of the slide its hard hooves broke through the surface and started the rocks sliding downwards, rolling over each other and pulling the hooves even deeper, soon the panicked horse was up to its knees in grinding stone. Screaming it kicked harder and slid deeper until its haunches were touching the surface, with a final huge effort it lifted its forelegs clear and plunged down hill , the front hooves smashed onto a large flat rock and heaved the hind quarters clear, of the rippling slide, another powerful kick and it was free, sprinting across the grass ahead of a spilling fall of rock and dust. Granger released what hold he had left on the slide and looked to the horse that was sprinting for the horizon, taking no notice of its many injuries. Namdarin slid from his saddle and told Arndrol "Go fetch." The big grey took off with a powerful surge and chased the other horse off down the valley.

"That didn't go exactly to plan." Said Stergin.

"We are down safe and that horse will be back in a little while, that's near enough for me." Said Mander.

"You are always easily pleased."

"Sometimes the simple pleasures of life are the best," Smiled Mander.

"The simple ones are the only one that you ever get."

"The simple ones are the only ones I ever try for."

"They must be simple to associate with you."

"At least there are some that will associate with me, I'm not a lonely old fool."

"Who are you calling fool."

"Are they always like this?" Asked Granger in a very loud voice, which caused both the men to turn and face him.

"I am afraid so." Said Jangor. "They can keep this sort of argument up for hours and hours."

"Why?"

"I believe that it is a fundamental difference in their life styles. One is a confirmed celibate the other has all the morals of a tom cat."

"They cannot just get along with each other? These sort of

arguments can turn very nasty."

"They have never actually come to blows over any of these issues, but that is probably because they only fight like this when there is somebody to get in between them."

"They seem to have stopped now."

"That is usually the way of it."

"Why do they bother?"

"Who can tell."

"We are here, you know." Said Mander.

"And here comes Arndrol, with the pack horse, so once Kern has seen to its injuries we can get on our way, can't we?"

Kern rapidly discovered that the horses wounds were luckily all minor, and easily treated. In only a few minutes they were all mounted and leaving the small valley, going down hill into the cold grip of winter again.

CHAPTER TWENTY

Kevana woke his group early, long before the sun had even started to lighten the sky. There was some grumbling but it was soon obvious that they had to leave if they were to make any distance on the thieves that were soon to be following them. Kevana was certain that Granger and the others would chase them in order to prevent them acquiring the kind of help that they so surely needed. Packing up their camp in the dark was not an easy task but they achieved it in a few minutes, with a breakfast of cold rations and cool water they left the valley and turn north in the snow. Progress was slow, the horses almost had the feel their way through the murk, placing each foot carefully hoping that the ground under it was solid, but not ice. As soon as the sky starred to lighten with the coming daybreak Kevana pushed the pace as fast as the horses could go. Now that he had a purpose in mind he moved at the limit of speed, pushing the horses to the ultimate of their endurance, never a full gallop, because the conditions would not allow, but always a fast trot down the hills and a good walk up. The urgency of his mission drove him on with a passion that could not be ignored, it burned in his heart, a hot fire that ate away at his innards, consuming his every thought, and his every action. He went over in his mind the things that he was going to say to ensure that he would get the help that he needed once they arrived at the mountain monastery. He knew that someone there could be convinced to help him, one of his associates from years gone by was there, he would at least listen, and hopefully consent to come along with Kevanas plan.

Worandana was a good friend for many years until their assignments moved them apart, they had shared many good times, and some hard missions, but always they survived unscathed, and usually victorious. Any mission that had Kevana and Worandana at its head had no shortage of volunteers, word soon reached the upper echelons of power and these decreed the rapid advancement of both men, and hence their separation.

Kevana had no doubt about his old friend, together they could not fail. Kevana's reverie was disturbed by a sudden shout from Alverana, up ahead was the valley that lead to the monastery, they turned south and soon started to descend, there would be forage ahead for the horses and maybe some short rest for the riders. Before noon they had dropped below the snow and the horses could not be restrained any longer, they had not eaten properly for some days and were starving, Kevana was forced to call a stop. A mid-afternoon camp and meal for the men while the horses ripped into the harsh grass, much of it brown and not very appetising for them, but still it was food.

"Do you think that they will follow us?" Asked Alverana.

"Yes." Nodded Kevana. "They must know by now that we have left and even if they think that they can beat us, they know that they have no chance at all against a larger force. They cannot risk us bringing a larger force to bare on them."

"What if they decide to run?" Asked Petrovana, munching on a piece of hard and only marginally mouldy bread.

"If they run then we will chase them to the end of the earth, they will not escape from me." Snarled Kevana.

"We are a day and a half from the monastery, we will probably spend a day there, and two days back, that gives them a five day lead, can we track them when the trails are so old?"

"Alverana can track anything anywhere, and the trail of so many people cannot be hidden. Worandana can hunt them from a thousand miles they cannot escape from both of us."

"You plan to recruit Worandana, that makes me feel better about this, his reputation is immense, almost as large as your own."

"Together we are unbeatable."

"Or as yet unbeaten."

"I cannot believe that these thieves are the force that can beat the pair of us."

"That we will have to wait and see."

"We rest one hour then we leave here. There is still a long way to go, and if we ride through the night we can save the best part of a day."

"Or kill us all."

"To die is no defeat."

"But no fun."

"Petrovana, you are beginning to depress me, your pessimism is very wearing on every one, so please be quiet." A hard edge to Kevana's voice stopped all conversation right there.

Once the rest was over Kevana set the same punishing pace through the mountains, pausing only to feed and water the horses, they rode on through the night, the full of the first moon made the night almost like day, that and the cloudless sky made visibility good but also cold, not like the cold they had endured a few days earlier but still enough to slow the horses some more. The heat of Kevana;s rage had no effect on the strength sapping breeze that blew up the valley, freezing their breath on their faces, cracking their lips and chilling their toes. On through the night they rode, in almost as desperate a fashion as their earlier chase through the snow. The only difference being that the weak ones had already died, the only people left are the survivors, the ones who will not just lay down and die, these are the ones who will always fight to the end, until there is not one more breath to be drawn, they will abide and survive. Even with the rising of the sun the temperature didn't improve and the wind became much stronger, it lifted the fallen snow into a blizzard of purest white. Not the white out of falling snow but intermittent flurries of such density that sight was curtailed to the occasional glimpse of a horses ears, but any further than that was too much to expect. Kevana was navigating by the map in his head, he knew the valleys quite well, or more accurately he remembered the maps of the valleys quite well. But the map is not the territory, and it was inevitable that they would become lost eventually, it was only a small error, but the minor wrong turn lead to a major precipice. Stumbling almost blind through the growing light of day Kevana became unsure when the track he was following kept going up when he was certain it should be descending.

"Alverana, take the point and be very careful, I think we are lost."

Kevana going over the map in his mind, he was certain that he was wrong, but where had the turn been wrong? Was there a way to get back to the right path without having to back track and waste an awful lot of time? Precious time. He couldn't work out where he had gone wrong, it could have been ten minutes ago , or ten hours. His horse was following Alverana's by pure instinct, Kevana, could not see the horse in front most of the time, but his horse knew where it was and followed in its footsteps, almost footfall by footfall. Because they had become useless Kevana had shut his eyes, thinking about a picture of the map and only listening to the world around him, he slowly became aware that the sound of the wind in the valley was changing, it was getting harsher and speeding up, as if something was restricting the flow of air, but the valley was no narrower than it had been. Suddenly the pitch of the wind fell, the pressure of it at his back seemed to lessen, but the snow was still streaming past at the same speed. ' Like a large open courtyard.' He thought. ' Or a cliff top.'

"Stop. Stand still. Something is very wrong here. Alverana, dismount. Check this place on foot."

"But I can't see properly, because of the snow."

"Walk forward very slowly. On second thoughts, tie a rope to your waist and to my horse then go forwards."

Alverana did as he was told, with a disbelieving look at Kevana, when he tied the rope to the saddle horn. "Is this really necessary?"

"I think so. Something feels very wrong here, I suddenly don't trust the ground you are walking on."

"It feels fine to me."

"Humour a crazy old man."

"As you wish." Alverana walked slowly forwards, up a slow incline, the snow obscuring every detail of the valley floor, when he had gone twenty feet past his horse the snow suddenly fell away beneath him. The rope rushed tight, and Kevana's horse was jolted forwards a step or two before the man's fall was arrested. Kevana eased the horse backwards and Alverana gradually re-appeared above the snow.

"Once through the crust it is almost vertical, for a thousand feet or so. Not a trip I would have enjoyed for very long."

"We go back. We must find the right route, in this weather we could all end up dead."

"More time lost, we should have slept rather than getting lost all night." Muttered Petrovana.

"You are beginning to irritate me." Snapped Kevana.

"Can't a man even talk to himself without being interrupted any more?" Tutted Petrovana with a large sigh, which brought a smile to some of the faces around him.

The descent from the cliff edge took them most of the morning, walking into the wind was much harder than walking with it at their backs, and the wind was increasing in force, though this did mean that in patches the snow was completely gone. Kevana decided that he had turned east too early so the headed south again and turned up the next valley. In daylight this was obviously the right one. The steepening slope led them up to the high pass. The afternoon was well under way when they passed the summit. The top was stripped of snow, down to the bare rock and hard soil underneath. Nothing much grew there even in summer, but at this time of the year there was nothing at all, just cold grey rocks and hard grey soil, and wind. Immediately they were over the top, the wind dropped and the temperature seemed to rise, even though the snow was much deeper, as they descended towards the monastery, more snow seemed to be falling, but it fell from a clear blue sky.

"Where is this snow coming from?" Asked Fabrana, looking over his shoulder into the sun, that was just above the mountain tops behind them.

"It is blowing up that valley and dropping out of the wind onto us. Once get far enough from the pass it will stop." Answered Alverana.

"Will we get to the monastery before the sun goes down?"

"Yes. You can just see its bell tower up ahead."

"That is still a long way away."

"We will be there while there is still light to see by."

"I have never been into these mountains before, I have heard some strange tales of them."

"So have I, but most of the tales are totally unfounded. Almost all the people who disappeared in these mountains were careless. They get caught by the weather, or fall off mountains, that sort of thing."

"Its the almost I don't like."

"I admit that some of those that got lost one would not have expected to make the simple mistakes, but who can tell, there is never any evidence to be found."

"No bodies, or anything?"

"No bodies, no horses, no packs, no anything, they just vanish. But it doesn't pay to dwell on these sort of things when one is up to ones knees in hard cold snow."

"Are you trying to frighten me?"

"Of course."

Fabrana turned away and muttered something unpleasant under his breath. Twilight was falling when they approached the gates of the monastery, it appeared to Kevana that something was seriously amiss, the walls were strangely deserted, the whole place felt empty, almost abandoned. The main gates were closed and locked, as Alverana found when he tried to open them. Alverana pounded on the oaken door with his sword hilt. There was no obvious answer.

"Fabrana. Find another way in." Ordered Kevana.

"I have never seen this place this empty." Said Alverana, as Fabrana set off along the wall looking for a place that he could climb it.

"Something very bad has happened here." Said Petrovana.

"You have a talent for the obvious, don't you." Sneered Kevana.

"That is indeed one of my many talents." Said Petrovana, with a mocking bow, and a wicked smile.

"Your sense of so called humour is going to get you killed, you do realise that?"

Petrovana merely smiled some more then turned away, his shoulders twitching as he laughed softly to himself.

A faint voice called from the other side of the gate. "Who knocks on our gate?"

"Kevana and some of his soldiers." Shouted Alverana.

"Can you prove that?"

"If you open the gate we certainly can, we may even be able to help with the cause of your fear."

"You are the cause, I suppose we must take a chance." The

bars on the inside could clearly be heard lifting from their latches. Slowly one section of the gate swung inwards. Kevana stepped forwards.

"I am Kevana. Who are you?"

"I am Helvana."

"What is your problem?"

"Everyone here was killed, some time ago. One was sent to investigate, he didn't return. We came to investigate the disappearance of the investigator. We have found many dead, there were no survivors."

"Who else came with you?"

"Our leader is Worandana, there are three others."

"Fetch your leader, he is known to me."

"One does not interrupt the master." Said the monk shaking his head.

"Shall I kill this fool?" Said Fabrana standing behind the short monk, who turned in panic, then retreated from the new threat until he was outside the gate standing amongst Kevana's men.

"No. He was just about to let us in, weren't you?" Said Kevana placing a heavy hand on the Helvana's shoulder. Fabrana open the gate wide and his friends walked in to find the courtyard stacked with piles of bodies, awaiting funeral pyres. Helvana followed them in, flapping around like a crow grounded with clipped wings. Squawking in a similar manner. Kevana made a simple hand signal and Briana grabbed the monk by the throat and shook him until he ceased his struggling.

"Be quiet, your noise is very irritating. Where is Worandana?" Demanded Kevana, in a quiet menacing tone.

"He was in the library."

"Lead on." As they approached the main door two more monks came out carrying a heavy burden between them, their surprise was evident, in the thud of a falling body.

"Carry on with your task, we mean you no harm." Said Kevana, as he barged past them into the darkness of the entranceway. There was little light, most of the torches remained unlit. A gentle push in the back reminded Helvana of his appointed labour, he rushed ahead along the corridor and into the library, a great many of the shelves showed that books were missing, the ones nearest the door were empty while those further away still held some volumes. A large monk near to cabinet shouted at them.

"Get on with the clearing out, I must find out which books are missing."

"You always were a bit of a worm." Said Kevana. The monk looked round.

"A book worm that is."

"Kevana." Shouted the monk. "What in all the hells are you doing here?"

"Looking for you."

"I am a little busy at the moment. Someone seems to have taken great exception to the presence of a few monks in this place."

"So I see, can we help in any way?"

"I don't think so. Though once I find out who it was that did this, I will gladly hand off the hunting and punishment to you and your men."

"I am currently hunting down one such and was hoping that

you could help me."

"Do you think that they could be one and the same?"

"I came across him and his friends only a few days ride from here, so it is possible."

"This one was definitely on his own when he came here."

"How can you be sure that one man caused all this?"

"Come with me." Said Worandana, leading Kevana out to the stable. "The abbot attempted to stop him with fire, and it would seem that he succeeded." The scar on the stable floor was unmistakable, it was the imprint of a man burned into the stone. The stones had a black glassy finish, the sure tell tale of the most intense heat.

"If he died here, how can you be still looking for him?"

"I think he came back again and killed our first investigator. Killed him then burned the body."

"How can that be?"

"There was no body here, the marks on the stones are irrefutable, a man died here. But then he walked away. All the other bodies in the area are bones, like they had been dead for many years, it is very strange. Also the abbot sent a somewhat garbled message about an attack by a lone man, a man of strength. At that point the abbot died, and the monk receiving the message was almost killed in the wash of flame that came with the message."

"Is there any way to find out more?"

"There is now, you are here and together we should be able to see this man."

"Is this something new from your research?"

"Yes. New and not truly tested yet."

"Risk?"

"There is danger everywhere, so why worry about another one?"

"True. We could find something interesting?"

"For certain. Or maybe nothing at all."

"How long will this take?"

"We need a few hours to prepare but other than that it should be quite quick. Rest and eat, we will make the attempt at midnight."

"Always a good time for this sort of thing, the witching hour."

"Sometimes you are so superstitious." Laughed Worandana. "Get your men to sleep a little we will need their energy as well, I will make sure that my assistants do the same, but they can do some cooking first."

"A great idea. Can we stable our horses in here or should we leave them outside?"

"Outside is best, they may interfere with the presence's in here."

Kevana turned and left the stable to collect his men and follow the instructions of his friend. A swift meal in the cleared but not cleaned refectory and then three hours sleep. Kevana was woken by Worandana shaking him, saying, "It is time." Kevana dressed swiftly and woke his men, they all went out to the stable together to find that Worandana and his four assistants were already there, they had been very busy. Most of the mess in the stable had been cleared, the damaged stones were marked off from the rest of the room contained within a white painted symbol. A seven pointed star and several circles each one bigger than the one before, all scribed around with strange writing, in a language that Kevana had never seen before. Placed right in the very centre was a white human skull, its empty eyes a plea of loneliness that tore at the soul.

"What do we do?" Asked Kevana. Worandana gave him and old piece of parchment saying. "This is a translation of a much older work, it is a summoning passage. I intend to summon the soul of the person whose skull that is, and contain it within the symbol, the hopefully it will answer some questions."

"This strikes me as one of the forbidden arts."

"Possibly, but this one is not actually proscribed. It is not mentioned in any of the texts. Perhaps it was too old to be included in the list. "

"It certainly breaches the spirit of the rules if not the letter."

"Spirit is what we mean to summon."

"How do we do this? Is it a circle or some other form of conjuration?"

"This one is triangular. You, I and the skull form the points of the triangle. Our men form a wedge shape behind each of us to feed the power we will need. You stand and that point and I will stand here, face the skull look it straight in the eyes, concentrate hard. You others fill your minds with the man at the point of your group, you must give all the strength that you can, this is going to be very costly for us all." Worandana look around the assembly, they each nodded as his gaze touched them. Kevana stood in the appointed place and positioned his men as per instruction. Worandana did the same.

"Ready?" Asked Worandana.

"Ready." Replied Kevana. Both men opened their minds to their accomplices, the flood of power took them a little by surprise, but once the surge was over the flow settled down to more manageable levels. Kevana saw Worandana lift his copy of the parchment and prepare to start reading, so he did the same. By a glance they started to read at the same time, holding to a slow steady pace, some of the syllables were unusual combinations that made pronunciation difficult, a single missed word could cause disaster. As they proceeded there was an electric feeling in the air around them, a slowly forming spiral of light spun gradually into view, centred on the skull. By tiny increments the spiral increased its speed, spinning faster and tighter, shrinking towards the skull, a tormented howl emanated from the coalescing form. Kevana felt the energy running out of him like water down a drain, he started to pull energy from his friends, he was not going to be the one to fail, his friends knew his need and fed it, though they were draining away, they kept pushing power from themselves into Kevana, until Kevana's need lessened to a level they could maintain with some difficulty. Worandana's plight was the same, the power needed for this incantation was enormous, very close to the limit of the ten men providing it. Slowly the gyrating spiral formed into the twisted shape of a man, the skull lifted from the floor and became part of the head, its whiteness clearly visible through the translucent substance of the apparition. Kevana and Worandana staggered as the energy demand on them fell to almost nothing, once the summoning was complete the power needed to maintain the apparition was minimal.

"Who has called me from my rest?" Spoke the ghost, in a voice filled with echo and reverberation, like a distant shout from the bottom of a huge pit.

"We call. We desire information about your ending."

"I ended is that not enough."

"We need to know the nature of your end. How it came about and who caused it."

The ghostly shape seemed to struggle in the restraining circles, Kevana saw sweat running down Worandana's face, just before his own eyes stung with salty fluid.

"The nature of the dead is that they do not communicate with the living."

"Inside the symbol you are not truly dead."

"Nor truly alive."

"Tell us who killed you."

"Not until you release me so that I can be alive again."

"You cannot be released, when I release you, you will return to your rest. Tell us what we need to know."

"I do not want to rest any longer, I want to live again."

"That cannot be, in life you were a servant of Zandaar, serve us now with answers in his name."

The shape twisted about itself turn round and round, distorting, fading, shifting its shape, trying to escape the symbol that held it in place.

"You cannot escape you are held by the symbol and the presence of your own skull, these will hold you until we decide to free you. You must tell us what we need to know or the pain of your imprisonment here in the land of the living will become unbearable, very soon you will start to feel the beginnings of the pain. It will start as itching that you cannot scratch, leading to a burning, that will not cool. Please tell us, I have no wish to cause a fellow servant of Zandaar such pain."

"Release me and the pain will end."

"We need to know who we are fighting so that we can avenge the deaths of all your friends, the one that killed you killed everyone else. I wish to make him pay, in more pain than you can imagine."

"All are dead?"

"Yes, everyone is dead."

"Everyone?"

"Yes, everyone is dead."

"Why did you pick me then?"

"You should have been logically one of the first to be killed, so you must have had the best opportunity to observe the killer, or killers, in your, shall we say separated state."

"That is true. He was alone."

"Are you sure?"

"He was alone. He poisoned us all with the water from the barrel, no not poison, more like drugged. Then he killed us."

"Can you tell us anything more?"

"He had been here some days before, he said that he was looking for a wizard called Granger." At this Kevana gasped. Worandana looked at him questioningly, but carried on with the interrogation of the spirit.

"Go on."

"He was very methodical, he was working to a plan, he started here then moved on to the main building, murder was written large in his heart, it was plain for any to see. He was filled with hatred, hot powerful hatred for all of us. Some fought back but failed, the Abbot locked himself in his room and wove the spell for the black fire, to kill the man, but the man set fire to the door and they couldn't get out, the man came out here it the stable and died in the black fire just here where you have brought me."

"Why are there none of his bones here?"

"A powerful force swirled around his body, though it was burned beyond any possible help, I was forced away and couldn't see clearly, but slowly his body was made well, and started to breathe again. The force dissipated and the man slept, a huge grey horse came and woke him, together they left, and I went on to rest. That is all I can tell you. Kill this man. Or he will kill us all."

"How can you say that?"

"He is the nemesis of Zandaar. He has strong friends that will help him to kill us all. "

"Surely if we kill him he only comes back to life?"

"Find a way. Release me, the pain is a torment. Let me pass on."

"Be gone. Rest in peace. Pass on to the next plane, with all our blessings, and all our thanks." With a cold screaming rush the spirit evaporated, and blew like smoke from the stable. The skull of the dead man dropped with a resounding thud to the stones and shattered into a hundred pieces on its second bounce.

"We are dealing with one man." Said Worandana.

"Not any more, he rides a large grey horse, has some friends and I believe that he was with Granger the wizard when we left the valley where he lives."

"You have seen him."

"No. We have met only indirectly. He murdered one of our watchers, one called Crandir, and stole a weapon, that I was sent to recover. I have chased him for many days and my troupe has been reduced to the number that you see here. I want that man with a passion, I want to eat his liver."

"If this is the same man, he must have some reason for this act of mass murder. To take on an entire monastery single handed is not something to do lightly."

"I care not for his motives, only his death, only his slow and painful death before these eyes."

"If we know what drives him we may be able to predict what he will do next."

"I have no idea of his motives, all I know is that he and his friends, killed a guardian tree, then the watcher, then a local bandit, then went to Granger's valley."

"If he is there, why are you here?"

"He and his friends are too strong. I am a soldier, not a magician. "

"He is a magician?"

"He is stronger than I am, his friends are stronger than I am, and Granger is probably stronger than you."

Worandana laughed. "He is a charlatan."

"Don't believe the propaganda. He is strong, he took my first blast of fire and pushed it to one side as if it were nothing, then I threw a lightning bolt, he let it run almost to impact then blasted it with blue fire, the blue absorbed the lightning and the backwash of power almost knocked me out. "

"As you say, you are a soldier. I will be able to beat this so called wizard."

"It is the man on the grey horse that I want." Said Kevana.

"How can you be sure that he is the one I am looking for."

"He rides a large grey horse, carries a weapon that belongs to Zandaar, and knows something of our mystical practices."

"What do you mean?"

"He is known to have killed at least one man with a dream."

"How can he have learned to do this?"

"Perhaps, surviving the attempt can teach one many things. Any trial that does not kill us only makes us stronger. He does not die, at least not permanently, so even trials that kill him make him stronger."

"We will have to do something about that."

"But what?"

Worandana looked around the stable and noticed for the first time that his men and Kevanas were prostrate upon the ground, some in various states of consciousness.

"First we must see to these poor wretches, then go hunt down this thief of yours."

"You believe that he is the one who destroyed this place?"

"He is the most likely person that I have heard of. From what you say it is the sort of thing that he would try, but we still need to know more about him, mainly WHY?"

"It must be something simple, he hates us."

"Hate is not simple. It has cause, how can we cause such powerful hatred."

"Some just take offence to the fact that we are different, and some call us witches, servants of the devils, but they don't understand the purity of service that we give to Zandaar."

"Have there been any reports of similar incidents elsewhere."

"I know of none, there has certainly been no general alarm, or calls for assistance, perhaps there are some references in the abbots reports."

"Look around you, these people didn't call for help, did they?"

"Maybe he has destroyed other places that we haven't heard of yet."

"Let's see if there are any outposts that have lost contact recently."

"How will you find out?"

"I will contact Mount Thornley monastery, they control much of the activity in this area, in fact it is my base at the moment."

By this time the other men were all capable of walking though they were exhausted, they staggered into the main building and went to eat, all the energy that they had expended needed to be replaced as soon as possible. A swift meal, followed by a slow one, had them all back to almost full fitness, though Kevana's soldiers recovered considerably faster than Worandana's scholars. Kevana and Worandana ate the first meal but decided against a second, they left and went into the chapel. Worandana used the fire and lightning symbol above the altar as a focus to contact Mount Thornley. Several minutes of silent conversation, then he turned to Kevana.

"They are more than a little concerned. Two outposts have been lost recently. One a minor village in the forest of Drangor, of no import and no return information from the follow up team, the other is more important. The mining village where our silver comes from was taken over by a very experienced priest, he has failed in the past but never like this. It appears that he was killed by a man on a grey horse, and a woman from the village. The follow up team was refused access to the area, and threatened with the same fate as Dorana."

"I know Dorana." Interrupted Kevana. "He is very good. He always knows which people to remove from any situation, he has a feel for the opposition."

"Knew, was and had. He is dead, beaten is seems by your simple thief. And this was before your thief stole your weapon."

"Did the follow up find out the name of this man?"

"No-one in the village would tell them."

"Melandius met him as well, but didn't get his name, he thought that he was subordinate to Jangor, who is a military man and seemed to be running the group."

"This gets more confusing, is the robber in charge or not? Does he guide the fate of the group, or is it the fighting mind that runs it?"

"And who runs it now that Granger has become embroiled?"

"Perhaps they don't have an actual leader. It could be that they decide things in a democratic manner, that should make them easier to predict."

"Have they done anything predictable yet?"

"No. They do the strangest things apparently without thought."

"We need to know who the robber is and why he is doing this," Said Worandana, waving his arms about the ruins of the chapel. "We must find him or find someone who knows him, anything else is just speculation, and we need information."

"Will you join me in my quest to destroy the robber?" Asked Kevana.

"Of course, he is the one who killed all our brothers here, that act cannot go unpunished."

"Will you tell your abbot about my involvement?"

"This sort of failure will look very bad for you, so I don't think they need to know just yet."

Kevana breathed a huge sigh of relief, he had the help that he needed and the council of abbots would not find out the extent of his failure, at least not for a while. Kevana tried to move things along quickly, but Worandana had much work to do before he could leave the monastery, he also had to report his findings to Mount Thornley. His report was sketchy and missing certain information that his superiors would have found most interesting, and resulted in Kevanas return for a serious investigation. As it would be several weeks before the monastery could be occupied again there was a lot of preparation to be done, perishable foods had to be removed from the stores, window and doors all secured, in a large complex like this it took two hours just to check all the windows. Kevana and his men were mounted and pacing around the courtyard for the best part of an hour waiting for the other group to be ready to depart.

They rode through the gate, which was then locked behind them, a lone monk climbed over the gate and dropped to the ground, mounted and followed them up the road to the high pass.

"What did you tell them?" Asked Kevana. Worandana was riding alongside him, their two groups strung out in line astern behind their relevant leaders.

"That I had a few leads to follow up, that the death of Dorana was probably caused by the same man, or group, and that I was going to follow that and another possible connection to a local mystic."

"Did they ask about the source of your leads?"

"They did."

"What did you tell them?"

"That they didn't want to know."

Kevana merely looked the question with a deep frown.

"Quite often they think that my methods border on the heretical, so when they ask, I say, don't ask because you don't want to know. That is usually enough to stop any further awkward questions."

This didn't quite suppress Kevana's disquiet, it had been many years since the two of them worked closely together, and he was putting a great deal of trust in somebody he had known, but who had certainly changed much in the intervening years of separation.

The weather remained fairly clear and the wind stayed light, so their journey back to Granger's home was uncomplicated. The monks gradually got to know each other and the rigid separation of the two groups slowly dissolved and they rode together more as a unit, they discovered that they had much in common, despite their very different duties in the Zandaar organisation. Their training had been equally rigorous, equally demanding, and at times equally deadly. Both military and scholastic arms of the order believe in selection of the fittest, in this process some must fall by the wayside, the fall being permanent sometimes, the fall from scholarship usually ended in menial labour whereas the fall from military service was death. Kevana and Worandana rode at the front of the column side by side, reminiscing and catching up on the things that they had both done since their separation. Kevana kept pushing the pace as hard as he could without risking the horses too much, and listening a little to the moans of Worandana's men, they were unused to the hard riding that was now being asked of them. The clear weather made the snow seem almost inviting, at least compared to their previous passage. Before sundown they set up camp for the night, Kevana felt no urge to ride through the night again, Worandana and his monks called the others to prayer as the sun was approaching the tops of the mountains, Alverana looked a question at Kevana, who merely shrugged by way of an answer. Worandana obviously was unaware of the fact that in the field these observances were considered less important than in the safety of monasteries. Once the prayers and food were over with Worandana explained that attention to these small details often increased the groups coherence and thereby their power in the field of magic. It was the discipline that held their minds together and greatly improved their efficiency, making the whole bigger than the sum of the parts. Kevana agreed to accept this as anything that might improve their chances must be tried. He took Alverana aside and explained this to him.

"The men are not going to like this. They are not used to this sort of rigidity, it is going to cause some friction. "

"It will be your responsibility to prevent this becoming a problem, we need these scholastic fools to further our purposes."

"You mean your purposes."

"You agreed to go along with the plan, just like the rest."

"We always have a way out, if we choose to take it. We are just following orders."

"How many times will that be used as an excuse by subordinates, especially when the leader in question has already died?"

"Until is stops working."

"Sometimes you are an incredibly cynical man, for a member of a religious order."

"Sometimes religion itself acts exceptionally cynically."

"Your words tread on the edge of heresy. Worandana would not allow you to speak like this."

"He would never hear me speak like this, his view of the world is very narrow."

"He himself sails very close to heresy much of the time, take as a fine example the summoning we performed only yesterday."

"Sailing close to the wind is where all the fun is, anyone can drift with the tide, I do not like to go with the flow. I begin to like this old friend of yours, he could even become fun, if he were to relax a little."

"He knows how to relax, take my word for it. Some of the things that we used to get up to when we were younger would really surprise you. What do you think turned his hair grey? It wasn't prayer, and it wasn't books, it was fast fun and hard living, and some of the entertainment that he used to enjoy would curl your hair. He used to be really wild, we used to be really wild."

"Is he really going to be able to beat this Granger when we catch up with him?"

"If anyone can, Worandana can, with our help of course."

"Then we must make the best we can of this situation then mustn't we."

"That is what I have been saying."

The two returned to the camp and Alverana took his colleagues into a small huddle and explained how things were going to be. They were unhappy, but could say nothing against the word of their leader.

The morning dawned bright and sunny to find the camp already dismantled and the men mounted and ready to travel, only one small thing was holding them back it was time for prayers. Worandana lead the prayers, making them short and quick, much to Kevana's relief, he had known morning prayers to last more than an hour, but in view of the mission that they were on Worandana had shorted things just a little, five minutes and they were moving down the valley, heading towards Granger's home, at a fast trot, a pace that the now rested horses should be able to sustain for some hours, though Worandana's men would have some trouble with saddle sores before the day was over. The saddles sores were their only problem, they arrived at Granger's home, just as the sun was going down.

"He lives at the top of this?" Asked Worandana.

"Yes. If he is still there. Well?" Asked Kevana looking at Alverana.

"No they left, some time ago. One or two days. They had some trouble getting down the slope, several small slides have occurred since we were last here. Though there is no blood on the stones, I don't believe that any of them were hurt."

"Which way?"

"I can see the hoof prints here at the base of the slide, but there has been some snow fall since they left, so where it is not melted I cannot tell."

"How many?"

"I cannot say, they walk in line, one behind the other, more than five less than twenty, that is as close as I can tell."

"Is there anyone left up there?" he nodded towards the top of the slope.

"More than five, less than twenty."

"We will have to get up there and find out." Said Worandana.

"It cannot be done." Said Alverana.

"Obviously it can." Snorted Worandana. "They have done it, they went up and then they came down. So it is possible, they know how, we have to discover how they did it, or invent a new way. Suggestions?" He asked looking to his own men, Kevana's men having already failed this test. Their failure was written plainly on their faces, and their embarrassment only just concealed.

"I saw a man, in my youth, set the surface of a river so that he could walk across, perhaps Granger used a spell like that, something that holds the surface so that it cannot move." Said Helvana.

"That might be enough. Though these rocks are going to tend to roll one over the other, it could work if the tension field was strong enough. Do you know the spell?"

"I was a child, it was one of the things that made me want to be a monk, but I have found nothing like it in the books I have read."

"So that doesn't exactly help us a great deal does it?"

"No. But it gives us somewhere to start."

"Anyone else?"

"There is a spell for freezing water." Came a quiet voice.

"Tell us more, Gorgana."

"I have seen it in a book, it makes the water hard but not cold like ice, just hard, " he looked from side to side, not really seeing, more like rummaging through his mind trying to find the words. " It was used for, erm, for, for catching fish."

"Do you remember the spell, and how it works."

"I think so." Gorgana nodded.

"You are going to use magic for catching fish to get us up that slope." Said Petrovana, in disbelief. "I am staying here."

"If I say you go, you will go." Said Kevana. To which

Petrovana simply turned away, hoping that he would not have to trust his life to their strange magic.

"Can you remember the spell?"

"I think so." Gorgana dropped to the ground, falling straight into a cross-legged posture, which was commonly used to aid concentration, he hummed a tuneless melody, a nasal droning that seemed to resonate in the air, gradually the sound filled their minds and they started to relax into the same sort of concentrated state that Gorgana was attempting to achieve. A state of intense self hypnosis over came Gorgana he held his hands in front of his body as if they held a book that he was reading, in his mind he was, the book was there in his hands as it had been the day that he saw the spell. He felt the same sense of disbelief, the need to read through the spell slowly, just be sure that it was real, and not some joke from the author. Sharing his hypnotised state with all around him they all read the spell just as he did, and they all knew that it almost certainly something that had worked in the past and could work for them today. Gorgana raised his head and breathed in sharply, breaking the hypnotic linkage.

"Ye gods." Exclaimed Petrovana. "How is that possible."

"Your studies were seriously neglected." Said Worandana. "You would have learned this if you had not branched out into the military."

"He couldn't learn that in a hundred years." Laughed Briana.

"I could. Well, I think I could, possibly, maybe, perhaps, no, never. That sort of thing gives me the shivers. I couldn't master that, not without shaking inside, and that would make it impossible."

"I agree." Said Kevana, "Some of us are just not meant for this sort of task, give us some heads to be separated from necks and we can enjoy ourselves, but this, just knowing it can be done makes me uneasy."

"Can one man hold this whole slide for the rest of us, or can he walk up it as well?" Asked Fabrana.

"I don't think that one can do it, not without some practise, I think that we should all fix the slide while our sword wielding brethren go up and find out what has happened to the residents."

"I can stand that." Said Kevana. "We will leave the horses here, they will cause unnecessary loading on the slide, we must give our magical brethren all the help that we can."

"I will accompany you." Said Worandana.

"Why?"

"You may need some help up there, who can tell."

Kevana nodded, thinking ' Who can tell indeed.'

"Worandana." Said Helvana, "the spell is directed at a fluid, we don't have a fluid here."

"The spell is directed at a specific fluid, water. Although this slide has certain fluid properties, it is rock with out a doubt. If we change the words, a little, substitute a symbol for rock instead of water, change the rhyming words to match, and make the rhythm more angular, to take account of the angular nature of the rocks, it should work."

"Should." Groaned Petrovana.

"I will be going with you." Said Worandana, " That should give you some confidence."

"Should again."

Kevana smiled and patted Petrovana on the back saying, as normal, "Do you want to live forever?"

"No. Tomorrow would be nice though."

"We will not take on the whole slide, half of it should be enough. A wide section right up the middle." Said Worandana.

"How about a strip up along the wall, that way it could be better anchored to the fixed points of the wall?"

"Good idea, which side?"

"This one." Said Helvana, pointing to the right hand wall, " It appears to be a shallower angle, and the wall in more uneven, that will give the wall more stabilising effect."

"Right side it is."

Worandana's four assistants sat in a row across the bottom of the slide one separated from the next by a few feet. Each chanting the modified spell in a smooth monotone. A steady beat that stilled the very air around them. Petrovana felt the hairs on the back of his neck start to rise, and the tension built around them, the electricity in the air became almost palpable. A mist of midnight sparkles climbed slowly up the fall until it reached the top, then the whole slide emitted a crunching groan like it was going to slide all at once, but nothing was moving. Worandana stood in front of his fellows and kicked the nearest rock. His foot recoiled like he had kicked a solid wall, the small rock unmoved by the impact. Looking closely at his men for any signs of strain, Worandana saw none. It seemed that they could hold this for some time.

"Let's go." He said to Kevana, in a quiet voice, not wishing to cause too much disturbance, to the stability of the spell. He set off up the scree as if on a stroll through a country meadow. It only took him and the rest a few minutes to reach the top, by which time they were all breathing fairly hard, especially Worandana.

"Rest a while." Said Kevana.

"No. They cannot hold that indefinitely, we must go on."

They went up the path to the cave very slowly, not certain that everyone had left, and not wanting to be caught by surprise. Walking carefully around the bubbling mud pot, they approached the cave mouth, a reeking steam rolled from the cave, harsh with sulphur and acid, it caught in their throats and made them all cough.

"There can be no-one in there." Said Alverana.

"But Granger used to live in there." Said Kevana.

"He must have done something to one of the gas vents from the volcano below our feet, perhaps opened it so that it fills the cave with this dreadful stench."

"Volcano." Shouted Petrovana, in between bouts of coughing.

"Where do you think the steam comes from to heat that pond of mud."

"Volcanoes are dangerous."

"It seems stable enough, for now."

"We cannot enter the cave, the area is empty, we can leave, as Granger as his friends obviously have." Said Kevana. Worandana nodded and turned towards the path to the slide. He lead the way back down to where his men were still sitting on the ground chanting, only now they were showing some signs of strain, they were all sweating and they voices were beginning to become somewhat ragged around the edges. Once everyone was down he stood in front of his men and faced them, turning his back on the slide.

"A slow release. If you release to sharply it could all come rushing this way." He stood conducting the singing of the spell like an orchestra, with steady hand signals he brought the spell to a slow and quiet end, the rocks at his back twitched a little and settled a little but they made no major moves. Everyone breathed a huge sigh of relief.

"We must rest a while, before we can go on." Said Helvana. Worandana knew the sort of tiredness that they were experiencing, and that it would pass in a few minutes though their mental strength would not return for some hours, physically they would be able to travel before an hour had passed. While they waited for the men to recover their strength the horses continued to feed on the lush green grass, it was certain that they were going to need all the food they could get inside them, the next real meal could be many miles away.

CHAPTER TWENTY ONE

Namdarin and Granger rode side by side as they left the small valley, Granger had said that he knew a way through the mountains that would entail some danger but would give them a good head start on the priests of Zandaar, who were sure to be following at some time. Namdarin was happy to surrender the leading of the party to the older man because it gave him some time to think of other things. The movement of his horse underneath him and the steady jingling of the gear that hung from all the horses was hypnotic, it caused his mind to slip into a strangely detached state, he was aware of everything that was happening around him, but it had no real importance to him. The hushed voices of his companions seemed to be so far away that they couldn't possible involve him in their meaning. He thought about what he had seen of the city of Zandaarkoon, so many miles to the south, his mind speculated slowly on the outcome of his impending meeting with Zandaar, there was no doubt that he would meet the god, he could not even consider that anyone could stop him from reaching the conclusion of his quest. The only question that had any real impact on him was, 'How many of his friends would still be alive at that time?' It was a certainty that some would die, but which could he afford to loose. Crathen, Mander, Stergin, Andel are all expendable, not be wasted, not thrown to the wolves for no real gain, but expendable none the less. Granger would become expendable as Namdarin learned more and more of his secrets, Kern next his calm strength was exceptionally useful, then Jangor, a strong man in every sense of the word, but Jayanne could never be spent, she could not be coin to be used to advance the quest, he knew that he could never bear that cost, without her the quest could die, and so could he. Whenever his thoughts turned to her his heart was filled with a soft warm light, it showed in his face and shone from his eyes, he was sure that everyone must know when he was thinking of her. Sometimes he felt like a teenager blushing at the pictures that raced through his mind, the hot steamy day dreams that brought a rush of blood to his cheeks and to other parts as well. Holding tightly on to the feeling of well being that these thoughts filled him with, he reached out with his mind hoping to find hers in a similar state, a warm dreamy feeling that he hoped would be full of him. As his head lolled forwards he made a gentle contact with a mind that was in a soft drifting state, it had the same sense of dislocation that his own did. If anything this mind was even more detached from the reality of a ride through the cold snow of winter. It was full of warm colours and soft green smells. Perhaps the mind that he had attached to was triggered by his own thoughts but it seemed to be thinking the same way that he had been about Jayanne, a beautiful face with sharp, hot green eyes was rushing around inside this mind, filling it with warm light and wonderful scent, the scent of a warm woman's body, that salty pungence of passion. Namdarin mind snapped to attention focusing hard on the thoughts all around it, the simple act of chasing the thoughts chased them away, the tenuous link between the minds was shattered in an instant. The memory of the thoughts was not, a seething rage of jealousy filled Namdarin's brain, the red fog of hatred came rushing to the fore to fill his sight. His head snapped around checking everyone in the party, hoping that the mind in question had felt his sudden departure and the body attached to it was reacting, there was no-one else looking round, Kern had sensed Namdarin's sudden alertness, and raise an eyebrow in question, Namdarin shook his head a little and Kern relaxed again, into his normal wakeful dream, Namdarin knew that the mind could not have been Kern, his was far to aware of everything that happened within the range of his senses, Namdarin doubted that anyone could invade Kern's mind with him being alerted. Namdarin ran through the things that he knew about his friends characters, it felt to him that the only ones that would harbour such thoughts of Jayanne could be Mander or Crathen. Mander is an obvious choice, his appetite for women is proven beyond doubt, Crathen on the other hand is really an unknown, Namdarin suddenly realised that he knew very little about the young man, the others all had a clear history behind them, but Crathen had never been truly forthcoming with details of his life, he had said almost nothing about himself, he was a mystery. Namdarin pushed the rage down, he couldn't react to every stray thought that he picked up, but he would work on Crathen, his past would be uncovered, if he were hiding anything Namdarin would find it. And if the secret turned out to be of a danger to Namdarin and his quest Crathen would die.

Before long they were on a road that only Granger knew, heading high into the mountains to the west. The valley that they were climbing was not steep but did appear to go on up to heaven, the white path on snow blended into the white of the clouds that spanned the gap between the peaks of the mountains.

"The peak to the left is Cragmoire." Shouted Granger over the rising wind. "It has some interesting history attached to it."

"What history?" Asked Jangor.

"It is said to be the home of a demon."

"Then why do we travel so close?"

"I haven't heard of this particular demon for some time, it might be nice to find out if the poor old fool is still alive."

"A demon. You want to find a demon deliberately. You are mad."

"The stories are of a demon, but many have considered me to be such in the past. I would discover the true nature of the demon of the mountains."

"What form does this demon take?"

"A large hairy monster, it could even have been the white bear that Jayanne killed not so long ago."

"So it might be dead."

"Yes. But then again if it was a bear, it has far outlasted the lifetime of a hundred such bears. Then it could be a family of bears, or a race of bears, or just a demon. Who can tell."

"Sometimes," Said Mander, "a little knowledge is a dangerous thing. I have no need of this knowledge, the mystery could remain for all that I care."

"For once we agree." Said Stergin. The two stared at one another for a moment or two then both said together.

"Let's find this demon."

"They both agree again." Laughed Kern.

"Then that must be our destiny, the demon of the mountains will be uncovered by Mander and Stergin. Those famous explorers of the wild places of the planet, the intrepid and fearless men who faced down the demon of the mountains, and brought him home for tea." Jangor then laughed at his friends discomfort, they were much more used to arguing over everything.

Higher into the mountain pass they went, the temperature

dropping all the time, the deep cold was soon all around them, the breath of the horses causing clouds of fog that hung about them in the still air, ice started to settle on the horses muzzles, and about the peoples faces.

"I wish we had skinned some of those black devils." Said Jayanne to Namdarin, who was looking in a very sorry state with white around his nose and mouth.

"That would certainly have been very useful at the moment, but at the time we didn't think that we would be going this high into the mountains."

"Do you think we will find this mountain demon?" She asked, her voice trembling with more than the cold.

"If we do then we will deal with it, if we don't then we won't worry about it. Those that follow us may find it instead. They can have the fun of chasing it to its lair and killing it."

"Will we have to kill it?"

"We cannot afford to leave something like that behind us, if it knows about us it will certainly not leave us alone, it will at least want to find out what we taste like."

"It is a cannibal?"

"No. I am not aware that it eats its own kind, but it is not our kind, so it may eat us." Granger said.

"That is not a very cheerful thought."

"This is not a cheerful place, in fact for some of the people who used to live hereabouts it was a place of dread, of fear, and of death. They believed that the demon was a supernatural force that fed on souls of people, I think it only fed on their bodies, there cannot be much game this high up to feed a predator of such a size. It must get very hungry waiting for its next meal to wander by."

"If this thing is real who would come up here?"

"You would be surprised how many thought that they could defeat the demon, some with physical weapons, some with spiritual, and some with only words. None ever returned, eventually the people moved further to the west where the mere act of survival was easier. I think the demon must have starved to death by now, the last of them left about forty years ago."

"If this demon was such a threat to the people why didn't they all band together and hunt it down?"

"Some races are just not designed to act in concert, I heard the story of one such attempt. A group of twenty or so of them decided that the beast must be killed, and while they were discussing the date of departure for the hunt, two died of old age, one raised a family of three children, one of which joined the hunting party. They sat around their fires for forty years before they came to the agreement that the hunt should depart in spring, after the initial floods of spring had subsided but before the fields had started to grow. Next which spring?"

"Did they ever decide?"

"When their number had reduced by natural wastage to ten they discovered that they were the only ones left who had not gone west, so the mission to kill the beast lost its purpose. They gathered their belongings and headed west after the others."

"They sound like very stupid people."

"They may have been but they made very few mistakes."

"They never did anything."

"That is also true."

Jayanne turned away from the old man in disgust. Namdarin laughed at the look on her face. He was unsure as to the veracity of the wizards tale, true or not it was an amusing story, but

Jayanne did not like to be gulled in this fashion. She had obviously believed every single word of it, her embarrassment glowed red across her whole face, until it nearly matched the colour of her hair. As she turned away Kern shouted. "Something strange up ahead."

Jangor kicked his horse and forged forwards to where Kern was standing up in his stirrups.

"What have you seen?" Asked Jangor as his horse skittered to a halt alongside the younger man.

"I am sure that something moved. Over there in those rocks."

"What was it?"

"I don't know, I am not even sure it was there. It may have been an illusion, a trick of the light, or some such, I am no longer sure that I saw anything."

"What did you see?"

"It was horse size and white. I saw it from the corner of my eye, by the time I focused on it, it was gone."

"Where did it vanish?"

"In those rocks." Kern closed his eyes for a moment and reviewed the incident in his mind. "It jumped over the rocks then dropped out of sight, I think."

"It fell into a hole, or dropped down amongst the rocks?"

"Amongst."

"Horse shape, move like a horse?"

"No." Kern paused then continued, "more like a goat. Stiff legged and all legs moving together."

"And it's in those rocks." Jangor waved his arm in the direction of the group of large boulders that Kern had indicated. The big man just nodded, staring with a rather puzzled look. The boulders stretched from high up on the left hand side of the valley and angled down to the valley bottom in an uninterrupted procession, they were large and irregular, the only break in them the large flow of ice that used to be a river in summer, then they continued up the opposite side of the valley until they reached into the jumbled snow field high to the south. Jangor turned to the others and said "It appears that we are to meet the demon of this valley. It is hiding from us somewhere in the boulders up ahead."

"Any ideas as to how we should deal with it?" Asked Namdarin looking straight at Granger.

"We could offer it breakfast."

"But it eats people." Said Jayanne.

"Do I hear any volunteers?" Asked Jangor, expecting and getting none, well none that were serious.

"I volunteer Andel." Said Mander.

"I think it would find Mander more to its taste, there is after all more fat on him." In truth the two weighed almost exactly the same, though Mander's waist was slightly the larger. A look, from Jangor, at the pair was enough the stop the pointless argument going any further. The soldiers spread out into a line and advanced slowly towards the boulders, the ones that Kern had indicated. The demon appeared when they had almost reached the first of the large rocks, Kern nearly had his hand on it, he was very surprised to see it leap over the boulders some yards to his left, it ran with a strange gait, like it was used to running on four legs or two, it ran almost sideways, but still with astonishing speed. It ran around the line of armed men and attacked the ones behind, who appeared to be less ready. Kern's shout caused Jangor to turn just it time to see the beast closing on the group. Granger sent a bolt of blue fire from his staff, it struck the thing in the chest and bounced to the side, reflected by a strange sparkly garment on the things body, Namdarin's arrow screamed shortly, for the distance was not great, it too was disdainfully discarded by the animals shining armour. The five soldiers started to run back towards their friends, Jayanne pulled her axe to strike at the things head, but one of its long arms swung first sweeping her to the side where she landed rather firmly on her behind. The demon followed the fall, moving in as if to kill, Crathen was the closest and without thought of weapon or anything other than Jayanne he hurled himself between the fallen woman and the beast, pinning her to the ground but protecting her with his own body. The demon stuck him with one heavily clawed hand. The bloodied claws went straight to its mouth, the taste seemed to make it smile.

"Namdaron." Screamed Namdarin, as he ran in the black jewelled sword of Xeron held high over his head. The beast swung an arm to beat the sword away, but the flat struck the arm with great force, causing it to rebound and the demon to howl in pain, the other arm struck and Namdarin parried it in the same manner, again the howl and the beast stepped back one shambling stride. Namdarin pressed forwards, and the demon stepped back again, now Namdarin was standing astride the two on the ground. The demon howled again more in frustration than pain and raised both arms above its head. Its large brown eyes staring, unmoving deep into Namdarins blue ones. Namdarin waited, he knew that the moment was almost upon them. The moment came the demon flung its arms wide and lunged forwards, the sword of Xeron flashed a blue arc that met with the head. An arm straining thump and the beast fell at Namdarin's feet, it sighed and went deep into unconsciousness.

"Why the flat?" Yelled Jangor, arriving at the instant the demon fell.

"I don't know, it didn't seem right to kill it."

Laid out on the snow its arms stretched wide it was bigger than anyone had expected, the arms were at least five feet long each, and the legs not much shorter, if it stood upright it would have been at least ten feet tall, but it didn't seem to be equipped to stand up, it moved like a large ape. Namdarin stared at its great chest, it rose and fell slowly, the beast was still alive. Jangor may have been right to want it dead, but staring down at its quiescent form, even he couldn't bring himself to kill it in cold blood. Crathen moaned softly as he rolled off Jayanne, he left a bright red stain on the white snow as he stood up, his hand reached down to help the woman to her feet. She spoke a single word of thanks, Namdarin's look was one of mixed concern for the woman and anger for the young man who had all but given his life for hers.

"Now what?" Asked Jangor, making some discreet hand signals to Kern, who went immediately to his horse to get some rope which he used to tie the demon with, its long arms secured at the wrists and lashed to its similarly tied ankles made them all feel a little safer, though the thin rope looked puny compared to the ridges of muscles in the things arms.

"How did it deflect your magic and my arrows?" Demanded Namdarin.

"Its body armour is something I have never seen before, though the movement of the colours does remind me a little of the silver that the Zandaars use for their weapons."

"It does seem to have a similar rainbow effect, but it moves like cloth."

"If it can reflect my magic perhaps it can reflect theirs."

"Then we must take it." All the time that they were speaking the demons breathing became stronger. As Namdarin reached closer to feel the silvery cloth around the demons chest, its large brown eyes opened, they tried to stare into Namdarin's blue ones. Namdarin froze, unmoving, staring into the dark eyes, the beast was clearly having some problems, its eyes would look deep into

Namdarin's, but then they would slide off to one side. It was obvious concussed, though the speed of its recovery suggested that it would soon be fully recovered, then releasing it would be a serious danger to everyone.

"We are going to have to kill it." Said Jangor.

"I had hoped to avoid that," replied Namdarin, "it has survived for a long time with no-one to prey on, so it must have a source of some other food that can obviously support it, it is certainly strong, and was very healthy before I hit with the sword. Perhaps it can be reasoned with. It looks very upset." The beast was starting to move, testing the limits of travel in its limbs. "It may decide to escape."

"That rope will take a 200 pound load, there are four turns round his wrists that 800 pounds to break those ropes." Said Kern confidently.

"The knots are weaker, they are always the weakest point of any rope," said Andel, "he could break a knot."

"Not one of my knots." Said Kern with a soft smile, a small joke that was echoed on all the faces around.

"It could be female." Said Jayanne, who had been staring at the creatures huge barrel of a chest. The others followed her eyes and were themselves a little unsure the shape was disguised by the shining cover of its strange armour, it was possible that it hid large breasts under its tunic. The demon twitched against the ropes, causing its rainbow hued tunic to ride up a little revealing the fact that it was most certainly male.

"Ye gods." Whispered Jayanne.

"Holy mother." Said Mander, suddenly feeling unusually inadequate.

The muscles of its legs stood out and the tension in its

shoulders increased enormously, its whole body seemed to swell with the effort. Corded tendons stood out clearly visibly through the soft white fur that covered it entire body, except for a prominent exception. The only sounds to be heard were the ragged breathing of the group and the groaning of ropes. The demon was not going to give up, it seemed to be only breathing in, swelling its body and increasing the tension on the ropes, with every passing second it became more certain that the ropes were going to fail, every moment the eventual failure of the bonds became more and more inevitable. Until with a loud twang a single strand broke, the rope unravelled from around the beasts arms with the force, and sound, of a heavy whip, even though the motion of those arms was stopped before it really got started. A small twitch was the only sign that the ropes had failed. The beast began to breathe normally, heavily but normally, slowly it unwound the shredded ropes from its wrists and legs, without ever taking its eyes off Namdarin's ready sword. Once it was satisfied that all the remnants were removed it sat upright and curled its legs around in front, sitting cross-legged before the one who had recently tried to kill it.

"Now what do we do?" demanded Jangor, his hand on his sword hilt, legs braced, wrist flexed, hair triggered for a fast draw, the beast ignored him utterly, though it never relaxed its gaze from Namdarin's eyes.

"Can you talk?" Asked Namdarin. The demon opened its mouth to reveal sharp teeth like a wolf, and a long tongue, a mouth shaped for tearing meat not talking, a soft growl was all that it emitted.

"He has intelligence." Whispered Granger. "He has escaped the ropes and sits patiently waiting to see what will develop, no animal would act this way. It shows reasoning intelligence like our own."

"How can we communicate?" Asked Namdarin, "Its mouth is no better fitted for talking than its claws for writing." Namdarin never took his eyes from the beast, as if it was the power of his gaze that held the demon in check.

"The crystals." Said Granger after a moment. He walked slowly over to Namdarin's horse. Arndrol was unsure whether to allow the old man to open Namdarin's saddle bags, he showed his discomfort by stamping his forefeet, the shock of the impacts made the demon twitch slightly, Kern walk over and held Arndrol's head, whispering in his ear and stroking his neck, this calmed the horse enough so that Granger could get the crystals from the bags. Granger walked very slowly to Namdarin, trying not to disturb the scene any more than was absolutely necessary. Namdarin took the crystals and held them out between the demon and himself. Namdarin looked down at the crystals resting in his palms, the colours slowly cycling, green, blue, red, when he looked up again the demon was staring at the crystals, hypnotised by the changing colours. Slowly it looked back up to Namdarin, a questioning look on its face. Namdarin smiled being very careful not to show any teeth. Once the demon had the stone in its hand and appeared to be settled with its constantly changing colours Namdarin held his own stone to his forehead with his right hand and waved with his left for the demon to do the same. It took a few demonstrations before the demon understood what was expected of it. Slowly the demon raised the stone in its hand, the group of people held the breaths, waiting for something to happen. As the demon's hand approached his head Granger muttered a quick prayer, and squeezed Namdarin's shoulder. The flashing crystal made contact with the white furred brow, and Namdarin reached with his mind to make contact with the demon, hoping to find some form or order within.

Cold white light flooded Namdarin's brain, white fire and hot pain filled his consciousness, with a scream he fell away from the demon dropping the crystal, and breaking the link. Through the fog of pain he heard a sound that he recognised, a sharp whistling. He struggled to raise his hand and shout, a cry that came out as a mumbled "Hold." Slowly Namdarin's eyes cleared to show that Jayanne's axe had indeed completed its back swing, and that the demons head was only a second away from starting a new existence in the creatures lap. Sitting upright and reclaiming his fallen stone he spoke shakily, "Hell. Its mind is strong, but I think I can get around that." Very slowly he touched his stone to his head, and waited for the demon to follow suit. Namdarin reached forth more slowly this time, carefully building the contact until the creatures mind made light contact. Namdarin was looking for emotions only not the real structure of words, just the feelings in its heart. Fear was the thing that came through the strongest, it was this fear that had totally swamped Namdarin's mind at the first attempt. Namdarin sent soothing, calming thoughts, hoping to allay some of its fear, knowing all the time that this was a vain hope for the fear was so strong. Never before had it been beaten, never in its memory had it been bested, not even by groups twice the size of this one. No foe had ever really tested it before, most didn't even see it until it was far too late, those that looked too strong never saw it at all, it let them passed without a challenge, but at the moment it was very hungry, this hunger had caused it to attack this group. Namdarin picked up on the hunger, and looked for the words in the creatures head, but he found none, there was no structure for language in its brain at all, it thought entirely in pictures. Namdarin sent it pictures on green fields full of cattle, and showed it sitting in the corner of a field eating a large cow. The demon returned with an empty field of ice and the sun rising and setting every few seconds, the same cycling picture showing many days and no food. Namdarin sent a picture of himself and his friends sitting having breakfast, as they had that very morning, then a picture of the creature eating, the food was a featureless blur, when the creature failed to respond, Namdarin sent the picture again this time the blur was brighter and stronger, he hoped that the creature would fill in the blank. The demon took the crystal away from its forehead, and stared at the man with its large brown eyes. 'It's hiding its thoughts from me.' Thought Namdarin. It seemed to take a long time, though it was only the span of one breath, before the creature slowly raised its crystal again, and re-established contact with the man. It had made a decision, it closed its eyes as contact was made, it sent pictures of itself hunting and killing and eating, it killed bears and horses and men. It was Namdarin's turn to break the contact. He stared into the demons eyes as they slowly opened, he knew that it was afraid for its life, and that it had still sent pictures that could only bring hatred in the men all around it, it had told the truth, even though this truth could bring about its own death. Or had it? Could this be mere bravado, an attempt to impress the people with the things fearsomeness? Namdarin reviewed the pictures and found no shading of meaning, they were clear and simple and so obviously true, that he couldn't question them at all. He wondered if it was possible to lie with ones mind at all. Voices can lie, but the mind always knows that it is telling lies, and no matter how well controlled the voice there are those that can hear the lies. No, in this situation the mind cannot lie, it can only tell the truth as it sees it, could the demons vision of reality be so different from the man's? No, the demon had told the truth and Namdarin was going to give it the chance to stay alive, he sent it a picture of his group leaving this place and the demon watching them go, then a birds eye view of a short flight down the valley to were another group of men, this time wearing only black, and a picture of the demon jumping out from a hiding place and attacking and killing them all, then the demon eat the choicest bits on the spot, before dragging the bodies off to the ice of the river and burying them in the ice. The demon return pictures of the bodies in the ice, the unspoken question why? Namdarin showed him many sunrises and the food still edible, preserved from decay and scavengers for many sunrises. The demon sent pictures of the men in black. Namdarin showed himself killing them with arrows and the creature killing with slashing claws and ripping teeth, and the demon killing the one wounded by arrows. The demon sent a slow sequence, very clear and very precise, Namdarin's group leaving, the demon watching, running down the valley and attacking the men in black. Namdarin returned the sequence adding a section at the beginning where the demon handed back the crystal and waited for a hand signal before leaving. The creature returned the extra sequence, then lowered the crystal, breaking the contact.

"We have come to an agreement, I will tell you about it later, this creature is going to get up slowly and leave, no one will interfere, is that understood?" There was a chorus of muttered acceptance and nodding. Namdarin held out his hand and the demon dropped the crystal in to, Namdarin made the agreed hand signal, a single raised right thumb, the demon stood, somewhat unsure of itself, looked around at all the people, then strode slowly away, with its unusual gait, until it disappeared amongst the nearest pile of boulders. Much to everyone's relief.

"How did you manage that?" Demanded Jangor.

"It was not easy, the thing does indeed eat people, but I convinced it that the ones following us may be an easier target. That may not be true but at least it gave us a way out of here without really harming it, it has lived a lot of years and many of those all alone. I taught it a thing or two and it may live a few years more, there hasn't been any food passing this way for some time, it is very hungry, or it wouldn't have attack a group as large as ours."

"How intelligent is it?" Asked Granger.

"For an 'animal' it is very intelligent, though it has no language at all, there are no words with its thoughts, it thinks entirely in pictures."

"That should make communication easy."

"Try it, think of something simple, say tell Kern to walk up the valley and across the mountain pass. Remember that he hasn't seen the pass." Granger thought for a few seconds without saying anything, then nodded.

"I would have to shown him a picture of the whole trip, from here to the top, and somehow give the impression that I wanted him to go that way. Not all that easy at all, why did you both break contact at some point?"

Namdarin told them all scene by scene what had passed between him and the demon.

"That is one clever monster." Muttered Mander.

"One very clever monster." Said Granger. "If it communicates without words, completely without words, then language has never been developed, but picture communication has. Which means that these things talk to each other, they must share ideas or the sort of intelligence that it displayed, would never have developed. Jangor, think what sort of weapon that could be on the battlefield, instant communication, perfect co-ordination. They would be unbeatable, wouldn't they?" Jangor nodded. "But then again, if they could communicate over any distance, then they would be the dominant species around here, if not in the whole world. No this form of communication has to be short range and more likely one to one only, that is why it sat still once beaten, hoping that we could talk to it."

"If it's so intelligent, how come it's the last of its kind?" Asked Stergin, a little irritated by Granger's lecturing tone.

"It knew nothing about preserving food," responded Namdarin, "I showed it how to freeze food in the ice of the river, it should live a few years more now, only a shame there aren't any more of them."

"Are you sure?" Asked Jangor.

"Certain, there was absolutely no suggestion of any others."

"Let's hope so, I wouldn't like to find a few of them just up this valley away. Mount up, lets move before it changes its mind." They all climbed into their saddles and started up the valley again, Kern in the lead as always, Jangor behind him, Namdarin alongside Jangor. The cold air formed plumes of white mist about the peoples faces and the horses muzzles. The boulders gradually closed in on the path that they were following, huge heaps filled with many hiding places, Namdarin kept his left hand on the bow that hung from his saddle horn, the quiver of arrows set across his back the green fletching's just above his right hip ready for a fast draw. The black gem in the hilt of the sword bobbed above his right shoulder, and his right palm seemed to itch for the feel of the rough wire windings of that hilt. Arndrol felt his riders unease, and skipped from side to side at the least noise, a kicked rock from one of the following horses, the clink of someone's gear, or even the tick of a falling pebble would make him prance. Namdarin's right hand would pat him on the arched curve of his neck just to calm him a little, but that hand never picked up the reins, Namdarin wouldn't embarrass his friend by doing that, he knew that the horse would settle down once the jumbled rocks moved further away from their path. Sure enough the path opened out and they didn't quite have to walk on the ice of the river, beyond the boulders the valley was wide and shallow. Here and there the odd stunted bush grew, now bare and covered with snow, but they must get enough warmth in the summer to grow.

"This must be a difficult place to travel when spring comes." Said Kern, to no one in particular. Jangor looked at him a little confused, Kern almost never spoke, even when spoken to. 'This adventure is changing us all.' He thought. 'Mander and Andel don't argue as much as they used, I am thinking far too much.' He shook his head and glanced across the river that was still to their right, its frozen state unchanged, but something else was different over that side, there was a small group of caves in the far wall of the valley, one of them had a dirty brown path leading up to it. 'The sort of colour that snow goes when people walk on it, people or white furred demons.' He turned to speak to Kern to find the big man's eyes fixed on the cave.

"I believe that Namdarin may have been deceived." Kern whispered. Namdarin look at the other two, then followed their stares.

"Ah. Kern may be right." He picked up his bow, and knocked an arrow, Arndrol tensed momentarily under him, waiting the instruction to stop or turn, the cave was on the wrong side Namdarin would have had to turn almost completely around to shoot an arrow that way. Nothing was moving around the cave, the entrance was a black pit in the grey rock of the mountainside, no smoke was visible, but then the demons have more than enough fur to keep them warm if they are out of the wind and the snow. The river widened out into a small lake, which appeared to be its source, for there were no streams feeding it. Beyond the lake the valley narrowed to a small path which passed between two high buttresses of black rock, almost like man carved pillars, as they passed between the pillars Namdarin was almost sure that he saw something move in the mouth of the cave, something shifting in the semi-dark, something that had been watching them to be sure they were leaving or maybe two somethings. The pillars seemed to lean in towards each other pressing down on the people and the horses as they walked slowly through, the horses heads drooped towards the ground as is a heavy weight was suddenly pressing them down, the people were equally depressed by the darkness of the rocks and the dim light of the passageway. Once past the pillars the passageway opened a little, but not more than a few yards each side of the path. Namdarin dropped back from his place beside Jangor until he was alongside Jayanne, as he moved in alongside her he glanced over his shoulder, there was Crathen. 'There is always Crathen, where ever Jayanne is there he is.' He thought a rage of jealousy filled him, but still he turned back to the young man, who was sitting a little crookedly in his saddle. "How are you doing?"

"I am fine. Kern says that cuts will heal in a few days, and that there are no broken bones."

"You were very lucky."

"Lucky would not have been so painful." Namdarin just nodded, his thanks unspoken, his wishes that the younger man had not been quite so lucky unsaid.

"You?" Namdarin asked Jayanne.

"I'm fine too, finer than him." She shook her hair backwards towards Crathen.

"You are going to have to be more careful in future. That demon nearly killed you. If Crathen hadn't got in its way it almost certainly would have succeeded."

"I don't understand how it beat me."

"It has really long arms, you missed with the first swing, and the follow through left you wide open for a counter attack, which is something you are going to have to watch, especially if you get to face a real swordsman, or a properly trained soldier. A good swordsman with a strong sword, or a powerful wrist, will beat an axe. If you miss with that first strike, he will get inside your defence, that is the problem with an axe, its not very manoeuvrable."

"How can I beat a swordsman then?"

"Two ways first let him strike first and then you counter, or strike first and don't miss. Sometimes a man may be surprised to see a woman attack in the way that you attacked the demon, all out savagery may win, it may force him into a defensive pattern, or it may not. If you were to let him strike, I am sure that your axe is as hungry for steel as it is thirsty for blood, looking back to Dorana's henchman, his sword didn't even slow it down, and that sword was good steel, the people in your village know about metal, don't they?"

"Yes, they do. It's not just silver they are good with, iron, steel, gold, when they find it. There are people who handle all metals well. But how do I judge when to attack and when to hold back?"

"Experience is the only way, one can usually tell by the look in a man's eyes which sort he is going to be, or the way he holds his sword, or the way he stands. There are so many things to take into consideration. Including the nearness of his friends and yours, if his friends are close by then you have to kill him quickly, you may not have the time to wait for him to attack, if help arrives too soon you will be outnumbered and quite soon dead, however the reverse is also true, it may be that you only have delay him for a while until one of us arrives to slip some steel between his ribs. The battlefield is a dangerous place to have to learn all this, which is why soldiers spend so much time training, on the field you don't normally have time to think, you can only react, and follow your trained instinctive responses. You don't have any real training behind you, so your responses will always be difficult to predict, even you don't know what you are going to do, this is an advantage, and a dis-advantage, you can't predict your opponents actions, so you are likely to be very surprised by whatever he decides to do."

"The axe always seems to know what to do. Sometimes it responds without my conscious thought."

"But you cannot always depend on the axe to do everything for you, it is quite possible that you will need to make it do things that it doesn't want to, it may come to the wrong decision and act the wrong way. I would certainly feel better knowing that you can override, its intentions."

"I will learn to do that, if you think it is necessary, but so far it hasn't been wrong."

"I can think of an occasion where it would have made a serious mistake."

"When?"

"Do you remember when we were back at Granger's and I lost control for a while, and attacked Kern."

"Yes."

"Then that axe would have killed me, had I been attacking you. But Kern knew the difference, he only rendered me unconscious. Do you see what I mean, the axe could get a friend killed because it has no friends, and it never has had any."

She nodded and looked away, seeing the truth in his words, knowing that she would have to control that axe more carefully in the future, she had few enough friends to begin with, and couldn't bear to loose any of them.

Up ahead Kern whistled his usual warning, they all stopped and waited for Jangor and Kern to investigate. Kern stood in the end of the narrow passage, just were it entered an open space, ahead of him was a wide flat area surrounded by steep rugged cliffs, which were not more than fifty feet high, open to the clear blue sky above, empty even of snow. Almost directly ahead of them was an opening in the opposite cliff, a small black shadow in the shadowy rock face. The sun shone down weakly into the open area, picking out the only thing there that was not grey stone, a gnarled and twisted tree trunk, its branches seemed to writhe in the air, like the arms of some deformed praying man, the tree was barely more than man height, it held no leaves, but that was no surprise at this time of the year, the only surprise was that it was there at all. Around the base of the trunk the rocks were lifted and cracked, the tree had obviously worked very hard to break through, or perhaps it had started in to small crevice which it had then widened, it was impossible to say.

"Why are you standing still?" Asked Jangor, "Is there some danger?"

"I don't know, it feels very strange. Like something I should know, but cannot quite get a hold of." Kern placed both palms against the side of his head, and stared hard at the tree, his fixed gaze brought him no more enlightenment. Eventually he shook his head, and walked into the open area, the deep shadows all around, the tree standing lonely in the clear light of the sun, its very shadow seemed to wriggle on the ground behind it. Kern didn't take his eyes from the stunted thing, he still felt that it ought to be telling him something about itself, maybe something from his past, something important that he had forgotten. Jangor signalled to Mander with a wave of the hand, Mander walked slowly towards the tree, he was unsettled by Kern's plain discomfiture.

"Stop." Called Namdarin. Mander stood quite still.

"What is wrong?" Demanded Jangor.

"Where are we going?"

"Into that cave, why?"

"What is Mander going to do?"

"Collect the wood from around the tree, to make torches so we can see in the cave."

"Any one coming this way would do just that wouldn't they?"

"So."

"Why is there so much fallen wood around such a small tree? It should be cleared out every time some one comes this way. No body has collected wood here for more years than I would care to think about. The demons cannot have stopped every group to come through here in the last fifty years, something else is protecting the tree."

Granger stepped forwards, and raised his staff above his head, he walked forwards slowly until the horizontal staff was in the sunlight, its shadow showed as a bar on the ground supported by two clenched fists. He began to whisper a soft prayer, something that the others couldn't hear. The staff creaked and crackled, gently, the sound barely audible above the breathing of the horses. "Mander stand very still no matter what happens." He whispered harshly, "There is surely something here, but I cannot feel it accurately, it hides in the shadows, and doesn't want to meet me."

Kern coughed, the noise reverberated about the cliffs, for what seemed to be a lifetime. "I have it now. I know who it is. This one is mine." Confidently he strode forwards, when he was level with Mander he said "Back with the others my friend." Mander needed no telling twice, above his shuffling footsteps an new sound was heard, a cracking rustle, that got louder with every step that Kern took, as Kern's head entered the sunlight and threw its shadow on the grey rock slabs, the sound was recognised by all, the beating of huge slow wings, the crackle of feathers in the wind. A Shadow appeared, a huge winged shape, that settled on the shadow of the staff, a huge bird, like a raven only from its shadow, it stood five feet high, though it wasn't on the staff, it merely cast it shadow from there.

"What is it?" Whispered Andel. Jangor shrugged. Namdarin shook his head. Jayanne shivered and flicked her wrist to bring the haft of her axe to her hand, her shivering stopped the moment that the axe snuggled into the callused palm. Namdarin reached over his head and drew the sword from its scabbard on his back, the sword rested across the saddle and Namdarin felt a little better. Kern continued his stately walk across the sunlight rocks towards the stricken tree. With a sound like the cracking of sails in a strong wind, the shadow bird snapped into the air, and sailed serenely to the tree, where it perched on one of the trees stunted arm. The branch clearly sagged under the weight of the invisible bird. "It weighed nothing when it was standing on my staff." Whispered Granger. Kern's sword remained in its scabbard, and his hand stayed very firmly away from it. The fallen branches crunched under Kern's heavy boots, he arrived at the tree, then turned his back to it, he leant against the trunk and placed his arms along the major branches until he had taken up the shape of the tree. The unseen shape that was loading the branch of the tree, could almost be seen to move to the raised arm of the man, the branch moved up and the man's arm moved down as it accepted the weight of the huge bird, the shadow barely changed at all, as if the bird had merely stepped across the short space to the man's arm, Jangor noticed the indentations of the birds claws in his friends sleeve, they were deep and terminated in extremely sharp claws. Kern moved away from the tree and walked into the middle of the open area.

"What is that thing?" Asked Jangor. Kern merely shook his head, a stern look saying 'Don't disturb me just now.' They all saw that Kern was speaking slowly in such a soft voice that they couldn't hear any of the words. The movements of his mouth took on the aspect of a chant, the steady pace, and the repetitive shape of the words, or if not a chant then a spell.

"Does Kern know any magic?" Asked Granger.

"Not that I know of." Was the quiet answer.

"It looks like he still has a few surprises for even his oldest of friends."

Jangor shrugged. Kern's chant became audible, and sweat could be seen running down his face, the strain was clearly displayed in his eyes.

"Can you understand him?" Asked Jangor.

"That is no language that I know." Replied Granger. The spell was building in power as they watched, the tension in the air mounting with every second that passed. The big man was snatching short breaths, so as to disturb the rhythm of his spell as little as possible, the tree was shaking from the tip of its branches to the base of its trunk, stirred by an insane wind that none of the witnesses could feel. Kern's voice started to shout and to shake at the same time, it crackled as if struggling with the unintelligible syllables. The effort finally had some effect. A smoky shape appeared on the man's arm, at first thin and grey, but rapidly it solidified into a huge black crow, fully five feet high that stood calmly, its cold black eye peering at the group of amazed people. It feathers glowing blue-black in the watery sunlight, the multicoloured shimmering of them was an almost mystical effect, but really only the shattering of the sunlight on the shiny vanes of the feathers. It rustled it wings then jumped to the ground, without spreading the glimmering wings at all. The clack of its claws on the hard stone of the pavement shattered the silence that had fallen when the bird had materialised.

"Craaaawwwk", the bird screamed its defiance at all around, the tree shook again and the very ground beneath their feet kicked and rocked, trying to throw them over, all the horses spooked and became difficult to control. By the time that the horses were back in hand and the people looked to their friend, he was deep in conversation with the bird. Speaking in squawks and squeaks. Jangor was watching with his jaw hanging open as the bird paced up and down in front of the man, who was now sitting cross legged on the cold ground, the bird was upset about something, its stamping feet and strutting walk, made that very clear for anyone to see. Kern was attempting to mollify the black crow, his head was hung down and he was avoiding eye contact with the bird. The bird screamed and raised its wings in anger, Namdarin snatched his bow from the saddle of the horse standing calmly behind him, turned nocked an arrow and pulled the string, even as he was bringing the arrow to bear on its intended target. Kern saw the movement and with astounding speed for a man so large, rose to his feet in a single smooth movement and put himself between Namdarin and the bird.

"Craarwwk". Spoke the Bird again. "You ask for my help and your friends think to threaten me." Jangor's jaw hung open even further for the Bird had indeed spoke words that they all could understand.

"Forgive them they thought that you were threatening my life, that is all, they are good people and the best of friends that a man could wish for."

"They don't seem to be friendly to birds." With every word it spoke, the words become clearer and less like the squawks of a trained parrot.

"Forgive them, they are mere mortals."

"And as such they deserve forgiveness?"

"Yes, they undertake a task that should be for the gods, not men, and as such deserve help, not just forgiveness."

"Help perhaps, but mine?"

"Help from any quarter is always gratefully received."

"What sort of help do you wish?"

"Any thing that can help us in the destruction of Zandaar."

"He is a god with many followers, his reduction will not be easily accomplished."

"We are fully aware of that, do you know of anything that would help us?"

"Perhaps. I feel that you have some old and powerful weapons, and some old and powerful friends, your cause could be assisted by a power that I know of though I have heard nothing of it for many a year. It is the mindstone of the elven lords. It was lost many years gone, after a huge battle on the eastern plains, the king of the elves wore it as decoration in his golden crown, I think that he knew not of its power, for the lore that it used was already long forgotten by the elven priesthood. It is a drab green stone like the black one in the hilt of the sword of Xeron, that I can feel very close by, its power is similar but much more free ranging. It may still be with the elven king in his funeral barrow, though I suspect it would have been stolen by one of your voracious brethren. The king has been dead for some hundreds of years and the protection of the barrow may have faded."

"What is the power of this stone and how is it protected?"

"I know that it is protected but how I know not, its power is the power of the mind, and is only limited by the mind that wields it."

"We will attempt it then, many thanks to you for this aid."

"Have a care, for the elven kings have been known to guard their treasures jealously." The crow spread is wide wings with a crack, and launched itself into the air, the back wash of its take off blew Kern from his feet, and scattered the others like the dried leaves of winter, the howling of disturbed air in the small space was like a tornado as it whipped every loose object around and around. The beating of great wings became no quieter but drifted slowly away, the bird covered no distance but dispersed slowly and faded from view, only when its shadow had completely gone did the wind of its passing subside with a raucous sigh.

"What was all that about?" Asked Jangor.

"What was that language you spoke?" Asked Granger simultaneously.

"The language," said Kern looking at Granger. "Is that of the priesthood of Gyara, a sect from the far west who worship the earth goddess Gyara. It was her that I spoke to, she has many forms but the black bird is one of her favourites. As soon as I heard her wings I knew that the tree was one of her creatures, this used to be a temple dedicated to her. The tree is shaped as it is so that it can be a former for the priests to use to shape their bodies and thereby enhance the power of their prayers."

"Where did you learn all this?" asked Jangor.

"It is something from my youth, I was training to be a priest, when things went wrong for me, I had to leave suddenly. Perhaps this was her plan all along, for me to come here and reactivate this temple, the gods sometimes act in the strangest of ways, they have a much longer view of things than we mortals."

"Well, can we leave now? This place is giving me the creeps."

Said Mander.

Kern nodded and collected his horse and led them all towards the cave opening to the left of the tree.

CHAPTER TWENTY TWO

Kevana and the rest set off from Granger's home, with the sole intention of tracking the thieves down and retrieving that which they believed to be theirs. The tracks where a few days old, and in places almost impossible for the skills of Alverana, he was tested to the limit on many an occasion, sometimes only holding on to the trail of the others by guess work and luck, though it soon became obvious to all that the path they were following lead up into the mountains, a path that had a history of terror, an un-named force held the valleys of these mountains in thrall, causing the disappearance of any that ventured into these passes. Petrovana and all the academics became progressively more and more nervous as they climbed up into the hard snow of the upper valleys.

"Do we really have to go this way?" Asked Petrovana. "We all know what terror lives up here." There was a subtle agreement from some of those around him, though none where terribly obvious, no one really wanted to ally themselves with a man who gave in to his fears so easily.

"How can you be a soldier of god?" Demanded Worandana, "You whine at the slightest threat to your miserable life."

"Miserable is certainly the word for it at the moment. Here in the frigid cold of the high mountains riding to meet the snow demon of legend, I have reason to fear for my life as do we all, no one really knows what is up here, the only ones that return have seen nothing at all, and should count themselves lucky. I would pray to all the gods if it would improve our chances of getting through these mountains alive."

"You talk heresy, that may be acceptable in some quarters of the world, but not anywhere that I am." Worandana snapped, then switched his stare to Kevana, the implication and accusation clear. Kevana shrugged, looked at Petrovana, with a hard stare.

"He is a good soldier, there are few men better to have at your back in a close quarters fight, he protects himself so well that you can totally forget about what is happening behind you, he can also find a way out of almost any situation, he knows every back alley in the world, and the little used exits of all the ale houses in every major city for more miles than any man can walk in a lifetime. He has his uses but sometime his mouth runs wild, especially when he is frightened, but that is also when he does his most devious thinking. He may just find a way around whatever it is that is ahead of us." Then he turned his gaze on Worandana, "Ignore him, he will shut up once his audience stops listening. I think he only does it to be the centre of attention, and perhaps to help him think more clearly."

Worandana looked around at his own followers and paid close attention to the ones that looked away. He grunted as the thought suddenly crystallised "He was testing all of you, he knows how his colleagues respond in a fight, he was trying to find out which of you would run when it counts most, and I believe he found out. You all failed his test, not one of you resisted the chance to turn round a go by any other way than this one." He shook his head slowly from side to side. "You are transparent even to someone as unskilled as Petrovana, he hooked you and played you all like little fishes, now you will have to prove to him that he is wrong about you all, I may even find some interesting ways for you to die." Then he turned away and heeled his horse into a surge that took him up to where Alverana was waiting for the arguments to stop. With a sharp shake of the head Worandana indicated that he wished to continue the trek into the hills. In only a few moments all of his acolytes had caught up and arranged themselves in a line abreast, a troupe of brave men heading off to battle.

It was this brave formation that approached the field of boulders that marked the hunting range of the snow demon, which was fully aware of them and had been for some time. None of them saw its white furred head against the snow when it came from its hiding place to check their progress up the valley, they were following the same paths that Namdarin and his group had travelled only a few days before, not changing its tactics too much the beast let the first, and bravest looking ones pass its place of concealment, then with an eerie silent surge it emerged, rushing with its strange four legged gait straight at the backs of the monks, much as Namdarin had shown, when they had mind linked. The soft snow and the light wind hid its headlong rush, only the horses seemed to twitch a little as it kicked snow about in its haste to close with its foes, soon to be its food. The first that the monks knew of it was the scream of Petrovana's horse as it was snatched out from under him, followed swiftly be that man's yell as he rolled to his feet drawing sword and cursing fluently in some of the worst language that was heard in any tongue. The beast slashed the horses throat with its clawed right hand then closed on Petrovana, all his friends were a little busy either trying desperately to stay on, or trying desperately to get off the stampeding horses, depending on the point of view. While Petrovana faced the beast alone.

The beast paused as the horse fell in a bloody heap, its legs kicking the last weak twitches as the life blood pumped from a throat that was no longer there, Petrovana held his sword low and wide ready for the rush of an unthinking beast, which was what he thought he was looking at. The pause gave both the man and the beast an instant to prepare, though Petrovana's friends very still struggling with panicked horses, the two combatants were no longer in the grip of the panic of combat, a cool intensity had descended on the man, a clarity of thought that only comes when the mind and body are pushed to the limit of time, the moment that reaches out to infinity, two minds thinking towards one purpose, death. The demon stepped forwards, almost to within reach of the man, the sword slashed round in a low sweeping and rising blow, intending to disembowel the white furred monstrosity that stood in its path, the belly twitched away from the sword in an uncontrolled reaction, an instantaneous retraction of the muscles was not enough to remove them from the path of the whistling blade, the rainbow armour flashed at the impact but received no damage and the beast stepped straight through the blow, its clawed left hand following the sword through and catching the man in the chest and throwing him to his knees, an explosion of breathe driven from his pained body. As the beast stepped in for what it believed to be the killing stroke, the man's sword rose and took it in the thigh, well below the skirt of the wondrous armour that covered its chest, Kevana had thrown himself from his horse, as was running as fast as he could find the traction through the snow towards the stricken man, the beast stepped away, a runnel of bright red flowing freely down its leg, it was unused to pain, almost none ever injured it at all, things were not going the way that Namdarin had shown they would. Pain, and rapidly approaching enemies with unsheathed swords, were too much for it to cope with, it turned away and ran, setting a pace with all four limbs that not even the swiftest of horses could hope to match over the slippery snow that was its home ground, once out of sight in the boulders it turned to watch the men as they regrouped, it stared for a moment to be sure that it was not being pursued, then turned and set course for its cave, higher up the mountain, it would have to take a circuitous route, in order to get around the men, that were even now getting their horses under control and re-grouping, into a more military formation.

"Worandana, one of your men will ride double with Petrovana." Was Kevana's first command, his own horse recovered by Alverana.

"What was that thing?" the question sprang from an unidentified mouth, for it was the question on all their lips.

"The Snow demon." Said Alverana, "I have heard many tales of this thing, but thought that most of them belonged to old wives, and warm campfires. If only half of what I have heard is true, in only loosing one horse we have done exceptionally well. It seems to know that the ones at the back are usually the most vulnerable, it deliberately avoided any contact with the brave troupes at the front." The sneer in his voice was clear, one of Worandana's monks made a move to protest but a snapped hand signal from the venerable priest turn the protest into a sudden fit of coughing. Though the moment was missed by none.

"How many of them are there?" Demanded Kevana.

"Stories vary, but the number is usually one or possibly two. There cannot be too many such large predators in this barren wasteland. There is almost nothing to eat for so large an animal, unless you count hapless travellers who need to cross these mountains just here."

"Will it come back?" quavered a rather timid voice, which received a harsh glare from Worandana.

"Petrovana tagged it real good, that wound is going to bleed hard for some hours and hurt like hell for some days, we should be safe, unless it decides that we are a threat to its family."

"Such a beast has a family?"

"Unless it lives for a thousand years, which is as far back as the tales go, then it has a family, to carry on the line, a proud line of killers, who unlike us, kill for food."

"You object to being a soldier of god?" Asked Worandana, a small grin on his thin mouth.

"No, I was merely observing that only men kill for something other than food."

"You don't believe that we should kill to defend our god?"

"You don't believe that our god can defend himself?"

"Of course he can, but what better test of faith is there than to die for ones god."

"But we are trained so that we won't die."

"No. You and your kind are trained to die, but at the highest cost to the enemy that can be paid."

"You are different?"

"No. We also die, just in a different arena."

"Then we are the same in so many ways, do you believe that we should kill to defend a god that can kill for himself?"

"I believe that we have been given a task to complete, by our god, that may take us all our lives and more, if we die before it is done, he will be glad for us only if we have done the utmost that we can, if we have cost our enemies the richest of prices, if we have gained the best there is for the high price that we pay, then victory will be ours."

"And the medals will be pinned to our unmoving chests, to be recovered after the funeral pyres are over."

"You have no wish to die in the service of your god?"

"I have no wish to die, if I stand alongside a man that wishes to die, I will grant him his wish, before his wish kills me. Do you wish to die old man?" A callused palm grips the black metal wires of a sword hilt, though the sword remains un-drawn.

"Enough." Shouted Kevana. "We have no need to bicker amongst ourselves, we have enough enemies baying for our blood without letting each others."

"Agreed." Answered Worandana. "We must move on quickly if we are going to catch up with our enemies."

"Their tracks are some days old." Said Alverana.

"I have gone a bit cold as well, "said Petrovana, "I am having no fun on this trip, what with avalanches, cold and white furred demons I have had enough and only wish for somewhere warm to hide, the inn by the red river would do nicely."

"Stop thinking of beer, in this cold even thinking of alcohol will bring on the sleeping death."

"I am also thinking of a warm, soft body to keep the heat in, or something else in."

"Those thoughts are not worthy of a priest of Zandaar." Said Worandana.

"These thoughts are most worthy of the most worth, I have heard of Zandaars, preference for virgins, of either sex. Not that they are virgins, or breathing, when he has finished with them."

"Such words are heresy."

"Nothing can be heresy when it is the truth."

"You speak about things you know nothing of."

"I know what the temple guards say, and they have no reason to lie to me, Zandaar uses virgins and spits out what is left, sometimes its not very pretty, some of the temple guards have the strongest stomachs in the world, for they always get to clean up his mess."

"He is god, his is the power, he does what he chooses, exactly as he sees fit."

"What fits him doesn't always fit the rest of us."

"Kevana, why do all your people speak heresy with impunity?"

"Because they fight and die, as they are told to. What better can a man do for his god?"

"There is nothing I suppose, but they could take a little less advantage of the price they know they are going to pay."

"You think what you want, we don't care about what people think. If they act rightly they can think what the hell they want, I don't care. If they step out of line, we will descend on them with sword and blood, we will kill until we are dead or they are. That is the law we live and die by, if it is too hard for you, then pick a different fight to be involved with, we tend to get very personal in battle, we get down and dirty, deep in the blood and guts of our foes, if that is too personal for you then quit now. Your choice."

"I have been in this for far too long to leave it now, I know of no other life, and would want no other, this life brings me everything I need, though the risks are sometimes higher than I would want, but then if a thing has no cost then it has no value. The price I pay for this lifestyle is less than the return I get from it, how else would I be allowed to practise and research the lost arts and magics of the past. If I were not a member of the priesthood, then you and your men would probably have been sent to kill me by now, I know that I take extreme risks, put the knowledge I gather is well worth it."

"You view knowledge as power."

"Of course, without knowledge one cannot control anything, and control is power."

"I disagree."

"You always have, which is why we went our separate ways and why we make such a good team, I know what to do and you know how to keep me alive while I do it, how can we ever lose?"

"There are always ways to lose. Lives are always lost, that is why you have no real friends but me, old man."

"I have many friends."

"How many of them would you trust to stand behind you with a knife in their hand?"

Worandana thought about that for a while, before replying slowly, "Point taken."

"A prophetic choice of words perhaps? That is the most likely end that I can see for you, stabbed in the back by a friend."

Worandana shrugged, "If that is the way I die then so be it. But I will fight for Zandaar until I draw that last breath, which is something I hope we both have in common, a thing that we all should have in common, this thing of ours, that binds us together, we take on the world, in the name of Zandaar."

"You take on the world if you want, I just want that damned sword back. I feel somehow that it is very important, did I tell you that I touched it with a search."

"No. What did it feel like."

"Steel."

"Just like any ordinary sword."

"No, definitely not. An ordinary sword has almost no reality in the astral realm, does it? You should have felt many a sword in all your experiments."

"No, I think of them but only in the background, usually one searches for people, men, minds, things that are bright and active in the astral reaches, cold steel is only a presence along with the man that carries it."

"This sword is not like that, it is sharp and hot. It almost shines with a cruel harsh light, it's difficult to explain, when your mind touches it, you can feel it but you know that it can feel you. It seems to suck energy from all around itself. But even that's not quite right, the effect is like a force sucking on your soul, it eats life, it doesn't just take life like other blades it actually feeds on it, and when it feeds it grows stronger."

"We cannot afford any more delays, that sword is indeed powerful, and cannot be allowed in the hands of these unbelievers. We must recover it." With these words he remounted his horse and set off up the valley without waiting for the others. Kevana nodded at Alverana, and the scout kicked his horse into motion rapidly catching up with the older man. Petrovana mounted double with Helvana, he being the lightest of the clerics, more accurately, Petrovana took the horse and Helvana hung on behind him. The whole troupe took off at a quick trot to catch up with those who were almost out of sight. Alverana was doing his best to subtly slow Worandana down, he didn't want to be too far from his friends when the demon came back, for Alverana was sure it would, it had too much resemblance to man, and not enough animal nature to stay away.

The afternoon was getting well along when they came to the

wide open flat, the frozen river to their right hand side, and beyond that the track riddled flat and the holes in the white cliff face, a huge escarpment, with a few deep black holes.

"The demons lair." Said Alverana softly, his words heard by all, as the intense nature of their surroundings had stilled all voices, even Petrovana hadn't complained about anything at all for some time.

"Are they at home?" Asked a shaky voice.

"Any ones guess. If they are let's hope they stay home if they are."

A piercing scream ripped the quiet air, the demon was not at home it was in the rocks above them, to their left, a large boulder separated itself from those around it and leapt into the air straight towards Alverana, using only his knees the large man moved his horse two quick steps to one side and the boulder smashed into the ground then slid across the river of ice, and already another was in the air coming towards them, and bringing many others with it, its was like an avalanche, rocks and ice pouring down on them. Alverana turned back the way they had come.

"No." Shouted Kevana, "Onwards! Move! " Alverana heeled his horse round and kicked hard, he snatched Worandana's reins on his way past and heaved the horse into motion by main strength. Petrovana, was close on his heels dodging round the crashing boulders, Fabrana's horse was almost felled by a glancing blow from a fast moving but small boulder, the air began to fill with white dusting of snow, that came along with the falling rocks, Kevana saw that the rocks were falling in two distinct patches, one where they actually were and another further back down the trail. Wasting no more time he followed the departing shapes of his men. The demons trap had failed, if they had turned back then they would have been ensnared between two demons, each one throwing heavy boulders, from an inexhaustible supply, down upon their heads. Into the narrow passageway they fled, the smoke of disturbed snow on their heels.

As soon as they were clear Kevana yelled for them to stop.

"Let's not rush headlong into something worse, shall we. I don't like the look of this passageway; it could lead to almost anything. Alverana, Briana, you two go ahead, carefully. We will rest here and look to the injured." The indicated two departed much more slowly, and Kevana turned to Fabrana, " Leave your horse here and go back that way, put as many arrows into whatever comes this way as you can, but don't take too many risks."

"In one moment you talk of giving your lives for Zandaar, then you say don't take risks. Sneered Helvana, his scholastic brethren milling aimlessly.

"Be quiet little man, only Petrovanas horsemanship kept you alive today, of course if he had dumped you off the back then his risk would have been considerably less, in fact all our risk would have been greatly reduced."

"How do you work that?"

"All a man needs when running from the tiger is a friend who runs slower than he does, once the tiger catches some food it stops hunting, but you would only have been a small snack for two of those demons."

"We only saw one."

"There were two throwing rocks, either that or one with arms fifty feet long, which would you prefer to meet in a dark alley?"

Helvana merely turned away. Soon the horses and men were patched where needed, though injuries were surprisingly light. Kevana waved Petrovana to collect Fabrana, then turned to the rest, "Mount up we move as soon as Petrovana gets back." Which took almost no time at all, the men returned at a gallop and almost collided with the stationary horses. "There are two of them and arrows don't seem to slow them down too much." Shouted Fabrana, waving an almost empty quiver. Petrovana pulled their horse up alongside Fabrana's, the archer crossed to his horse that Helvana had been holding, hoping to be riding alone, the Petrovana hauled him upwards and dropped him onto the saddle behind him.

"Move." Shouted Kevana, before he had noticed that he was almost the last one there, the reverberation of his voice had barely subsided when he heard the growls of approaching demons, he took his own instruction and left at speed. The twisting canyon held many pitfalls for horses, but Kevana's sure footed stallion didn't let him down, it caught up with the smaller horses in a few seconds that felt like a lifetime.

Kevana soon became impatient of the horses ahead, though there was no room in the narrow passage for him to pass, he heard no more of the demons but there was so much noise from the hooves of the horses that he really didn't expect to. Before long the leader, Alverana reached the end of the passage and hauled his horse too a sliding halt, the following horses merely ran into the back of him, Kevana was the last to join the pile, though his skill ensured that he didn't fall, nor did his horse.

"What in all the seven hells is going on now?" he shouted, picking his way slowly to the front of the seething mass of bodies. Alverana was standing beside his horse, stroking its neck and whispering in its ear, which seemed strange to Kevana because the horse appeared to be totally unconcerned; it showed none of the usual signs of fear.

"Speak to me." Said Kevana softly.

"I don't like this place, there is something strange here, I can feel it, like a hunger, not hunger like the snow demons hunger, but something older and colder, something that has been hungry a long, long time. "

"All I see is a withered tree."

"Yes a twisted tree, with no snow on its branches, high in the mountains in the middle of winter there is no snow here at all."

"Perhaps there is some form of heat to keep the place warm, like the volcano at Granger's cave."

"If there was enough heat to melt the snow there would be water around us, puddles and rivers of it, there are none, and have been none for many years."

Kevana nodded, he knew that Alverana's senses were to be trusted always, sometimes the man seemed to occupy a different plane to the rest of them, he felt things that no one else could, and was almost never wrong. "Worandana." He called. "This might be something for you." The old monk came forward from the now disentangled group.

"I feel something too. What it is I am unsure, it has something to do with that tree and the cave over there." Both Alverana and Kevana were surprised, they hadn't even noticed the cave, their vision had been captured by the tree.

"If they came this way, they went into that cave." Said Kevana walking towards the cave.

"Halt." Shouted Worandana. Kevana stopped mid stride, years of military commands brought the instant reaction. Worandana's shout sounded so like a drill sergeant on a parade ground that Kevana couldn't help but obey. The shout echoed around the rock walls, it bounced backwards and forwards, in increasing reverberations, building in intensity, then slowly it faded, into a rustling murmur that continued to move around the open ground in front of the men. Kevana turned back and walked slowly to where Alverana was rooted to the ground, his head moving slowly from side to side, tracking the soft rustling sound, it was like a physical being moving at random around the area between the cave and the tree, physical but non-visible.

"What is that?" Whispered Kevana. Alverana merely shook his head, though his eyes never left the place the sound emanated from.

"It will take some thought, I feel some power here, some very real power at work. We must be very careful, it will take some study." Answered Worandana.

"We don't have time for study."

"But we have time to die?"

"What do you mean?"

"I feel a power here, it may be resting but it is not sleeping, it is aware if not truly awake. If it takes umbrage at our passing I would like to be ready for it."

"How much time do you need?"

"Minutes, perhaps."

"Do it."

Worandana walked slowly towards the tree, that was the only presence to be seen, his senses were tuned to feel the vibration in the ether of any other presence, but only the dead tree impinged on his perception. 'Its not really dead.' He thought, 'It has a life that is not its own, it is borrowed from something else.' He stepped carefully through the few remaining broken pieces of wood around its base and stroked the grooved and gnarled trunk gently with his left hand, holding his walking staff firmly in the right. He felt the surge of electric charge as his fingers touched the tree, then the steady tingle that grew slowly, he felt the hairs on his neck stand slowly to attention as the charge built, the tension raising between himself and the tree. 'An old and very strong power, which has been dormant for many years, but what sort of power?' His touch could feel it but nothing of its nature reached his mind.

"Power of this place and this tree come forth, show yourself that we may honour you." He called, in a clear demanding tone, the only response was the crackle of the wind.

"Power of this place and this tree come forth, show yourself that we may honour you." He called again, a crackle of wind and the rustle of leaves, 'There are no leaves but I hear them.'

"Power of this place and this tree come forth, show yourself that we may honour you." A surge on energy came from the tree and coursed through his arm, leaving his fingers numbed to the bone, the tree shook and darkness fell across the sun. 'A god, an old one but a god none the less, and powerful.' Thought the old man.

"Form a defensive circle, and start building energy in it, cycle it around as fast as you can." He called to the men waiting by the entrance. Kevana saw to the arrangement of the circle, he knew that this sort of defense needed balance to maintain its integrity, he placed each man in order, one soldier then one monk, before taking the last place for himself, each man was facing outward towards any danger that might befall them. Kevana started the energy surge in the ring, he built a small charge in his mind and passed it on to the man on his left, who did the same, every mind adding a little to the energy pulse that traveled around the ring. While the ring was forming the tree shook itself from the tips of its empty branches to the bottom of its trunk, and for all anyone knew on down to the very ends of its roots, though what un-imaginable place they may reach who can know. Worandana watched the circle building power, a cycling energy that traveled around the ring in less than a second, anything trying to break into the circle would collect that dreadful energy, energy to which it was not attuned, energy for which it was not prepared, energy that would end its life, if life it had. Worandana was not at all sure that what they faced had life at all. The darkness across the sun assumed a shape, a huge black bird, like a raven or crow with ragged looking wing tips was approaching out of the sun, the light seemed to pass straight through it though it was much diminished in the passage. Worandana had a few moments of calm contemplation which he used to search his memory for any reference, however obscure to something like this, nothing came to fore. As far as he was concerned he was utterly in the dark, a dark that came ever closer. The ghostly sound of rushing wings came ever closer until it seemed to fill the sky above them, Worandana faced it with some trepidation in his heart. 'Sometimes I feel really old.' He thought as the black shape hardened before his eyes, its huge claws shrinking into solidity, the blackness of the feathers densified into the glossy blackness of the true bird, the beak blackened and revealed its chipped edges, almost as if the bird had been sharpening it on a rough stone.

"CRAAAWK." Its cry filled the space around and inside their heads, words came from all around, from the blue of the sky and the grey of the rocks, from the withered branches of the tree and blackness of the bird, "Who are you to disturb my rest?"

"We are the priests of Zandaar, we search for some thieves that came this way only hours ago. Can you tell us anything of them?"

"Why should I help Zandaar, who should be long gone from this realm, he should be in another dimension with all the others of the old ones."

"Are you not an old one who should have gone with them?"

"I was old when they were young, I will remain while there is life in this realm, only when all life is extinguished will I move on, to that other realm."

"Tell us of the thieves." Worandana signaled to Kevana with a concealed hand gesture, a sign to prepare, be ready to release the energy of the circle.

"They carry the cure for all ills in this place."

"What is the nature of the cure?"

"There is only one way to relieve the suffering of this realm, and to release me from my task here."

"They can destroy all life?" Worandana's question brought another signal. Hold.

"Such that it is, they can end it and my servitude here."

"How?"

"CRAAAWK."

"How?"

"I'll not say, you could stop them, or you could help them to achieve that which I desire, I cannot influence either way, there is a possibility that my action could tip the balance on way or the other, until the outcome is definite I will not influence it in any way."

"So you will let us pursue them?"

"As far as my divination's go, your activities can cause both outcomes, the banishment or destruction of Zandaar, or the ending of all life. On the other branch, if your actions cease in this place, both outcomes remain equally valid." Worandana signaled an urgent readiness. "It seems that you are not as important as you like to think you are."

"You will stand in our way?"

"You think that you can threaten me, you have not the power to end all life, only they can threaten me, for in the ending of life there is an opportunity to destroy this form, and hold my spirit in the lifeless realm. That I cannot allow, the thieves, as you call them, do not know this and will never know. You cannot tell them the path that leads this way, nor can any living soul. You have not the strength to walk the path, or weave the pattern of death. Your endings will be a small thing, something of note to no-one."

"Will you stand in our way?" Worandana spread his arms wide in readiness for the energy burst that he was about to accept from the circle behind him.

"Perhaps, a small demonstration." The bird's wide wings snapped forwards generating a huge clap of sound that disrupted the concentration of the circle; in the moment of the rings collapse its energy burst was released in an utterly uncontrolled manner. The birds wings snapped backwards sucking all that burst into themselves, the glossy blackness of the underside of the feathers glowed even more, a rich dark light emanated from them, dark rays scattered through the disorganized group of black robed figures, the rays darker than the robes, the robes scattered about, the monks falling over each other. Worandana staggered but did not fall.

"I shall let you live, because I am no longer hungry, there are few in this world that can feed my hunger to any real extent but you have done very well today, go not in peace, but go anyway."

The huge wings snapped forwards and the black bird flew away, not in the manner of birds in general, but its flapping wings blew the air around and caused it to slowly fade from view, until only a single black feather was left, caught upon an irregularity in the bark of the tree. Kevana was the first of the fallen ones to regain his feet, staggered by the intensity of the energy discharge and astounded by the way the bird absorbed it all into itself, Worandana looked on in silent amazement as the others slowly picked themselves up from the cold grey rocks, the exception being Helvana.

"What is wrong with him?" Asked Worandana. Fabrana knelt beside Helvana and turned the unconscious cleric over and then dropped him, backing away on all fours like a crab scuttling for its burrow, a look of shocked fear on is face. A look that would never again appear on Helvanas face, for he had no face to speak of. Blackened and burned there were no features to mention, only two totally white eyes stared emptily out of the ruined face.

"He's just a little dead." Said Petrovana. " What did that to him?" Asked another voice.

"We were all facing away from each other," replied Kevana, "I didn't see anything and I doubt that any of the rest of you did either. He must have been the one holding the charge when the circle broke, he had no where to pass it on to and was unable to contain it all, it just got away from him."

"You are wrong," Said Worandana, "I have seen the result of that sort of accident, the head burns from the inside, his head was burned from the outside, that damned bird did it, it took the energy of the circle and stole it all, then gave Helvana some of it back. It killed him to show us that its power is greater than ours."

"In this place and at this time it was most certainly right, however this to can change." Snarled Kevana, "Once we have finished with the thieves I intend to come back here and destroy that god forsaken crow."

"This may be a bad time to make threats, I would prefer some distance between us and this place, which is obviously sacred to the crow god, before you start to incur his wrath." Whispered Worandana.

"You think it was a god?"

"How much energy did you have in the ring?"

"It was definitely starting to get very warm, a touch hot for some perhaps." Kevana looked down and the rapidly cooling monk.

"Who but a god could feed on that much power and not be sated?"

"None. Let's move."

"What about him?" Asked Petrovana. "We can't just leave him here, the demons may come and eat him, or that crow may decide to feast of flesh not power."

"Lash him to the back of your saddle, or his saddle as yours is down the valley in the snow with your horse." Petrovana nodded and Fabrana helped him with the corpse, while the rest gathered the skittish horses.

"We will bury him at the earliest opportunity." Said Worandana, with no real idea when that would be.

Alverana passed the reins of his horse to Fabrana, and walked slowly into the darkness of the cave mouth, once the roof of the cave was overhead the darkness thickened until it was almost impenetrable, almost but not quite. Once his eyes had accustomed themselves to the darkness it was possible to make out the shape of the passageway, which descended at a very gradual slope into the mountain, the path was plenty wide enough for the horses though they may have some trouble with the darkness. After a hundred or so paces he turned round and went back to assure the others that the way was clear. The descent continued for some considerable time, though time itself appeared to lose its place, on the surface that great timekeeper, the sun, was always there to mark the passage of the days, however once in the subterranean depth there was not such indicator for the travelers. Hunger told them when it was time to eat but that is not an accurate measure, the boredom of the journey, and lack of external stimulus makes the internal so much more powerful, and empty stomach takes on huge proportions in an empty mind.

The passageway opened out into a huge cavern, the echoes of the horses iron shoes rattled on and on, the sparks those shoes struck from the hard edges of the rocks added flashes of light that illuminated nothing but hurt the overly sensitive vision of the horses and the humans. The uneven walls of the cavern were festooned with strange mineral growths, huge shiny stalactites reaching down to stumpy stalagmites below, strange veins of crystalline colours were scattered through the walls filling the emptiness of the cavern with vaguely coloured light, never enough to see properly, but plenty to change the grey light of the underground to blue and red and green. The gentle sound of running water told them of its presence but they couldn't see any evidence of a stream, other than the pathway itself which must become a waterway when the rain falls above ground or in the thaw of spring which floods all the rivers.

"We rest here for a while." Said Kevana, there were no arguments for some reason the mere act of walking through the darkness drained all, even the horses were hanging their heads, perhaps looking for food that they knew they were not going to find. With a few simple hand signals, Kevana distributed tasks amongst his men, Petrovana was to look to the horses, Alverana started to search around the perimeter of the cavern, leaving alone the most obvious exit, Briana and Fabrana set about a fire and food for all the men.

"What is he looking for?" Asked Worandana, waving a hand in the general direction of Alverana.

"What ever he can find, but water would be good, we don't have much left, unless you want to go back and get us a few loads of snow, that may just give us enough for a few days."

"Water would be good." It was now Worandana's turn for hand signals, two of the monks, separated from the huddle and started a low slow chant, a deep sound, not unlike the grinding of huge rocks, one rubbing slowly against the next, the monks raised their arms and the sound rose, until the very air of the cavern thrummed, a deep tone almost below hearing that set dust and dirt to jumping in strange patterns wherever it lay. The two turned towards one wall of the cave, which began to shake so hard that one of the smaller stalactites fell with a resounding crash. Out of the depth of the sound came a different noise, the soft liquid trickling of water flowing over rocks. The monks focused on the noise, bringing it to the fore, the deep rock sound diminished until only the water could be heard, bright and sharp, the sound itself making the men thirsty, bringing images of cool clear streams into everyone's mind. The monks walked slowly towards the rock face, the sound sharpening all the time, with every step it became clearer, until its intensity was unbearable, the thirst it engendered was driving the horses to distraction, Petrovana was struggling to keep the horses from running towards the sound, the men were struggling with themselves. Thirst has always been an incredibly strong driving force in man, if not one of the most fundamental. The two monks reached the wall of shimmering rock their arms spread across its face, their song deeper and more powerful by the moment, gradually the rock that was directly between them began to change, it shone more wetly than before, almost as if it was bleeding from its heart, slowly the liquid accumulated on its face and began to flow downwards, forming a small puddle, the rocks life blood was being squeezed to the surface by the song, the puddle grew with astounding speed and once the monks started to get their feet wet they shared a moment of eye contact and ended the song, the flow didn't stop, it continued to grow, slowly for several minutes then steadied into an even stream, small but most obviously useful.

One of the singers turned and spoke with a drained and shaky voice. "It is done, this should flow for a day or two."

"Grandly done." Praised Worandana. "Is that enough water for now?" His question was aimed at Kevana.

"Most definitely, we are only going to stay here long enough to get some rest then we must make up some of the time we have lost. How close are we?" He shouted the last towards Alverana, who was standing at the far end of the cave.

Alverana walked slowly towards the two ranking priests, slowly, almost insolently. It seemed that he had no wish to disturb the peace of this place with a raised voice, and felt that their noise was somehow an affront to the denizens of the cavern, his voice was as quiet as it could be and still be heard over the trickling of the new spring.

"We are definitely on the right path, they left by that large opening over there, but how long ago I cannot really guess, there is nothing here to degrade their tracks and so no hint as to how old they are, though I cannot believe that we are more that a day or so behind them now."

"Are we gaining or loosing ground?"

"I cannot tell." Alverana shrugged and turned away.

"We have a quick meal then a few hours sleep, we must catch up very soon, if our enemies make it to the open air before we catch them they could go almost anywhere, we may not be able to track them because the ground on the other side of this mountain system is very rocky." Kevana spoke clearly so that all could hear, Worandana, merely nodded his agreement, there could be no dissension in the ranks. A fast meal was prepared and eaten with some gusto, but with little chatter, the horses were given some grain, and water enough to keep them happy for a short while. The soldiers unrolled the blankets and were soon asleep, the monks were not, they didn't have the training to sleep anywhere at the drop of a hat. Soon the only sounds to be heard in the cavern were the snores and whispers of the men, the horses moving softly from side to side, as horses often do when the darkness is all around them, and the soft babbling of the new formed spring, where water still bubbled to the surface of the rock, and dribbled into the growing pool. The darkness of the cave was by no means complete, soft pools of milky white light were scattered about, one or two of the stalactites glowed with an eerie inner light, there was no pattern to the light, and no obvious source. Gorgana, not being able to sleep like some of the others, watches the lights, and sees that they are slowly changing, only by closing his eyes is he actually aware of the changes, when he opens his eyes things have changed for while he cannot be entirely sure. So he memorises a particular patch of the floor of the cave and the light patterns on it, closes his eyes and counts slowly to a hundred, when he opens them again the lights have definitely moved. Carefully observing the changes he repeats the process, until a real pattern begins to emerge, there are only two stalactites that seem to glow with an inner light, it is of such a low level that it is really hard to discern any difference between the active ones and the inactive, as Gorgana becomes more attuned to the lights he can tell a difference between them, one has a red tinge and one green. Slowly the green one fades, and for a while disappears completely, Gorgana is almost convinced it has gone when it slowly starts to grow in a different stalactite, very gradually the colour grows in the new stalactite, and equally slowly the red one fades. 'They seem to be on the move.' Thinks Gorgana, then berates himself for imbuing these phenomena with intelligence. Now the gradually growing lights are directly above the horses, the intensity of the lights grows far stronger than any he has seen before, so strong in fact that he can now see multi-coloured shadows under the horses. The animals are certainly disturbed by the lights. They are moving from side too side pressing against each other, as if to reassure each other that they are not alone. Soon the muscle definition in the rumps of the horses became very obvious in the increasing light. The only horse that didn't seem to be too disturbed was Kevana's stallion, he was as aloof as always, his demeanour showed that he didn't want to associate with these lesser horses at all. Though he was beginning to have a little problem, as were all the others, manes and tails were starting to stand up, bristling and waving in an un-felt breeze. The stallion tried very hard to shake his tail into shape, and twitch his mane to make it lie flat, until in frustration he picked up a foot to stamp in on the hard rock, as the hoof lifted a huge blue spark jumped from the iron shoe into the rocks below, the crack caused the other horses to twitch in annoyance, and the stallion to snort loudly. This seemed to make his tail behave but only for a few moments, very shortly it was growing into a huge bush all over again, and the light from the stalactites was getting brighter.

"Worandana." Whispered Gorgana.

"What?" Snapped the elder, who had been on the brink of sleep.

"Something disturbs the horses, striking sparks from their hooves and making manes and tails stand up."

"I see that, but what is causing it?"

"The light in those stalactites was moving around some time ago, but now is fixed above the horses and getting brighter all the time."

"That could have something to do with it."

"It seems like a tension field, in some respects, but how to stop it, I know not." Gorgana sat upright, and stared around the cave, looking for some source that could possibly make any sense.

"I could damp it down with water or some such," Said Worandana, "but the stalactites are wet already."

"Wet with heavily calcified water. I thought it was impossible to build a tension field when the air is damp, let alone as wet as it is in here."

"They weren't wet earlier, all the stalactites were dry, and now only the lighted ones are wet."

"The ones that were lit earlier are drying, not quite dry but very close."

"There must be something moving around in the rocks, something that causes wetness, light and a charged atmosphere, something that can charge the air, no matter how wet it is."

"What could it be?"

"We have seen enough unusual things on this trip, it could be almost anything, but one thing is for certain, it doesn't meet many people down here, nor much in the way of light. How fast did the lights move?"

"Hundred counts, five times, that's how long it took for them to move from the original two stalactites to the ones they are in now."

"The only real question is 'Were they being stealthy or moving as fast as they could?' Let's hope it was the latter. Kevana." The last near a shout to wake to other man.

"What do want?" Mumbled Kevana.

"We have a problem, we need to move the horses from where they are and attack the strange lights in the rocks above them, but it all has to be done at the same time, understand?"

"No, but that isn't necessary. Petrovana, Fabrana, stand by to move the horses." The two moved with concerted purpose, each gathering a handful of reins. Petrovana nodded to indicate their readiness.

"How do we attack these lights?" Asked Kevana.

"You have lightning bolts ready?"

Kevana reached inside his jacket, to the hidden pocket and brought out a clenched fist. Nodded.

"The red one is nearest to you, so you take that one," Kevana just stared hard, stating something so obvious only showed the older man to be lacking experience, "as soon as you release the bolt shut your eyes and hit the ground, we don't want to damage our eyes." The stare got harder. "Everyone else shut your eyes now and cover you ears." Though Worandana thought it impossible Kevana's stare became even harder.

"You forgot something." Sneered the soldier.

"What?"

"Breathe in, breathe out." Worandana looked around the cave the only people with their eyes open were the two with the horses and the two holding quiescent lighting bolt in their hands, the others had all found what cover there was and were taking advantage of it. Worandana looked at Kevana, with an apology in his eyes, then he followed Kevana's eyes, there was Gorgana trying to wriggle into a gap between two huge rocks, a task made more difficult by the fact that his eyes were squeezed tight shut and his hands were over his ears, he looked like a black rabbit trying to get into a mouse hole, kicking his legs in the air. Kevana just shook his head.

"Are you ready?" asked Kevana. Worandana nodded, as did the other two. The strange lights pulsed slowly, like the beat of a huge heart, a heart made of light and rock. "Fine, wait until I give the release command." Kevana nodded at Petrovana and the horses start to move, slowly at first, they were much disturbed by all the confusion around them, but they quickly got the message, and a swift kick in the ribs for any serious resistance. Immediately the lights started to fade, but very slowly. Once the horses were clear of the immediate area Kevana shouted "Now." Two arms flashed forwards, two lightning bolts streaked and formed in the air, two flashed as one and one thunderclap filled the cave with a wall of sound that was felt more than heard, a compression wave that ripped around the cave in a gradually decreasing fashion, shaking rocks and men alike, driving horses beyond the limits of panic. Two men almost concussed by the noise hung tightly on to a double fistful of reins, the only restraint other than the sudden darkness that filled the cave. Kevana shook his head, and lit a torch, huge pink flares filled most of his vision, but he could see something of the chaos around him, dust was still falling from the roof, along with the occasional small rock, dimly he could hear a man screaming, but in the confined space had no idea which one it was, it was a strong scream so therefore nothing to worry about, he helped his two men bring the horses under some semblance of control, his own horse merely stood against him and breathed hard. He made no attempt to talk to the two holding the horses, he helped them to their feet, and checked them for injuries, hand signals were all they could manage, their hearing had fled in fear. Worandana was just staggering to his feet, shaking his head, wondering were all the bells were coming from.

"Please remind me never to do that again." He shouted to Kevana, who nodded, having trouble with his own bells. Together they followed the screaming, which was beginning to sound more and more urgent. Gorgana had managed to squeeze between the two huge rocks, but then one of them had moved a little, to make the gap even smaller and he was still in there. Kevana sat on one rock and pushed against the other with both feet, while Worandana pulled on the trapped monks feet, with only minor cuts and bruises the monk was rescued from his hiding place.

"Thank you." He said, though his quiet words went unheard, nothing short of a shout would be audible for some time yet. Worandana looked upwards and found that the lights in the rocks had gone, or at least subsided to the point of invisibility, he had no real way to be sure, because the flare of the lightening bolts had total wiped out his night vision, it would be many minutes before this returned, if at all. Hearing was even worse, the hard ringing in all their heads meant that vocal communication was as near to impossible as makes absolutely no difference. Kevana working with only the hand signals, that he and his men normally used when silence was the order of the day, assigned guards to both entrances and one to watch the roof for any intrusion of light beings, he had no doubt that they were indeed such. Worandana assigned one of his men to each of the soldiers, sharing tasks in this manner could only help the coherence of the group, that was his hope at least, though Kevana thought that it was a vain one, he knew that these two disparate types of men, could never think as one, at least not when there was no time for thinking, soldiers do not think with their brains, they merely react, in a way that they all understand, their training is the glue that holds them together, the clerics use a different glue, one that requires thought and normally discussion, things a soldier has no time for. The group will hold together for a while, but when the stress hits the level where thought becomes counter productive, at that time the clerics will die, because they cannot respond fast enough to whatever it is that is going on around them. Worandana thought that it was a vain hope, he knew that the soldiers could cope with anything at all, so long as it was something they had been trained for, if something out of the ordinary happened then it would be up to the clerics to hold the group together and keep it safe, and the way things had been going in the last two days, he knew that ordinary was not going to be a problem that they would have to deal with. Kevana and Worandana returned to their respective beds, their thoughts running on exactly the same line, but at opposite ends of the spectrum.

Kevana opened his eyes, and heard nothing, which made a big change, the ringing in his ears had stopped, then he realised that he did indeed hear nothing, nothing at all, fearing for his hearing he snapped his fingers beside his head, the resounding crack of his middle finger hitting the base of his thumb echoed through the gloom of the cave for what seemed an eternity, he mouthed an apology to the raised eyebrows of Alverana.

"How long have I been asleep?" he whispered.

"Not much over a couple of hours, I divided up the guard duties so that everyone got some sleep."

"Including you?"

"Including me, though can't really sleep in this place, it makes me very nervous, I don't know why, but it does."

"What about the others?"

"Some have no problems sleeping, but they are in the minority, most just rest, thinking their own thoughts, and saying nothing. How do you feel?"

"I feel surprisingly good, my hearing is back to normal and my vision is clear, and that is something I wouldn't have bet on two hours ago."

"Time to move on?"

"I think so, get them moving."

Alverana nodded and rolled to his feet, with the gracefulness of a cat, he had certainly benefited from the rest. He moved around the group shaking those that were asleep and nudging the ones that weren't. He spoke not a single word but they all knew that it was time to get going again. Worandana stood up before it became his turn to be shaken or nudged. He nodded at Alverana and started rolling up his bed. Almost no words were spoken during the breaking of their camp, canteens were all filled to the brim, from the spring, then drunk from and filled again, the water should no sign of lessening, its flow was as strong as when it was formed. Kevana waved Alverana into the lead, and held his torch high above his head, until he was the last one to leave the cavern, looking back in the flickering light of the yellow burning torch he saw the remains of their camp, and the tracks they had left behind, hoof prints from the horses and footprints from the men. 'How long will it be before someone else comes this way?' He wondered. 'It must be many years since anyone else did, we are following one set of foot prints and leaving our own behind us, footprints in the sands of time.'

CHAPTER TWENTY THREE

Jangor lead the way down into the gloom of the cave, after only a hundred feet or so, the path took a tight turn that totally cut off all the light from the surface, Jangor had to get off his horse and lead it with one hand while the other hand trailed along the wall, feeling his way. "We need some light." He said, "Anyone got a torch or two?"

"Will this do?" Said Granger, as a soft blue glow issued from the tip of his staff, it lit the path with strange colours, though the light was blue to look at, some of the rocks reflected other shades, some red, some green and some colours that were impossible to give names to. The black jewel of Namdarin's sword reflected none of the blue light, instead it shone with an unusual red light, a red that showed only those things that it touched directly, and only those things that were alive, the horses stood out, the men were red against the blue background, but the swords were utterly dark, slowly Namdarin noticed that though the living things reflected the red light strongly the leather of the saddles reflected some of the red, 'Perhaps because they were living once.'

After an hour or two's careful walking they entered a cavern where many stalactites hung down, Granger's blue light scattered around, reflected off the many planes of the rock formations, occasionally it seemed to flare up and burn harshly into their eyes, Granger gently turned down the intensity of the light until it was barely any stronger than a lonely firefly, but still the blue light seemed to bounce around the cavern, almost with a life of its own. Granger quenched his light completely, fully expecting darkness to engulf them all, but the blue continued to flash around the caves edges, flaring slowly from one stalactite to another, a self perpetuating illumination the like of which none of them had ever seen before.

"Very strange." He said, to no one in particular.

"Indeed," Replied Namdarin, "Have you noticed the light that comes from the black jewel on my sword?"

"No."

"It lights up everything that is living with a red light that is so dark it is almost too dark to see."

"No, I haven't seen anything like that at all."

"But your own horse is so bright that I can see the rocks underneath it lit up red."

"I see nothing, not reds anywhere, only the blue that comes from these rocks. Perhaps you can see it because you hold the sword."

"That could be it I suppose, I have noticed that living things stand out really bright and the once living show up slightly, saddles and such." He paused. "But why do those stalactites shine red too?"

"Stalactites, are not and have never been living."

"But they glow red, almost as strongly as the horses, it seems very strange."

"This is all very strange." Said Crathen.

"Can they be alive? Or perhaps conceal a life within them?" Asked Jangor, looking at Granger.

"How would I know? This is as new to me as it is to you. Can you imagine a life form that lived inside solid rock?"

"No. And I certainly wouldn't want to meet one, let's get out of this place, it feels very bad."

Kern took the lead, and the rest followed him from the cavern, down a dark and narrow tunnel, which lead them after some small time to another open area, one with no strange lights, other than the ones they brought with them. A few small rock formations that looked a little unusual but nothing out of the ordinary.

"This looks like a good place for a rest." Muttered Kern, not willing to make any un-necessary noise. Jangor nodded and the others found places to rest.

" Any water about?" Asked Andel.

"I think I can hear something in amongst those rocks over there." Said Kern, waving a hand in the general direction. Andel walked over, and returned with his canteen full. "There is a small pool over there, I think it has a spring that fills it, should be more than enough for our needs." He sat down on a sandy patch of ground with his back to a smooth rock formation, in a moment or two he was sound asleep, his gentle snores echoing around the cavern, causing the horses ears to twitch, they knew what the sound was and where it was coming from, all the echoes seemed to give it more than one source, as if they were surrounded by a hoard of sleeping men, even Arndrol was unhappy about all the snoring, he flicked his ears, one way then another, finally he stamped a heavy hoof, which stopped the snoring by waking the man. Mander laughed, and the others smiled.

"What have I missed?" Asked Andel.

"Nothing much, just a horse expressing an opinion about someone's snoring."

"Why? Who was asleep?"

"You were, fool."

"I don't snore!" Everyone laughed. "I don't!"

"I think we should take an hour or two to rest here." Said Jangor. "We all seem a bit tired."

"But what time is it? I can't tell down here in the dark." Asked Mander. Jangor looked at Kern.

"Not yet sundown, but not far off."

"Good enough for me." Said Andel, returning to his recent bed, only this time taking a blanket with him.

"Kern, how does the perimeter look?" Asked Jangor.

"Fine, two real exits, the one we came in and the way onwards, I presume, all the other holes are just that, nothing bigger than a rabbit could move around in any of those."

"Great a couple of hours, then we move on. The horses can stand guard, I don't think that anything could be creeping up on us down here."

It was a little more that two hours when Jangor woke up again, looking around he saw nothing out of the ordinary, but was surprised that he could see anything at all, no-one had lit any torches and Granger's staff was not giving off any of its blue light, so where was the light coming from? It seemed to be a general glow that came from above, though he could see no real concentration anywhere, only a very low pinkish glow that lit the cave up with the strangest of colours, things he knew to be one colour were showing as a different shade. Moving slowly so as not to disturb anyone he went to where Kern was sleeping and just touched his shoulder, the big man woke instantly, fully alert in a moment, as always.

"Strange lights again." Whispered Jangor.

"I can't wait to get out of these damned caves, nothing is ever as it should be, strange lights, strange noises, strange breathing."

"What strange sounds?"

"Some time ago, I heard a sound like soft breathing, but far too slow to be any human breath, slow long and deep, almost as if the rocks themselves had lungs to draw breath."

"I'm glad I didn't hear that, when did it stop?"

"I'm not sure, I fell asleep listening to it, a very hypnotic sound."

"But what about the light?"

"Some sort of growing thing that gives off light as a natural by product, like rotting logs in a forest."

"Yes I've seen such, but what can this sort of life live on, there is nothing to feed it here."

"Who can tell, there must be something it feeds on."

"Let's not worry about it, it's time to move on anyway. I'll check on the horses, you get the rest moving." Kern merely nodded and set about his assigned task, waking some of the sleepers wasn't easy, they had had a hard time recently and only been asleep for a short time. Andel even needed a kick to be sure he was moving, not actually awake but mobile. Before long everybody was ready to leave the cave, Kern took the lead as usual, and they headed out in single file, Granger was directly behind Kern, so that his staff could light the way if required, Namdarin was close to the back of the line, immediately behind Jayanne. He noticed that she looked quite relaxed, her axe was hanging on it's thong from her saddle horn, not in her hand but certainly only an instant away. He was very soon hypnotised by the swaying of her hips as she walked slowly in front of him, her trousers weren't very tight, but occasional would show the smooth curve of her buttocks as she stepped forwards. Her long hair swayed in perfect counterpoint, the red picked out by the soft pink light all around them. 'I wonder how she does that?' He thought, 'Does she know the effect that has on men?' He dragged his eyes away, not wishing to embarrass himself with the arousal he could feel building, though there was precious little else to look at, Arndrol's slowly nodding head, the walls of the cave, the swinging tail of Jayanne's horse and back to Jayanne's hair. He draped the reins across Arndrols saddle and quickened his pace until he was directly behind the young woman, he could smell her hair even above the all enveloping stink of horses, it smelled of pine, and forests. 'How can she smell so good, we have been out in the wilds now for days and days, yet she manages to smell so fresh?'

"How are you doing?" He asked his voice a little rough.

"I'm fine, tired but fine, this cave is starting to get very boring."

"You should try standing where I am, it's a lot better."

"How can that be better, it's no difference at all."

"Take my word for it, it's a whole lot more exciting, in some ways far too exciting."

"I don't see it, even if we were to change places the only difference would be that you would be in front of me rather than behind me."

"Exactly. Then I would be looking at Stergin's back not yours, nothing like as nice a view."

"It's just a back."

"But it moves so nicely."

"What did you think of the crow, and Kern?" She asked, changing the subject to another one she was more comfortable with.

"It was very unusual, but then perhaps the unusual is normal for us."

"I've certainly never seen or heard of anything like it before, not even in the oldest tales."

"I don't know about that, I seem to recall something about a crow god, I can almost hear my grandfathers voice saying something about it's feathers, 'Blacker than the blackest of nights, yet still shimmering like oil on water.' Yes. That was it."

"An accurate description of the feathers without a doubt. Can you remember anything else?"

"No, I was very young when my grandfather died. Perhaps only four years old I think, it was the picture of black shiny feathers that stuck in my mind. He was a really good storyteller; his tales seemed to come to life in your head. I was too young at the time to really appreciate them, but some of the older children on the estate told me that he was the best of storytellers."

"Sounds like a really nice man."

"I don't know, I didn't know him at all really, but my father was distraught when he died."

"Your family all seem to have been very close."

"I suppose, but then the old ones die, until I was the oldest left, then they all die, and I am alone."

"Not alone any more." Her hand reached out to his, as the distress intensified on his face. They walked along for a while hand in hand, saying nothing, but thinking many thoughts, him about his family now dead, and about her of the hard eyes and the soft skin. She thought about her empty life that was now filled with friends, and excitement. Despite her recent misfortunes she was beginning to enjoy her new life, with all its risks, and terrors.

Namdarin felt her warm hand in his, and knew hope, a hope that he thought was dead, a hope that the house of Namdaron could rise again, a vague hope, a hope years down the line, the sort of hope that the human spirit clings to when all others are lost. But still it was a hope that filled him with warmth, a warmth that he could quite well do without, the harsh reality of his life, and the quest that is his life, gave him no room for the softer emotions, he has to remain resolute, and focused, or the Zandaars are going to kill him, but at times like this concentration isn't at all easy. His thoughts turned to the weapon that the crow goddess mentioned, what could it be? Would they find it?

"I have to talk to Granger." He said, squeezing her hand gently, then he passed he to go down the line to where the old man was lighting the way for Kern.

"What to you know of the Elven weapon the bird mentioned?"

"I may have heard of it, or read of it, I think it could have been in one of the books I left back at my cave, but I cannot be entirely sure, I would have to see it to be certain. Though there is no way we are going to go back for the book, so I'll just have to make do with what ever we find, if anything."

"But you can remember something?"

"Yes, but it's all very vague, the mindstone is a crafted stone, that intensifies thought, or strengthens it. It could be that it helps the user to see into the minds of others, or through their eyes, on the other hand I could be thinking of something entirely different, if it exists we have to find it, Gyara says it is important to us, and I tend to believe her, though I sometimes feel that she may have a different purpose in mind for us."

"Why do you think she is playing us false?"

"She is a god, but a god with few followers, perhaps she wants to increase her following by taking some of the Zandaars to herself."

"No," Said Kern, "she has enough followers, she has never been a god to seek after more people, I would say she is exactly the opposite."

"But a gods power derives from his, or her followers." Said Namdarin.

"Normally, yes, but in the case of Gyara, I think her power comes from something else, something older than people, she was here before the people were, and she will probably be here long after all the people are gone."

"Why should she be here when she has no followers, surely that is when a god moves on, once no-one believes in them, they fade away, don't they?"

"Not in her case." Said Granger "She was here before men came into being, perhaps she had some part in the birth of man, but if she did, she's being very coy about it."

"Why would she create a race of men and then almost ignore them?" asked Namdarin.

"Perhaps she is a goddess to the elves, they were here before men."

"Then why create man, by doing that she has sealed the fate of the elves, they are dying out, they have few children, though they do have considerably longer lives than ours, they still don't breed fast enough to replace their losses, not something that can ever be said about men." Said Kern.

"If she is a god to the elves, then her power from them is failing, maybe once they are all gone she can switch her 'allegiance' to men."

"I don't think so." Said Kern, "I've know of her for many years, and though her temples are small, almost crude to some peoples eyes, her people are very devoted to her. None of her people are of the elven race. There is nothing of elven lore in her teachings anywhere that I can remember."

"I still feel she is playing some form of double game with us, something so subtle that we have almost no chance of seeing it." Granger grumbled, shaking his head slowly from side to side.

"The god's do indeed work in strange ways sometimes, they play their own games and have their own set of rules, rules more flexible than we could ever work to." Said Kern, as he turned his eyes back to the twisting tunnel that they were following. It lead steadily downwards, and Kern was fairly sure that it still tended eastwards, though his sense of direction was becoming more uncertain with every passing hour, even he needed to see the sun now and again to reaffirm his location instinct. Before long he saw a light ahead, it was soft at first, but soon overcame the light from Grangers staff, he stopped and waited for Jangor to catch up.

"What is the problem?" Asked the ex-captain.

"I don't want to blunder into all that light, at least not unprepared as we are now."

"Agreed. Namdarin get your bow, Stergin, you go too. You

three check out this light, the rest will wait here, Go quietly."

The three set off, Kern his sword at the ready, Namdarin the huge bow strung and an arrow set to the string, Stergin his sword swaying gently in his hand, creeping slowly towards the light, came upon a huge boulder that stuck out into the tunnel, almost blocking it, beyond this the light was intense, it seemed to be coming from everywhere. The three waited a minute or two, until their eyes had become accustomed to the new intensity, then they stepped carefully around the boulder, into a huge cave, with a high ceiling, no stalactites or stalagmites were visible, but a different sort of rock formation was clearly the source of all the light in the cave. Six huge pillars, of a crystal that looked like quartz, reached down from the roof and carried on down through the floor, some of the individual crystals in the columns were at least twenty feet tall and five feet across, with the typical hexagonal cross-section of quartz, each one shone with an internal light, a light that seemed to be scattered off the internal fracture planes within the crystals, a captivatingly beautiful sight.

"I wonder where all that light comes from?" Asked Stergin.

"Looking at the scattering, there is little on the roof, and a lot on the floor, so it probably comes down from above, perhaps these pillars extend all the way to the surface, and their tops are currently in sunlight." Said Kern.

"They are beautiful." Said Namdarin, unable to take his eyes away from the slowly changing light, it seemed to fade, then grow, in a pattern that bore no relation to time. The changes were small, the brightness of each pillar only changing a little, and they were all changing at the same time and rate. "Could the changes be clouds passing over the sun above?"

"It's possible, but look here." Said Kern, pointing at a flatter section of wall between two of the brightest pillars. The wall was covered with drawings and paintings, of animals and hunters, of stars and ships, they were all mixed up, some painted on top of others, in some places it was almost impossible to tell exactly what was being depicted, some of the drawings were readable but very stylised, stick figures and deer shown only by the antlers, the rest of its body just a few vague lines.

"What are they?" Asked Stergin, the other two just gave him a look that said, 'Did you really ask that?'

"I meant, what do they mean?"

"Who can tell, they could have been here thousands of years, this could be millennia of religious art work, or a hundred years of someone's doodling." Said Kern, "I see no altar, but that doesn't mean that this wasn't a place of religious significance to someone."

"Why 'wasn't'? It could still be a place of worship for someone."

"I don't see any recent signs, but that doesn't mean that no one comes here anymore, I'll go and get the others." Kern walk back the way they had come, leaving the two to marvel at the light and the paintings. Very soon they were all gathered in front of the painted wall, Granger was more vocal than the others, he insisted on pointing out every little part of the pictures that he deciphered, much to the annoyance of the others, who wanted to find the images for themselves.

"Granger." Asked Jangor. "Any idea who painted all these?"

"No, not really, but we cannot be far from the surface now, this must have been a regular meeting place for the people who drew these. I can't make any sense of these ships, they look like ships, but there is no reference to water, or any real sails. Very strange."

"Perhaps their ships didn't sail on water, or use wind for motion." Said Mander.

"Don't be ridiculous." Said Andel. "All ships sail on water, and have sails, any fool knows that."

"And any fool knows it's dark in a cave, but look around, fool."

"You know what I mean, this is a special place and a special case."

"Maybe their ships were a special case as well."

"Where else could they sail then, if not on water?"

"I don't know, maybe on land, like a carriage, that doesn't need a horse."

"But they would need wheels like a carriage, these pictures have no wheels, and no roads."

"If they didn't use wheels they wouldn't need roads, they could just sail to where ever they wanted to go."

"Without wheels and roads, they would be sailing in the sky like birds, that's just plain stupid."

"Who are you calling stupid!" shouted Mander his hand dropping to the sword at his side.

"Who else. Flying carriages indeed!" Andel's hand was on his sword hilt in an instant.

"Stop it you two." Yelled Granger, both looked at the old man with shock on their faces, it was usually Jangor that interrupted them at this point. "You may actually have been getting somewhere, an almost intellectual discussion, not something I would have expected from you two, but it was happening, until you descended to your usual name calling." He heaved a huge sigh, "I have heard of flying carriages, but these are old tales, and perhaps not true, but these pictures do cast a different light on the stories, maybe they did exist. That would be a much better way to travel, rather than walking on two feet, or borrowing four from a horse. Would you rather ride a horse or fly? You choose." He turned his back on them, and went back to his studies of the pictures.

"Fly." Said Mander.

"Ride." Said Andel.

Jangor threw up his arms in disgust, "You two just wont ever agree on anything, will you?" They both shook their heads. "Except that. Kern find us the way out of here, we cannot stay here for ever, much as some would want to." Kern checked all around the cave, and found three exits, carefully he examined each one in turn. Returning to Jangor he said, "I'm not sure, all the exits show some traffic, I can't tell how old the tracks are, I cannot decide which one is the way out, it could be any."

"But they all must go somewhere, right?"

"Yes, but where, we want to get out of this mountain, we don't want to go on a sightseeing trip through the bowels of the earth. I mean, they could lead to more caves with drawings, or old meeting places, or even the place where the people who used to use this place lived, or live."

"If the path leads to the place where they lived, then it should logically lead on from there to the outside, logically the place where they worship their gods or whatever, should be further into the mountain, than where they live. Extending that logic a little, every one of the paths could reach eventually to the outside. Perhaps one of the others can give us a clue."

"Granger." He called. "Can you help us we have a bit of a problem."

"What is it?" Was the irritated reply.

"Kern isn't sure which is the best way out. Can you shed any light on the exits?"

"There is plenty of light around here as it is, why would you want more?"

"What with those two squabbling all the time, the last thing I need is to be lost inside a mountain with a sarcastic wizard. Can you tell us which is the quickest way out of here? Kern says that all the passages have signs of many people using them, we cannot tell which one to use."

"I'll have a look." Granger went to each exit in turn, carrying a candle he had just lit, he muttered a few words as he stood in the mouth of each. Finally he blew out the candle and declared, "It's the middle one."

"Sometimes magic does have it's uses." Said Crathen.

"Magic," Snorted Granger, "I used the flame of the candle to measure airflow in the tunnels, in the left hand one the air was blowing out of this chamber, in the right hand one, there was very little movement, in the centre on the air was blowing into this chamber. These tunnels will act much like a chimney, air drawn in at the bottom and pulled out at the top. Seeing as we want to find an exit low down on the mountain then we must walk into the air currents, simple logic, no magic at all."

"But is there any way your logic could be wrong?" Asked Crathen.

"Oh yes, if the path we take goes down to the bottom of an underground waterfall, then the falling cold water would generate a large updraft, but that is very unlikely, it would have to be a long way off for us not to hear it."

"So you're not certain." Sneered Crathen.

"No," Granger shook his head slowly, "but then I am equally uncertain that the sun will rise tomorrow."

"The sun always rises."

"You mean the sun has always risen so far, who can predict

what the morning will bring, perhaps you rely too much on your own magic." Granger turned away, looked at the paintings one more time, and sighed before mounting his horse.

Kern lead them into the centre path, Granger close behind him, a few yards from the cavern a turn in the tunnel blocked out all the light, and Granger lit his staff again. Namdarin positioned himself behind Jayanne again, now that she knew why, she would look back occasionally and smile at him. Crathen was directly in front of Jayanne, he glanced back occasionally as well but there were no smiles on his face, only a look longing, an urgent lust that filled his eyes. Soon the roof of the tunnel dropped so that they had to walk alongside the horses, Namdarin could trust Arndrol to do as he was told, even steeply twisting downwards path. The presence of so many people and horses kept the grey calm, he needed no hand to sooth him, so Namdarin was free to walk alongside Jayanne again. Jayanne was happy of the company, even though they spoke little, if at all, Crathen still glanced backwards occasionally but Namdarins position at her side only made him angry, and he didn't want Namdarin to know how he felt, somehow he needed to keep his emotions hidden for a while longer. 'Soon,' he thought, 'soon, she'll understand how I feel, and she'll want me, not that old man.' For this was how he viewed Namdarin, an old man, one foot in the grave, far to old for the young Jayanne, who had obviously been tricked into liking him by his experienced tongue, she would see through the tricks soon enough, and he would be there to pick up the pieces, he would even help her break the spell the Namdarin had over her. He wasn't sure how he was going to do that, but was certain that the chance would come his way, after all it was only right that she should belong to Crathen, he thought that he was just what she needed, he was a little amazed that she had resisted his obvious charms for so long, the only reason that he could come up with was a magic of some sort, a love potion, or a spell of some sort. Crathen spent the quiet times of the journey planning how he was going to make Jayanne his own. Crathen reverie was suddenly disturbed by a loud snort from Arndrol, who stamped his fore hooves with a noise that echoed long and harshly in the confined space, Namdarin turned to look back at the agitated horse, who snorted and stamped again.

"What's wrong with that horse?" Demanded Jangor.

"Something's upset him." Said Namdarin.

"Any idea what?"

"I'll try and find out." Namdarin walked back to his horse, and placed a calming hand on his flank, which twitched and flickered as if trying to shake off a fly, Namdarin leant against his old friends flank and whispered softly, words that meant nothing, more sound than verbal communication. Slowly he reached out with his mind to make contact with the horse and the herd consciousness that the horse was part of. With an almost impossible ease the contact was made, every time he tried this it became easier. 'Must be practice, as with everything else.' He thought, this thought shredded the connection, Namdarin shook his head and started again. The feeling of the horses was one of creeping terror, something dark and hidden. A quiet killer in the night, stirred by an unwary foot. The images made little sense to Namdarin, they seemed very confused, perspective and distance were totally wrong, as Namdarin tried to get more from the images, the horses all started to become disturbed, they didn't like to focus so intently on their own fears, for them fear is something that people usually deal with for them, fire chases off most of the things that horses are afraid of, but only when fire has people with it, at other times fire is one of their greatest fears, it is one of the things that can run faster than they can. By this time most of the riders were holding tightly onto their reins, trying desperately to control the agitated horses.

"Namdarin, stop. What ever you are doing is only making things worse."

Namdarin slowly pulled his thought away from the fears that

was now gripping all the horses, he sent calming images of open pastures and sunlit meadows. Immediately the horses began to calm down.

"Well?" Demanded Jangor, with his arm around his horses neck.

"I can't make much sense of whatever it is. It's a killer of horses, it makes no noise, and is very," he paused for a while grasping for a word that would fit the feeling of the horses, "short, no, close to the ground, I'm making no more sense than they are. Their fear is real, and something has triggered it." He shrugged.

"Ideas?" Asked Jangor loudly. The response was more shrugs, until Stergin spoke softly, almost diffidently.

"Snake?" All eyes turned to him.

"Have I said something stupid?" He asked.

"I think not." Said Granger, "I believe that the images that Namdarin was trying to describe could easily be the way that horses would see snakes. But what has set off that fear here."

"Whatever it was, I am now frightened of snakes." Said Mander looking carefully around, before reaching into his saddlebag for one of the torches that he kept there.

"Kern, any signs of snakes?" Asked Jangor.

"Now you mention it, I thought that the curved ruts were caused by running water flowing down here occasionally, but in light of new information provided by our four legged friends, I believe that there is at least one, quite large ophidian down here somewhere."

"What do you mean by large?"

"Maybe two feet."

"That's not a big snake." Said Andel, Jangor knew, and dreaded what Kern was to say next.

"Across. More light please." The last was aimed with a glance at Granger, who obligingly increased the light from his staff.

"Is that enough?"

"Perhaps too much, but it will do for now."

"What do you see?" Asked Stergin.

"Two feet." Muttered Andel. "That could be ten or fifteen feet long."

"Two feet." Murmured Mander, "It could swallow something four feet across, it could eat a horse."

"Or a man." Replied Andel.

"Gods." Whispered Mander.

"Quiet, you two." Said Jangor. "What do you see?"

"Definitely, at least one, perhaps two, big ones and some smaller ones as well."

"Carry on, slow and careful."

"How can snakes live down here, it's far too cold and they are all cold blooded?" Asked Andel of no-one in particular.

"Haven't you noticed that it has been getting steadily warmer for the last hour, for some reason as we go deeper it gets hotter, perhaps there is a volcanic vent down here, like Granger's cave." Said Mander.

"There are just far too many things living in this cave system, it should be empty and barren, I've seen less life in some forests."

"How many caves have you traveled through?"

"Well, this is my first."

"So, you actually have no experience of caves and the life that inhabits them, you just believe that there is no sunlight down here, so nothing can grow?"

"Well, yes I suppose so."

"It is as much a surprise to me that there is so much living down here, but on the other hand, life seems to find a way any where at all. Deserts, icy wastelands, it matters not to life, something will live, and thrive in almost every environment."

"I suppose so, but that is no excuse for snakes. Why not something small and furry, with whiskers and a tail, why does it have to be snakes?"

"Perhaps there is something small and furry, with whiskers and a tail, perhaps that is what the snake eats, when it can't get something bigger."

"Something like us, you mean?"

"That's the sort of idea."

"Can you two can the chatter, some snakes can hear sounds, and our first warning is likely to be the sound of it moving across the sand, but we'll miss that because of your babbling." Jangor interrupted.

"Snakes with ears, it gets worse." Mumbled Mander, before lapsing into a watchful silence. The others were equally as alert as Mander, Jayanne had her axe in her hand, swinging slowly in time with her stride, Namdarin had his bow strung and loaded, the sword of Xeron hitched high in its baldrick, ready for a quick draw should the snake get too close for bow work, Stergin's slender sword was whistling softly to itself, as it snapped form side to side. Crathen couldn't make up his mind, on moment he was holding his bow, the next his sword. The only ones who seemed relaxed were Kern and Jangor, Kern because of his certainty in his own tracking abilities, he was sure that there was no snake of that size that could surprise him, and Jangor because he was always ready to draw his sword, and that was all he needed. Jangor couldn't help thinking that someone was working very hard against them, they were meeting just too many dangers while traveling, they had enough to deal with, Zandaars behind them, and ahead too. Weren't they enough danger for anyone. Bemoaning his fate would get him exactly nowhere, he knew that, but it was hard to avoid the impression that the risks were getting ever bigger, with every step they took, perhaps he should turn round and pick another path, not another path through this cave, but another path through his life, maybe it was time to cut his loses and move on. How was Namdarin different from Morndragon? Both seem intent on getting him and his friends killed. One in a fight over a few scrawny cows, the other in a fight with a god. One crazy, the other stupid. What is the difference? He shook his head slowly, as if to rearrange the things inside. 'The difference, you old fool,' he thought 'is that one is right, the other so wrong as to be stupid. I'm stuck with the crazy one, and no honourable way to back out. Do you want to live forever?'

"No." He shouted, then looked at all the confused faces turned towards him. "Sorry. Just arguing with myself, please feel free to carry on."

"Was the outcome of the argument satisfactory?" Asked Namdarin.

"Only time will tell."

"I'm sorry if you have become ensnared in my problems, if you and yours wish to turn away from this path, I will understand."

"Can you read my thoughts?"

"No. But it's not exactly difficult to guess what is bothering you."

"I can see no way that I can turn away."

"Simple, just turn round and go back, a quick fight with some monks and you are free."

"I see no way I can turn away and live with myself. We are stuck on the same course, death or life are all that await us."

"Trust you to look on the gloomy side."

"There is a happy side to this?"

"Perhaps the Zandaars will listen to our arguments, see the error of their ways and fall on their swords."

"Your argument is the song of steel."

"Their swords, my sword, I care not which."

"It's not your sword, and it's not very likely."

"True, but a possibility none the less."

"Sometimes you amaze me, how can you be so carefree when a good percentage of the people in this world want you dead."

"Not just dead, slowly dead, and I disagree, most of the Zandaars know nothing about me yet, I still have the element of surprise in my favour."

"If the time comes when most do know about us, then we will be very dead, very soon."

"Do you want to live forever?"

"I asked myself that earlier, you heard the answer, it was no then, is no now, and will be no as long as I live."

"Let's hope that we both live a long time, I think that one of the secrets of living is knowing when to stop."

"What do you mean by that?"

"I think that some people don't know when to stop, I cannot see myself laying in bed being waited on hand and foot, being nothing but a burden to those around me, I couldn't do that. That is not the way I should die."

"How would you wish to die?"

"In battle is only way for a warrior to die, all the men in my line have died that way, at least all the ones that I knew."

"In battle is the best way for a warrior to die, but then most don't get their wish, unless they actively seek it. Is that what you are doing? Seeking for death? As befits a true warrior."

"No. Perhaps at the start, but I believe I have found something else to live for, or maybe something else to die for."

"Often the two are linked."

"Nothing in this life is ever simple."

"That, I believe, depends upon the type of person that one is, simple people live simple lives, the rest of us seem to fight every inch of the way, it is because we cannot accept the role that life has chosen for us, we have to go our own way, which only makes things more complicated, but also more interesting."

"For a soldier you are quite a philosopher."

"For an aristocrat you're quite a soldier."

"I have a tendency to learn things from those around me, my father taught me to use all the talent that I could find, he said that one day it could well save my life, he has been so right, so often recently."

"So I am just a talent to be used up then discarded?"

"I don't feel that I could ever treat anyone like that, and I can't believe that you would think so of me."

"That was in the days before your oath, I sometimes think that you will consider anything at all disposable if it suited your cause."

"No. I don't think that I could ever be like that, to act that way would make me no better than the damned Zandaars."

"But you are willing to act just like them."

"Only against them, I try to speak a language that they can understand."

"But they never survive the conversation, and cannot learn anything from it."

"We cannot afford for them to learn anything about us, I can feel them breathing down my neck, even though they know almost nothing of me."

"How close are they, when you feel them?"

"I'm not sure, it is just a vague feeling that they are closing in or reaching for me."

"Reaching?"

"Like a long arm is stretching out to grab the back of my neck, sometimes I even look round for it."

"Right now?"

"No. I cannot feel anything from them at all. Here in these caves the horses can't even feel the others, which is probably why they don't really like caves, they don't like to be out of touch with the rest of the herd."

"They always get very restive as they go underground."

"Perhaps the contact slowly fades, and they don't like it."

"Could be."

The conversation lapsed into silence, as the men returned to their own thoughts.

CHAPTER TWENTY FOUR

    Deeper and deeper into the darkness they walked, leading horses that couldn't be ridden, the roof was far too low in patches and far too dangerous in others. Alverana confidently leading the way, his small torch picking out the tracks they were following, Kevana bringing up the rear, his own torch shedding little more light than was needed to be sure that no-one had been left behind.

    "Can someone tell me if my eyes are open?" Said Apostana from the middle of the line, his question had no real target, it was merely an attempt to lift the depression caused by the unending blackness.

"Perhaps I am deaf as well." He said when the first question remained unanswered for a short while.

"You can't be deaf, you make too much noise." Replied Petrovana.

"Why should him making noise mean that he isn't deaf?" Demanded Fabrana.

"Deaf people are always quiet."

"No they aren't, they only sound quiet to themselves."

"That's ridiculous. There was a deaf man lived in the town I grew up in, he was the quietest man I have ever known, he moved with less noise than Alverana, and his voice was a soft as a whisper. When ever he was around the room took on the aspects of a church, voices dropped to reverent mutterings, people would apologise for any sudden loud noise, and almost any noise seemed loud."

"I knew a man who was nearly struck by lightening, his hearing was taken away by the noise, and ever after, he always shouted at everyone, he stamped his feet and was exceptionally clumsy, always knocking things over, any place that he was always turned in the busiest, loudest tavern that you have ever heard." Snorted Fabrana.

Gorgana laughed heartily.

"What is so funny?" Asked Petrovana, unseen in the darkness a cold hand strayed to a knife hilt.

"Yes, what's funny?" Demanded Fabrana, black gloved hand resting softly on black bound sword hilt, in the inky blackness that surrounded them all.

"You both have met a single deaf person and come to a generalised view of how deaf people are, two totally opposite points of view. Viewpoints that you are probably willing to fight to defend." The guilty rustling of fast moving hands caused him to laugh even louder.

"Are you saying that we are both stupid?" Asked Fabrana, his voice cold and quiet. Gorgana knew that the hands had returned to the weapons even though there was no sound to reveal the movements.

"No." The amusement was obvious for all. "I am just amazed how such convictions can be born. The more I think about it the clearer it becomes, I believe that the 'quiet' deaf man had never be able to hear. He was feeling the vibration of his voice in his head, a whisper produces a lot of internal vibration but little noise, for him this was the loudest sound he could make, the 'loud' deaf man on the other hand, had been able to hear, his ears were destroyed by the thunderclap, or very nearly destroyed, he could probably hear a little, and thought that he was speaking normally, and failed to notice the noise of things falling over."

"So the 'quiet' deaf man thought he was being loud." Said Petrovana.

"And the 'loud' deaf man thought he was being quiet." Said Fabrana.

"And both were wrong, as were you to jump to the conclusion that all deaf people were the same. A priceless piece of confusion." Gorgana laughed harder than ever.

"There is another possibility." Said Briana.

"Which is?" Asked Gorgana.

"Everything you have said is logical, but pure conjecture none the less, you could be wrong as well."

"This too is true." Gorgana laughed even harder, his mirth was so loud that the horses were beginning to get frightened.

"Does this discussion serve any purpose?" Asked Worandana.

"None at all, it merely passes the time in a slightly less boring manner than silence." Replied Gorgana, "A little light debate is good for the soul."

"A little light would certainly be good for our sanity, let ours souls look to themselves." Said Petrovana.

"We have a limited supply of torches, they must be conserved until we are in desperate need." Was Kevana's gentle response, he was fully aware of the effect that continuous darkness can have on men, especially those who aren't used to it. He handed his torch to Petrovana saying, "You take the last place in the line, I'll move forwards a little where it is darker. Does that make you feel better?"

"I think so." Replied the younger man, a little uncertainly.

"Great." Said Fabrana, "Any one that sneaks up behind us will find him and his light first, then we will get some warning."

"Suddenly I don't feel too good again."

"What are you worrying about? The enemy is ahead of us, they couldn't get behind us."

"This place is a rabbit warren, there are tunnels everywhere, they could easily get behind us, then I would be the first to die."

"That is a bad thing how?" Asked Fabrana.

"Be quiet you two, if the enemy have got behind us they are sitting in the dark waiting for us to start killing each other, and make their task so much easier." Said Kevana.

"Are your men always this combative?" Asked Worandana.

"I like them this way, they react fast and are always ready, they have a habit of staying alive, no matter how chance throws the dice against them."

"You believe that luck keeps them alive?"

"Of course, in our line of work, much depends on the luck of the moment, or the instant trained response, and the luck that it is the right one."

"Don't you believe that Zandaar looks after his own?"

"I have seen too many good men die," snorted Kevana, "to believe that Zandaar pays any particular attention to the foot soldiers of his war."

"What about the higher ranks, like ourselves?"

"I have never felt Zandaar breathing down my neck and throwing off the enemies aim, I prefer to rely on my own ability to duck when the arrows come flying my way. A tree makes a better shield than my belief in Zandaar."

"Again you risk charges of heresy."

Kevana stared hard in the eyes of his old friend, for a long moment, then said softly. "Fabrana stick an arrow in this old fool." Fabrana moved with instant obedience, the arrow flowed from the quiver to the bowstring with a movement that spoke of years of practise, the string creaked softly in the sudden silence as it was drawn towards the man's mouth.

"Hold." Shouted Kevana. Fabrana had the string kissed to his lips, the merest moment away from release, though Kevana had not taken his eyes from his old friend's, he knew exactly how long it took Fabrana to ready an arrow.

"Don't you trust Zandaar to protect you?" He asked quietly. "Your hand is on a lightening bolt in your pocket, detonation of which in this confined space would probably kill more than the archer. Though I do believe that the arrow is going to be quicker than you."

"Actually chance chose flame, which would certainly have been a bad move in these close quarters."

"You may think I risk charges heresy, but I live in the real world and wish to continue doing so, Zandaar is a busy god, he has much to look after, I prefer not to bother him with protecting my life, and you are the same, as your flame testifies, however, I make no pretense of trusting Zandaar to protect me, and make that very clear in all my dealings with people, that way there is less chance of a misunderstanding." He turned to Fabrana. "Stand down, soldier." Fabrana breathed out slowly and relaxed the tension on the bowstring, he returned the arrow to the quiver, nodded to his commander and turned away.

"Can we be a little more careful with charges of heresy please?" Asked Kevana.

"Sure." Said Worandana, turning away and waiting for Alverana to start the line moving again.

"Anything changing up there?" Asked Kevana. Alverana merely shook his head, a small movement that was visible in the light of the torch he was holding high above his head. The line started moving at a slow but steady pace, Alverana being very careful about checking ahead, he didn't want to walk into an ambush, though he really didn't think it was likely that the ones they were following would set such a thing, his feeling was that they merely wanted to keep ahead of the chase, and he had long learned to trust his feelings, up to a point, the point where his life didn't depend on a feeling of others intentions. Slowly they proceeded downwards, deeper into the darkness of the cave, though the darkness itself was unchanged, except by the temporary light that they brought to the passageways, brief moments of illumination, accompanied by the small sounds of people and animals. The overall effect on the cave system was negligible, nothing the people could do would have any major effect here, and this feeling wasn't lost on them, the perpetual darkness of the place made them feel very small, and kept their voices down to the absolute minimum, mere mutterings in pitch, mumblings in the dark. As the quietness increased it became self enforcing, gradually making the people quieter and the noise of the cave louder, until the cave appeared to have a life of its own, a deep throbbing not unlike a heartbeat, huge and slow, deep and sorrowful, was the pulse of the depths, like a huge slow drum, though in another way unlike a drum. The sound didn't have the beat of a drum, it was more like a deep breathing, but so powerful that the change from in to out was like a beat of a drum.

"What is that noise?" Asked Petrovana, of no-one in particular, he was voicing a question they all had in their minds.

"It certainly has a peculiar resonance." Said Gorgana. "I've never heard its like before."

"Nor I." Said Apostana.

"I have heard something a little like it." Said Kirukana. "There was a bell in the town where I grew up, when the wind was in the right direction it use to sing softly, not the same sound it made when struck, but a soft almost breath like noise, it used to breath all night sometimes. Some people used to say it was a demon trapped in the bell, others that it was the spirit of an ancient monk, who had been killed for preaching against the gods of the time. I know it was just the wind, I once made it stop breathing by touching the edge of the bell with my hand, under the lightest of touches I could feel it vibrating but it didn't ring enough to be heard."

"Are you saying there is a huge bell somewhere near?"

"No, but it certainly sounds a little like that bell, a pulse that isn't a heart or a drum."

"If it is only bell then it is nothing to worry about."

"Very true." Said Gorgana. "If it is a bell, if it is not a bell, then it must be something else, then it could be something to worry about."

"What do you mean?" Asked Petrovana.

"Have you seen the small green snake from the plains to the south, it lives in farm land usually?"

"Yes, what of it?"

"Have you seen the small green snake, with the pointed nose and the bright green stripe along its back, that lives in the swamps to the east?"

"No, but I have been warned about that one."

"They are like the bell that isn't a bell, both would escape from your approach if they could, both will hide from you when they can, both will bite you if you step on them, but only one will kill you with that bite. Just because it looks like a small green snake doesn't mean it is harmless, just because it sounds like a bell doesn't mean it can't hurt you."

"You talk in riddles, I know what you mean, but you make it seem so trivial with all this talk." Said Petrovana.

"You were the one that was worried about the noise first."

"No. I was just the first to say something about it."

Their progress continued at the same pace despite the sound from below, though as their caution had increased with the tension in the air caused by the sound, their pace slowed somewhat, this started to irritate Kevana, more than the noise. He didn't care about the possible threat of the sound, he only wanted to recover the sword and kill those carrying it, and do it quickly.

The gloom of the downward march only deepened, and depression took the mood of all the men, Kevana was suffering the most, it seemed to him that at every turn something more went wrong, almost as if the gods themselves were plotting against him. Despite his earlier protestations he was beginning to think that Zandaar could at least send him some aid, and improve his luck just enough to give him a chance of getting the blade. His frustration was starting to get the better of him, he kept drawing his sword at the tiniest of noises and making the others jump to face the new danger, a danger that wasn't there.

"Kevana, can you please calm down a little, we will catch them when we catch them, no amount of panic in the mean time is going to get us there any quicker." Said Worandana.

"I know that, but I can't help feeling that they are getting away from us. Their tracks aren't getting any fresher, they could even be dead by now, taken by some force in these caves. If they are we aren't likely to find the sword."

"What ever their fate, we will track the sword until we find it. It is only a matter of time and patience."

"Somehow I feel that time is something we don't have much of, I can feel it running away, like sand through the fingers. We must hurry or we will be lost."

"We could try another search, we are closer than before so it should be easier."

"Even I know that these rocks will make a mental search very difficult and exceptionally unreliable, even dangerous to try, there is life down here that could perhaps snare the searching mind and never release it."

"I thought you weren't afraid of anything?"

"I believe I have faced death often enough to prove my bravery, but the thought of being trapped in a rock or some such is just unbearable to me."

"We are very different then, I would struggle to face a swordsman like yourself, but a mental challenge I would never run from."

"Different, but the same, each to his own field, you wish to try a search in this place?"

"If it will allay your fears as to the criminals escape."

"Do it. Alverana stop. Our clerical brethren are going to attempt something that I wouldn't dare."

"Which is?"

"Mental search for the sword."

"In here?"

"Yes, Worandana thinks they can do it, and believes himself to be equal to any challenge that might come his way."

The two groups separated and gathered around their individual, and individualistic leaders. There were some quiet words spoken in both camps, though it was only stern looks from Worandana that kept the clerics in line, though it hadn't been his idea for him to be the centre of the search, Kevana had given him no way of avoiding it without some serious loss of credibility.

"This has to be very dangerous in this cave system, the density of the rock itself is going to resist our search, and those luminous life forms we met earlier could cause other problems, Kevana's fear of imprisonment in solid rock is a definite possibility." Said Gorgana.

"I am fully aware of the risks, and they will be mine alone, I will make this search alone, I will expect each of you to give me enough energy, but I want no piggy back consciousnesses, no-one tags along, is that very clear?" Demanded Worandana. The clerics all nodded or spoke their assent.

"I wouldn't risk that sort of thing if my life depended on it." Said Apostana.

"Your life could depend on this, we need to know what is ahead." Muttered Worandana. "Prepare for energy cycle, I want you all to give the best you have." He continued in a louder voice.

In the other group there was as much consternation. Kevana spoke quietly. "Get a fire going, they are going to need rest and food when this is over."

"I think they are mad to try that sort of thing in here." Said Petrovana.

"I think you were more than a little unwise to goad him into this rash course." Said Alverana staring hard into Kevana's eyes.

"He was irritating me."

"That is a good enough reason to alienate one of our best allies. If he fails or is harmed the already shaky coherence of this group will be totally destroyed." Kevana stared open mouthed at Alverana as he turned away, such insight was utterly unexpected, and the forcefulness of the words something unheard of, from the soft spoken man. Still a fire was kindled in moments, its cheery flames chasing off the gloom of the cavern, the shadows leaping in yellows and reds, casting strange looks upon the faces of the clerics as they sat on a circle, all facing inwards except for Worandana, who was facing in the direction of the search.

Worandana sat with his head bowed waiting for his clerics to prepare themselves, there was no visible signal of readiness, they all sensed each other, and each others state of readiness, together they built their awareness into a solid unit, and as a unit they reached out and touch hands, each hand clasp a gentle melding of skin on skin, mind on mind. Worandana started the energy surge with a huge blast of his own, he was not for wasting time building slowly, he knew the capabilities of those in the circle, and he knew they could cope with a rapidly building energy pulse, he felt it go around the circle, until it came back to him, almost twice as powerful as he started it, passing it on after a brief moment he added some more of himself to it, just as all the others had done, and round it goes again. Round and round the pulse went, growing bigger and hotter with every revolution. It seemed to reach a maximum, a limit, but Worandana wanted no limits on this search, he wanted it all, so he threw another massive jolt into the pulse on his next turn, and waited expectantly for it to come around again, indeed it came back at a level that he had never experienced before, he almost jumped with the intensity of it, perhaps it was the passion of the moment, but his friends had exceeded is expectations, next time round he lifted his head opened his eyes and triggered the launch. Riding out from the confines of his mind he leapt through space, through rock and void, water and air, reaching for a sword he had only ever heard of, no written records of it exist, only secret word of mouth, he was looking for a strange sword, one which almost had a life of it's own. By the time the next surge of power came to him from the circle he was out of the mountain in open air, the sun was shinning on the bracken and sparkling in a waterfall, but these momentary distractions he could not afford, the power drain was intense, pushing back into the mountain was hard, like swimming through molasses, focusing on the sword was very difficult, like trying to see in utter darkness a black cat, but he found it, it was lit with a strange fire, a light that came from within, the pommel stone was glowing with a dark radiance, hot purple light flowed from it, a cool blue light also filled the cave where the sword was, the gentle lights of people were there as well, in all the colours that people carry in this plain of existence, there was another thing with the group, it was only visible by absence, it was an absence of light so deep, so dark that it showed against the dark background as a darker patch, a hot blue human shape was carrying it. It was like nothing he had ever seen in this sort of search before, he tried to touch the blackness, but drew back before contact, he could feel it sucking in energy, energy in all the bands where it existed, he felt that it would have swallowed him whole. He touched the sword instead, felt a fear and an eagerness for battle, touched the blue light, which came from a staff of wood, and felt something very similar, though there was less eagerness in that one. The others were merely ordinary people, not worth the attention considering the energy being expended to keep him here, as he pulled back easing towards his own form, some distance away, he felt something else. There was cold green radiance, a long green light that seemed to stretch a long way, its intelligence seemed strange, it looked like a lower animal but carried far too much energy for such a thing. He touched it, and felt it's cold heart, felt its hunger, felt it's frustrated rage, he was amazed by the intensity of its emotion. As he looked into it, it also looked into him, it turned and tracked him as he retreated. The snake followed the white hot firefly that had no existence in the real world but in the astral spectrum it was a meal the like of which it had never sensed. Worandana returned through the thickening stuff of rock and soil and water until he reached his own body, settled his consciousness inside where it belonged and lowered his head, the circle broke, the energy flow stopped and the clerics staggered where they sat, Apostana fell face first into the circle, asleep before his head hit the floor, the others weren't in much better state, for that had indeed given their all to the search.

"I found it." Mumbled Worandana.

"Where?" Asked Kevana.

"They are still in the caves, though they are getting close to the outside, the sun is shinning by the way."

"I care nothing of the weather, how far away are they?"

"They are not far in distance only a few miles, but the path is most confused, it turns many times, they are perhaps a day ahead of us."

"So we keep pace with them?"

"Yes. They are carrying some other strange weapons, one

man has a staff of wood that glows with a cold blue fire, another has a weapon that sucks energy out of the world, it is so black that it is only visible by occlusion of light behind it."

"The staff belongs to the wizard Granger, but the blackness I know nothing of."

"There is something else."

"What?"

"Another life down here, a cold and hungry life, I have never felt hunger so intense, I think it is a snake, but such a snake."

"What do you mean?"

"It must be tens of feet long, and far more intelligent than a snake has any right to be, I fear it wishes to eat them all, and then us."

"How can it know of us?"

"When I touched it, it knew me."

"How can that be?"

"Who knows, but it did, without a doubt, it turned towards me as I left. It knows we are coming, and it waits."

"What can we do about it?"

"I don't know but I feel we will have to face it before we can get out of this cave system."

"But they will have to face it first?"

"And very soon."

"If it kills them will we be able to find the sword, and the other weapons?"

"The sword will be no real problem, it has a life of its own, the others are something else, I think the wizard will most likely drain his staff completely before he dies, and the black one is going to be hard to find even if one knows where to look."

"Well, the sword is the only one that really matters. Rest now and we will continue the chase as soon as you are able." He waved Petrovana to bring over the soup that had been made, and the clerics greedily ate, for their efforts had seriously depleted their energy reserves. Kevana paced pack and forth waiting for the clerics to rest enough to continue, all the time thinking about the sword getting further and further away with every moment that past.

"Relax," Said Alverana, "pacing isn't going to catch them any quicker, and we cannot proceed until our friends have recovered from their search."

"We are close, so close I can almost taste their blood."

"You are taking this far too personally, they probably aren't even aware of the thing they carry."

"No. They are aware, and they have plans for it."

"What plans can they have?"

"Why would Zandaar set a team the size of ours to guard a sword that is buried under a killer tree that no-one can reach?"

"I never really thought about it, I just looked on it as an honour guard duty, a reward for good service, more a ceremonial duty than anything else."

"On the surface yes, but why has this duty always gone to experienced and skilled combat units, and always the whole team transferred in at one time? There is something really important about that damned sword, and I think it is a major threat to Zandaar himself."

"Who or what could threaten a god? It is after all in the hands of a mortal man."

"If this sword is a weapon of a god, then a man could conceivably use it to kill a god."

"So we are set as watchdogs to snatch the thing if someone takes it?"

"No, and yes. The watchdog is the mystic, he's placed close, close enough to feel when the guardian dies, he warns us, and we race in to steal the sword from the thieves."

"But we were delayed by the snow and the thieves managed to get a good enough start on us, a start we haven't yet overcome."

"Yet. When we do they will pay with blood and pain, they have killed enough of my team, and made us look like fools, for that they will wish they had never been born."

"Worandana may be up for a little simple butchery, but anything more 'elaborate' he's not going to stand for."

"He'll stand just were I tell him to, have no fear."

"Any plans come to mind?"

"There is a woman in their party, fancy a little sport with that one?"

"What, while the rest of the survivors are forced to watch sort of thing?"

"Yes, you are getting the sort of idea."

"I'm sure you can find a taker or two for that, it has been a while for most of us."

"Then butcher her, and the others really slow."

"We don't have that much time, we need to get that damned sword back to Zandaar, so he can destroy it, or what ever he plans to do with a sword that can kill him."

Kevana let plans of torture run though his mind for a little while, but he knew in his heart that in a case of face to face combat there were unlikely to be any survivors, at least for whichever side lost. The woman is almost certain to die before she can be captured, she knows what capture can mean. Still he played with the idea of rape and torture, unlikely as it was, it amused him, and helped him to forget at least temporarily that torture and death are probably his fate if he returned to Zandaar without the sword. The more he thought about Zandaar and the sword the more he began to worry, another thought came suddenly amongst the general fears, 'What if Zandaar already knew that the sword was loose?' Then things could already have taken a bad turn, there would be another team on their way to find the sword and the first team, in fact it was very likely that the message that sent Kevana after the sword, also was passed on further to set the second team after the first. 'Perhaps there is even a third team?' Taking this line of logic even further, the first team are a small force of soldiers, if they don't show up quickly they have failed and the second team would be dispatched, the snow slowed their task to extent that any normal force would have been classed as overdue and probably dead. If a small force of soldiers fails then the second team should logically be clerics. 'Has the second team already arrived?' Worandana would be a logical leader for such a team of clerics. 'How long before the third team are sent?' The third team should be a mix of soldiers and clerics, such as we have now, but Kevana could think of no such team already in existence, unless knowledge of such a team was deliberately hidden from him. 'All this thinking is getting me nowhere, it's just making me angry, and it is pure conjecture anyway.' With this thought he decided to ask Worandana if he knew of any team of soldiers and clerics that could be better suited for this task, Worandana would know, it is very difficult to hide any sort of information from the old weasel, the mere act of concealment attracts his attention. Kevana realised that he had to talk to Worandana these issues have to be sorted out before they could carry on. Kevana couldn't bring himself to believe that his force was an expendable first attempt to capture a simple sword. Or that his friend Worandana had lied to him.

A few hours later the clerics had recovered from their exertions and were beginning to wake up. Kevana touched Worandana lightly on the shoulder and gestured for him to follow, which he did with a frown. Kevana walked slowly away from the main group, with a wave to Alverana, a wave that told the soldier there was no problem, just a little privacy required. Alverana nodded and set about cooking for the whole group.

"What is the problem?" Asked Worandana.

"I've been thinking."

"Not always a good sign."

Kevana frowned deeply.

"Sorry, carry on, what thoughts have obviously disturbed you."

"I've been thinking about the nature of my mission."

"Your particular mission as regards this damned sword or you mission in life?"

"The sword of course."

"And, what of it?"

Kevana paused for a moment trying to marshal his thoughts and questions, this was very important, it had to be done just right or he could alienate his only 'friend'.

"If you were a god, would you trust the recovery of an important weapon to a group of soldiers?"

Worandana raised his eyebrows in astonishment, a surprising question, not something he comes across often, he looked away so as to think clearly. After a moment or two he turned to look at

Kevana again.

"No. This is an important thing to Zandaar, he couldn't possibly give its recovery to only one small group of soldiers."

"So the soldiers fail, or are delayed long enough to appear to have failed, remembering that they are recovering something that Zandaar himself cannot recover, from a group who have taken it. What sort of group is next to try for this sword?"

Again Worandana thought for a few moments, not rushing something he now felt to be of importance to his friend.

"Clerics, a team that have proved their worth and their teamwork."

"A team such as yours?"

"Yes, my team would be adequate to the task."

"Is your team the one sent to replace me?"

"No. I was investigating the destruction of Mount Indran monastery, however I feel that there is another team that could be used in such a case, I have heard of a monk of skill akin to my own, however, he takes a more orthodox line, he would be a better choice as far as the council of Zandaar are concerned, he questions nothing that is already known, or has been decided by the council. He is waiting for a seat on the council, he wants the power and prestige that such will bring, not something that I want or that I will ever achieve."

"So this man and his group could be on our trail, tracking the sword and hoping to steal our prize?"

"Could be. Last I heard he was stationed in some obscure back water somewhere, he is called Stevrana, have you head of him?"

"Yes, I've heard of him, I met him once, a pompous ass as I

remember."

"Definitely, if you think that of him then you've met him."

"Is his team any good?"

"Yes, in the view of the council, he is the best there is."

"That statement begs a but."

"But, his knowledge though extensive is restricted to the dogma and dictate of religion and religious observance. Give him something like this to deal with and he will certainly fail, it is too far outside his experience."

"So if he is on my trail he will be falling behind?"

"Almost certainly."

"If he fails who will be in team three?"

"Team three would have to be a mix of soldiers and clerics, and task force size, I know of no such, and I believe that anything on that scale would have to be arranged at the time, not something to have standing around doing nothing waiting for someone to recover that sword, it could have been there for hundreds of years, perhaps even thousands, how long a history does your posting have?"

"The list goes back as far as memory, written records go back so far they are unreadable."

"So that station has been there, waiting for the sword to surface for a few hundred years at least?"

"I'd say so."

"This sword is of some serious importance, so much so that I would have thought that Zandaar would have found some way to get it himself. Where there any special instructions upon recovery."

"Yes, capture the sword, take it to Zandaarkoon and put it into the hand of Zandaar. A chance to meet our god face to face, not something that happens to most people."

"So the sword must be placed willingly in his hand?"

"Yes, is that important?"

"Sometimes, the power of these things can depend upon being given freely. If that is the case then this must be a thing of real power, and he wants it all, or perhaps he fears it to go to someone he doesn't control."

"Well what can we do about this potential team that may be following us?"

"I don't think there is anything we can do, but you should think that Stevrana is a favoured one of the council, and as such can probably call on far more forces than either of us, so he could quite easily have expanded his usual team of seven to include many soldiers as well. The council will have no problem backing him in this matter, they cannot lose, if he gets the sword then they have helped him, if he fails then despite their help he failed, his fault not theirs, a good no lose situation to be in."

"So we can only act as if we are the only group after this sword, until we have real evidence to the contrary."

"I believe that about sums up the situation, if this other team exists we can do nothing about them, other than offer our help if they show up."

"Let's get on with our task then, we have some thieves to catch."

The two joined the main group and started the journey again.

"What of this snake you found on the search?" Asked Kevana.

"It was huge, whether this was actual size or just astral size I have no real idea. Either way it's a monster of a snake, and I don't believe its entirely a snake, it feels like a higher intelligence, not the normal cold sort of mind that one would expect from a snake, this mind had an intensity that I haven't felt in anything other than a man."

"So what in all the hells is it?"

"I know not, it is snake shape, it has snake hunger, only on a larger scale, but it's mind is in some ways human, and it saw me, and looked into me, it probably knows as much about me as I know about it."

"Except that you are a simple man, and it is a complex animal. It saw you and knew that you are a man, you saw deeply into it, and still have no idea what you saw."

"Can we please stop belabouring the fact that it probably learned more from the encounter than I did? I am not perfect yet, I leave that sort of thing to the soldiers in this world. They seem to manage perfection in a matter of moments, it has taken me years of study to achieve this level of ineptitude."

"Sometimes you can be really touchy, I was merely saying."

"Well please stop saying."

Kevana turned to his own men and said. "Alverana, you take the lead, Petrovana you take the rear everyone else somewhere in the middle, I feel no need to specify any more than that, but if anyone feels like arguing, I'll be more than happy to oblige." He stared directly at Petrovana, as this would be the usual person to argue. Petrovana just shook his head and walked slowly to the back of the line. They walked as quickly as they dared in the cramped confines of the tunnel, Kevana was fully aware of the painfully slow progress that they were making, however, he still believed that they were actually going fast at this point than the ones they are pursuing, they were at least aware of the dangers ahead, the search had told them this much, the others however had no foreknowledge, so they would have to be much more cautious, there can be many hidden dangers in caves, this one was no exception, at least one huge snake lived here, and that was certainly danger enough. Kevana went over in his mind the dangers that were normal in caves, and that his team didn't have to worry about, rockslides, narrow places, waterfalls, rivers, all these things they didn't have to fear. Then another thought crossed his mind.

"Worandana, when you performed the search, did you look for all dangers, or just the sword, and living dangers?"

"I was looking for the sword, as you asked, I came upon the snake by pure chance, it was in the area and I felt its presence."

"So you didn't actually check out the path from here at all?"

"No. I targeted straight onto the sword, its influence is unmissable, in some ways it shines like a beacon."

"Alverana, caution please. We actually have no idea about dangers on this path Worandana didn't bother to check the tunnels." Alverana just nodded, but didn't slow down at all, he was quite confidant in his ability to see any dangerous place before it became a problem for those following him, all he had to do was keep following the tracks, the rocky floors did make this a problem but there were few turnings and whatever people do horses always leave a certain sort of trail behind them, unless someone is willing to shovel it up and carry it along with them, a thought of roses growing on the back of a horse flashed through his mind and he laughed out loud.

"What has made you laugh so suddenly?" Asked Gorgana.

"I just had a picture of roses growing out of the back or a horse."

"That could be amusing but please explain why you had that thought?"

Alverana explained briefly the line of reasoning that brought him the image.

"Even if they did that they would still leave a trail we could follow."

"How?" Asked Alverana.

"Just follow the smell of roses." They both laughed out loud this time.

"What has cheered you two up in this dismal place? Asked Fabrana.

The two just looked at him and laughed, then Gorgana explained it and Fabrana joined in with the general amusement. They progressed quite quickly until they arrived at a junction there were four exits from the small cave, Alverana was unsure which one to take, there were no tracks to follow, the floor was solid rock and even the iron shoes of the horses would leave no marks at a simple walking pace.

CHAPTER TWENTY FIVE

At this point the line of people suddenly stopped moving.

"What is the problem?" Called Jangor.

"These damned snake tracks are getting so confused I'm not sure which way they are going, there seem to be more and more of them."

"More snakes, or more tracks?"

"Yes."

"Which?"

"Either would have the same effect."

"You can't even guess which?"

"No." Kern shrugged, and turned setting off again along the narrowing passageway, it felt like the whole mountain was slowly sinking on them, as the walls came nearer and the ceiling sloped downwards. The light from Granger's staff threw harsh blue shadows everywhere, the path started to turn upwards, getting even closer to the roof, and the sand beneath their feet was replaced by sharp edged rocks. Kern called back over his shoulder, "No tracks at all now." The tension in the group rose quite quickly, until they were all twitching at the slightest sound, jumping at the merest touch. Arndrol started to get agitated, his ears were flicking around so fast that everyone could hear them crack as he shifted from listening to the front and listening to the rear. He started to stamp his fore hooves.

"Wake up everyone, Arndrol thinks that something is near, and he certainly hates snakes of any size at all."

"Even Mander is awake, I can hear his knees knocking from here." Joked Andel.

"I'm surprised you can hear anything over the chattering of your teeth." Was the attempted cheerful reply.

"That's not my teeth, it's the bones in my neck, they rattle like that when I'm trying to look both ways at once."

"Anyone would think these big brave soldiers are frightened." Said Stergin.

"Only someone who knew them." Said Crathen.

"Or someone who had met them." Said Jangor.

"Or someone who had seen them from afar." Said Stergin.

"We are not frightened." Said Mander.

"No," agreed Andel, "we're petrified, just because you are too stupid to know when to be afraid, is no reason to take it out on us."

A rock rolled slowly away from the wall to the left of Mander and Andel. Two hands flashed, two swords streaked through the air, shrieking defiance at the world, two bright yellow sparks lit up the cave to the instant that was their life, and a nine foot long snake was chopped into three equal pieces.

"Check the walls for loose rocks." Yelled Jangor, before the portions of snake had finished falling to the ground. As everyone started inspecting the walls more closely Arndrol sidled over to where the snake had dropped, and stamped the twitching pieces into bloody submission. A few loose rocks were found but none with any snakes hidden inside.

"Nothing quite like fear to keep one sharp." Said Granger.

"Fear is something we aren't exactly short of at the moment." Said Jangor, "I'm beginning to hate these damned caves."

"Beginning?" Asked Namdarin.

"It's just that they seem to go on forever, I get the feeling that we will never get out of here, do you know what I mean?"

"Yes. I hope that we get out soon, or I am sure that we will all go completely mad."

"Not for to go for some of us."

"Speak for yourself."

"I was."

Kern suddenly held his sword high above his head, and silence fell on the group, like a blanket that obliterated all sound, even the horses appeared to be holding their breath.

"What's wrong now?" Whispered Jangor.

"Everything," Was the soft reply. "I felt a sound, more like a pressure wave, like when someone slams the door on a well sealed room, only this one stopped all the air flow in this passageway, there is something moving nearby that blocks these ways completely."

"Ideas?"

"None of them good."

"Granger, how much power have you got stored in the staff? We may have to frighten the snake off."

"There has been a lot of drain recently and no time for a recharge," came the whispered answer, not the one that any wished to hear. "I fear my staff is almost empty, though there may be another way if it gets close enough."

"Say on."

"We have with us some weapons of great power, perhaps they could dissuade the snake from it's intended meal."

"I feel very little power in my sword." Said Namdarin, Jayanne merely nodded.

"They are weapons in their own right, my staff is only a conduit for power, if these can strike the snake, then they will steal its power, and energise themselves."

Jayanne looked sideways at the old man, Namdarin said in words what she said with her eyes, "That is awfully close to a big snake, far too close for my liking."

Jangor chuckled softly to himself, "Do you want to live forever?"

Namdarin shook his head.

"Kern." Said Jangor, "which way is the blockage, ahead or behind?"

"Not sure. Ahead I think, or it felt like that way when the air stopped."

"Namdarin, Jayanne to the front, Granger just behind them, keep the light low, a sudden flare may distract the snake enough for them to get in close, Crathen with Granger, keep that bow ready, arrows may cause a better distraction. People move like we have a plan." Jangor's orders were softly spoken, but with all the authority of his years as a commander of men. A hush descended, 'Quiet as a grave.' thought Mander, 'hope it's not going to be mine.' The only sounds were the shuffling of feet and the thud of hooves, even Stergin's sword ceased is interminable swishing, Kern was walking with his eyes almost closed, though Granger's light was now so low that there was little to see, Kern's ears were trying to pierce the covering of silence, hoping for a hint, a suggestion of the snake, that they all knew was hunting in these galleries, the longer they walked along this tunnel the more Kern became unsure as to the location of the snake. Then a thought struck him, 'What if the snake and the blockage were different?' he racked his brain, trying to find some reason for the air to stop in this passageway, something that didn't involve a snake, 'This place is like a chimney, only closing it with something like a damper would stop the air moving.' There was something nagging at the corner of his mind, something he had seen, something half remembered, but what was it? His mind turned in tight circles, like a dog chasing its tail, determined to remember. 'Chimney. It's something to do with a chimney.' Namdarin and Jayanne, turned a sharp corner, and Granger followed, darkness as well as silence, 'Dark, quiet, and a fire that wont light.' Kern cursed under his breath, "Damn it." 'What is this memory?' 'Where was the fire that wouldn't light? It was in a dark barrack room, in winter, the wind was howling round the eaves, but all the doors and windows were tightly sealed against the cold.' Crathen stumbled over a protruding rock, almost stabbing Jayanne in the back with his arrow. A harsh stare from the green eyes, and a downwards glance from him. Kern's memory suddenly sprang into sharp focus, an old sergeant, long term resident in the barrack, spoke softly so as not to wake the soldiers who were still sleeping, not yet woken by the falling temperature.

"It happens sometimes, when the wind blows from a certain direction and at a certain speed, the chimney just stops working, when a fire is burning and it does it, this place fills up with smoke in a minute or two. Light a candle and I'll show you something amazing." Kern lit a candle and gave it to the sergeant. The man held it in the mouth of the chimney, a place were it would normally have been blown out by the updraft, the flame jumped and twitched but it was not extinguished. "Do you see the way the flame pulses, it has a rhythm, it jumps to the beat of the chimney. This chimney is acting like a flute, a huge flute, the air in the chimney is singing, but because of the size of the pipe, the pitch is so low that we cannot hear it, this also prevents the normal flow."

"How are we going to keep warm then?"

"It is possible to stop the flue singing and start the air flow again."

"How?"

"Change the shape of the pipe."

Kern frowns. The old man smiles and takes a shield from beside the fire and puts it over the mouth of the chimney, almost completely blocking it, suddenly there was a boom as the shield was sucked hard against the chimney breast. Then a loud whistling sound came from the constricted opening to the chimney. "See." Said the sergeant looking into Kern's open jawed face. Then he removed the shield and the flow in the chimney stopped with a soundless thud, a compression of the ears that was so physical that it hurt. Kerned looked at the man with raised eyebrows. The man placed the shield in a groove that ran each side of the chimney mouth, smoky side down, slowly he pushed it into the slots and slid it across the opening, at about half way across the whistling returned.

"You can light a fire now, but only a small one. Try not the burn the shield, it's the only one that fits those slots, I'd have to make another one."

"How often does this happen?"

"Very rarely, but I've been here a lot of years, and I was shown this by a man who had been here more years than I have now."

Kern opened his eyes and returned to the dark tunnel, free from the revealed memory. "Stop." He said softly. Jangor frowned at him, Kern ignored the look, and took a candle from inside his jacket, then he lit it, and set it on the floor amongst the rocks of the passageway.

"What is going on?" Asked Andel, "Are we having a séance?"

"Well?" Demanded Jangor.

"Quiet a moment, please, let the candle settle, it is important, I promise." He watched the yellow light slowly establish itself, though it didn't actually settle, it jumped, slowly, up and down, in time to some beat that only it could hear, with a pulse of about two beats a second. Kern nodded and blew it out, returning the cooling wax to his jacket.

"This chimney is open at both ends, though the wind at one end is making it sing like a flute, the singing is so low that we cannot hear it, and normal air flow is suppressed by the tone."

"And this means?" Asked Jangor.

"There is no blockage in the pipe, there is no snake in the tunnel."

"Damned thing could be anywhere then?"

"Yes. Anywhere it chooses to be."

"Gods! Just when I think we've got things sorted out, everything changes, has anyone any good news?"

"If the snake blocks or nearly blocks the tunnel, then the air flow may start again, and that will tell us that it is close." Said Kern.

"That's good news?" Snorted Mander.

"Good as it gets, I'm afraid."

"Namdarin you take the lead, Jayanne, you the rear, that should help a little when the damned snake shows up." Said Jangor.

"I really don't like that 'when', an 'if' would have been better." Said Mander.

"I think the 'when' is far more likely than the 'if'." Said Jangor. "We must be getting close to the exit by now, and the closer we get the more likely the snake is to show itself. It probably hunts outside as well as in here, though I don't think a snake would like to be outside in the winter."

"Unless it's a warm blooded one." Said Andel.

"Are you trying to frighten me deliberately?" Muttered Mander.

"No, but its working." Whispered Stergin.

"Why does it always have to be snakes?" Shuddered Mander, " I hate them."

"Why do you hate snakes so much?" asked Stergin.

"They sneak up and bite you when you're not looking, they can bite you without you even knowing, and you die slow and painfully. What is there to like about snakes?"

"They usually only bite people in self defence, there are some who's bite can kill, but they are very rare, especially around here, further south that is different. They usually eat rats and other vermin, a few large snakes in a grain store can kill more rats and mice than any number of cats."

"But cats are so much more friendly."

"Only when they want to be, they'll bite you for far less reason than any snake."

"That is beside the point, the snake that is here somewhere, doesn't eats rats, it eats horses."

"No. It could eat horses, perhaps the rats are bigger down here."

"Yes, they've got long legs and hooves." Stergin shrugged his shoulders and turned away, he went back down the line towards the rear, Jayanne, was trying to watch behind herself and walk forwards, a difficult task at the best of times.

"You just be ready, I'll keep my ears on the passageway, it cannot sneak up on me, at least not now that fool isn't babbling at me."

She returned his smile, glad to have someone to share the burden of watching everyone's back. The relaxed swing returned to her stride, and the supple swing of her hips was totally wasted, because there was no-one behind her to see, unless you count a hard, black pair of eyes, more interested in the heat of her body than its actual shape or motion, hungry with a appetite that can never be quenched, never be sated, a truly elemental force, moving so slowly that it made no sound at all, at least none audible over the noise of human feet, and animal hooves and the infernal humming. It's belly scales picked up the vibration of the footsteps despite the noise in the tunnel, it was these that had brought it to this place, it had been surprised to hear a sound so loud, it had been a long time since it heard such a meal on the move. It had almost raced here, to a place it knew well, there was no better place for an ambush, it could check out the meal before it moved ahead, and then wait for the meal to come to him. This snake had been alive in this cave system for more years than most men can count, more years than any two men can count, though he had no real idea about the passage of years, these were things from his past, a past when he had a different shape, one with two legs, for this snake had indeed been a man. The shapes moving ahead meant nothing more than food, enough food for many months, but deep in the snakes brain, he knew, no gorging would stop the eternal hunger, only death would end that, and there wasn't enough humanity left for him to wish for that end, for no human mind could bare the pain of this hunger. Now that it knew enough about the party traveling through his domain, he entered a concealed side tunnel, and moved at a pace more suited to his form, along a path that his form had basically shaped by friction over the years, the smooth passageway turned and twisted in a smooth pattern that perfectly fitted its form, giving the snake incredible speed, with little expenditure of energy. As he entered the hunting pathway, he heard the low thrumming sound of the main passageway die away, this sound had been hiding the noise of the group, but now the sound of their footsteps came through the rocks with such an intensity that venom started to leak from his fangs, a bitter taste in his mouth, but a precursor to a meal, hopefully a meal such as he hadn't eaten for many a year.

    Namdarin felt it first, the sudden decompression in the ears then the rush of air, a momentary gale, that settled to a soft breeze, blowing into his face. "Something has changed, the air is moving again, everybody stay awake." He called, he head turned partially to those behind but his eyes firmly locked on the passageway ahead. An acrid odour rode up the passageway on the breeze, a harsh dry sort of smell, musty but dry.

"Beware." Shouted Kern, "Something moves I can feel it."

"What do you feel?" asked Jangor.

"I don't know, but it's big and coming our way. It feels strange, not human, but not entirely something else."

"Which way?"

"I can't tell, its seems to be everywhere, and nowhere." The tracker threw up his arms in disgust, never before had he been put into such a state of confusion by any animal he had encountered.

"I feel it." Said Granger, "It is definitely not entirely ophidian, it has an real intelligence behind it."

"If it's not a damned snake, what the hell is an ophidian?" Demanded Mander.

"An ophidian is a snake, fool." Said Andel.

"Why can't people speak plainly?"

"They do, it's just that you are too stupid to understand them."

"Shut up." Yelled Jangor. "We don't have time for that crap now. Mander front, Andel rear. Move!" The two jumped in the directions they were instructed, without even an instants hesitation, they both knew when they could push Jangor, and when to back off. "You two that feel this thing, where and what?"

"It's everywhere, and I can feel mainly snake, but a shadow of something else." Said Kern.

"I agree, though it feels more ahead than behind." Said Granger, looking at Kern for confirmation.

"It's moving ahead, almost certainly." Said Kern.

"Almost certainly, is that as close as you can get?"

"Yes, it's a very vague feeling, and the harder one tries to focus on it the vaguer it gets, it's illusive." Said Kern.

"I agree." Said Granger. "This thing really doesn't want to be found or known, it relishes mystery and illusion, I feel its hunger more than anything."

"That's it, hunger." Nodded Kern.

"Namdarin stay sharp, they think it's ahead of us somewhere, but it's probably hiding, so check everything, and watch the corners."

"Where the hell can a two foot wide snake hide?" Demanded Namdarin.

"Any where it damned well pleases. Keep looking, because it certainly is."

Namdarin paid very close attention to Jangor's words, and slowed the pace down to a crawl, checking every dark recess and corner, but his searching was fruitless, wherever this snake was, close as it might be, it was not going to be found easily, at least not until it was ready, and by then it could be far too late. With every second that passed Jangor became more and more nervous, he knew that a large snake was most likely to ambush them, he was racking his brain, trying desperately to remember something someone had told him about the biggest of snakes. It had been in the hot jungles of the far south, a story of a hunter who was after a solitary huge cat, the hunter tied a calf to a tree, and then climbed a nearby tree to wait for the cat to come to the bait, but the snake had also been hunting in the area, and it was waiting in the same tree as the hunter, only the snake was higher up, the hunter soon became lunch.

"Namdarin." He called, "Check above, big snakes like to fall on the prey, check for ledges high up on the walls, or anything like that where a snake could be hiding."

"It could be in any one of a thousand places, I'm most unlikely to see it, there could easily be ledges on these walls that are completely invisible from down here, especially in the sort of light we have to work with. You really like to make things a challenge, don't you?"

"Not me my friend, life, that is what the challenge is."

"Yes," Mumbled Mander, "keeping a tight grip on it is getting harder and harder around here."

"Then you just run on ahead, I'm sure we'll catch up it time to see your feet vanishing from view." Said Jangor.

Namdarin looked carefully around the next corner, the tunnel they were traveling in widened out suddenly into a huge cavern, with many stalactites hanging down from a ceiling that seemed to be shrouded in mist, a vapour drifted across the ceiling as seeking a way out, the dry musty odour was much more intense once Namdarin had stepped away from the tunnel mouth, craning his neck so he could scan the wall above the opening, he thought it was the most likely place for the snake to be waiting for them. All that he could see was the strange fog rolling around the stalactites. 'Anything could be hiding up there.' He thought. 'Even a huge snake.' Looking back he saw Granger and Mander leaving the safety of the tunnel for the open floor of the cavern, a floor made quite treacherous by the stumpy stalagmites sticking up, Namdarin thought, 'This is not a place to be trying to run.' Granger increased the intensity of the light from his staff, trying to illuminate the whole cave, trying and failing. The hard blue light seemed to cast twitching shadows that only confused the eye, Namdarin looked up to see the fog shining an intense blue, almost as if it was throwing the light off, in pain or disgust. The occasional crystals in the wall of the cave threw the blue light back in many colours, brief flares of green and red, but nothing that was usable to the eye.

"Can you feel the snake?" Asked Namdarin in a soft voice.

"Yes," replied Granger even more softly, "it is all around us, everywhere, anywhere. This is hard, not the feeling but finding the words, I can feel it's hunger all around us, almost as if it has no centre, it has no mind, like it is a diffuse being, spread all around this cave." He shook his head, giving up the attempt, words are just not enough some times. Granger reduced his light, slowly at first, gradually reducing the blue glare until the fog was just out of it's reach, high against the roof the roiling mass disappeared from view.

"That feels better." Said Granger.

"What. The fact that you can no longer see the snakes hiding place, that makes you feel better, you would rather not think about it. That all right for you, but I can't stop thinking about a snake the size of a mountain, just waiting in the smoke, waiting to reach down and eat me." Said Mander.

"Size of a mountain?" Asked Namdarin.

"The way it feels." Namdarin frowned at this answer, hoping that Mander would elaborate.

"Ask Andel about the size of the spider that crawled out of his boot yesterday. He feels about spiders the way I do about snakes. That spider was the size of a horse, even though it crawled out of his boot, so that snake is the size of a mountain to me." With this Mander turned away, and searched for dark corners, thoroughly expecting to be eaten at any moment. The first of the horses reached the exit of the tunnel and balked, planted both fore hooves firmly on the rocks and leaned back against the reins, it was a gesture that they had all seen before, one that on many occasions had actually saved lives, but in this case, they couldn't go any other way, this was the road that the horse had to take like it or not, there was a resounding crack, as the flat of Jangor's hand hit the horse firmly on the rump, the horse surged forwards with a backward glance of disgust. The sound of hooves skittering on the rocks of the cavern floor filled the air with sharp echos, the noise shattered into a confusing buzzing, a sound that came from all directions, causing even more distress to the horses, who became more and more restless, as the noise hummed around their heads, until Arndrol came out into the cavern that all the others were so afraid of, he tossed his head and shook his mane, the crack as the long hairs of his mane moved from side to side momentarily drowned the buzzing, then the grey slowly, deliberately, picked up one of his fore feet and slammed it down, a boom that made the other horses jump, and one or two of the people start. Slowly the hoof rose again, paused then slammed down, a hard echoing boom filled the cave, a challenge to any that could hear it, Namdarin shook his head, 'One day that horse is going to get us all into a heap of trouble.' As the echo's died away, the rest of the sound in the cave went with them, until there was almost nothing to be heard, the people started to hear their own heartbeats, and ragged breathing above any other sounds, this did nothing to calm the tension that they were feeling. Arndrol snorted his contempt of the denizens of the cave, they were far too frightened to rise to his challenge. Jayanne walked into the open and saw the frozen scene, all eyes were on the horse, waiting to see what he would do next, she knew, she stepped forwards, even as the horses rump lowered, and slapped him on the flank. "Stop showing off." She said gently, he looked round and snuffled softly. "Men!" she said.

"What do you mean?" Asked Stergin.

"He was going to paw the air with both feet, scream and slam both feet down together, just to make a big show, and to be sure that everyone is looking at him. I would rather that people were looking for a snake than staring at this animal making a fool of himself."

"You're saying that all males are like that?"

She merely raised her eyebrows and turned away, a quick glance at the tunnel, just be sure that there was no snake following, and she turned to follow one of the walls, looking carefully for any place that a snake could be hiding. The others followed suit, Stergin keeping close to the young woman, for some reason he couldn't fathom he felt safer if she was near. The more he thought about this feeling the stranger it seemed. He should be protecting her, not the other way around. He kept close to her, his sword drawn, his step light and balanced, this journey was putting his nerves under severe stress, he appeared to be permanently on alert, stepping over anything that could make a noise or displace his footing. 'It's hard, all this, but it certainly keeps the heart racing, though living at this sort of speed has got to be paid for at some time.' He thought this as he watched her move with that fluid grace that only a woman or a cat is capable. 'Some say that horses move with that sort of fluidity, but I don't see it, horses are just to heavy and solid, even at full gallop there is still something harsh and angular about their motion, cats are always smooth and slinky, even at their fullest speed, they still maintain that poise that is peculiar to their species.' His thought caught him looking around at the others, one pair of eyes flashed away as soon as he saw that they were watching Jayanne as closely as he had been. Crathen looked quickly at the ground, like a schoolboy caught with his hand in the biscuit barrel, he almost blushed, before lifting his head to look in an entirely new direction. Stergin swung his gaze from one to the other, and thought, 'Crathen is always in a place where he can see Jayanne, not always close, but always in line of sight. He never takes his eyes off her, Jangor must be told. He may already have noticed, but I will tell him anyway, the young mans lust for Jayanne was clear in his eyes, and the feeling between Namdarin and Jayanne was evident for all to see, this sort of thing can tear apart a small group such as this. Jangor will know what to do, I'll tell him as soon as I can.' Stergin stayed close to Jayanne, not giving Crathen any chance to move in, his lust was running out of control, the last thing that Stergin wanted was a confrontation before Jangor had an opportunity to sort this out. Namdarin moved slowly over to where Jayanne was searching a particularly confused jumble of boulders, with lots of openings and potential hiding places.

"I don't' think it will be hiding under any rocks, if it is going to ambush us it needs the ability to attack quickly, it can't do that from under a pile of rocks, it will need to be concealed but in the open."

"That is a contradiction." She smiled.

"I know, but that is the way I feel about this snake."

"What if your feelings are wrong?"

"My feelings aren't often wrong."

"What, just your feelings about snakes?"

"No, I tend to be right about almost everything."

"Don't you think that your head is a little small for a statement like that?"

"Perhaps, but I tend to trust my feelings especially when there is no more accurate information to work with."

"Let's hope you can feel the damned thing before we feel it, if you know what I mean?"

"I understand, but I can't really feel the snake at all just now, it's almost like it's trying to hide, even from itself."

"How can that be?"

"I know not." He shrugged and turned away, scanning the rest of the rocks around quickly but knowing that he wouldn't find anything there, the snake wasn't going to be down amongst the rocks.

"If this damned snake gives off such a presence that so many can feel it, how come it's never been killed before now?" Asked Mander, of no-one in particular.

"It's probably that this is a very strange group of people." Replied Granger, softly.

"You speak for yourself, I'm not strange."

"Have you ever traveled with a group as complex and mixed up as you do today?"

Mander looked round slowly, then nodded. "No, usually it's just soldiers, with a few officers or gentry mixed in, well mixed in but separate, if you get my meaning. This group is just so mixed up, most of the characters don't even fit into a single group, lords who are warriors, women who are warriors, wizards like yourself, and soldiers, if temporarily out of work ones."

"Out of work? I feel that our current employment will outlast most of our lives."

"You want to life forever?" Mander returned to old soldiers cliché, almost to boost his own confidence, which is what it was intended to do in the first place.

"I was giving that a good try, but it was getting boring." Granger chuckled, a deep soft sound in his throat.

"This is anything but boring?"

"Very true, but still not very good for an old mans bones."

"You are as old as you feel."

"Sometimes I feel mighty old indeed, but right now I'm thirty again."

"Only until the excitement of this impending snake dies off."

"Perhaps, but one should grasp these moments with both hands, they could so easily be our last."

"My grandfather once said, 'Life passes like dry sand through your fingers, the tighter you hold on to it, the quicker it flows away.'"

"A wise man, your grandsire." The old wizard nodded and turned away.

The exploration of the cavern proceeded without any sign of the snake, though Kern did admit that the tracks on the soft dirt of the floor were so confused they could be almost anything, the large curved ruts were certainly the snake, but the other tracks could be men or horses or something else entirely, the snake trails ran over the top of everything, and all but obliterated the other tracks. The only thing he could say for sure was that the snake was alive when it left, the others, who can tell. The exit was soon discovered, it was narrow and the sand at its opening had no snake tracks at all, the air blowing in was cold and clean smelling, Kern declared that they couldn't be very far from the outdoors.

"Where is that blasted snake?" He asked, looking at both Kern and Granger. One shrugged and the other glanced at the floor. Jangor thought for a moment and came to a decision. "Kern you lead, Jayanne, with him, Mander and Andel next, you take the horses. The rest of us bring up the rear, the snake is most likely here somewhere or behind us, Kern set a steady pace, let's not get too strung out in here."

"Shouldn't Jayanne be here at the rear?" Asked Stergin.

"No, her axe may be the only thing to hold off the snake until the rest of us can catch up." Stergin nodded and nudged Crathen, "Keep that bow of your's ready." Hearing this Namdarin started to string his bow.

"Not you," Said Jangor, "I don't think that a bow is going to do much more than irritate a snake of this size, sword work is definitely called for."

"Then why?" Asked Crathen, a bow in one hand and an arrow in the other.

"Your sword work isn't up to much and you could get lucky and take an eye." Said Stergin. Crathen was quite distressed to have his skills disregarded is such a casual fashion but knew better than to question the swordsman. Jangor nodded, and turned to Kern, "Move out." He said, softly, more a whisper than a command, thought he whisper carried with it the hardness of iron. Kern punched Jayanne gently on the shoulder and moved into the tunnel that they all hoped was to be the exit. Namdarin became gradually uncomfortable, he felt that someone, or something was staring at the back of his neck, he kept looking back over his shoulder, but he saw nothing unusual.

"What is wrong?" Asked Jangor, trusting Namdarin's instincts more with each passing hour.

"I feel that something is behind us, and it's getting closer, I don't know what it is but there is something out there."

"Could it be the Zandaars catching up?"

"Perhaps, but I'm not sure, I'm not really sure there is anything out there at all."

"Let's just try and keep as sharp as possible, you could be right, I think that the snake is ahead of us and the Zandaars behind."

"Sound's like rock and hard place to me."

"It could get unpleasant very soon I think."

Namdarin sheathed his sword, and strung his bow, readying an arrow.

"This bow packs more punch than you realise, and I feel better with the extra reach it gives, I can always use the sword when things get to close for the bow."

Jangor merely nodded, in some ways he agreed with Namdarin, but his mistrust of bows was deep seated, a sword would never turn against it's wielder, and he had seen arrows turn many times after leaving the bow, it worried him to have two bowmen in his party.

Suddenly Kern stopped, the tunnel had opened into a large cavern, with a fairly level floor area, but many stumpy stalagmites scattered about, each one with a mirror stalactite hanging from above. There was a subtle change in the air, Kern could almost taste the freshness of open fields, and underneath that an acrid mustiness, a scent that he knew only too well, the snake was here somewhere. The horses sensed the presence of the snake, they began to get very restive, the was much stamping and snorting, even Arndrol had a stamp or two before Namdarin's glare made him stand still, and satisfy himself with some serious twitching of his mane.

"Crathen, Stergin, you look to the horses, if that snake puts in an appearance here, they are going to go mad." Commanded Jangor, another command in the shape of a single nod prodded Kern, Namdarin and Jayanne forwards, Namdarins bow half drawn, Jayannes axe swinging slowly in her hand, like the pendulum of a large clock, Kern's sword was upraised, but he had no more target than Namdarin. Granger followed them, his staff held firmly in both hands across the front of his body. Jangor followed his hand on his sword hilt. Some distance away was the exit from this cavern, unmistakeably lit from outside, slowly they moved towards the exit, Jangor was the first to notice the fog that shrouded the ceiling of the cavern.

"Look up, anything could be hiding up there." He whispered, just loudly enough for those closest to hear. Namdarin pointed his arrow towards the fog, but didn't draw the string any further, pulling on the huge bow took a great amount of effort and he didn't want to tire himself. Jangor waved to those waiting in the tunnel mouth and indicated that they should guide the horses towards the exit, keeping close to the wall. The horses were extremely nervous, they knew what was in this cavern, and they were afraid, but the presence of the men, helped to calm them a little, that calm was shattered when the snakes head appeared from the fog, a huge grey mottled head, with hard black eyes typical of snakes the world over. Only Arndrol's lead kept them all alive, he headed straight for the echo of sunlight in the exit, he turned at the last and pawed the air screaming while the other horses ran through the opening, then his fore hooves crashed to the ground and he turned and fled.

"Show off." Muttered Namdarin, his bow thumped as he released the string, the green fletched arrow sang straight towards its target, the snakes head flinched at the last instant and the arrow was buried almost to the fletching just behind the eye. The snake hissed and struck, Kerns sword swung to meet that strike, the heavy sword barely cut into the thick scales on the nose, but it was enough to stop the mouth from opening, the head however carried on and knocked the man to the ground, Jayanne swung at the top of the head and just caught it as it was recoiling, the axe opened a long cut from the top of the head down almost to the tip of the nose, not deep, but enough to bleed some. Grangers staff spat a bolt of blue fire at the head, and Namdarin put another arrow into it, this time through the bottom jaw and up through the top one. Kern staggered to his feet, and as a group they started to edge towards the exit, never taking their eyes from the snakes, the head stayed out of reach of the swords, and kept swaying away from the arrows, Granger's bolts were too fast for it to wholly avoid, but they were only causing irritation not real damage. A coil of mottled grey snake descended from the roof, between Jangor and the exit, it was fully four feet thick and blocking the way. Jangor stepped towards the loop of flesh and drew his sword in a single fluid movement, the two handed slash that he delivered to the body of the snake should have opened it up like an old wineskin, but the tip of the sword only struck a few sparks from the scales on the flank, one scale cracked and revealed a shiny new scale underneath. His second stroke did no better, the only reaction was for the coil to move to encircle the man, Jayanne saw the coil about to close on Jangor and rushed to his aid, leaving Granger and Namdarin to deal with the beasts head. She struck the closing coil with a huge overhand blow, the axe carved through the tough scales like hot oil on snow, as the body flexed away from the wound it opened like a gory mouth, spilling red blood and black ichor across the floor. The flexing of the body released Jangor from his fleshly trap, as he moved away from the snake Jayanne struck it again, trying for the same wound as the first time, but she missed by quite a way, the snake was moving quickly now, the coil went up into the fog swirling on the roof, spilling its crimson life fluids as it went. Jayanne turned to Namdarin and yelled at him.

"The exit is clear." Behind him she saw black robed figures come into the cave, after a moments pause they started to advance towards the snake, she noted that they moved a little strangely, almost like marching but somehow out of step, one of their number started shooting arrows up into the roof, then another threw a huge lightening bolt upwards, the roof exploded in fragments and splinters of rock. Either the arrows or the lightening attracted the snakes attention, the head turned away from Namdarin and Granger. Namdarin took full advantage of it's distraction and stepped back, lowering his bow, and waved Granger to follow, the noise in the cavern was intense, the occasional shout from the monks was only adding to the confusion of sound, Namdarin ran to the exit, and stood by it as the others passed he held Jayanne and Granger, turning back into the cave he saw that the monks were now fully engaged with the snake, he reached his hand out and recalled the arrows, like a flock of homing pigeons they returned to his hand. He drew the sword from its place on his back, it almost howled into his hand, he felt energy rush into him. The crackling of the Zandaars fire bombs was filling the cave with a mind destroying noise, hand signals were the only communication available, but the others got the idea really quickly, on a waved count of three, they struck, Namdarin one wall, Jayanne the other, and Granger the roof, the rocks around the opening moved and started to slide, they all turned and ran for the exit with the dust of falling rocks chasing on their heels. Coughing and spluttering they made it into open air, the valley they found themselves in was warm and dry, the grass was soft a green under their feet, a few paces from the mouth of the cave the others were sitting on the grass, Jangor was checking for injuries while Kern was making sure the horses were ready to ride, the horses weren't exactly helping this process, it had been a few days since they had actually seen any grass, let alone eaten any of it, they were taking full advantage of the sudden abundance of food.

Jangor turned to Namdarin, Jayanne and Granger, all of whom were sitting on the grass coughing as if they would never stop.

"What happened in there?"

"We put a little something in their way." Said Namdarin laughing and coughing at the same time.

"What?"

"A mountain." Spluttered Granger, "I'm too old for this sort of thing." He muttered further.

"How long will it hold them?"

"Who can tell, it should give us a few hours to get our breath's back, but nothing in this world is certain."

"That's for sure. We'll eat then make tracks. Which way are we going?"

"East, that bird thing said there was a weapon that way that could help us, elven mindstone, or something wasn't it?"

"Mander." Shouted Jangor, "Make something to eat, let the horses eat for a while as well, we'll move on in a while."

Namdarin looked around for the first time since they had emerged from the darkness. The valley was broad and wide, the cave system exited through a large outcropping of grey rock that thrust upwards through the valley floor, not far away was a wide river, slow flowing and meandering across the valley, small clumps of trees were visible, there were none of the signs of cultivation but the valley somehow managed to give the impression that people lived here, or had lived here.

"Jangor. What do you make of this place?"

"It looks strange, feels odd, I can't quite work out why."

The smell of wood smoke indicated that a fire was already burning and Andel returning from the river with a large water skin that was so obviously full stopped conversation until Namdarin had washed the dust from his throat.

"Any signs of nearby habitation?" Asked Namdarin.

"I see nothing, but again this place makes me uneasy." Said Jangor.

"If there is anything it will be downstream." Said Kern.

"Why downstream?"

"The grass gets shorter that way, so cattle or sheep come this way to feed, but no too often."

"That's it." Said Namdarin. "The damned grass looks like a partially cut lawn, far too green to be just natural and wild."

ABOUT THE AUTHOR

My name is Michael Porter, some call me Roaddog. Formal training for writing, I have exactly none, I did start reading early, generally before breakfast, I actually learned to read before I started school, many thanks to mother for all the hours she put in. Of course this wasn't popular with the school at that time, some fool had just introduced an new learning system, some sort of phonetic garbage. When asked "Why should children have to learn English twice?" They had no answer. I didn't bother with that phonetic junk, they had to get some old books out of storage for me to read. Yes a trouble maker from the start. I was only at that particular school for one year, but before I left I had read every book they had, well, all the ones that were spelled properly. This pattern continued through every school I attended, grammar school was no different, they had a huge library, which I read in less than three years. Much to the despair of my teachers reading didn't help me in my English lessons, spelling, punctuation, these things aren't important it's the story that counts. I'm sorry Miss Boll, Cider with Rosie is boring, I'm not reading it. David Eddings, now he's good. I'm making no friends amongst the English department here. English exams were obviously interesting, mock 'O' level I scored a massive -30%. This was in the days before students got credit for just being there. The scoring system was simple, you start with 100 points, for every spelling, punctuation or grammatical error a point is deducted, it seems that in only four pages of writing I managed an impressive 130 errors. The real 'O' level was unclassified. No real surprise there. I managed to pass on the second attempt, but only by twisting the proposed essay title, and plagiarising large chunks of the sci-fi novel I was currently reading. Enough ancient history.

For those that don't know me I'm getting along in years, I'd be approaching retirement if the government didn't keep moving the goalposts. I've been writing this story for many

years, but only got around to publishing it recently due to pressure from she who must be obeyed. I started this mammoth project after reading a particularly dreadful fantasy novel. I decided that even I could write something better than that. I noticed that most books of the genre were lacking in real violence and proper sex, so this series is definitely for a more adult audience. I'm hoping to have the complete set finished before the end of 2018, I have a day job that takes up a lot of my time, I also have an evening job as sound and lighting engineer for a local rock band, which eats a big chunk of my weekends, so time for writing is somewhat restricted. I'll try to get Doom finished on schedule, as there are a couple more projects in the pipe. For me reading and writing is all about the story.
Enjoy.

Printed in Great Britain
by Amazon